Morgan Clyde Series #4

	DATE DUE		
966			

Too Proud to Run

A MORGAN CLYDE WESTERN, BOOK 4

Too Proud to Run

Brett Cogburn

FIVE STAR
A part of Gale, a Cengage Company

LIBRARY OF CONGRESS CATALOGING-IN-PUBLICATION DATA

Names: Cogburn, Brett, author.
Title: Too proud to run / Brett Cogburn.
Description: First Edition. | Waterville, Maine : Five Star, a part of Gale, a Cengage Company, 2022. | Series: A Morgan Clyde western ; book 4
Identifiers: LCCN 2021035984 | ISBN 9781432831943 (hardcover)
Subjects: GSAFD: Western stories.
Classification: LCC PS3603.O3255 T66 2022 | DDC 813/.6—dc23
LC record available at https://lccn.loc.gov/2021035984

First Edition. First Printing: February 2022
Find us on Facebook—https://www.facebook.com/FiveStarCengage
Visit our website—http://www.gale.cengage.com/fivestar
Contact Five Star Publishing at FiveStar@cengage.com

Printed in Mexico
Print Number: 01 Print Year: 2022

Too Proud to Run

Chapter One

He stopped and crouched in the darkness among a jumble of moss-spotted gray boulders at the foot of a sandstone bluff. The mix of adrenaline and fear had left him breathing harder than all of the running and dodging, and the stock of his rifle was sweat-slick under the grip of his hands. It was too dark to see anything, but his eyes scanned the night, anyway. His senses heightened and on edge, he listened for the slightest sound that might give away the location of the men he hunted, and who in turn, hunted him.

The first gust of wind on the storm front was a big one, swaying the treetops and rattling and roaring like a phantom highball train passing across the dark face of the mountain. There was a crack of thunder and a dazzle of jagged lightning, and for an instant, the world was lit up in a shade of electric blue.

In that brief moment of weird illumination, he thought he glimpsed the feral shadows of men moving through the timber and the maze of boulders and ledges downslope from the foot of the bluff. There were four of them, and maybe more, spread out in a wide, loose skirmish line, like a pack of trailing wolves that had struck his scent.

He shifted his position slightly until he stopped against the fat trunk of an ancient, gnarled pine tree growing straight up the face of the bluff. He tugged his black hat down more firmly on his head as the next gust of wind tore through the timber and howled over the mountaintop. The rain would come soon, but it would likely all be over before then, one way or the other.

There came the sound of a turkey's gobble. Not a real turkey, but a man doing a good job of imitating one. Cherokee warriors sometimes gave that call during a fight as a challenge to their enemies, and others in the territory, not only Indians, had taken it up as it suited them.

"Hey, lawman!" A voice shouted at him from somewhere down the mountain and spaced wide of the turkey caller.

He eased his rifle's barrel in the direction of that voice and readied himself with its buttstock pressed to his shoulder, waiting for the next flash of lightning. The world around him narrowed with each passing moment, until all that remained was to be found looking down the barrel of his Winchester. It was a world that smelled like burned black powder and gun oil.

"Hey, Clyde!" The same voice called. "Come out and fight, you son of a bitch!"

Someone laughed from a different spot, and then came the turkey gobble again. They were toying with their cornered prey, savoring the hunt. Thunder drowned out whatever else might have been said. He pointed his rifle where he thought he last heard the voice calling to him. Whoever that was talking, he was a damned fool or too brave for his own good.

He held the high ground for the moment, but his back was also against the wall in more ways than one. It was a good place to make a stand, but also offered little chance of retreat. He had been looking for a way up or around the bluff before, but those below him weren't going to give him the time he needed.

The next bolt of lightning broke the night sky into a thousand splinters. It was then that he saw one of the outlaws hunkered down on top of a large boulder only fifty feet below him. They saw each other at the same time, and both of them already had their guns up and ready.

He was a shade quicker, and his Winchester's boom was drowned out by the drum of thunder and another bolt of lightning. The outlaw, struck hard, threw his arms wide and toppled off his perch. His rifle clattered to the rocks below him. By then, the man they called Clyde was already up and running along the foot of the bluff.

More guns flamed below him, and he heard bullets striking the rock face around him as he ran. He worked the lever on his Winchester and fired again from the hip at one of those gun flashes. He kept running and firing with his teeth gritted against the bullet that was bound to eventually find him.

He came to the end of the bluff, where the high wall of sandstone gave way to a slope slightly less steep and a jumble of rocks that had broken free from it and slid downhill. A great slab of the same rock, pockmarked and weathered by erosion, leaned upslope and provided his first chance to climb.

A bullet struck his rifle and knocked it from his grasp so violently that it stung his hands. Still, he kept going. Another shot knocked chips from the stone slab right below his heels and ricocheted away with a nasty whine as he scampered upwards, bent at the waist and with arms outflung for balance. The higher and farther he went, the harder the climb became. Both hands and feet fought for purchase as he neared the top, and he clung precariously like a spider with the guns banging away at him.

He threw out a hand and took hold of a holly bush growing in a crack in the stone and heaved himself the last few feet upwards where he rolled over the top of the slab and onto a flat bench of ground level with the top of the bluff. The guns below him went silent as the first spattering of raindrops fell from the sky and popped against his hat brim. He inhaled deeply and got his legs back under him.

He leapt over a wide crevasse and ran along the top of the

bluff until he found a place where he could see down into the boulder field below. He bellied down and waited with his Colt revolver resting on one forearm.

Alone on the mountain with a gun in his fist, he asked himself how a man came to such a point in his life. There were some that said every decision led you to a different fate, as if a string of consequences could be plotted from the then-and-there to the here-and-now. But the map of his life's regrets was far too convoluted and twisting to ever backtrack.

A bitter chuckle sounded from somewhere deep in his chest. Maybe it was the first day he pinned on the badge and hung a pistol on his hip that started it all. As for more recent ill-advised turns on the road of fate, maybe it was a shotgun and a hanging judge that were to blame . . . and a woman, or rather a woman's scorn. But wasn't there always a woman involved?

And then the lightning flashed again and was followed by the roar of guns. He fought hard, like a cornered animal rather than a man. For despite what some will say, there is no such thing as a good day to die.

Chapter Two

Fort Smith, Arkansas, on the Border of the Indian Territory, One Week Earlier

Morgan Clyde was well into his third glass of whiskey and slightly and pleasantly drunk. He slapped his next domino tile down on the table and smiled. "Give me another dime."

The drummer on his left gave a grunt that was more like a growl and shoved his bowler hat back on his head. He frowned at the last two dominos in his hand and then glanced across the table at the woman who was marking Morgan's score down on a scrap of a brown paper sack with the nub of a pencil. She was a rounded, buxom woman, just plump enough and more than amply endowed to push the limits of the robe she wore, especially considering that she wore nothing else under that thin silk.

"Your turn," the woman said to the drummer.

"I wish you would go put on some clothes," the drummer replied. "Hard enough to concentrate without you hanging out of that robe."

The woman, the madam of the house, placed the fingertips of one hand at the exposed crevice between her large breasts where the neck of the robe showed that V of bare skin. She gave him a shocked, mocking expression. "Am I bothering you?"

"That's what I get for letting you con me into a game for a penny a point," the drummer said. "At this rate I'll lose a week's commission before I get out of here."

The madam smiled at him. "I'm doing better then, aren't I? Usually you hand over your two dollars, spend five minutes with Claire, and then you're gone again until the next week."

The drummer growled again, studied his dominos, and scraped at the stubble of whiskers on his chin. "Kitchenware sales are slow this time of year, I tell you. Been to Little Rock and back this week and didn't sell but two little orders."

"You could always go home to your wife. She's probably keeping the blankets warm for you right now," the madam said.

"You don't know my wife. That woman's got a backside that would chill beer. Winter or summer, she'll back that big rump up against you and it's like cuddling a frozen ham."

"I bet she thinks the luster went off you a long time ago, too."

"I think you and the marshal are partnering me. You keep it up and Claire is going to have to give me one on the house."

"Not a chance. Quit stalling and pass. You don't have a six and you know it."

Morgan's attention had drifted away from the table while the two of them bantered. The table where they played was against the far wall of the parlor opposite the front door, and near the interior doorway leading into the kitchen.

The brass kerosene lamp on the wall above him lit the table, and other such lamps cast the rest of the room in a soft glow. Morgan smoothed one corner of his thick mustache with his fingers and then pushed back the lapel of his black frock coat and pulled a cigar from his vest pocket while he studied the room before him with his intensely blue eyes.

House business was slow, and there were few customers that he could see. Two of the doves were over on one of the parlor couches trying to coax the fire chief into going upstairs with them, but the fireman was having too much fun with them fawning over him and was playing hard to get. Two other men stood at the bar built against the stairs and were visiting over glasses of whiskey and ignoring the girls who pouted and lounged above them on the stair landing or stood in clusters about the room trying to be noticed.

The drummer had noticed the same thing while he drew a domino from the boneyard. "Your girls are having to work for it tonight. Either they've given everyone the clap and put them out of action, or you need to cut the price of your liquor and find some new chippies."

"I've got the best house in town, and you know it," the madam said. "Water's still too high, and I'm not getting my usual customers from across the river."

The drummer nodded at that. "Been a rainy spring, that's a fact. I hear the *Harold B.* has been tied up over at the Van Buren dock for three days now, and the ferry down on the Poteau isn't operating, either."

"The captain of the *Harold B.* says he'll start crossing again tomorrow if it doesn't rain tonight and the river keeps falling," she answered.

"Well, you'll be back to picking high cotton then, won't you?" the drummer said with a grin. "What we need is for the railroad to finish the job and build a bridge across the river. Things will boom then and this city will grow like you've never seen. You mark my words."

It was an old discussion, and one that had worn thin long ago for Morgan. Though Fort Smith's inhabitants were quick to tell any newcomer that they were standing on what would one day become the next St. Louis, the last good jumping-off point at the edge of civilization. However, that grand plan had yet to come to fruition, if it ever would. Talk of brick paving and streetcars and gaslights was nothing but talk for the moment, and the city's streets were still muddy and rutted, no matter how often the city fathers tried to grade them. The only lights were fueled with wood or kerosene, and the town proper, from the river landing to the Church of the Immaculate Conception at the top of the hill, was still as rough-edged as any frontier town. But it was busy and bustling with traffic, and it was growing. Maybe that's what led to such optimism.

First was the emigrant wagon trains of those bound for California during the gold rush, but that traffic played out as soon as the boom was over. And then the war came and shot everything to hell. When the Union Army had closed down the fort at the end of the war, many said that it was the end. However, the river trade made the location a natural shipping point and market for the farms scattered along the fertile river bottoms and for those in the Indian Territory to the west. The importance of that trade was evident in the goods and produce stacked along the wharf ready to be loaded on riverboats and barges and delivered to points in the east, or hauled by wagon to be distributed among the merchants' storefronts lining Garrison Avenue. And just across the Arkansas River was the railroad, teasing bigger and better things to come, the same railroad that kept promising a bridge across the river to truly connect Fort Smith to the wide world.

The floorboards creaked above Morgan, and he looked up and saw a new girl stepping out onto the stairway landing on the second floor. She was a tall, skinny blond, and she was wearing nothing but her bloomers, naked from the waist up. Her rib bones showed like slats in a corncrib.

The drummer looked up at her. "Now see there, Jesse, Claire is the best hustler you've got. She'll make her wages tonight if anybody does. Maybe I ought to get some sales and advertising advice from her."

Morgan bit off the suck end of his cigar, spit it into the brass cuspidor against the wall near him, and struck a match with his thumbnail. He lit the cigar, squinting up at the blond on the landing through the tobacco smoke while he puffed the burning tobacco to life. She stared back at him and gave him a challenging, impish smile.

"You better get to Claire quick or I think Morgan's going to beat you to her," the madam said to the drummer as she played her domino and wrote her score down on the piece of brown sacking paper beside her. "That'll be another five for me."

"Damn," the drummer said when he saw that the madam had scored again. "No, Morgan won't steal my Claire. He doesn't come down here for the ladies. He's like you and only wants to take my money."

Morgan looked away from the bare-breasted prostitute above him and took up his whiskey glass and held it up to them. "It's the whiskey and conversation that keeps bringing me back."

"I like'em skinny," the drummer said, still thinking about the blond prostitute hovering over them.

Morgan played his last domino with relish and leaned back in his chair and took another sip of whiskey.

"Your luck's running hot tonight," the drummer said.

Before they could go farther with their conversation, a black woman in an apron came through the kitchen door. "Ma'am, there's somebody out back."

"Who is it?" the madam asked.

"Don't know. Some man that says he's got to talk to you."

"And he can't come talk to me in here?" The madam scooted back her chair from the table and stood.

"No, ma'am. He says he needs to talk to you in private."

The cathouse madam and the cook disappeared into the kitchen.

Morgan poured himself another single finger of whiskey from the bottle on the table. The drummer's attention had gone back to the blond dove above them. He finally looked away and pulled out a coin purse from his vest pocket. He glanced at the score sheet, frowned, and then pitched his losings on the table with a rattle of coins.

"Are you calling it quits?" Morgan asked.

"I'm done for the night. Believe I'll go up and see how Claire is doing," the drummer said.

"All right. I'm about played out myself."

The drummer was halfway across the parlor to the foot of the stairs when Morgan threw down the last of his whiskey and stood and took his black felt hat off the peg on the wall beside him. He readjusted his coat, and for a moment the tin badge pinned on his vest was revealed, as was the butt of the engraved Colt revolver worn at a cross draw on his left hip.

He ran a hand through his thick black hair to push it back from his forehead, and then put on his hat. He spent some time adjusting the hat to the proper angle and fit, and then took his share of the drummer's money according to the score. He hadn't been back from a manhunt into the Indian Territory for more than a few hours before their game, and he was in bad need of some sleep. The bed he had rented at a nearby boardinghouse was calling his name.

He had barely taken a step towards the front door when it flew open. A shotgun roared and belched flame, and a load of buckshot struck the tabletop and scattered dominos and splinters of wood in every direction.

One of the whores screamed, and by then Morgan was already sprinting across the room towards the bar. Without stopping, his left hand flipped back his coat while his right hand went for his pistol. The man at the door was far enough out on the porch that darkness almost completely masked him, but Morgan saw the flame leap from the shotgun's second barrel just as he dove over the bar top.

The second charge of buckshot struck the walnut bar and

knocked chunks from it. Morgan rolled over the top of the bar, landed behind it, and then came up with his revolver pointing at the front door.

The man with the shotgun was gone. Morgan came out from behind the bar and crept to one side of the open front door, then paused there with his Colt cocked and ready. He scanned what he could see of the dark street fronting the brothel, but saw nothing. Still, he wasn't about to step into the doorway and silhouette himself.

"Put out the lights," he ordered without looking back at the room behind him.

Most of the doves and Johns had fled to the kitchen or up the stairs during the shooting, but apparently there was someone still in the parlor. He heard them moving, and the lamps started going out one by one.

The parlor went black, and he waited for a count of ten before he ducked out the door. He moved down the porch to the end of it and leapt off of it into the yard. His boots sank to his ankles in the sodden muck and he almost fell.

There was a boarded picket fence separating the brothel from the billiard hall next to it, and he stopped at the end of that fence where it touched the edge of the street. He waited there, watching and listening.

After some time, he stepped out on the street, but whoever had shot at him was already long gone. He holstered the Colt and went back to the parlor. The drummer and the madam were relighting the lamps by then, and a few of the doves were coming to the upstairs landing to peer down at him.

The madam glanced at her torn-up bar, and then at the top of the table where they had been playing dominos only moments earlier.

"You get him?" she asked.

Morgan shook his head and then looked down at his fancy,

high-topped black boots, now filthy with mud, and frowned.

"Who was it?" the madam asked.

"Couldn't make him out in the dark."

"Well, he about fixed your wagon."

Morgan looked at the table where he had been sitting, and then at the scattering of buckshot holes in the wallpaper about perfectly in line with his chair. "Who was at the back door wanting to talk to you?"

"He was gone when I got there," she said, and then it showed on her face that something had dawned on her. "You think that was a ruse to get me away from the table where he had a clear shot at you?"

That was exactly what Morgan was thinking. He took his pocketknife and dug into one of the holes in the wallpaper. He had to dig into a second one, and then a third to find where one of the buckshot pellets had hit a stud and was still embedded there. He popped it out with the tip of the knife and looked at it in his palm.

"Number 1 buck," he said as he examined the lead shot pellet. "Cluster of that will make a mess of a man up close."

Except for a few stray pellets, the brunt of the buckshot pattern had hit the table. It wasn't hard to see that if that charge had taken him in the chest he wouldn't be standing there.

"You've got a hole in your coat, Marshal," the drummer said.

Morgan took hold of one side of the tail of his coat where the drummer was looking, and examined the frazzle of threads that revealed a tiny hole where a single buckshot pellet had passed through it. A little farther to one side and it would have been a hole in his flesh.

"Who do you think it was?" the drummer asked.

"Why should I have any idea?" Morgan snapped at him.

He immediately felt bad for that, and took a deep breath. He was cranky and tired, and his nerves were still jittery like they always were after a fight.

He gave the drummer an apologetic look. "Sorry."

"No need for an apology," the drummer said. "It's just with your line of work and all . . . Thought you might have somebody in particular in mind."

"Maybe they were going to rob me and weren't even after you at all," the madam said like she didn't believe her own suggestion.

"Case of mistaken identity?" the drummer asked with the same disbelief apparent in his voice.

"You know anybody that could be mistaken for this long, tall galoot?" the madam asked and tipped her head at Morgan. "People here, they see him coming down the street from blocks away in that black hat and coat and they all know it's Marshal Clyde."

"Maybe whoever did it was drunk," the drummer continued.

"Listen to what you're saying," the madam scoffed.

Morgan didn't believe it was a matter of a misunderstanding, not with him sitting in a well-lit room and with the little act to get the madam to go to the back door. But that didn't mean the shotgunner hadn't been three sheets to the wind, nor did it make such an assassin necessarily any less deadly. He had known lots of badmen who had never pulled a trigger except when they were drunk. The liquor had a way of steadying nerves, and for some, it set free the meanness in them.

None of the house's customers had come back into the room other than the drummer. The madam had noticed that, too.

"Afraid they'll get caught here when the police show up," she said. "Coppers don't usually come down along the river after nightfall, but this'll likely bring'em."

"Sorry about this," Morgan said as he started once more for the front door.

"Where are you going?" the madam called after him.

"I'm done for the night," he said over his shoulder.

"I can't believe you're leaving me alone when you know the coppers are bound to be here soon. What do you want me to tell them?" she asked.

Morgan paused in the doorway, his tall lean frame outlined there, and looked back at her. The left side of his coat was still tucked behind his pistol butt. "Tell them they should find whoever shot at me before I do."

Chapter Three

Judge Isaac Parker leaned back in his chair and stared at Morgan across the office desk between them. The grandfather clock on the wall behind the judge ticked steadily, and Morgan counted every tick while he waited for the judge to say something. The morning sunlight struck the window across the room from them and spilled a little ways onto the battered and dented hardwood floor.

The judge was nearing forty, but his bearing was still straight as a fence rail and not a gray hair showed in his well-combed hair. Too much time spent behind a desk or in a courtroom and too little exercise was beginning to show itself at his waistline, but he was still an imposing figure. Even in the relaxed setting of his office, his demeanor was that of a trial judge, as if he could not shed himself of some of that formality. Or perhaps he was simply mad at Morgan and about to pronounce sentence, considering he had summoned him to his office so early in the morning.

"Mr. Clyde, what are we going to do with you?" Judge Parker finally asked.

Morgan had come to know the judge only well enough in the short time he had ridden for his court to understand it was better not to say anything, not yet. Let the judge talk first so that he could find out how to best defend himself. A new session of court had begun, and the judge was always a little cranky when under the burden of his trial docket.

"What do you mean?"

"Don't try to play innocent with me," the judge said while he knocked loose a biscuit crumb left over from a late breakfast that was stuck to the whiskers of the fashionable mustache and goatee that covered his lip and chin.

"Are you referring to what happened last night?" Morgan asked while he played with his hat in his lap.

"What else do you think I'm referring to? The whole city is talking about it."

"I was down at Jesse's house and somebody took a shot at me," Morgan said.

"And what were you doing in a house of ill repute in the first place?" the judge asked.

Morgan's only response was to look up from his hat and to arch one eyebrow at the judge.

"Granted, that's a rhetorical question. Sustained," the judge said. "But I can't have deputy marshals representing my district patronizing such establishments. It's not a good look, not to mention that it's illegal. I've already got every trial defense lawyer working my court running down to the newspaper offices and pushing stories that you and some of the other marshals are no better than the outlaws you're sent into the Indian Territory to apprehend. I have to hear that blather almost every day in my courtroom."

Morgan stared back at the judge and gave no reply.

"You have nothing to say in your defense?" the judge asked.

"What do you want me to say?"

The judge rested his hands on the top of the desk and clasped them together. His expression was thoughtful as he looked away from Morgan and gazed out the window. The brick building that held the federal jail and courthouse had once been soldier barracks before the old fort was closed down, and it sat on a wide lawn dotted with oak trees and bounded by a low rock wall in places. From the office window, a man could look out across that lawn towards the timber lining the high banks of the Arkansas River after it turned in a wide, muddy bend around Belle Point before turning again and resuming its way westward into the Indian Territory. The territory was the reason that the judge's court existed at all, and was the source of most of his headaches. It was a common saying that there was no law west of Fort Smith, but the judge had been appointed by President Ulysses S. Grant to change that.

The judge took a deep breath and exhaled before he spoke again. He also changed tactics in that single breath. "I had some reservations about you joining the marshal's office, despite the numerous recommendations that were attached to your application."

"That so?" Morgan asked.

The judge went on, "You were with the New York Police Department for a time until you quit to join up with the 1st U.S. Sharpshooters, Berdan's regiment?"

"That's correct."

The judge began to spill off items from Morgan's past, touching the fingers of his left hand with the pointer finger of his right, checking those things off one by one. "Following your previous stint as a deputy marshal under Judge Story when he ran this court, I believe you were employed as the city marshal of Sedalia, Missouri, and then Baxter Springs, Kansas."

The look on Morgan's face was unreadable. The more the judge talked, the more certain Morgan was that the judge wasn't entirely reciting the facts from memory. It sounded too much like reading from a file or resume. Either somebody had been talking to the judge about him, or the judge had taken a special interest in him for some reason.

The judge glanced at the ceiling, and then went on again as if he had remembered the rest of it. "Hmm, let's see. Chief of

Railroad Police for the MK&T where I'm told you cleaned up their construction camp at Eufaula, stopped a riot, and somehow prevented an assassination and a payroll robbery all at once. Remind me to get you to tell me about that some time. Must have been a doozy, because you're the only man riding for my court with a personal letter of recommendation from the Secretary of the Interior on record."

"You might say I was a bit busy that day," Morgan said.

The judge ignored Morgan's dry sarcasm and rambled on. "Worked as a deputy city marshal at Dennison, Texas, and last but not least, a brief term as an officer for the Secret Service where you helped build a case against . . . no, no, shall I say, you helped remove some of the more nefarious members of my predecessor's court. That's a more polite way to describe that bloodbath you took part in at Eufaula last year, isn't it?"

"The inquiry found my actions to be just."

The judge grunted again, louder this time. "The newspapers had a ball covering that one. Three of Judge Story's corrupt marshals downed in a gunfight, and three more civilians with them. Buildings burned down or shot to pieces, and you, sir, right in the middle of it all, smoking pistol and box of matches in hand."

"The way you put it, I come off sounding pretty bad," Morgan answered.

"No, on paper your law enforcement experience is really quite impressive," the judge said. "It's what's between the lines that concerns me."

"Has someone been talking about me?"

"You're a man with, let's say, a sizable reputation, and it's a bloody one."

"It's a dangerous job."

"Some of your fellow peace officers say you're too hot tempered and have a tendency to be a little too quick to shoot."

"Some that have said that about me aren't with us anymore because they didn't shoot when they should have," Morgan said. "You've hired how many deputy marshals since you first took over this court? And how many of those have been killed in the line of duty since then?"

It was the judge's turn not to answer.

Morgan let out a scoffing chuckle. "Our dearly beloved government, in its usual wisdom, evicts the Indians because the white man wants the land, and then sets aside another big swath of country for the Indians only to find out you can't keep the white men out of the new place, either.

"Thirty something tribes all forced from their native lands and thrown together in the Indian Territory. You've got the civilized tribes with every one of them thinking their constitutions and tribal governments make them a real nation. And then you've got the wild, stick-a-feather-in-their-hair, asses-hanging-out-their-buckskins tribes out west still trying to live by the old ways and surviving on reservation handouts under the watchful eye of the army until they can be . . . What do we call it? Assimilated? Going to make farmers or preachers out of all of them."

"The only way for the red man to survive it is to adapt," the judge said.

Morgan rolled his lips tight together and shook his head. "They think they are finally going to be left alone, but we won't let them prosecute a trespassing white man, no matter what he's done to them. And all we wind up with is a damned no-man's-land and a place for every two-bit thief and killer to run and hide and do what he pleases while lawyers squabble over jurisdiction and all the other technicalities."

"That's a simplistic overview of the situation, but not one I entirely disagree with," the judge said.

"Judge Parker, it's more than four hundred miles from here

to the far side of the territory, and that's a long way for even the long arm of the law to reach. Fancy talk about the finer points of law and order is fine for your courtroom, but out there in the territory, the men you send me after do their talking with a gun or a knife and they couldn't give two spits for such niceties."

The judge turned his face away from the window to once more look at Morgan. "We have been charged with cleaning up the territory, and as you say, it will take men of action to do that. However, with God as my witness, we will do it under the letter of the law."

"Six cents a mile while on court business, and two dollars per arrest when we deliver a prisoner to Fort Smith, plus expenses, that's what you're paying me and the rest of the deputy marshals. Not much of a price to put on a man's life, is it?"

"I'm currently trying to get your pay increased, perhaps even a regular salary put in place," the judge replied with a hint of irritation creeping into his voice.

Morgan waved a hand at the thought, as if it didn't matter. "One year, that's all the jail time a man gets for resisting arrest. Not much to risk, is it? Not if you were a man I was after. Myself? Things go wrong and somebody's digging a hole to bury me. I wear the badge as best I can, but if a man pulls on me, I put him down. I'll do my job, but I intend to stay alive while I do it."

"How did a man like you come to make your living the way you do?" the judge asked. "In a lot of ways, you don't fit with the rest of my peace officers."

"What do you mean?"

"Amongst the other things I've learned about you, it's said you are a Yale graduate, and that at one time you were considered one of the young up-and-comers on the New York business scene."

Morgan wondered who had told the judge that. It was something from his life long before the war, and not what he readily shared. He shifted in his chair to a more comfortable position. "Maybe I found that I'm a lot better lawman than I was with a dollar."

"Is that a humorous way of saying you went broke?"

Morgan grinned in a way that had multiple meanings. "I promise you there was nothing funny about it at the time."

The judge shuffled a stack of papers on one corner of his desk and pulled forth a single sheet and held it for Morgan to see. "Do you know what I have here? It's a petition requesting your removal."

Morgan took the petition, gave a brief glance at the dozen signatures on it, and then handed it back. "Six of those signatures belong to men I arrested and brought in last month. I believe two of them are still locked up in the jail below us at this very moment."

Speaking of the basement jail, the smell of it was wafting up through the floorboards strong enough to be unpleasant. That usually happened only on hot summer days in the judge's courtroom, as the jail was immediately below it, but the two flagstone-floored common cells that sometimes held as many as a hundred prisoners must have been especially rank that spring morning for the odor to creep into the other end of the building. Perhaps the wet conditions had exacerbated the smell of what many in the city called *the dungeon*. The judge must have smelled the same thing, for he got up from his desk and cracked the window open to let in a little fresh air.

Footsteps sounded in the hallway outside the judge's office, and another man in a neat suit appeared in the open doorway and leaned one shoulder against the doorjamb. He was a man of pale complexion, with a long, thin nose and a mustache and goatee to match the judge's. A short-brimmed hat sat on his head, and his open coat front revealed a gold watch chain that was draped across his vest front below the U.S. marshal badge pinned on his breast. He wore no sidearm.

"You're late, D.P.," the judge said to the marshal. "Where's Mr. Clayton?"

D.P. Upham was the recently appointed United States Marshal for the Western District of Arkansas, the man Morgan directly reported to. He had made a name for himself as a militia officer fighting the Ku Klux Klan in the eastern half of the state after the war. He was a man with strong opinions, but so far he had been a reasonable boss, even if he was more of a fire-eater than the judge.

"Your district attorney said to tell you he's tied up this morning and couldn't make this little meeting, and I'm only here for moral support. You told him yet?" Marshal Upham said to the judge.

"Told me what?" Morgan asked. "Am I about to get fired because of that sorry excuse for a petition?"

"The judge sat back at his desk and propped both elbows on it and leaned closer to Morgan. "The reason we've been having this little discussion is because Marshal Upham, District Attorney Clayton, and myself want to know if you're the right man for a job we have in mind. I know you can handle yourself in a scrap, but I need to be sure that you are capable of judgment and discretion."

"What is it you want me to do?" Morgan asked.

The judge hesitated as if he wasn't sure how to properly frame what he was about to say. "Your ex-wife is holding a party or a meeting of some kind for some very influential businessmen and tribal leaders at her hotel in Eufaula three days from now. J.J. McAlester and the owners of the Osage Coal & Mining Company, as well as Chief Cole of the Choctaws are said to be among those attending. It's also rumored that

Superintendent Huffman from the Katy will be there, possibly Manager Bond, as well as a few other of Jay Gould's heel hounds and henchmen."

The Missouri, Kansas & Texas Railroad, the MK&T, was simply known as the Katy in the territory.

Morgan took a few seconds to let what the judge had said soak in before he replied, "And what's that got to do with me?"

"I'm sending you and two other deputy marshals to Eufaula to make sure nothing unexpected happens," the judge said.

"Unexpected?"

"Something I wouldn't like."

"You have a particular worry?"

"Chief Cole stands in staunch opposition to any intervention by white men in the Choctaw Nation and has already tried unsuccessfully to return ownership of all coal claims back to the tribe. As you might imagine, there is no love lost between himself and the mine owners, especially between he and J.J. McAlester."

Morgan considered that. J.J. McAlester was a known name in the territory. He had started out with a little trading post on the Texas Road, and then, years later, the Katy train tracks had been laid across his front door. Through hook or crook—mainly by gaining tribal citizenship through his marriage to a Chickasaw woman and his friendship with some ambitious and wealthy Choctaws—he had somehow gotten his hands on coal claims within the Choctaw Nation. The Katy was hungry for coal, and McAlester found a ready market. So ready that it wasn't long before the Katy bought into his mining company. And he was using those profits to add to his land holdings and mercantile business and turning what was once a sleepy little trading post into a real town—a town that bore his name.

And the trouble between Chief Cole and McAlester was not unknown to Morgan. The chief's attempt to nullify McAlester's coal claim rights and to have him arrested for illegally selling tribal resources was already becoming a legend within the territory. As the tale went, Chief Cole sent a force of Choctaw Lighthorsemen to apprehend the owners of the Osage Coal & Mining Co. and they surrounded McAlester's store. Some versions of the story claimed the Lighthorsemen informed the white men they were to be executed. But somehow, McAlester and one of his partners managed to get away from their captors and make use of the railroad handcar to escape up the Katy tracks to Eufaula in the Creek Nation where they hid out for a couple of months until cooler heads prevailed and the warrants for their arrest were done away with.

"Putting Chief Cole and McAlester in the same room might be like tying two old tomcats' tails together," Upham added. "Not to mention Gould's boys being there to stir the pot."

The judge nodded and sighed at the mention of Gould, the New York robber baron and railroad magnate. "Do you know what the newspapers are reporting? They're saying that Gould doesn't only own Wall Street, but also owns the Indian Territory. Only yesterday I read where they're calling it Gould's Territory and telling jokes about Gould's Indians."

"I thought this new man, Bond, is heading the Katy board now," Morgan said. It hadn't gone unnoticed on his part how often the judge mentioned the newspapers.

"Bond is nothing but Gould's puppet, same as Superintendent Huffman. The Katy going into receivership and the restructuring gave Gould the chance to put his people in place. He's taken it over behind the scenes, even if he isn't officially in charge, yet. Not to mention that he is now one of the partners in J.J. McAlester's coal company, through the Katy, of course," Upham added. "I read the papers, too."

The judge grunted and shook his head. "If Gould thinks the territory is his playground, then he is in for a rude awakening."

"The only railroad in the territory and all the coal," Morgan said. "I'd say he's already playing pretty hard."

"You understand the situation then," the judge said. "This court is under the constant scrutiny of both the Congress and the President, as well as our every action and decision being tried in the court of public opinion according to what the newspapers see fit to put on their front pages. I have no doubt there will be reporters tagging along with Gould's representatives and looking for salacious scraps. I want you to make sure nothing salacious happens in Eufaula while they're there."

"That's all?" Morgan asked. "You want me to referee a meeting?"

Judge Parker and Marshal Upham shared a look between them that Morgan couldn't decipher. Whatever silent conversation they held ended, and the judge looked back at Morgan.

"What has Helvina done this time?" Morgan asked.

"Too put it bluntly, Helvina Vanderwagen is a royal pain in my backside," the judge said. "I've got three cases involving her and her, ummm, *associates* for this court session. Members of the Creek tribe have grievances against her for illegal grazing, and I'm recently informed that she's bringing more Texas cattle up the trail as we speak. The other two cases involve a sawmill that the Choctaws claim is processing stolen timber, and a meat packing house at Muskogee for which one of her companies pays a license fee to the Creeks and where one of our marshals found five head of stolen cattle belonging to a Cherokee rancher."

"Shut her down," Morgan said.

"It's not that simple," the judge said. "While all those accusations may be true, your former wife is very adept at covering her machinations. She put one of the best lawyers in this city on retainer more than a year ago, and I'm told one of our state senators arrived by train at Van Buren yesterday. He is waiting for the river to go down to make his way to our fair city on Ms. Vanderwagen's behalf."

"Don't underestimate Helvina," Morgan said. "She's blatant about what she wants, but she's quite devious about how she gets there."

"Oh, I don't underestimate her. She has already shown an impressive knack for complicating the paper trail for the ownership of her businesses and has demonstrated an astounding knowledge of every legal loophole in existence that might be to her benefit. Not to mention that she seems to have friends in high places," the judge said. "There are rumors floating around that she is not above bribing or blackmailing certain tribal officials, and just a few days ago a reliable source told me that she has offered to purchase a cotton gin that she would allow the Creek tribe free use of in exchange for their granting her a 100-year lease on a thousand acres of prime bottom farm ground near Checotah Station. Not illegal, of course, but it is a sign of the expansive nature of her intentions."

"And where do I come in? Putting me on anything involving her is a defense lawyer's dream."

It was Marshal Upham's turn. He pulled a handful of roasted peanuts from his vest pocket and began to shell one of them. "We talked about that already."

"If you're investigating Helvina, you must think I have information you could use."

"No, that's not what we're asking. We wouldn't put you in that predicament, for both personal and legal reasons," the marshal replied.

"If I were you, I wouldn't trust me, not if I was looking at it from your end. How much of this is you wondering if I'm involved in Helvina's money grabbing? There are plenty of people in the territory that still think we're all crooks after what Judge Story and his boys pulled while they were running things."

The marshal shook his head. "We trust you, or we wouldn't be talking with you right now. Your history in Eufaula and your connections there might be viewed as a handicap, but we see them as the best way to have someone in place who knows the lay of things. Plus, given your background, we hope you will be better able to carry yourself with the proper deportment among some of Ms. Vanderwagen's guests, not to mention that you once worked for Superintendent Huffman and he trusts you."

"Still . . ." Morgan started to argue.

The marshal cut him off. "And we're sending Gus Chapman and Ted Tabor with you. They'll meet you in Eufaula two days from now. Chapman will be in charge."

"All right. Are we only working security for Helvina's social, or are we spying on her and the railroad boys while we're at it?"

Marshal Upham cleared his throat before he spoke. "Your job is to see that nothing happens to her guests until they get back on the train and on their way home, and to ensure that business arguments do not get out of hand. Any investigations pertaining to other matters, should such exist, will be handled by other officers of this court."

Marshal Upham straightened in the doorway and made as if to go back to his office. "Any idea who took a shot at you last night?"

"Not a clue," Morgan answered.

"The jailer tells me you brought in three prisoners yesterday afternoon."

Morgan nodded. "I had to go down in the Chickasaw Nation near Tishomingo to serve some subpoenas and take depositions, and then I picked up the Craven boys by accident on my way back."

"The Craven boys? That's good work," Upham exclaimed. "I don't mind admitting a personal grudge against those three, ever since they killed Deputy Marshal Hagerman after he arrested them. Knocked him over the head with a chunk of firewood one night in camp, choked him with their shackle chains, and killed his night guard with a butcher knife. But you knew that, didn't you?"

Morgan nodded.

"Damn good work, Clyde," Upham added. "I'll dance a jig and piss on their graves the day the judge stretches their worthless necks."

Judge Parker frowned at Marshal Upham, not hiding his displeasure at those harsh words. No one Morgan knew had ever heard the judge use profanity.

"They didn't give me much trouble," Morgan replied to the marshal.

Both Upham and the judge gave Morgan a knowing look that said how much that bland reply downplayed what it took to get three violent prisoners halfway across the territory with no help. While many of the marshals went out in groups in search of wanted criminals and used the aid of posse members and a prisoner wagon with guards, Morgan usually worked alone.

"Turn in your expense reports before you head out again," Marshal Upham said as he started down the hallway. "You're always concise with your figures, and I appreciate that."

"Tell that to your clerk so that he doesn't reject half my expenses like he usually does," Morgan said to the retreating marshal.

The judge rose from his chair and went to stand at the window when the marshal was gone. His back was to Morgan. "You think I look at you and judge you a violent, reckless man, but I understand more of what you face out there in the territory than you think. If there is one thing I have come to learn since I arrived in Fort Smith, it's that a coward can be highly moral, but he cannot serve as one of my peace officers. And you, Clyde, of all the things said about you, are no coward."

"I'm no saint and no devil. Only somewhere in between like the rest of us, I suppose," Morgan said while he rose from his chair and smoothed the hang of his black frock coat on his wide shoulders.

"Do you know what the newspapers back East are already calling me?" the judge asked. "They're calling me the 'Hanging Judge.' Can you believe that? As if I were worse than the murderous villains I sentence."

Morgan considered the serious, bright man from Ohio standing at the window, and he recalled the four men hung simultaneously on the gallows alongside the courthouse after the judge's first court session a year earlier, not to mention six more that the judge had sentenced to the same fate so far during the current court session.

"Seems like I'm not the only one with a reputation," Morgan said.

"Would it surprise you to know that I do not personally hold with capital punishment?" the judge asked. "But I will do my job. Equal and exact justice, that is my creed and motto, no matter what the papers say. If the adage of an eye for an eye and a tooth for a tooth written into our laws requires I sentence murderers to their deaths, then I will not quail or falter. The people of my district will look to Fort Smith and know that here lies a fair and just court to stand against the criminal element."

"Nice speech." Morgan put his hat on and slid a cigar from his vest pocket. He clenched the cigar between his teeth and gazed at the judge with his intense blue eyes. "Don't let it get to you, Judge. We'll get it done. You've got your ways, I've got mine, and to hell with the newspapers and the crooked lawyers."

Chapter Four

It was late in the morning by the time Morgan left the courthouse, gathered a few belongings from the boardinghouse where he resided during his intermittent stays in Fort Smith, and retrieved his horse from a corral at the stockyards. By then, the latest round of storms had moved on, the rain had quit for the time being, and the sun was threatening to break through the smoky gray clouds overhead.

Sun or no sun, it was going to be a muddy trip, and he had begrudgingly packed his black suit in his saddlebags. He now wore a light sheepskin, hip-length jacket, a flannel shirt, and a pair of tan ducking work pants tucked into the top of his fancy boots. There was also a Winchester rifle in a saddle boot beneath his left knee, and a canvas bedroll and oilcloth raincoat tied behind his cantle.

He was riding past the Hole in the Wall Saloon when somebody waved at him to get his attention. It was Harlan Dix, a local drunk and sometime swamper at the saloon. Morgan reined over to see what Harlan wanted.

"You look like somebody poured you out of the bottom of the bottle, Harlan. Rough night?" Morgan asked.

Harlan made an effort to tuck in a stray bit of the tail of his shirt that looked like it hadn't been washed in a long time, and rubbed at the whisker stubble on one cheek as if he only then realized that he hadn't shaved in almost a week. He grimaced and looked at Morgan out of bloodshot eyes.

"I hear somebody took a shot at you over to Jesse's place," he said.

"They did."

Harlan rubbed his cheek again, and then adjusted his grimy, battered hat on his head, as if whatever he was about to say made him uncomfortable. "Might interest you to know that I'm pretty sure I heard somebody trying to buy your killing."

"Did you now?"

"Oh, I know what you're thinking," Harlan said. "Damned right I was drunk, but I know what I heard. Sometimes when I'm short of spending money they let me help out 'round here. Last night was busy as the dickens, and I was supposed to be carrying a box of empty beer bottles out the back door. Guess I decided to sit and rest a spell, or maybe I just plain passed out. Next thing I knew there were two men talking."

"Who were they?"

"Couldn't see. They were standing in the dark, like maybe they came around back to have some privacy."

"And you're sure they were talking about me?"

"I might have been drunk off my ass, but I ain't deaf. I didn't catch it all, 'cause they were talking too quiet. But I'm sure I heard your name mentioned. And I heard one ask the other what it would cost to put an end to you," Harlan said. "And then the other says it would cost two hundred dollars and that he'd blow any man to hell for that much money. The fellow asking said that was about the most expensive shotgun shell he ever heard of."

"That's all they said?"

"All that I could make out."

"And you don't have any idea who it was?"

"Didn't recognize either of their voices, but when they left one of them walked through the edge of the lantern light by the back door. I was piled up inside a stack of packing crates, and down low like that all I could see was that he used a walking cane. Walking cane with a silver hand knob on it."

"Anything else?"

"That's about it. I haven't told anybody else."

"Appreciate you telling me."

"I reckon if the sheriff's men knew, they could go 'round looking for a man with a silver-handled walking cane. Can't be too many of those."

"Doubt it would come to much," Morgan said. "What say we keep this to ourselves. No since bothering the sheriff."

"Makes no never mind to me. You're the one who almost got his head blown off."

Morgan dug in his jacket pocket and pulled out a dollar and flipped it to the man. "You see anybody with a silver walking cane again, you take a good look at him so that you'll remember what he looks like the next time I'm back in Fort Smith."

"I didn't call you over here to go begging for money. Just thought you might like to know."

"Keep the money," Morgan said. "Helps sometimes to have a friend."

"Everybody says you ain't got no friends, Marshal. Maybe that's why you think you have to pay me."

"Keep a lookout for that silver walking cane." Morgan nudged his horse's belly with his spurs and rode off and left Harlan standing in front of the saloon.

He was soon past the outskirts of the city and struck the Skullyville Road. That road stayed south of the Arkansas River after it made its turn to the west, and headed toward the border with the Indian Territory.

The dun gelding with the peculiar leg stripes he rode, what some called a zebra dun, and with an unusual lightning bolt brand on its right shoulder, was a touch on the small side for such a tall man, but still a fine-looking mount and a good traveler. He let it choose its own pace, and it clipped down the road at a ground-eating trot, splashing through the mudholes and pinning its ears at the occasional dog that came to greet them along the edges of the byway.

The border between the Indian Territory, what some called the Indian Nations, and Arkansas was marked by the Poteau River immediately west of the city. There had once been a plank bridge built across the Poteau upstream a ways from where it spilled into the Arkansas, but that crossing was destroyed during the war. Now, the only means of crossing the Poteau without a dangerous and uncomfortable swim was by means of a ferry.

That ferry was nothing more than a sturdy-built barge of logs and oak planks with peeled pole handrails down two sides. A heavy cable was strong across the river and secured on each bank, and a steam engine and winch-and-pulley system provided the necessary propulsion to drag it across the water.

He was thankful to find that the ferry was operating again when he rode up to the notch in the riverbank where the road dropped down into the channel. If the river was not crossable near Fort Smith, then it meant he would have to go south towards the Winding Stair Mountains in hopes the river was lower closer to its headwaters, and that would take him miles out of his way and could add days to his trip.

The river was still high, but it had fallen some and was now several feet below the flood bank. No longer was it rolling with the fury it had been the two previous days, and the surface was flat, though still flowing strongly. It was nothing during such floods to see whole trees and other large debris being washed downstream on waves that resembled ocean surf, and no ferry operator or passenger in their right mind was going to ride across the river in such conditions.

The owners of the ferry had built a small log cabin just back from the riverbank to provide a place for travelers to wait out weather, but it had been washed away a week earlier and scattered bits of it were no doubt now on their way to the Mississippi. While the weather may have turned for the better, it was still a brisk spring day, and the wind was starting to blow. No matter, most travelers going to and fro in that country were used to such hardships. Several of those hardy souls were waiting under a white-trunked sycamore tree. They stood around a campfire, and several saddle horses were tied to a picket line nearby. There was a wagon parked a little farther back from the timber along the river and a farmer and his family had their own fire built, as if they might have been camped there since the previous night.

Morgan marked the location of the ferry, now on the far bank and loading two wagons, and made a quick calculation of how long it would be before it was back on his side. He was anxious to put some miles behind him, and didn't relish the wait before him.

He tied his horse with the others and went to the fire. Those gathered around the fire lifted their chins from their coat collars to nod at him in greeting, and he nodded back.

There were two young Indian men there. To what tribe they belonged to, he wasn't sure, but thought them Choctaws if he had to guess. Both were dressed like cowboys with their blue denim pants tucked into the tops of the tall-topped boots with spurs strapped to their heels and big-brimmed hats on their heads. That was not unusual in the eastern half of the territory for most of the Civilized Tribes, though the sight of such might have shocked some tenderfoot's notion of the wild red man. The territory was like that, and a place full of such flip-flopped expectations and stereotypes. The Indians often dressed like cowboys or farmers or bankers, while there were white men who acted more savage than any Indian ever written about in a dime novel.

Along with the Indians, there were two freighters who had come down to the river to check its condition, with the intent to come back the next day with their wagons if they found the ferry operating. While that mission had no doubt been completed, they seemed to have decided to stay and enjoy the conversation they found around the campfire. That, and perhaps shared a fondness for the bottle of whiskey being passed around to ward off the chill. One of those freighters held out the bottle to Morgan. Morgan's badge was hidden beneath his jacket, but apparently, the man recognized a lawman when he saw one, badge or not.

"Best we finish it on this side of the river," the freighter said. "Wouldn't want to take it into the territory and break the law, now would we, Marshal?"

Although Morgan, like the rest of D.P. Upham's force, was only a deputy United States marshal, the general slang for such peace officers was shortened to simply *marshals.* The man's companion and the two Indians laughed.

It was illegal to take any kind of alcoholic beverages into the territory or to possess it there. Running down bootleggers, whiskey peddlers, and busting up whiskey stills occupied a lot of the marshals' time, but it was not a crime on which Morgan focused his energy or efforts. The government wanted to keep whiskey and other spirits out of the Indian Nations because of its detrimental impact on the tribes, and most of the tribal leadership was equally intent on keeping the territory dry. However, in his opinion, that was an impossible task, no matter how well intentioned. Plus, he often imbibed, and persecuting other men for the same weakness felt entirely too hypocritical to suit him. Maybe picking and choosing what laws he was willing to enforce was wrong of him, but he had enough failings that he could live with another small one.

Morgan waved off the bottle. "No thanks."

Two men in a red-wheeled buggy came rolling up to the crossing. The buggy was pulled by a single horse charging down the road at a high trot. The driver brought the horse to a stop too close to the campfire, and some of the spray off the buggy's wheels splattered the two Indians. One of the Indians made as if to threaten the driver, but looked at Morgan and then kept whatever he was about to say to himself.

"Good, just in time," the driver said when he saw that the ferry was on its way back across the river.

The driver laid his ribbons on the seat, stepped down from the buggy, and went and dropped a cast-iron tie weight on the ground and snapped the piece of rope trailing from it to the snaffle bit ring on the horse. He was a petite man with a thin mustache, and wore a long oilcloth coat with caped shoulders and a bowler hat. Morgan had seen him somewhere before, but couldn't quite place him. The driver saw Morgan looking at him.

"Long time, no see," the driver said as he made his way towards the fire. He was young, and his walk was almost strutting, like a cocky little rooster showing off in the barnyard. "Marshal Clyde, isn't it?"

The other man in the buggy perked up at the mention of Morgan's last name, but Morgan's attention was too intent on the driver to notice.

"I'm afraid you have the advantage on me," Morgan said to the driver. "Have we met before?"

The driver gave a slight frown when Morgan did not shake his hand. "Charles Dunn. We met a year or so ago in Eufaula."

And then it dawned on Morgan who the kid was. "Charlie Dunn? Weren't you the bell boy at the Vanderwagen Hotel?"

"I was the manager, and my name is Charles, not Charlie," the man said with his annoyance plain in his clipped, Midwest accent.

"Oh?" Morgan's face was as bland as his speech. He could see the butts of two pistols through the open front of Dunn's oilcloth coat, one under each of his armpits in shoulder holsters. For a hotel fellow, he went mighty well-armed.

Dunn stood a little straighter as if that would make him taller. "I don't work at the hotel anymore. I've gone into business for myself."

"What business is that?" Morgan tried to remember what little he could of the Bantam rooster before him. From Chicago, as best as he could recall. Nosy, stuffy, presumptuous little devil. Tenderfoot with a bad attitude, the kind Helvina was likely to employ.

"This and that. You know how it is chasing a dollar," Dunn said.

"Sometimes takes a man a while to find what suits him," Morgan replied.

"Oh, I think I've found it."

The buggy springs creaked behind Dunn, and his passenger stepped down on the far side of it. When he came around the buggy horse he was revealed as an elderly man in a tan, three-piece suit. A mustard yellow silk tie was tied around his collar with a diamond stickpin in the center. A short stovepipe hat of the same color topped his head, with a thick thatch of gray hair and sideburns spilling from it.

He made his way carefully to the fire, making sure to avoid the worst of the mud to keep his polished shoes as clean as possible. He nodded at each of them stiffly and formally when he stopped at the edge of the heat cast by the fire, and gave a disgusted look and waved a hand in front of his face to ward off the smoke when a gust of wind washed it his way.

His attention fell on Morgan, last of them all, and it stayed there. Morgan's gaze was no less intense, his face taut and the tendons in his jaws visible. Unlike he had with the driver, Morgan had no problem at all recognizing the passenger. It had been a long time since he had last seen the man, but he would have known him anywhere.

"It's been a while, Morgan," the old man said. "Or should I say, Marshal Clyde?"

"Not long enough." The strain in Morgan's voice was evident.

Of all the men Morgan might have met on the riverbank, Adolphus Vanderwagen was the most unexpected. He was thoroughly caught off guard, the same as he had been by his ex-wife's arrival in the territory years earlier. It had been the lure of a crooked, lecherous railroad superintendent's money that had first drawn Helvina from the East, and he shouldn't have been surprised that the old man was coming to get in on the action now that his daughter had a foothold in the territory. The whole damned family was like that, feeding off and driving each other to the worst.

"I hoped that we might be past this, should we ever meet again," Adolphus said.

Morgan heard in the old man's accent a touch of his own, though his had faded over time.

"You put the damned Pinkertons on me," Morgan said, and held up his right hand where the knotted joints of his slightly crooked pointer and the middle fingers could be seen, as well as the tiny scars on the back of his hand. "They gave me this and broke my jaw. Made sure to tell me the message was from you."

The old man nodded thoughtfully. "I'm afraid I was a bit rash in that matter, passion of the moment and all. Would it help if I were to tell you I regret that decision and apologize? Helvina chose to make a new life for herself, and I merely wanted you to leave her alone."

"What makes you think I won't settle this here and now?" Morgan asked.

The other men at the fire began to back away from it, wanting no part of what was coming. They were men used to hard ways, and it was a country where disagreements were often settled with violence.

"You won't harm me, because like me, you have matured and understand that to let bygones be bygones is sometimes the only course of action left to us, and that the only way to get on with one's life is to let go of the past," Adolphus said.

Morgan looked at him and was reminded of nothing but bad memories and old hurts still not healed. They settled in the pit of his stomach like kerosene. So long ago that it sometimes felt like another life and another world, but Adolphus's presence was bringing it all back as if it were only yesterday.

"Go back to where you came from, Adolphus," Morgan said. "Go back if you want to keep the peace between us."

"I've come a long ways to visit my daughter and to see the fine hotel she has built," Adolphus said. "Whether you believe it or not, I bear you no ill will. Not anymore."

"Once a liar, always a liar."

Charlie Dunn's posture stiffened. "He's got no call to talk to you like that, Mr. Vanderwagen."

Morgan looked at Dunn from head to toe, and there was disdain written all over his face. "Did you say something?"

"Mr. Dunn, please stay out of this, if you would," Adolphus said before Dunn could do anything, the same stuffy politeness and snobbery dripping off his every word. "Some men, given the slightest authority, can't help abusing their position. I'm sure Morgan is trying to bait me in order that he may drag me off to some God-awful jail, or otherwise bully me as a matter of revenge. You see? He and I have a history. A regretful history, but it is what it is."

"I don't like how you're talking to Mr. Vanderwagen," Dunn said.

"You can go to hell." Morgan felt the black, bitter rage rising within him, a thing that he welcomed as much as he feared it.

Dunn took a slow step backward, as if physically struck, and a flush spread over his face.

Adolphus held up a hand, the gold and ruby ring on one of his fingers so large and gaudy it was impossible to miss. "Mr. Dunn, again I admonish you to remove yourself. This is a family matter. If you are too greatly offended, then I suggest we report Marshal Clyde's behavior to the authorities back in Fort Smith. I'm sure they would love to hear how one of their peace officers is accosting innocent travelers."

"You, innocent?" Morgan scoffed.

"Come, Mr. Dunn, let's go back to our buggy and wait for the ferry," Adolphus said. "Do not stoop to his level."

Dunn hung back for a moment, staring at Morgan. "You think you're a big man, don't you?"

Morgan only stared back at him.

Dunn blinked his eyes and looked up at Morgan's hat as if it intrigued him. It was a John B. Stetson in black beaver felt, and with a flat brim and a four-inch rounded crown.

"Nice hat. One like that would look good on me." Dunn gave a sick little grin and then turned on his heel and started for the buggy.

Adolphus shifted his weight as if to go after his driver.

"Be careful, Adolphus," Morgan said. "You aren't in New York anymore."

Adolphus made a mocking show of looking around at his surroundings, as if only then realizing where he was. "A bit primitive, but I would venture a guess that a man with the experience and the ambition might go far here. Getting in on the ground floor and all, you know?"

"The territory doesn't need your kind."

"It's a shame. You once showed so much promise," Adolphus threw over his shoulder as he walked away. "And now here you are like this. I don't even know how to describe the state to which you have fallen. You really should look at yourself in a mirror, Morgan Clyde. You might not like what you see."

Morgan watched him climb back into the buggy. Dunn drove it closer to the ferry landing.

One of the freighters let out a low whistle of relief and came back to the fire. The others followed behind him. No one said anything, all of them simply staring into the smoke and flames, and only stealing occasional glances at Morgan.

Finally, the same one that had whistled looked up at Morgan. "Thought there was about to be trouble."

"Huh?" Morgan asked, still watching Adolphus and his henchman sitting in the buggy overlooking the river a few yards down the road.

"I said who was that fellow, if you don't mind my asking?"

Morgan thought about the question for longer than he should have, thinking of just how to sum up Adolphus Vanderwagen. And it was his turn to grimace. "Well, he used to be my father-in-law."

"Thought it was something like that," the freighter said, and then let out another low whistle like a sigh. "No trouble like family trouble, is there?"

"No, there isn't," Morgan replied.

What was it that old lawman had once told him? It was the people that were hard, not the job.

"Well, the territory's a big place. It's likely you two can keep your distance," the freighter said, and then took a slug from his whiskey bottle.

Morgan gave a bitter chuckle at the irony of the freighter's words. The freighter heard him and looked a question at him, but Morgan said nothing to let him in on the joke. Instead he surprised the freighter and reached and took the whiskey from him. He turned up the bottle and took a long pull from it.

The freighter watched him with one eyebrow cocked, and then nodded his head as if he understood. "Won't fix what ails you, but it'll sometimes cut the edge off things."

Morgan took another slug of the whiskey, watching the ferry coming from the Indian Territory. It was nearing the landing and pushing a wave the color of weak coffee in front of it. He looked across the river to the west. Seventy miles in that direction along a course of bad roads and trails lay a sleepy little railroad town called Eufaula. The whiskey settled in the pit of his stomach and mixed bitterly with bile already churning there.

"There isn't enough whiskey in the whole wide world to take the edge off what's bothering me."

Chapter Five

Cumsey Bowlegs was anxious to see his sweetheart again, and he touched up the little paint gelding he rode with his spurs and put him down the rutted, muddy lane at a fast, ground-eating walk. It was eleven miles as the crow flew from his cabin on Choate Prairie to Canadian Station, and he was impatient to make it there with plenty of daylight left and in time to catch the next northbound train.

He didn't usually take trains, much preferring overland travel on the back of a good-looking, sweet-traveling horse that he could show off to anyone he passed on his way, but the train was his only recourse if he wanted to avoid a dangerous river crossing. He had forded many a river in his time—waded them, swum them, floated them with reckless disregard—but given all the recent spring rain, the South Canadian was no doubt running out of its banks. And he had more than a healthy fear of that particular river, feeling that it had some special vendetta out for him.

Some years before, when he was still a boy, he had tried to ford it on the rise and had lost a horse and a good saddle to the boggy quicksand of the flooded river bottom, not to mention that he had barely gotten away with his life. Since then, he avoided crossing the South Canadian except during dry times, and felt as if he would live much longer due to that sensible decision.

The stiff breeze fluttered the bandanna tied loosely around

his neck, cowboy style. It was brand-new made of red silk, and he had chosen it especially for this trip. The new dove gray felt hat he wore was set at a rakish angle on his head, and his high-topped boots shined with a fresh coat of polish. And not only had he polished his boots, but he put on his cleanest white shirt. A man going courting needed to look his best.

He was an unusually handsome man, at least according to the testimony of many a maiden scattered across the territory, no matter whether they be black, red, white, or somewhere in between like Cumsey himself was. His mother had been a black slave woman, and his father a Seminole full-blood, and that blend of heritage had left him with a square, dimpled chin, big brown eyes with long, soft eyelashes that many a woman would have envied, and skin the color of dark honey. His teeth were perfect and white, and he was a man that smiled often.

Thoughts of flashy horses and equally pretty women occupied most of Cumsey's time, and right then, Cumsey was smiling and showing those pearly whites while he thought about a certain pretty schoolmarm that awaited him at the end of his journey. The paint gelding covered another mile while Cumsey daydreamed.

The next thing he knew they came upon a farm set right alongside the road, and he wasn't sure if his paint had somehow stopped of its own accord or if he had reined it in.

The farm didn't look prosperous, simply a little cabin whose logs were old enough to have turned gray, termite tunnels already showing in the wood. The corncrib, barn, and hog pen looked equally run-down and poor. The black filly standing in the corral was of such a fine quality that she looked entirely out of place.

He considered himself an expert judge of horseflesh, and he took in the filly's fine lines, the deep chest and strong hindquarters, yet still with the refinement of head and neck. She was short-backed and long underneath, and he guessed her a sprinter. A three year old, or maybe four, only then blooming into the prime of her looks. Steeldust blood in her, unless he missed his guess. She cocked one smart ear in his direction when he moved his paint over closer to the fence. There wasn't but one white speck on her, and that was a single star squarely between her soft, intelligent eyes.

"Now ain't you a lovely lady?" Cumsey said to the filly.

The filly came to the fence and stretched her neck over the top rail.

"Oh, you little temptress," Cumsey said with a grin.

There was no sign of anyone stirring around the farm, and he couldn't help it that his gaze drifted to the corral gate. It would be such an easy thing to open that gate. A halter and lead rope hung on the gatepost as if those items had been left there specifically for him.

Again, he looked for any sign of someone watching him, and shook his head at how easy it would be and at the incompetence of whoever owned the filly. Anyone living in the territory and owning a horse like that was a fool not to keep her better secured.

He thumbed his hat farther back on his head looked up at the sky. "You testing me, Big Guy? Well, I ain't going to do it. There was a time when I would have, but I won't."

He congratulated himself for his newfound willpower and ability to stay on the straight and narrow, and urged his paint gelding down the road again. He was humming snatches of a favorite tune when he passed through a stretch of timber atop a hill where the road came out on the edge of a little prairie. Before him in the distance was McElhaney's Store.

Despite its humble appearance as a one-room cabin, the store was a popular place and a drawing point for people from miles around, and not only because it was situated at a crossroads.

There were several saddle horses tied out back of the store under the spreading limbs of an oak, and Cumsey guessed it must be mail day. While not an official post office, volunteers brought the mail to the store by horseback from Canadian Station a couple of times a week.

He stopped his horse to get a good look at who might be hanging around the place. There was still the matter of a certain warrant hanging over his head, a little confusion and misunderstanding about the ownership of a team of stout gray wagon horses that he once briefly had in his possession. The new Choctaw sheriff lived nearby, and had already promised to have him whipped and run him out of not only Tobucksy County, but the whole Choctaw Nation. If the sheriff or any other lawman was there, he wanted to see them first.

The gloomy weather must have driven everyone inside the store, for he saw nothing other than the saddle horses under the tree. Somebody's hound had a squirrel treed down in the creek bottom, and its bawling voice rang in the still air. A handful of chickens scratched in the middle of the road beside the store, picking worms driven to the top of the ground by all the recent rain.

He was about to ride on in when he caught a glimpse of a buggy coming towards the store at a high clip from the south. The top of the buggy was up and made it hard to see who was driving, but there were two outriders on saddle horses loping along with it, one on either side.

He considered the bright splotch of color, almost white, showing behind the buggy's dashboard and decided that it was a woman driving it, a woman wearing a pale dress. And she was a reckless driver, for he could make out the flick of the driver's buggy whip over the buggy horse's back.

Normally, he might have taken more time casing the store or avoided it all together, but his curiosity got the best of him. He had been alone at his remote hideout at the far end of Choate Prairie too long, and he wanted to see what kind of woman might be traveling with two guards.

A gunshot cracked the air, and at first Cumsey thought someone was shooting at him. The paint beneath him, startled by the noise, bolted of its own accord, not back over the top of the hill, but towards the store where the shot had come from. Cumsey reined it towards the cover of timber and the thicket along the edge of the road. He pushed his way through the tangle of growth until he had put both he and the horse behind the large trunk of a walnut tree.

More gunshots sounded, and he flinched and shucked his Winchester '73 rifle from the saddle boot beneath his left knee. It took him a moment to realize that none of the shots were aimed his way. Taking a deep breath, he watched the fight playing out before him.

No, it wasn't a fight. It was a plain and simple ambush.

Whoever those horses at the store belonged to had waited until the buggy was almost upon them before they opened fire with no warning. One of the riders with the buggy never even got his gun into the fight, and was blown out of his saddle with the first killing shot. As Cumsey watched, the woman driving the buggy and the other rider somehow managed to turn around and flee back down the road under a hail of gunfire. Cumsey could see the burps of muddy water splashed up from the flooded wheel ruts in the road where bullets struck. The buggy bounced and careened wildly, and the surviving rider racing along with it snapped wild shots with his rifle at the store behind them.

The buggy didn't make it far before that rider's horse was shot out from under him. The horse went down and its rider went flying over its head while the buggy kept going. The rider must have been a brave man and uncommonly cool in a fight, for he crawled back to his dead horse and forted up behind it with his rifle across its side. Once, twice, his rifle boomed, and little white gun smoke clouds hung as thick and fluffy as cotton bolls around him in the damp air each time he fired.

And then a bigger gun boomed from inside the store. Not the pop of a saddle carbine loaded with pistol cartridges like a .44-40 or .44 rimfire, but a big bore caliber like a Sharps or a Remington Rolling Block. The man down behind the dead horse in the road was a good one hundred and fifty yards from the store, but the bullet struck him squarely in the forehead. He flopped backwards and didn't move again.

The road south doglegged around the corner of some farmer's corn patch, and the buggy made the turn on two wheels, almost tipping over before it went out of sight. In a matter of seconds, men were pouring out of the store and getting on their horses. There were six of them, and they raced down the lane after the buggy, whipping and spurring their mounts to greater speed.

One of them paused in the road long enough to put a second bullet in the first rider they had downed before he spurred after the rest of his counterparts. Like the buggy, the gang soon disappeared around the corner of the cornfield. Cumsey heard no more shooting.

He rode from the timber and to the store with his Winchester ready. Both the back and front doors were wide open. He went on down the road to the first body. It was a white man. One bullet had struck him in the hip and he might have survived that, but another bullet had been put in his back square between his shoulder blades while he lay facedown in the road. He wouldn't be getting back up again.

A little farther along was the dead horse, its flesh pockmarked with bullet holes, and behind it the body of the second rider, an Indian. Most of the top of his head was gone.

There was still no sound of further gunfire, and he stared down the road in the direction that the buggy and its pursuers had gone. He grimaced and cracked open the action on his rifle enough to make sure there was a round in the chamber, and then put the paint to a lope towards the corner of the cornfield.

The road past the field dropped off gradually to where a little shallow branch cut between the low, rolling hills on the far side of the prairie. Thinly scattered post oak trees dotted the waist-high grass, and when he found the buggy a mile farther on, it was barely visible lying on its side several yards off the road. The horse that had pulled it was gone along with the driver. The grass was smashed flat and the ground was chewed to pieces with hoofprints where the buggy's attackers had encircled it. And he found several imprints of a woman's small shoe amongst the tracks, confirming that the buggy's driver had been a woman.

The hoof tracks led across the branch and up a long slope towards a dense stand of timber. He had barely gone halfway up the hill following them when, almost simultaneously, his horse groaned and staggered, and the boom of that big rifle echoed across the hills again.

The bullet struck the paint squarely in the chest, and it dropped out from under him in an instant. He barely managed to kick free of his saddle to avoid being pinned beneath it. Fully expecting more shots fired his way, he scrambled on his hands and knees for cover.

Close by was a tree downed in some past storm, and he tucked in behind its upturned root ball and peered around one side of it with his rifle ready. He assumed the shot had come from the forest at the top of the hill, but if so, his attackers were too well hidden for him to make out. He ducked back behind the root ball, not liking the thought of leaving his head exposed too long.

He cursed the pinch he found himself in and the moment of rash decision making that put him there. Nobody but a fool went against six guns.

Some time passed with not so much as another single shot fired his way. He was leery to expose himself, no matter that he assumed that whoever had taken the woman was likely to be in a hurry to get out of the vicinity of their crime. Such assumptions could get a man killed in a hurry.

When he finally broke cover, he went to his fallen horse and stripped the saddle and bridle from it. He started walking back to the crossroads with his rifle in one hand and his tack slung over the other shoulder.

He had almost made his way back to the store when he saw someone coming out of the cornfield. It was young McElhaney, the storekeeper. He was on foot and carrying a shotgun, and he was as nervous and jumpy as a cat in a storm.

"Cumsey Bowlegs, you're a sight for sore eyes," the storekeeper said. "I thought you were a goner when you went down the road after them."

"They shot my horse out from under me."

The storekeeper shook his head. "When I saw that bunch coming up the road, I knew they were no good."

"So you ran into that field?" Cumsey studied the mud that completely coated the front of the storekeeper's clothes, and then he eyed the cornfield skeptically. The new corn was barely ankle high, and thin and died out in places where too much standing water had damaged the planting—not much of a place to hide.

"I ran to the house to get my shotgun." The wood forearm on the shotgun was loose, and the storekeeper was shaking so badly that it rattled.

McElhaney claimed to be Cherokee, but like a lot of the more well-to-do Indians among the Five Civilized Tribes, he was as much or more white than red, as was evident by his last name and his pale complexion. Cumsey didn't care, and it also happened to be one thing he liked about the territory. Being a half-breed didn't carry the stigma it did in a lot of places, especially amongst his own tribe. Black folks had always lived around the Seminole, some free and some as slaves, even back when the tribe was still in Florida.

But a Cherokee full-blood—Cumsey knew plenty of them—would have said it was the white part of McElhaney that was doing the lying. Not that some Indians wouldn't lie, but only a white man would look you in the eye when he spoke with a forked tongue. It was obvious that the storekeeper had taken one look at the outlaws headed toward his store, grabbed his shotgun, ran out in the field, and laid down on his belly hoping not to be seen.

"Did you recognize any of them?" Cumsey asked.

"Not a one," the storekeeper said. "What about Mrs. McAlester? Did she get away?"

"Mrs. McAlester?"

"She came by here yesterday and bought a few things. Said she was on her way to Eufaula for some kind of party, but was going to visit a friend and stay the night first."

"She kin to J.J.?"

"His wife," the storekeeper said. "You think they were out to rob her? Everybody knows her man's got money."

"Found her buggy turned over down the road a piece," Cumsey answered. "Looks like they took her with them."

"Lord Almighty, I knew that was a bloody bunch the instant I laid eyes on them, but I never . . ." the storekeeper said. "Stealing women in the broad daylight, and her baby boy with her."

"Baby?"

"Little one, maybe three or four years old. You need to ride down to the Tobucksy Courthouse and tell the law what's happened. Judge is holding court today, and Sheriff Choate is likely to be there. If you can't find them, look for one of the federal marshals or leave word for them at McAlester's store. Send a message on the wire about what's happened."

"You know that wouldn't be a good idea."

"What wouldn't be a good idea?"

"Me going to the courthouse, that's what."

"Goodness gracious, they just shot down two men in cold blood and ran off with Rebecca McAlester!"

There was no way Cumsey was going to hunt up a lawman of any kind, white or red. The storekeeper knew his situation. From what Cumsey had heard, the man spent a good deal of his spare time gossiping about him.

"You ride after the sheriff," Cumsey said.

"I can't go off and leave my store unattended."

"I don't have a horse."

"I'll loan you mine," the storekeeper said. "Think about that poor woman. The Lord only knows what she's going through right now."

Cumsey found it more than a little ironic that the same man who had hidden on his belly in the mud during the ambush was now lecturing him about moral duty. He slogged his way toward the store with the storekeeper on his heels and nervously chattering away like a songbird.

"You're going to be the last thing on Sheriff Choate's mind when you tell him what's happened," the storekeeper added. "Might even be a good thing for you, riding for help. Any judge couldn't help but consider that. I'll tell them how you tried to go after her and get her back until your horse got shot."

"I told you I'm not going."

"Well, at least ride over to Canadian Station and give the word. Have the depot house send a wire to her husband at Eufaula. She told me she was going to meet him there."

Cumsey pointed down at the dead men in the road as they walked past the bodies. "You know him or the other one?"

"No. You think they were her kin?"

"Who knows?"

"What do you think they're going to do to her? Them that took her, I mean."

Cumsey sat his saddle and gear down by the store's front door. "If you bring me a horse I'll ride to Canadian Station and give the word."

The storekeeper hesitated. "I'd appreciate it if you brought him back."

Cumsey scowled at the storekeeper. "What's that supposed to mean? You implying something?"

"It's just that . . . Well, you know . . . He's the only horse I've got."

"You think I wouldn't bring him back?"

"I didn't mean anything by it. You can leave him at Canadian Station if you aren't coming back here."

The storekeeper left, and wasn't gone long. When he returned he was leading a saddled bay horse. Cumsey had helped himself to a stick of licorice from one of the jars on the counter inside the store, and he stood leaning against the doorjamb and chewing the candy. He recognized the horse the storekeeper was leading as belonging to the first rider shot in the ambush.

"I found him standing at my barn door wanting in with my stock," the storekeeper said. "Must have ran that way during the shooting."

Cumsey studied the leggy bay gelding with a critical eye. The bay was thin after a long, cold winter, as if its owner might have been stingy with the feed. But a little corn and another few weeks of green spring pickings and the gelding would flesh out nicely, even if Cumsey guessed him a little slow. Not a horse he would have picked for himself, but it would do in a pinch. He swapped his own saddle and tack for that on the horse while the storekeeper held it.

"Any men close by that you can gather?" he asked.

"You mean a posse?" the storekeeper asked.

"That bunch will be long gone and their trail cold by the time the law gets here."

"Everybody knows you're on the scout, but me . . . I'm no fighter, and neither are my neighbors," the storekeeper said. "Oh, I can bust a squirrel or a rabbit when you give me time enough to aim and a good rest for my shotgun, but I've got a wife and a new baby myself."

Cumsey nodded. "Well then, I don't guess either one of us is going to be a hero today."

The storekeeper took a deep breath. "I don't mind admitting that I'm scared. Scared as all get-out. What if those men come back?"

"If I was you and they come back, I would run. Most wouldn't tell you that because it doesn't make for a good story, but being scared beats the hell out of being dead every time."

The storekeeper frowned and shuffled his feet. "Hard to think about that poor woman and her child in such a scrape and not trying to help her. Like you said, maybe there's a couple of men I might could get to help."

"You do that," Cumsey said as he started the bay horse down the road to the east.

He left the storekeeper staring after him, and two hours later rode into Canadian Station. He had started the morning feeling like it was going to be a lucky day, but he was wrong and it only kept getting worse. Not only did the depot agent inform him that the recent flooding had washed out the telegraph line both ways out of the station, but also that he had missed the northbound train by an hour and there wouldn't be another run until the next day.

He shared word of the ambush and the taking of Rebecca McAlester and her child, and then moved out again on a lathered horse, following the Katy tracks north towards Eufaula. Maybe the day would get better.

And it came to him that if the ferry on the South Canadian was out of commission he was going to have to take a swim.

"Hasn't rained since yesterday," he said to the horse he rode, mainly because there was no one else to talk to. "Maybe the river's gone down."

He was nearing the river bottom when he came across an Indian boy driving a wagon back in the direction of Canadian Station. He and the boy stopped in the road.

"How's the river?" Cumsey asked, and the smile he gave the boy was intentionally optimistic.

The boy actually laughed at him. "Where do you think I'm going, mister? She's running bank to bank or I wouldn't be turning back for home."

Cumsey rode on, at a loss to think of some good thing that might change his day. He tried to focus on his sweetheart instead of the river, and how he was going to surprise her with a visit. And he tried not to think about the stolen woman and her child, or having to risk getting himself arrested in order to find her husband and give him the word. And he also tried not to consider the fact that he was once again riding a horse that didn't belong to him. Being a reformed man was harder than he ever expected.

Chapter Six

It was a day later than Morgan intended when he finally rode into Eufaula, once known as Ironhead Station when it had been nothing more than an end-of-the-tracks tent camp during the construction of the Katy railroad. He had spent three days on the road from Fort Smith, and it had rained on him most of that time. And even now, the sky was overcast and gloomy.

Eufaula had grown a little since his last visit more than a year earlier, but under such lighting it was still a gray, drab little frontier town. No two buildings matched in style. Some were log, some were framed with rough-sawn lumber, and only a few were painted.

Both he and his horse were covered in a splattering of mud, and they followed the Katy's roadbed along the storefronts and shops lining it until they reached a white, two-story frame building standing catty-corner at a street intersection. A long front porch fronted it, and a sign over that porch proclaimed it the VANDERWAGEN HOTEL.

He did not stop there, but turned down the side street between the hotel and the Katy depot and went on to the place he sought. A false front of rough-sawn pine planks daubed in a thick coat of red paint presented itself before him. Behind that front was only a large canvas tent, and it had once been home to a saloon known as the Bullhorn Palace back in the days when Eufaula had been nothing but a hell-on-wheels boom camp. The sign nailed to a post in front of the false front marked the place as MOLLY O'FLANAGAN'S BARBERSHOP, what most locals simply referred to as Red Molly's place. A red and white striped barber's pole was hung to one side of the front door, and it hadn't been there the last time Morgan was in town.

Morgan glanced at the slow trickle of woodsmoke floating out of the chimney pipe above the barbershop, and then left his horse at the hitching rail and went inside. Tent or no tent, the warmth of the room he entered immediately struck him as he closed the door behind him.

A thin man of medium height, with his dark hair oiled and parted neatly in the middle, was the only one in the shop. He was wearing a paisley vest, and his white shirtsleeves were bound at his upper arms by black garters. He came across the room with his hand held out. One of his legs was stiff at the knee, and his limping stride thumped on the puncheon floor with a distinct sound.

"Long time, no see. Eh?" the barber said. "That is what you say, no?"

"Noodles, your English is getting better," Morgan answered as he shook hands with the man.

The barber shook his hand with a smile on his face. "I practice, you know. I talk it all the time."

"That's good." Morgan took off his jacket and hat and hung them on the coat tree by the door.

Noodles, whose real name was Salvatore Finocchiaro, had been one of the early comers to town, first working with the Katy crews until he got a railroad iron dropped on his leg. Since then, he had served as a bartender and now a barber.

"Signor Clyde, do you come for a haircut or a shave?" Noodles asked.

Morgan ran a hand over the dark whisker stubble on one

cheek and nodded. "I could use both, but how about a drink first?"

Morgan started for the canvas sheet that divided the front of the tent from the back. Noodles stepped in front of him to stop him.

"We don't have a back room no more," Noodles said.

Morgan was surprised, and first thought Noodles was kidding him. The barbershop had always been nothing more than a front for Red Molly's real business, which was a saloon.

Barbershops were one of the businesses legally allowed for non-tribal members to own in the Indian Territory. Taking advantage of that loophole, and operating under a license from the Creek tribe and paying an annual fee to them, the barbershop occupied the front room, but the back room had always offered a respectable supply of various liquors and a few card tables where visitors might be invited if it was deemed they could be trusted. It had been a flimsy cover and not one that had been much of a secret, but Molly tried to keep a low profile and most looked the other way. Noodles's nickname had been given to him due to the pasta he sometimes cooked for the free lunch the saloon used to offer its customers. That, and nobody in Eufaula could pronounce his real name.

Over time, Molly's place had become as much as a social club as it was a barbershop or a saloon. Not only was it a place to get a drink or one of Noodles's lunches, the men who came there had come to expect the best collection of the latest newspapers and Eastern periodicals, which were taken straight off the trains and piled on a table in the barbershop for all to catch up on the news. A good selection of cigars and pipe tobacco was on hand for sale, not to mention that the owner, Red Molly, was once the best-known dove on the Katy line from Kansas to Texas, and a woman who was very easy on the eyes. There were men in the territory who would ride a long ways for no more than a look at a pretty woman.

"Come on, quit pulling my leg," Morgan said.

"I don't understand. I don't pull your legs. No, not me."

"What's the joke, you little Italian? Did Molly put you up to this?"

"I have told you many times. I am Sicilian." Noodles leaned aside and made a fake spitting motion in disgust.

Morgan had forgotten how touchy Noodles was about that, and couldn't keep down a grin. "Sorry, I forgot."

"We don't serve whiskey here no more," Noodles said. "My family lives in the back room now."

Noodles had once spoken of bringing his family to America as soon as he saved enough money. "How long have they been here?"

Noodles shrugged. "Three months. My children, they already speak English better than me, but their mama, she teach them from this little book since before they get on the ship. And the priest, Monsignor Pickins, he teach them at his church. At first we think it maybe a bad thing to go to such a place with the Methodists, for we are Catholics, but they learn fast and we want most for them to be good Americans."

Morgan nodded. "Sounds like a good plan."

"My wife, she a smart woman."

Morgan gave one last regretful look at the canvas walls dividing the two halves of the place. "Now, you mean to tell me Molly really shut down her saloon?"

"Too many *poliziotti* come around," Noodles said and pointed at Morgan's badge. "They all no like you, and *Signora Testa Rossa,* I think all the trouble make her think she don't want to take so many chances no more. No more selling the whiskey."

"Well, where's she at? I wouldn't mind seeing her. Been a while," Morgan replied.

"She don't feel so good. Sick all the time. This winter . . . the wet and the cold, it was hard on her." Noodles gave a fake cough into his hand, as if that said it all. "You know she get married? She don't live here anymore. She and Signor Dixie, they stay at their farm. I rent the barbershop now."

"Married? She and Dixie?"

Noodles nodded. "I thought you know this."

"Times change," Morgan said. "I guess if you don't have anything to chase the damp from my bones, I'll take you up on the offer of a haircut and a shave."

Noodles picked a white cloth up off the barber's chair, gave it a brisk snap before folding it over one forearm, and gestured for Morgan to take a seat in the cast-iron and nickel-plated barber's chair.

Morgan started to sit, but Noodles pointed at the revolver on Morgan's hip. "You do not take off your *pistola,* even to get a haircut?"

"Carried it so long I suppose I feel funny without it," Morgan said and left his gun belt on when he sat down.

Noodles shrugged. "*Pistolas* make me jumpy, ever since the trouble, you know. I hear someone shoot and for a little while I think it is all happening again."

Morgan gave Noodles a look. While timid on the outside, he recalled that the unassuming, nervous Sicilian had held his ground quite well during the trouble of the previous year. He and a few others had been the only ones to stand with Morgan during a gunfight at the hotel with some outlaws and a trio of crooked deputy marshals.

"It's not a gun you have to watch out for so much as the kind of man that happens to be carrying it," Morgan said as Noodles settled the cloth over him and secured it around his neck.

Noodles spun the chair until it was facing a mirror on the wall behind it, and then reclined the backrest. Morgan relaxed as Noodles laid a hot towel over his face. The cast-iron, potbellied stove in one corner of the room ticked pleasantly from the heat of the bed of coals inside it. He must have almost fallen asleep, for the next thing he knew Noodles was taking the towel off his face and the little bell on the door was ringing as another customer came in.

Morgan looked in the mirror and saw a redheaded, stocky man hang his hat on the coat tree as the door closed behind him. Both his sleeves were rolled up to his elbows, and there were faint traces of coal dust and brown rust on his shirtfront and the thighs of his pants. He took a seat in a chair across the room behind Morgan and nodded at him in the mirror.

"Saw you ride into town," the man said to Morgan.

Noodles was rubbing shaving cream on Morgan's face with a brush, and reclined like Morgan was, he had to look along his chin to see the man in the mirror. "That you, Hank? From the look of you, I take it I'm addressing the blacksmith and not the undertaker today."

Hank Bickford served Eufaula in both capacities, no matter how unusual of a combination it was. He also was a fine woodworker and carpenter, and quite possibly the hardest working man Morgan had ever met. Like Noodles, he once worked for the Katy, but he and his family had remained behind once the tracks moved on to Texas. And like the Sicilian barber, he was one who had helped Morgan in the fight the year before, not to mention some other troubles before then.

Noodles put a finger under Morgan's chin and scraped the straight razor up Morgan's throat.

"How's business?" Morgan asked Hank.

"Which business do you mean?" Hank replied.

"You tell me."

"Fine. Fine. But it's liable to be better now that you're back in town," Hank said with a twinkle in his eyes, and unable to suppress a hint of a grin.

Morgan caught the inference in those last words. "Will it now?"

Hank looked over the top of his newspaper. It was a copy of the latest edition of the *Indian Journal.* "Do you know what they call the cemetery up there on the hill now? They call it Clyde's Orchard, seeing as how you put most of those there under the ground. Go against Morgan Clyde, they say, and he'll plant you in his orchard and grow another tombstone."

Morgan gave a scoffing grunt to show his displeasure, causing his head to jerk slightly, and he felt the nick and the sting of the razor on his throat.

"Hold still," Noodles said to Morgan. "You make me cut you."

"How are Lottie and the kids?" Morgan asked Hank.

"Lottie's fine. She's still doing laundry for the train men and baking for the hotel on the side. Kids are growing like weeds," Hank answered.

"Can't see her being able to work for Helvina," Morgan said.

"Got to have a lot of irons in the fire to make a living," Hank said. "Ms. Vanderwagen's money spends just as good as any, even if she's a witch to work for."

Morgan closed his eyes again while Noodles rubbed the last traces of the shaving cream from his face and prepared to cut his hair.

"How long you in town for?" Hank asked while Noodles was snipping with his scissors.

"Couple of days, maybe," Morgan said. "I hear Helvina's throwing a party."

"I'll bet you anything she didn't send you an invite. That woman hates you like pure poison," Hank replied.

"Any of her guests in town yet?"

"You're late. Don't know the half of them, but they're all up there at the hotel mingling and doing whatever muckety-mucks do," Hank said.

"Maybe they argue about who has more money," Noodles said, and then frowned over his most recent cut with the scissors.

Hank nodded. "Could be. All I know is that she went whole hog and then some revving things up to impress them. Got that hotel lobby all decorated up even more than usual. Real high-toned. Had me make her a big table. Fine a piece of furniture as I ever built, ten feet long and made out of quarter-sawed ash. Must weigh three hundred pounds. She called it a banquet table."

"Anybody else in town?" Morgan asked.

"Like who?" Hank answered.

"Any other marshals?"

"No. You expecting some?"

Instead of answering him, Morgan looked down at a long lock of hair that fell into his lap and then caught Noodles's attention in the mirror. "I thought you were only going to take a little off the top."

"I cut good. Make it short," Noodles said.

Hank laughed and got up from his chair and put his hat back on.

"Where are you going? Thought you were waiting for a haircut?" Morgan asked.

Hank made a show of studying the job Noodles was doing on Morgan's hair, and grimaced critically. "No, after I've seen what Noodles is doing to your head, I believe I'll pass. I admit he's getting better at his barbering, but he's off his game today."

"What? I give good haircut," Noodles said while Morgan frowned at his own image in the mirror and turned his head this way and that to see what damage had been done.

Hank laughed again and went out the door.

"That Hank, he tease me, but he is good man," Noodles said

as he rubbed some hair tonic through Morgan's shortened locks and combed them.

"That he is," Morgan replied.

When Noodles was through, Morgan rose from the chair, paid him, and went to the coat tree and put his jacket and hat back on.

"You go to the hotel?" Noodles asked somewhat dubiously.

Morgan winced. "Bad as I hate to. She might as well get it out of her system now."

Noodles laughed.

"What are you laughing at?" Morgan asked.

"They say what a brave man you are," Noodles said. "Everybody say that, but I think you scared of her."

Morgan opened the door and stood inside the doorway and looked up the street. "Have you ever had a tooth pulled?"

Noodles shook his head.

"Well, I guess it's about like that. You do what you've got to, but you're sure not looking forward to it, either."

With that, Morgan went out and closed the door. Noodles went to one of the windows and watched him lead his horse towards the Vanderwagen Hotel. He shook his head, then went back to his barber chair and took up a broom and began to sweep up the cut locks of Morgan's hair left on the floor, whistling a Sicilian sailor's tune while he worked.

Chapter Seven

"What are you looking at?" Charlie Dunn asked.

The woman staring at him didn't look away. He could see her in the dim glow on the far side of the fire. She sat on a rock with a wool blanket wrapped about her shoulders. The little boy sat on her lap wrapped in her protective arms. He, too, watched Dunn, his round little face peering from the blanket that all but hid him.

"Why are you doing this?" the woman asked.

"Because I can," Dunn answered.

The woman didn't say anything else, but she kept staring at him. The look she was giving him irritated him almost as much as the pitiful excuse for a fire he was attempting to warm himself by.

Dunn didn't even know why they had bothered with a fire. The rain had set in again no sooner than they had crossed the Katy tracks headed east. Not a hard rain, but a light mist. It was the kind of rain that didn't seem so bad at first, but eventually left everything heavy and sodden and dripping wet. His caped oilcloth coat was supposed to be waterproof, but somehow the water crept in past it and he was saturated down to his skin.

The only firewood they could find that would burn in such conditions was pitch pine, or what some called lighter wood or pine knots. Normally, that pitch pine would flame up with the single touch of a match to it and a pile of it put off a heat hotter than Hades, but in such damp conditions, even chunks of almost pure yellow pine resin burned sluggishly and reluctantly. It gave off a dark, heavy smoke that hung heavily around the fire and refused to rise. There was only the slightest hint of a breeze, intermittent and constantly shifting directions, and he had moved several times to different locations around the fire to avoid the smoke hitting him in the face. No matter, each time it followed him.

One of the other men chose that moment to throw another chunk of wood on the fire, and caused a puff of ashes, ember sparks, and choking smoke to wash over Dunn. He jumped to his feet and took off his bowler hat and fanned at the smoke.

"Can't somebody find something to burn besides pine knots?" he said.

It was Injun Joe who had thrown the wood on the fire, and he had nothing to say about it. Instead, he squatted on his heels and stared at the fire. The other men to either side of Injun Joe were equally quiet, as if the rain had turned any words they might have said into mud balls in their throats, as thick and choking as the smoke that lingered over them.

The breeze picked up slightly. Not enough to clear the smoke altogether, but it gave a little relief. Dunn mumbled to himself, most of it profanity.

"I always hated the wind in Chicago, but I'd welcome a good gust of it right now," he said.

"I'd settle for a day or two without rain, and maybe a dose of sunshine. I think I've got moss growing on my back," one of the men answered.

Dunn stared back at him, trying to make him out in the dark and through the smoke. He couldn't remember the man's name, for he had only joined them two days earlier.

Bledsoe, that was it. A pimple-faced scarecrow with stringy blond hair and an Adam's apple as sharp and knotted as if he had swallowed a chunk of glass and it had stuck there in his scrawny neck. A stupid farm boy in a ragged cloth cap and a patched homespun shirt, and with a big LeMat pistol in a holster sagging his waistband and pulling at his suspenders. Said he was from Missouri, and claimed he was on the scout after trying unsuccessfully to rob a bank, or some other such big talk.

The woman shifted under her blanket and pulled his attention back to her. Many a cardsharp and gambler would have envied her poker face. It was absolutely void of expression, and whatever she was thinking was hidden behind that still mask—that and those damnable dark eyes. But most of the Indians he had met were like that. You never could tell what one of them was thinking. In his experience, the red heathens would rather grunt than talk.

And the woman was no different. Other than the few words she had spoken at the fire, she hadn't said anything. She had cried some at first, but since her tears had dried up, she was taking her ordeal more calmly than was to be expected.

She was pretty, Indian or not, and even if she was a little on the old side. Somewhere in her thirties if he didn't miss his guess. Straight, even features, strong jaw that was almost regal, full lips, hair as black as a crow's feathers. And she was short. He was only five-foot-four standing on his shoe heels, but he was easily a half a head taller than her.

He waved his hat at the smoke again, and thought he saw a hint of a smirk at one corner of her mouth. "What do you think is so funny?"

The corner of her mouth straightened, but once again she did not look away.

He stomped in a half circle around the fire and stopped when he stood over her. She kept eye contact with him, but did clutch the boy more closely to her.

He slapped her hard. So hard that she almost fell on her side. He cocked his hand back again, daring her to look at him.

"Think you're really something, don't you, squaw?"

The blank-faced stare she was giving him altered slightly, and he saw her fighting to hold down her fear. It was as defiant as it was laughable.

"Are you stupid, or are you deaf?" He started to slap her again, but she scooted away from him.

Her back struck the trunk of a tree behind her and brought her to a stop. The child in her arms whimpered. He covered the ground to her so quickly that she had no time to evade him.

"Put a fancy dress on you and you think you're as good as a white woman? Like you aren't as brown as muddy water?" He was a man unusually quick with his hands. He snatched at her, but she flinched away and he only managed to grab one sleeve of her dress. It ripped it from the shoulder to her wrist, and she cried out.

A couple of the men around the fire shifted positions or turned where they could watch what he was doing. He was aware of their stirring and felt the intensity of their watching, so palatable it was like the light touch of a hand on his back.

He reached for her again, but she tried to kick him in the groin. He twisted and took the blow on one of his knees.

"Damn you!" he said as he reared back a hand to hit her again.

It was Injun Joe's voice that stopped him.

"Thought you said we aren't supposed to lay a hand to the woman," Joe said in a flat tone.

His name was Joe Jackson, but everyone called him Injun Joe. He was well over six feet tall and built like a draft horse—a big, slow talking, slow walking man with a look on his face like he was either always thinking or never thinking. It was hard to tell which.

Dunn realized he was breathing hard, almost panting, and collected himself while he considered Injun Joe. Had there been scorn in the Choctaw's smug tone?

"Nobody asked you, Joe," Dunn said after a few breaths.

Injun Joe stared at him through the smoke. "You rough her up, maybe we don't get our money."

Dunn scratched at one side of his chest, putting his hand closer to one of the Colt revolvers hung beneath his coat under each armpit. He knew he shouldn't let the challenge pass. "We'll get our money, exactly like I said."

Dunn did his level best to stare down Injun Joe. He had found that even big men often had trouble holding eye contact with him if he stared at them hard enough, and making Injun Joe look away would be a small victory to help him save face in front of the men.

Injun Joe merely stared back at him. After a time he said, "Four thousand dollars, that's what you said. You kill her, then what are we going to get?"

"I call the shots, Joe," Dunn said. "I put you on to this, and I call the shots."

Joe nodded in his slow way, his head like a ponderous weight on his shoulders. "All right, you're the big chief, but we've all got a stake in this. There'll be hell to pay when the law finds out we've taken McAlester's woman and young'un."

Dunn kicked a clod of dirt and pine needles at the woman. "I'm only making sure she understands that the only way out of this is doing like she's told. You get it through to her if you want. Tell her in that Choctaw gibberish you speak if that's what it takes."

"She's Chickasaw."

"Huh?"

"I said she's Chickasaw."

"I just wish we'd get to the caves." It was one of the Love

brothers who spoke. The two outlaw cowboys looked enough like each other to be some sort of twins, and it was hard to tell them apart in the dark. But Dunn thought it was Jesco talking. "Liable to be every law dog in the territory hunting us come daylight."

"Hell, for four thousand dollars I'd shoot a wagonload of law dogs." That was Budge Love. His Texas drawl was the same, but his voice slightly whinier and higher pitched.

The Love brothers had come up from South Texas with a King Ranch trail herd, only they never made it to Kansas or wherever they were going. That trail herd trampled through a couple of farm fields and a few gardens, and when one of the farmers rode out to meet the herd and make an issue of the damages the brothers shot him down. Since then, the two of them had been on the dodge, hiding out in the territory and getting into whatever trouble suited their fancy. Nothing seemed to faze them, and they were a joking, laughing pair, even if, at times, they were more than a little crazy.

The McAlester woman's kid started crying. The sobs were muffled under the blanket she held him in.

"Shut that kid up," Dunn said.

"He's cold and wet, and he's hungry," she answered.

"This kind of weather is hard on a young'un," Injun Joe observed out loud.

Dunn shifted the focus of his anger to the man sitting to Joe's left. "John, you said we'd be to the caves tonight."

John Rabbit was another Choctaw Indian like Joe, though half Joe's size. A man of no signature feature other than a fondness for knives and the floppy brimmed hat he wore with a turkey tail feather sticking out of the hatband, John Rabbit claimed to know every trail and hideout in the eastern half of the territory.

"Wait 'til tomorrow when I can see, and then I'll take you to the caves," John said.

"An Indian that can't find his way in the dark?" Dunn threw back at him.

"No good trail. High water," John said. "Best we wait 'til tomorrow."

"He's right," Injun Joe said. "Best we wait 'til it's daylight."

"No, we're getting out of here," Dunn said. "Put the woman on her horse."

Most of the men got up and started for their horses. Only John Rabbit and Bledsoe remained by the smoking fire.

"Didn't you hear me?" Dunn asked. "I said let's get going."

"We were just talking about the caves," Bledsoe said.

"You've been there before?" Dunn asked.

"Couple of times," Bledsoe said.

"Then you can lead us there if Rabbit can't."

"Never come on them in the dark. Don't reckon I could find my way any better than Rabbit."

"But you could find your way in the daylight?"

"Reckon I could."

Dunn went to his horse, dug in his saddlebags, and returned carrying a brown paper envelope. He handed it to Bledsoe.

"I want you to ride back to Canadian Station. There will be a man hanging around the depot waiting for you in the morning," Dunn said.

"Who's gonna be waiting for me?" Bledsoe asked.

"Not sure, but he'll be wearing a red garter on his left shirtsleeve and checkered pants so you'll know it's him," Dunn said. "You be careful and look things over good before you approach him. Ask him friendly like if he's waiting for the train. If he says no, he's waiting for a telegram from Chicago, then you'll know for sure he's the one."

"Kind of like a password like you hear about in those stories," Bledsoe said.

"Exactly like that," Dunn said.

"What if somebody recognizes me?"

"Nobody's going to recognize you. You meet any lawmen on the trail, you just play dumb and you'll be fine," Dunn said. "Stay off the roads and well-used trails if you can. Don't talk to anybody you meet on your way unless you have to. Go straight there and then get yourself to the caves. Hear me?"

Bledsoe nodded.

"I expect you at the caves by tomorrow evening at the latest. Make sure nobody follows you."

Bledsoe mounted his horse and spurred off into the darkness. Dunn listened to the retreating sound of the outlaw's horse until it was gone. By then, some of the others had the woman and her child up on her own mount. The horse she rode had formerly pulled her buggy, and there was no saddle for it. She rode it bareback, with her long dress draped down either side of it and her high-topped lace-up shoes and the skin of her bare calves exposed. She still had the blanket, now covering her head, and the child clutched in front of her within the binding of that wool to shelter them both from the rain as best she could.

Dunn got up into his saddle, and with some trouble, kicked around with the toe of his shoe until he found his off stirrup. He was not a good rider, and envied the other men's ability to immediately get their foot in their off stirrup upon mounting, and without even having to look down at it, all in one smooth motion. He had purposely picked a gentle horse that would stand still for him to get on it, but still he couldn't seem to get the knack of threading his toe into the stirrup once he had his leg swung over the saddle. It was a skill he was determined to master.

John Rabbit was easy to spot. The gray horse he rode stood out plainly, even in the gloom. He led them off, out of the timber and out onto the prairie of Reams Valley. The Love brothers were next to strike out.

"Get going," Dunn said to the woman.

"You should let me go now, while you have the chance," she said. "My husband will put the law on you. They'll catch you and hang you for sure."

"Your husband better hope I don't get caught, or he won't ever see you or that kid again," Dunn answered. "Maybe you're used to getting your way, but right now, doesn't matter how much money you've got or who you think you are. Understand? Mrs. J.J. McAlester or the Queen of Sheba, doesn't matter. This goes wrong, I leave you under a rock somewhere to rot, and the world goes on. If you don't want to go off to the happy hunting grounds, or whatever you Indians believe, then do like I say, right when I say it."

"I understand," she answered.

He slapped her horse on the top of its hip and set it off before him. Injun Joe sat his horse as if waiting for Dunn to go first. Dunn wasn't about to let Joe behind him, not the way the Indian was acting.

"No, you go ahead of me," Dunn said. "I'll keep watch behind us.'

"You worry too much, *na hullo.* Nobody follows us. Not yet," Joe said before he kicked his horse after the woman's.

Dunn reined in behind him. There were no Choctaws where he had grown up, nor had he known any Indians of any kind until he came to the territory. But even so, the way Joe had said *na hullo* let him know it wasn't a term of endearment. He studied the dark form of the big Choctaw in front of him while his hand slipped inside his coat.

Joe wasn't the only one. The rest of the ignorant, backwoods fools thought they had his measure, too. Perhaps they didn't come out and say to his face, but he could tell it by their demeanor at times, the subtle looks they occasionally passed between them when they thought he wasn't watching them, and the way they sometimes whispered to each other. Maybe they were still a little unsure about him, unsure enough to maintain some caution where he was concerned and to do as they were told for the time being.

But that had always been the way of it, even when he was still back in Chicago walking the stinking streets of Packingtown on the outskirts of the stockyards. Any place that smelled like blood and guts and hog shit was bound to be a hard place to live, but Packingtown was even harder than it smelled.

He had always been the smallest in any group from the time he was a child, and being a small boy in such a place had taught him things. You had to fight for what you wanted, and winning was always more a matter of who applied the most violence the fastest than it was an issue of physical power. Secondly, it wasn't always bad to be underestimated, because it could give you the advantage of surprise. And last, but the most important of all, was that people only truly respected what they feared.

Dunn slid one of his Colt revolvers out of its shoulder holster and cocked it. The others were already far ahead, but Joe was only ten feet in front of him. There was no way he didn't hear the sound and know it for what it was.

"Hey, Joe," Dunn said loud enough for only Joe to hear him.

Injun Joe's horse slowed slightly, as if the sound of Dunn's cocking pistol had caused him to tense enough to draw back on the bridle reins.

"What you want?" Joe's asked.

"What's *na hullo* mean?"

Joe let his horse go a few more walking steps before he answered. "Don't mean nothing."

"Nothing? I don't think so. Might mean you think I'm a low-down, dirty shit heel," Dunn said. "Might mean a man that'll let people talk to him any way they please."

"It's only our words for a white man," Joe answered. "No different than you saying I'm an Indian. Just words."

"Keep riding, Joe. Don't you stop, and don't you turn around," Dunn said.

He waited until they had ridden a ways before he spoke again, letting the Choctaw's nerves work on him. "Would you let a man talk to you like that? Especially with the other men listening and maybe thinking they could talk to you the same way?"

"I didn't mean anything by it," Joe said.

"That's good, Joe. If I thought a man was insulting me there's no telling what I would do."

"I helped you steal the woman, didn't I?"

"Maybe you've been thinking on how to make your cut of the take bigger. Thinking on how it easy it would be to put the little city fellow out of the game. Pull a nasty trick on the *na hullo.*"

"Wouldn't work. Without you we don't get paid."

"That's right. Best that you don't forget that."

"I wouldn't turn on you."

All right, Joe. I guess we can get past this little misunderstanding, don't you think?"

"Never was a misunderstanding on my part."

Dunn uncocked the pistol hammer, then cocked and uncocked it again, the mechanical clack of it like breaking glass. They rode a little further before he holstered the Colt.

"Are you still holding a gun on me?" Joe asked.

"What gun?" Dunn replied. "Your nerves must be getting to you, or else you've got a guilty conscience. I was only making sure that I could count on you. Hell, Joe, if I was going to kill you, I wouldn't have said a word to you before I did it."

He heard Joe let out a heavy sigh, and then they rode on in silence. Soon, they were strung out on the prairie, five desperate men and a captive woman and child. The only sound was the plod of their horses' hooves on the wet ground and the occasional creak of saddle leather.

The rain quit after a while, and some time later the moon slid out from behind the clouds overhead long enough to cast the San Bois Mountains to the southeast in black shadows. They rode straight for those mountains, headed to a hideout known as the caves.

Chapter Eight

Despite Morgan's bold words, he didn't immediately go to the hotel after he left the barbershop. He ate a meal at the café and lingered long over a cup of coffee afterwards. He glanced at the hotel when he left the café, and admitted to himself that he was intentionally stalling and putting off the inevitable.

He was taking his horse to the livery when he heard the train coming from the south. He looked that way and soon saw the black column of coal smoke rising above the timber between the town and the South Canadian River, and soon the dull glow of the engine's headlamp was visible in the waning evening light. The engine's steam whistle sounded, and that long lonesome call brought a scattering of people out of the businesses and houses along the tracks.

By the time he made it to the livery barn and rented a stall for his horse, the train was clanking up to the depot house. He tended to his horse, gathered his rifle, bedroll, and saddlebags, and stepped back out on the street just as the train came to a stop. The engineer opened his valve to dump some excess boiler pressure, and a cloud of steam rolled along the sides of the train cars, obscuring parts of them from sight for a moment. He could make out the faint shapes of people getting off the train and gathering luggage.

The hotel once more loomed before him. He studied the double front doors as he went up the porch steps, noting that the large glass panels in them had been replaced, and the bullet holes in the front wall patched or puttied over and repainted. He winced at the memory and thinking about what waited on the other side of those doors.

He went inside, entering the main room that served both as a lobby and a restaurant. A huge wrought-iron chandelier bearing at least fifty lit candles hung down from the high ceiling, and a banister-edged stairway led up to the second floor and the balcony overlooking the lobby. The walls had been covered in floral wallpaper, and the kerosene lamps lining them were mounted in brass sconces. New rugs covered the hardwood floor in places to give the room extra color. It was said that the Vanderwagen Hotel was the nicest in the territory.

She could have been elsewhere, but she wasn't. He turned toward the register desk and there she stood, Helvina Vanderwagen, once Helvina Clyde before she reverted to her maiden name.

She had always been an uncommonly pretty woman, beautiful even, and the years hadn't taken much from her. Green had always been her color—green dresses, emerald jewelry, silk and ribbons the color of an Irish spring—but now she wore a dark maroon dress edged with white lace. She was not quite as slender as she had been in her prime, but the fit of the dress and the tightness of her corset exaggerated her bustline and gave her a waspish waist. Her blond hair was piled high atop her head and coiled in ringlets. That hairstyle and the dangling gold earrings exaggerated the taut, slim line of her neck. His arrival in her hotel had not escaped her notice, and the way she stared at him did not come off as regal, no matter how much effort she had put into her look for the evening.

"You," she said when she saw him.

He considered all that she might have left out with that single word, all that was between them and all that had been. "Good evening, Helvina."

"I told you to never come in here again," she said, and then she realized how loud her voice was and looked around the lobby to see if anyone had noticed her loss of composure.

"I simply need a room," he replied and sat his bedroll and saddlebags on the floor and leaned his rifle against the desk.

"I have no rooms to let."

He saw how hard she struggled to regain her cool composure, and was surprised to find that he himself felt almost nothing looking back at her. All the anger he had once spent on her was now only a vague numbness too far away to reach. Even the regret was fading.

That had not always been the case. There had been a time when she had been coal oil poured on his fire, so madly had he desired her. Perhaps it had been so easy for that same fire to turn to something else, and perhaps the two of them had always walked a fine line between love and hate. She was that kind of woman, the kind of woman like Helen of Troy must have been, the kind of woman who could drive men to their worst.

He looked around the lobby, making a show of the fact that there was no one else in the room. "Doesn't look too busy to me."

"There are no vacancies," she said. "As much as I would like to stand here and argue with you, I have some very important guests who are expecting a lavish dinner that I must attend to."

"I take it you wouldn't care to entertain these guests of yours with one of our spats. First impressions are everything, aren't they?"

Her green eyes measured him and accused him, wet and gleaming under the lamplight softening the gray dusk creeping through the hotel's window glass. "Do you know it has taken me almost until now to make this hotel presentable again after what you did?"

He started to reply, but she cut him off.

"All new front windows. Fix the bullet holes in the walls." Her voice was rising again. "Do you know how hard bloodstains are to remove? All the time I've spent building the reputation of this business, and you turn it into a slaughterhouse."

"I believe I have already apologized to you, and for far more than the damage to your hotel."

"Your apology isn't worth anything. You say you're sorry, but you never change."

Looking for whatever verbal spears they could pierce each other with was an old habit between them, and he ignored her stab. He watched the faint tremble in her full lips above the dimpled chin he had once been so fascinated with. A beautiful woman physically, yes, but Helvina had always needed to be reminded of her appeal. At times it bordered on a need for worship, and her vanity was only exceeded by her ambition.

"It would be like you to make a scene simply to embarrass me," she said.

"I'll be on my best behavior, and we'll avoid a public spat."

She reached on a board behind the desk and took down a key and held it out to him. "Room 12 upstairs."

He took the key, but did not move. "Is that a new perfume you're wearing? Which of your guests do you seek to woo?"

He cast that small spear without meaning to.

Her gaze was like glass. "Hold up your end of the bargain. No matter how much we might both enjoy a brawl, this is not the time."

"As you wish." He took up his gear and started for the stairs.

"The restaurant will be closed tonight," she called after him. "Feel free to stay in your room."

He kept on walking toward the stairs.

"I know you won't grant me even that small favor. But if you must show yourself in my lobby while my guests are here, please do me the favor of taking a bath and changing into something more presentable."

He mounted the foot of the stairs without looking back at her and revealing the slight grin on his face. Like his, hers had only been a small spear, and he did not hold it against her. He was at the top of the stairs when she spoke again.

"I think it fair that I tell you Ben will be here tonight or tomorrow," she said. "Have the decency to leave him alone if he does not wish to speak with you."

He hesitated as if struck between the shoulders at the mention of their son's name, and then moved on. The secret to winning a fight with her was sometimes as simple as not showing it when she had struck a blow, even if it was a large spear cast straight for his heart.

As he was working the key to his door, Adolphus Vanderwagen stepped into the hallway from the room directly across from his. The two of them looked at each other for a moment.

"After so many years, what are the odds that we should meet twice in the same week, and in a backwater place such as this little hamlet?" Adolphus asked. "You did not mention that you were headed here when we met outside Fort Smith."

"You didn't ask."

"I trust that you and my daughter have mended your grievances with each other enough that you will behave yourself in front of her guests," Adolphus said. "She has put a lot of work into the preparations for this meeting, and I would not care to see you disrupt her efforts."

"Helvina and I have made as much peace as we ever will. I think both of us are content to keep that truce."

"And yet, she tells me you followed her here to the territory. That doesn't seem like the actions of a man who has lost his infatuation for her."

That was a lie, and Adolphus knew it as well as Morgan did. Morgan had been working in the territory long before Helvina ever touched a single dainty foot there with the notion it was her next big chance to strike it rich.

"If your wit was only as sharp as your tongue," Morgan said.

Adolphus's condescending, scornful smirk changed to a flat-out frown. "I tried my best with you. Really, I did. Tried to help you make something of yourself."

"Something like you? A bitter old man with a fake diamond tiepin? How come you're here, Adolphus? Did your creditors back in New York finally catch up to you? Couldn't find a rich widow to latch on to your next fortune, so you come to pick up the scraps around your daughter's table?"

"I will brook no more of your insults," Adolphus said with a grunt of disdain.

Morgan watched him go, and then went inside his room. He locked the door behind him and pulled both curtains closed on the single window overlooking the street below it. He did not light a lamp, nor did he undress, but simply took off his jacket and hat and boots before he lay down on his bed with his revolver on the lampstand beside him.

He was bone tired, but sleep was a long time coming to him. His mind was too restless and fitful, although it wasn't thoughts of Helvina or Adolphus that bothered him. Ben was coming, his son, the best thing he ever did and also a reminder of his greatest failing. And not for the first time he wondered if a man's past could ever truly be left behind.

Chapter Nine

Morgan woke the next morning feeling that he had only taken a brief nap, but surprised that the rising sun was already lighting his window curtains. There was a basin on the dresser, and he brushed his teeth and bathed himself with cold water as best he could. Having combed his hair and swapped his trail clothes for his black suit, he buckled on his gun belt and went downstairs.

Only two of the tables in the restaurant were occupied. A group of four men sat at one of those tables situated near the front windows overlooking the train tracks. All of them were dressed like businessmen except for one. That man, a short Indian, wore a tall silk top hat, what some called a bee gum hat, and hunting coat made of small squares of different colors, as if it had been put together from scraps like some grandma's quilt.

Morgan recognized Superintendent Huffman from the Katy sitting next to the Indian in the top hat. Huffman had once been his boss when he worked as a railroad policeman and detective. The superintendent was too caught up in the ongoing conversation at his table and didn't notice him.

Morgan looked out the windows and saw two men loitering on the porch, also Indians, and both of them loaded down with boots and spurs and pistols. He assumed the men on the porch were Lighthorsemen, tribal police, and their presence told Morgan that the Indian in the funny hat and coat at the table with Huffman was probably Chief Cole of the Choctaws. The chief was said to be as eccentric as the way he dressed. While many of the past chiefs were as much or more white than they were Indian, and were also quite wealthy, the chief was a full-blood and notorious for living and holding court at his backwoods homestead in the mountains.

Adolphus Vanderwagen sat alone at the other table. He was trying to act like he was reading a newspaper, but watching the chief's table and doing a poor job of hiding the fact. The old man barely took time to scowl at Morgan before he dropped his eyes back behind the newspaper.

Morgan went past Adolphus and found his own table at the far end of the room away from the hotel entrance and where he could sit with his back to a corner. A young Indian girl dressed in a well-starched light pink dress and with a white apron tied over it brought him a cup of coffee and took his order before she hustled back to the kitchen. Another girl dressed in an identical dress and apron came into the room carrying a plate of food for the chief's table. Helvina's hotel wasn't the only one in the territory, but it was the only one he knew where the staff wore matching uniforms. And it hadn't been that way the last time he was in Eufaula. It seemed she was pulling out all the stops to impress her guests.

He was nursing a mug of coffee and taking in the room when one of the front doors to the lobby swung open. Through it strode a tall young man dressed in a blue soldier's uniform. For a moment, it seemed as if his gaze locked with Morgan's own.

For Morgan, it was like looking at a younger version of himself. How old was Ben now? Twenty-four? Other than a brief meeting between the two of them the previous year when Ben had been posted with a Fifth Infantry detachment at Fort Gibson—an accidental reunion that had gone horribly—most of Morgan's memories of him were images of a little boy that in no way matched the stranger standing there.

Lieutenant Benjamin Clyde took off his officer's forage cap

and then started across the room toward him. Morgan rose from his chair while his mind raced for the right words to say.

"You look good, Ben," he said.

And then it dawned on him that his son's attention wasn't on him, but instead aimed at Adolphus. He had no doubt that Ben saw him, but was ignoring him on purpose.

Ben stopped halfway down the length of the room at Adolphus's table. "It's been too long, Grandpa."

He leaned over his grandfather, and the two of them shared a quick hug and patted each other's backs.

"We'll have more time to spend together now that you're getting out of the army," Adolphus said.

Only then, did Ben acknowledge Morgan with a look of scorn.

"You might have warned me," Ben said to Adolphus.

"It's as much a surprise to me as it is to you," Adolphus replied.

Ben turned to face Morgan. "Does Mother know you're here?"

Morgan nodded. He hated the unsure, awkward feeling that came over him. He was an assertive, decisive man, but he was at a loss facing his estranged son.

Ben took a seat in a chair across from his grandfather. He hadn't inherited Helvina's fine blond hair, and his was as black and thick as Morgan's. He drummed the fingers of one hand on the tabletop, watching Morgan.

"I have made it plain that I want nothing to do with you," Ben said.

"I only want to talk," Morgan answered. "Hear me out, and I won't bother you again if you still feel the same afterwards."

"We've nothing to talk about."

"I think there is plenty that needs said."

"You know something?" Ben asked. "I realized a long time ago you aren't worth the trouble."

Morgan inhaled and let out the breath slowly. If he flinched at all, it only showed in the tight set of his face. "I went to war. Your mother decided she would not wait for me to come home."

"You're actually going to blame it on her? All these years and that's all that you can say?"

"No, the blame belongs on me alone. You get a little older and maybe you'll look back and realize there are lots of things you should have done differently."

"I'm nothing like you."

"Good." Morgan walked closer, not stopping until he was standing near his son and looking down at him. "Do you know what my greatest regret is? What I'm most to blame for? I hunted for you for years after I came back home and found you gone, but what I'm most ashamed of is that I didn't keep hunting . . . that I didn't do whatever it took, no matter how long it took, to find you and say I'm sorry and that I was there if you needed me."

"Sorry doesn't cut it," Ben said. "You say a few words and I'm supposed to forgive you? Is that how it goes?"

"I don't expect you to forgive me. Not at all."

"Do you know how hard Mother struggled to make ends meet?"

"Easy, Ben," Adolphus said. "I like this no more than you do, but hear your father out."

"My father?" Ben scoffed. "You're more of a father to me than he ever was. You know the things he's done . . . how he abandoned us. You said it yourself. The best thing I can do is to forget he ever existed and go on about my life."

"You told him that?" Morgan said to Adolphus. "I bet you didn't tell him how you tried to get his mother to divorce me even before the war."

"Don't drag me into this," Adolphus said.

"Drag you into this? Oh, you've been in the thick of it all

along," Morgan said.

"I only told him the truth. You were never a good provider. You had lost almost everything, even before the war."

"Everything? No, that was just money, but I expect you don't know the difference."

"Your business, your house, all gone. Not an asset to your name. Debts and bills that you couldn't pay, and a family you couldn't support. My daughter and grandchildren living in a tenement apartment not fit for dogs."

"Shamed you, didn't it, that I took a job as a common policeman?" Morgan said. "What would everyone down at the club say? Such scandal and embarrassment when you were trying so hard to revive the mighty Vanderwagen name after your schemes all but ruined it."

Adolphus scooted his chair back from the table in anger, and the chair legs grated loudly on the hardwood floor. That sound, along with their steadily rising voices, caused the men at the chief's table to stop their own conversation and stare at them.

Adolphus noticed the attention they were drawing and smoothed his coat front as a way of gathering himself. He waited until the others in the room politely looked away, and lowered his voice when he spoke again. "You simply quit trying. One bad business decision and you let it drag you down, even though I told you I had connections that would help get you through your bankruptcy."

"Bribing a judge and breaking my word to those that trusted me? That was your solution?"

"I told her you would never amount to anything. Told her from the first time I met you, but she had to see it for herself."

Morgan felt his temper rising. Felt it in his breathing and in the tightening of his chest and the building pressure in his head, but tried hard to keep it down. A fight with the old man was only going to push Ben farther away, yet there he was doing just that. He had simply intended to say a few words to Ben, and to maybe lay the groundwork where they could talk again. But he could tell by the look on Ben's face and the tone of his voice that he had gone too far, even if he hadn't intended to.

"Do you know how hard losing her baby was on her?" Adolphus asked. "And you gone off playing soldier when your wife and your son needed you most."

The words Morgan sought hung up in his throat. Ben wasn't even looking at him anymore.

In a last-ditch effort, Morgan tried to shift the conversation back to Ben and away from the old history between him and Adolphus, a history in which Ben's only part was as a victim. "Are you still at Fort Gibson? I heard your grandfather say you were getting out of the army."

Ben didn't answer him.

"I wrote you a letter when I found out that you had been accepted to West Point," Morgan said, pushing on against the feeling he was losing his son all over again. "I sent you lots of letters after that. Don't know if you got them all, but I wrote them."

Ben quit looking at whatever he was staring at across the room, and his gaze slowly landed back on Morgan. "I got your letters."

"Good."

"Burned them. Never opened a one."

Again, for Morgan, the look on Ben's face was like looking at a younger version of himself, and he recognized the stubborn set to Ben's jaw and the disconnection in his gaze for what it was. It was like a steel door falling into place, stubborn and impenetrable.

"You said you would go and never bother me again once I heard what you had to say," Ben said. "Well, I've heard you."

Silence settled between them. Morgan remained standing

over their table.

At that moment a young boy came running into the room. He paused, spotted Morgan, and came to him.

"Are you Marshal Clyde?" the boy asked.

Morgan nodded.

"I'm supposed to give you this telegram." The boy held out a folded piece of yellow paper.

Morgan took it from him and gave him a nickel. The boy left and Morgan unfolded the telegram and read it. It was a message from Deputy Marshal Chapman informing Morgan that both he and Deputy Marshal Tabor had been sidetracked with some other business up on the Kansas border and would not be able to make it to Eufaula.

Morgan was still frowning over the telegram when Ben rose from the table. "Come on, Grandpa, let's go down the street and have our breakfast at the café. I could use a walk and some fresh air."

Ben rose and started for the front doors without a backward glance. There was nothing Morgan could do other than watch him go.

Adolphus followed his grandson. He paused at Chief Cole's table long enough to give a slight tip of his hat brim to the gentlemen there. "Pardon us if we've disturbed your breakfast. A little family squabble, nothing really. You know how those things can be."

Adolphus was barely gone when there came the sound of a commotion from the porch. Something had the Lighthorse officers out there in a stir. They were talking to somebody on the street, and Morgan could detect the tension in their voices, even through the hotel walls.

He went out on the porch and found the two Choctaw lawmen standing at the top of the steps and having a conversation with a man sitting a bay horse in front of them. Both of the

Lighthorsemen had their hands on their holstered pistols, but hadn't yet pulled leather.

Morgan wasn't surprised at their reaction, for it was Cumsey Bowlegs riding that bay horse, but he was surprised that Cumsey had the gall or the necessary stupidity to ride up to a pair of lawmen in the broad daylight. The young horse thief was as reckless as they came, but he was usually more cunning than he was showing then. That clever nature was the reason Cumsey was still running free when so many lawmen were looking for him.

"Damned, don't you pull on me," Cumsey said to the two Lighthorse. "I came here to tell you something, and you're grabbing at your pistols like I'm going to burn the town down."

"Don't try anything stupid, Cumsey," one of the Lighthorsemen said. "Get off that horse and come peaceful. There doesn't have to be trouble."

Cumsey, seemingly oblivious to the tension, grinned at them. "I didn't come here to turn myself in, and if you had any sense you'd see I'm not looking for a fight."

Cumsey had a point, though the Lighthorsemen were slow to realize that. Cumsey wore no pistol, and the only firearm he carried was the Winchester rifle stuffed down in the rifle boot strapped to his saddle. A man wasn't going to put up much of a fight, nor was he going to last long if he did, with his rifle so unhandy and slow to get to.

"I've got a warrant for you, Cumsey," the same Lighthorse fellow said. "More than one, I reckon."

"To hell with that. This is what I get for trying to do a good deed?" The grin disappeared from Cumsey's face and the edginess he had been hiding showed through.

"I ain't telling you again, Cumsey. Keep your hands away from that Winchester and get down off your horse," the Lighthorse officer said.

"I came to tell you the news, and when I'm done, I'm riding out of here the same way I came in."

Morgan had stood behind the Choctaw lawmen quietly to that point, watching it all play out. Knowing Cumsey, he was about to put the spurs to his horse and make a run for it. And it was also plain that he was so full of bad news that he was fairly bursting to tell someone.

"What is it you came to tell us?" Morgan asked.

"Is that you, Clyde?" Cumsey asked like he only noticed Morgan at that moment.

"You know damned good and well it's me. Quit stalling and thinking about putting the spurs to that horse, and say what you've got to say."

"Well, I guess I really stepped in a hornet's ncst this time," Cumsey said. "Two Lighthorse and a federal marshal, now ain't that just my luck?"

"Speak your piece."

Cumsey cocked one eyebrow. "Cranky as ever, ain't you? How would it strike you if I told you somebody stole Rebecca McAlester and her baby and gunned down two men that were with her?"

"You keep an eye on him," one of the Lighthorsemen said to the other, and then ran inside the hotel.

"Where did it happen?" Morgan asked.

"McElhaney's Store west of Canadian Station," Cumsey said. "About noon yesterday, or thereabouts."

"Who did it?"

"No idea, but there were six of them, white men and Indians. Tried to follow them but they shot my horse out from under me."

"That horse you're riding doesn't look wounded," Morgan said.

Cumsey found his grin again. "You know how it is. Ain't

hard for a man to find another horse if he knows where to look."

Morgan was about to ask more questions, but a broad man in a suit and string tie, and with his whiskers shaped into a goatee, charged out the front door. The Lighthorseman who had gone inside the hotel earlier came out right on his heels.

"Marshal Clyde, what do you intend to do about this?" the man in the string tie asked with a great deal of bluster and a quavering voice.

Morgan knew J.J. McAlester well enough to recognize him, and not much more. His peace officer work often took him through the town named after the man, and the two of them had occasionally exchanged a few words when Morgan visited McAlester's store. It was understandable that the man was distraught, given the news he had just learned.

Morgan shifted his attention back to Cumsey. "Who else knows about this?"

"Some of the locals around McElhaney's Store are getting a posse together, or maybe not. And the telegraph wires were down and no way to get a message out of Canadian Station when I went through there except for the train man there saying he would spread the news when he could," Cumsey said.

More people were coming out on the porch. Chief Cole motioned the two Lighthorsemen over to him, and they gathered slightly away from the rest and talked in hushed tones.

"I said, what are you going to do?" McAlester threw at Morgan again.

"We'll do our best to get your family back," Morgan said.

"What does that mean?" McAlester asked.

"It means I'll go after her, but the first thing we need to do is spread the word and see who else we can put on the trail."

More people off the street were wandering over in front of the hotel, and the word of the taking of Rebecca McAlester and her child was already spreading fast through the little town.

"You said you chased after them before they shot your horse out from under you," Morgan said to Cumsey. "Which way were they headed?"

"Southeast," Cumsey replied.

A man in the crowd spoke up. "Hurley over at the depot said this morning that the wires are working to the north, but he still can't get anything through south of here. Said the high water must have knocked the lines down somewhere."

Morgan motioned at the two Lighthorsemen with the chief. "I expect you aim to get in on this seeing how it happened down in your country."

"We're with you," one of the Lighthorse answered.

"Well, I need one of you to catch the next southbound train and go to McAlester and put together whatever kind of posse you can. Get men out on every road and trail you can think of. Spread the word farther south in case our fugitives have already gotten past there. Make sure Major Harlan at Caddo Station and Red Hall at Dennison know what's happened. They'll know what to do."

"All right," the same Lighthorseman answered.

Morgan took a small notebook and pencil from inside his coat and hastily scrawled a note. He gestured at the man in the crowd who had spoken up about the state of the telegraph wires. "Get back over there to the depot and tell him to send a message for me. Tell him to make sure Marshal Upham at Fort Smith gets this, and both the Creek Lighthorse and the Cherokees. Chickasaws and Seminole forces, too. We need to make sure everyone up and down the line is on the lookout for Mrs. McAlester and the men who took her."

"They could be a hundred miles away by the time your arrangements take effect," J.J. McAlester said.

"We'll do our best," Morgan answered.

"Your best? My wife and child have been abducted, and two

of my employees murdered."

"I understand your grief, but all I can promise you is that I'll try."

McAlester turned to the crowd facing the porch from the street. "I'll pay a thousand dollars to anyone who can bring my wife and child back to me safely. And two hundred dollars a head for the men who accosted my family and took her from me."

"Are you paying for those outlaws dead or alive, J.J.?" somebody in the crowd asked.

"I'd rethink that, Mr. McAlester," Morgan said before McAlester could answer. "That's a lot of money. Word gets out what you said and you'll have every man who owns a gun out beating the brush."

"That's my intention," McAlester said.

"All you're going to do is muddy the water. Keep the amateurs out of this and let us do our job."

"My wife and son may not even be alive at this moment. And if they are, Lord knows what they're going through."

Morgan handed his handwritten message to the man who had come from the depot. That man started to head back across the street, but McAlester stopped him.

"While you're delivering Marshal Clyde's message, you tell that telegraph operator to send one for me. Tell him to send it out that J.J. McAlester is offering the rewards just like I said, word for word, dollar for dollar."

Their volunteer messenger took off for the depot at a run, with Morgan's piece of paper wagging in his hand and fluttering like a kite. Morgan watched him go and heard him calling out to those he passed to tell them about the reward J.J. McAlester promised.

McAlester got Chief Cole's attention. "We've had our troubles, you and I, but I suppose I can count on you to be of assistance in this matter."

The chief nodded. "I will put the Lighthorse out and try to get word to all the sheriffs and constables in the Choctaw Nation."

"You have my thanks." McAlester shifted back to Morgan and gave him a frowning look. "I suppose you intend to form a posse?"

"That's my thinking."

"You hear that?" McAlester asked the onlookers. "Marshal Clyde is forming a posse."

Morgan held up a hand to those same people. "Go back to your homes and your shops. If I need your help, I'll let you know. Go on now. This is a matter for the law."

Very few of the people left, most of them simply waiting and watching the show, or gathering in small clusters to talk excitedly.

"Don't tell me you intend to go after them alone," McAlester said to Morgan.

"If that's what it takes."

"You do what you will, but I warn you I will be sending a message to Marshal Upham and Judge Parker making them aware of what I see as a weak response on your part in this matter."

Morgan reminded himself again that McAlester was under a great deal of duress, and simply turned away and found the two Lighthorsemen.

"Which one of you is going with me?" he asked.

"I'm going with you." The one who spoke was the taller and older of the two, with a pale gray hat pulled way down on his ears and his thumbs hooked in a gun belt sagging down on his right hip from the weight of a long-barreled Remington pistol and lined all the way around with loops studded with brass cartridges. He had long hair cut off bluntly at his shoulders, and one lazy eye that pointed off to the side and caused him to turn his head peculiarly when focusing on you while talking. "Name's John Moshulatubee."

"Glad to have you with me, John."

While Morgan was talking to the Lighthorseman, and while the rest of the folks gathered around were busy with their own discussions, Cumsey Bowlegs was easing his horse out of the crowd—not bolting off, but doing it kind of easy and subtle as if his departure might go unnoticed.

"You hold up, Cumsey," Morgan called out.

Cumsey stopped his horse with his back to Morgan. "You holding a gun on me, Marshal?"

"Will if I have to," Morgan replied.

"Don't tell me you intend to hold those old warrants over my head," Cumsey said.

"There's that."

"What if I told you I haven't stole a single horse in almost a year. Reformed is what I am. Repented of my wicked ways."

"That's a matter for a judge."

Cumsey turned his horse to face Morgan. "I guess this is because you're still sore at me for getting away from you last year."

Morgan chuckled.

Cumsey's flippancy fell aside, and his tone became more serious. "You aim to arrest me and take me to Fort Smith?"

"You're going with me, one way or the other."

"That old hanging judge will send me up the river, sure enough, and I don't think I could stand being locked up in that Detroit prison. Hell, I don't even know where Detroit is, other than it's a long ways from home. No, sir, stone walls and steel bars ain't for me. Reckon I'd rather you shoot me dead in my tracks."

"I'm not taking you to Fort Smith, at least not right now.

You're going to help me go after the men that took McAlester's family, and then we'll talk about your situation after that."

"Say that again."

"You heard me."

"You're saying you're swearing me in your posse?"

"That's right."

Cumsey thought about that a moment. "What are people going to think about you riding with an owlhoot like me?"

"I don't care what they think."

"Have I got any choice in the matter?"

"Not a lick."

Cumsey's grin came back to him. "Marshal Clyde, you're just plumb full of surprises."

"It's been that kind of morning."

Chapter Ten

Cumsey and John Moshulatubee were in front of the general store packing some hurriedly gathered supplies into the saddlebags on their horses when Morgan came back from having another talk with J.J. McAlester and gathering his belongings from the hotel. He shoved his Winchester down in his rifle boot, butt pointing up beside his saddle swells, and then busied himself tying his bedroll and saddlebags behind his saddle. His black suit had once more been traded out for his trail clothes.

"You about ready?" he asked Cumsey and the Lighthorse officer.

"I'm ready to ride," Moshulatubee said and untied the palomino mare he rode. She was little bigger than a pony and still shaggy with winter hair that she had yet to shed.

"We're packing awful light. How come you didn't take that hostler down at the livery barn up on his offer to loan you a packhorse?" Cumsey asked.

"Don't plan to be out that long," Morgan answered.

"You figure this to be over quick?" Cumsey asked as he swung up in the saddle.

Morgan unwrapped one bridle rein from the hitching rail. "One way or the other. We're going to ride hard and fast. Packhorse would slow us down."

Cumsey reined his horse around so that he could look at both of them. "Now I'm usually on the other end of this posse stuff, mind you, but finding them might take a while. Big country and all, and them with a head start on us. Rain last night is liable to wash out their tracks."

Morgan swung a leg over the zebra dun's back, and rocked his saddle back to center before he answered Cumsey. And his voice was quiet enough for only the three of them to hear. "I won't say it to her husband, but I think the McAlester woman and her baby are likely already dead. Regardless, we'll do our best."

Cumsey lifted his hat from his head with one hand and scratched at his head with the other while he frowned over what Morgan had said. "I told you there are six of them that took her, best I could count. You got any more help?"

"Better a few good men than a bunch of amateurs. Like to know I can count on those with me.'

Cumsey settled his hat back on his head and pointed down the street behind Morgan. "No worries, Marshal, either way. I just thought that man coming yonder might be joining us."

Morgan turned and saw what Cumsey was looking at. It was Ben, and instead of his uniform, he too had changed into some rough clothes suitable for travel, a light tan duck jacket, brown pants made of heavy corduroy, and a red wool shield shirt. The only thing besides the black felt fatigue hat on his head that hinted of his being a soldier was the Colt pistol he wore at a cross draw in a military flap holster and the trapdoor Springfield hanging in a scabbard. That, and the fact that he was riding a good chestnut gelding about fifteen hands tall and with a U.S. brand on one shoulder and a McClellan saddle cinched on its back.

Morgan took note of the bedroll tied behind Ben's saddle. And then he looked to the hotel and saw Helvina out on her porch watching them. She was too far away to make out her face, but he could tell by the way she was standing that she was upset.

"Looks like you're going somewhere," Morgan said.

Ben stopped his horse in front of Morgan's. "You're short-handed, and I'm going with you."

Morgan weighed his words carefully. "I appreciate the offer, Son, but you'd best sit this one out."

Ben sat more upright in the saddle, his spine as stiff as a rod and his shoulders thrown back as if he were on a parade ground posing for inspection. His tone was that of a man as used to giving commands as he was taking them. "My detachment of the Fifth Infantry is in the territory under the orders to help the Indians prevent the encroachment of those seeking to unlawfully settle on their lands and to act as a protector and buffer against any other activity from white criminals against them. I think you would agree, Mrs. McAlester's abduction falls well within the duty defined by those orders."

"Thought you mustered out of the army."

"My enlistment will not be over for another month, and even if I were already a civilian, I would consider this a matter of civic duty. Were that my wife or mother who was taken, I hope there would be good men to volunteer their aid."

"You stand to get yourself in trouble if you go with us, if not outright court martialed," Morgan said.

"I have already sent a telegram to my post informing them of my intention to go after Mrs. McAlester, and my commanding officer has approved my efforts. Had we a cavalry detachment at Fort Gibson I'm sure he would put them in the field to help our cause."

"Son . . ."

Ben cut him off. "Do not call me son. In the future, I would appreciate it if you referred to me as Lieutenant Clyde, or Ben if you must. I assure you, my wish to accompany you has nothing to do with any desire on my part to spend time with you."

"That all?"

Ben looked over his shoulder at his mother on the hotel porch. "I suppose I'm going to have to go over to her and hear her out one more time."

Morgan watched him ride his horse to the hotel. In the meantime, Cumsey came alongside Morgan and pointed at Ben's back.

"That fellow talks about as stiff as he rides, like he's got a corncob up his ass," Cumsey said.

"I guess that half that officer and a gentleman's show is meant mostly to try and put me in my place," Morgan replied.

"I take it he's some kin to you. Favors you, he does."

"He's my son."

Cumsey scratched at the side of his head again and twisted his face. "Sort of figured that. I sense a real loving relationship you two have got going."

"Let it lie."

"Never aimed to do anything different. You actually going to let that tenderfoot go with us?"

"Wouldn't if I could do anything about it."

"He that stubborn?"

"And then some."

"Well, I guess he comes by it naturally, kind of like his pa."

"Cumsey, I suggest you talk less."

"Riding after them outlaws ain't going to be much fun with you and that son of yours all bowed up and growling at each other the whole way," Cumsey said. "What about you, John Moshulatubee, are you fond of a little friendly conversation to pass the miles?"

Instead of answering, the Lighthorse officer simply gave Cumsey an irritated look, then kicked his shaggy yellow Choctaw pony down the street.

"You think he's ignoring me?" Cumsey asked Morgan.

"I think he had the good sense not to egg you on."

"I couldn't tell if he heard me or not, no more than I can tell whether he's looking at me or not. You looked him in the eyes yet? Just like the Choctaws to hire a crooked-eyed lawman. Likely the reason they never could catch me."

"Moshulatubee strikes me as a steady man. I imagine he'll do fine."

Morgan nudged the zebra dun forward to put an end to Cumsey's talk, but instead of going after Moshulatubee, he rode towards the hotel porch. By the time he reached it, Adolphus had joined his daughter there. The two of them were talking to Ben. Both her face and Ben's were flushed.

"You put a stop to this right now," Helvina threw at Morgan.

"I think his mind's made up past changing it," Morgan answered.

"Morgan, you leave him here or I swear . . ." Helvina's voice was steadily rising and her lower lip and chin were quivering again like they did when she was angry.

"I'm going, Mother, and there's nothing you can do to change it, as much as I love you and as much as I know you don't like to hear that," Ben said.

"Benjamin, you leave this to Morgan and the others that get paid to hunt down outlaws," she said.

"What kind of man would I be if I stayed here while other men do their duty?"

"Duty? Would you listen to yourself?"

"I'm an officer in the United States Army."

"You make it sound like it's some kind of camping trip. Tell him, Morgan. Just one time, think about someone besides yourself."

"I already tried to talk him out of it," Morgan answered. "But like he says, he's a grown man."

Adolphus cleared his throat to get Ben's attention. "Think of your future and all the things we talked about after you quit the army. Your mother needs you here."

"I'm sure you and Mother can do without me for a few days."

"Listen, I'm not so old to have forgotten what it's like to be a young man," Adolphus said. "So exciting to think of riding off to rescue the damsel in distress, but you need to stay here and take hold. This territory is ripe with opportunity for a smart young gentleman such as yourself."

Ben turned to Morgan. "No doubt we should be on the march instead of sitting here talking ourselves in circles."

Morgan nodded.

"You're actually agreeing with him?" Helvina asked.

Morgan shrugged. "It's best we get going."

"Goodbye, Mother." Ben reined his horse around and started down the street towards where Cumsey and Moshulatubee had stopped to wait for them.

"I swear, if you let something happen to him . . ." Helvina said to Morgan.

"I'll look out for him as best I can."

"Oh yes, you've always been so dependable," she scoffed.

Adolphus hobbled a few steps along the porch to where he could better see Morgan. "We have done all that we can to ensure Ben is given every chance to be a success. Nurtured him and pushed him at times, and watched him grow into the upstanding man he is now. West Point has polished him and prepared him in many ways, but I'm afraid that although he considers himself some sort of professional warrior, he still has led a quite sheltered life."

"Spit it out, Adolphus," Morgan said. "I haven't got all day."

Adolphus hobbled another step closer to the edge of the porch, and there was a distinct limp in his stride that hadn't been there earlier. "Ben is not you, and you would do well to remember that."

Morgan barely heard Adolphus. It was only then that he had

noticed the limp and the walking cane Adolphus was using.

"Fancy cane you have there," Morgan said.

Adolphus tapped the end of the cane on the porch and gave his version of a tired smile. "I see you think this some pretentious bit of costume on my part, but I'm afraid the years are catching up to me and there are days when my hip bothers me fiercely, especially this cool, wet weather."

Morgan did not reply.

"Glare at me all you want, Morgan Clyde," Adolphus continued. "Go ahead and needle me with more of your petty insults and mock me if that makes you feel like the better man. My only concern is Ben's well-being, and despite all our differences, I bear you no ill will. No matter what you may imagine to the contrary."

"That so?"

"On my honor."

Morgan grunted at the irony of that, and reined his horse around and left Adolphus leaning on his walking cane—a walking cane that just happened to have a silver hand knob.

Chapter Eleven

It was in the gray light of morning before true dawn when Charlie Dunn's gang came to the creek in the bottom of the mountain draw. They splashed across the rocky shallows and snaked their way uphill through the timber in single file. No one talked, and they approached the odd little mountain meadow that appeared out of nowhere with the caution of hunting wolves. Not a natural meadow, but a small flat at the foot of the ridge where someone had chopped down the trees and cleared the underbrush.

On the far side of the clearing stood two boulders the size of railroad boxcars, and in the faint moonlight they could all see that the trail they followed passed between those two huge rocks like giant sentinels daring them to enter. Beyond that, more big rocks and high ledges loomed over them.

John Rabbit reined his horse to a stop, and the rest of them did the same while he tilted his chin up and sniffed the wind. Both of the Love brothers had their rifles out and laid across their laps ready and easy to hand.

Dunn eased his horse past the woman's and stopped alongside Rabbit's. "What's the matter?"

"I smell smoke," John Rabbit answered.

Dunn had smelled smoke most of the night, for his clothes and the lining of his nostrils seemed to be permanently impregnated with it after their pine knot fire, but he knew that wasn't what the Choctaw meant.

"You think somebody's up there?" Dunn whispered.

"I do." Rabbit answered him in the same hushed voice.

"Think they've seen us?"

"They see. You don't ride in here without somebody knowing it."

Injun Joe rode up alongside them.

"Who do you think is up there?" Dunn asked him.

"No telling. There's most always somebody at the caves, either passing through or laid up for a while and cooling off their heels," Injun Joe said. "Never know who you'll run across."

"Might be lawmen," Jesco Love observed behind them.

"No lawmen ever found this place, or if they know about it, they ain't never made a try against it," Injun Joe answered.

The hideout some called the caves was an outcropping of high sandstone ledges and jumbled boulders hidden in the San Bois Mountains some twenty miles south of the Canadian River, unknown to all except the outlaws who used it and a few roving Indian hunters who might have stumbled across it over the years. On a ridge overlooking the headwaters of Fourche Maline Creek, the bare, weathered gray rocks mottled with lichen and moss appeared like some kind of castle or fortress sticking up out of the dense hardwood and pine timber.

"We wouldn't stand much of a chance against somebody up there in those rocks," Budge Love threw in.

"Easy place to ride around, hard place to ride into," Jesco answered.

"You said it, brother. I don't mind having a little powder friction burned over my head, but I like the chance to shoot back."

"John, you go ahead and ride on in and check things out," Dunn said. "Make sure anybody that's up there knows we're coming."

When John Rabbit kicked his horse out onto the meadow, Injun Joe went with him. The rest of the gang and their captives remained where they were, waiting.

The two Choctaws soon disappeared and all that was left was the clatter of their horse's hooves on the rocks. It wasn't long before even that sound went silent.

It was a good half hour before Injun Joe rode back to the meadow. "Come on."

"Who's there?" Dunn asked.

"Some I know, some I don't," Injun Joe answered. "Should be all right."

The Love brothers put the woman's horse between theirs and started up into the rocks. Dunn made as if to go behind them, but Injun touched him on one shoulder to stop him.

"What's the matter?" Dunn asked.

"That's Chicken Whitehead's bunch up there. They tried to rob a bank down in Texas and got shot to pieces. They're worried the Rangers might come into the territory looking for them."

"Are you giving me some kind of warning?" Dunn asked.

"Chicken ain't so bad, but he ain't here. He's gone across the Canadian to Briartown to fetch some supplies," Joe said. "Would have been better if he had taken Big Henry with him."

"Who's Big Henry?"

"Big Henry's touchy sometimes. Give him plenty of room and mind what you say around him, and it should be all right."

The trail climbed and wound up the ridge, becoming more difficult as they went. The sandstone formations consisted of large ledge blocks, slabs, and a jumbled mix of boulders. For the most part, all the soil was eroded away, leaving nothing but bare rock with large crevasses and tunnels winding throughout like some kind of crazy maze.

A man up on top of one of the rocks above them suddenly stepped out where they could see him. He was carrying a rifle propped on one hip. Dunn knew without asking that the guard had been watching them from up there the whole time.

They came through a narrow corridor between two enormous boulders and a flat stretch of ground opened up before them. Topsoil eroded from higher up had apparently washed down and been caught there, enough for a few trees to grow. Sheer rock walls twenty-five or thirty feet high surrounded the little park on all but two ends, the one they came through and the other opposite them. Those gaps were filled with rail fences made of peeled oak poles. A number of loose horses stood within the stone corral.

They unsaddled their horses and turned them into the enclosure and piled their saddles and tack underneath the protection of a little overhang. Dunn was gathering up his bedroll and saddlebags when he noticed another guard standing on the tallest of the bluffs, a sheer wall of smooth stone. The guard continued to watch them as they went out one end of the stone corral and climbed higher.

The foot of the bluff the guard stood upon angled upwards and they followed its course until at the last turn they came into sight of the mouth of a cave. The top of it was curved like a Roman arch.

"Howdy, boys," Injun Joe said as they approached.

There was a campfire burning a little ways downhill from the front of the cave, and there were men loafing about it, either gathered to watch the newcomers' arrival or because they had nothing else to do. They were a mix of white men and Indians, the same as his own party. All of them bore weapons on their persons, and he noticed that one of them had his arm in a sling and bloodstains on his shirt. All in all, they were a hard-looking lot.

The Love brothers and John Rabbit were already talking with them, either introducing themselves or perhaps greeting old acquaintances. Dunn's eyes sought out Rebecca McAlester, and he saw that she had taken a seat on a rock as far away from the men as she could. The pale yellow dress she wore was soiled and stained by their travel, and one sleeve of it ripped away. And her black hair had come unbound and hung in tangled disarray over part of her face. Her boy child sat on the ground at her feet playing with a handful of pine needles.

Dunn glanced at the guard up on the bluff again, thought of the other guard he had seen earlier, and then shifted back to the men by the cave, doing a mental count. There were nine of them if there weren't others yet to reveal themselves, which was a possibility, for he had counted more horses than that in the corral.

"You the one Joe told me about?" A booming voice called out.

Dunn's eyes tracked beyond the group of men. There was a black man sitting at the top of a leaning slab of rock to one side of the cave mouth behind them. If Injun Joe was big, the man there was a giant.

A sleeveless, long-tailed buckskin shirt showed off the massive muscles of his arms, and was cinched about his waist with a Mexican belt of hammered silver conchos. He wore no hat, and his woolly black hair was shaved into a mohawk. His right eye had been ruined sometime in the past, and was nothing but a sightless, milk white orb.

It was easy to tell that the black man thought highly of himself, for he had no doubt intentionally positioned himself at an elevation where he could look down on everyone. His pose and bearing were that of some kind of bandit chieftain, and Dunn guessed him none other than the one called Big Henry.

"You hearing me?" Big Henry called out to him again.

The rest of the men went quiet at those words.

"I hear you, like I guess anybody on this mountain did," Dunn answered.

Big Henry looked Injun Joe's way. "Cocky little runt, ain't he?"

"His name's Charlie Dunn," Joe said in an attempt to divert the growing tension.

"I prefer Charles." Dunn's appeared calm and relaxed and unfazed by Big Henry's insults, and only someone who knew him well might have detected the slight hint of strain in his voice.

"You prefer Charles, do ya?" Big Henry tried an imitation of Dunn's clipped Midwestern accent, but it didn't come off funny. He laughed, anyway. He was the kind to laugh at his own jokes.

Dunn noticed the Yellowboy carbine leaned between Big Henry's knees. The weapon looked all out of proportion to the big man's frame, like some kind of scaled-down toy.

"What brings you up in these hills?" Big Henry asked. "You don't look like no outlaw I've ever seen. Especially not the kind I expect some salty old boys like Joe Jackson and those others to follow. You're more like some kind of bank teller or maybe one of them piano players in a whorehouse. I can smell the hair tonic on you all the way up here."

"Matter of fact, I most recently sought my fortune in hotel management," Dunn said.

"Hotel management?" Big Henry laughed. "Now that's a first at this old hideout, I guarantee you. What changed your mind?"

"It finally dawned on me that I don't own any hotels."

Big Henry laughed again.

"Plenty of room enough for all of us here," Injun Joe said. "We'll go down to the low cave and stay there if you don't want company."

"I ain't talking to you, Joe Jackson. This dude's doing fine talking for himself," Big Henry said. "First off I thought he was a little standoffish, but I'm warming up to him."

"I guess I was only trying to decide what I was looking at," Dunn said.

That pleased Big Henry. "Likely you ain't never seen nobody big as me. Well, I ain't neither. You see, I eat regular sized people for breakfast. Don't even bother chewin' 'em just butter their heads and swallow'em whole. Got this cave here filled up with folks so's I can reach in and have me a snack when I gets hungry."

Dunn could feel the other men's eyes on him, all of them waiting and watching to see what he was going to do. He knew Big Henry's game, and that it was more than merely testing him. It was a bully making sure Dunn knew his place in the pecking order, and reminding the others who was the toughest kid on the street. Some things never changed, no matter where you went.

Dunn forced his body to relax and managed a smile that might have looked real. "That so? Well, I hope you already had your breakfast this morning."

"I like this one, Joe. Real corker," Big Henry said.

Dunn guessed the distance between them to be about fifteen yards. He took another step closer to Big Henry, and then another, his moves casual and calm.

"Well, Mistuh Charles Dunn the hotel manager, Joe there tells me your looks are deceiving, and that you're some kind of professional woman stealer now."

"I'll take a turn at whatever will make a dollar." Dunn came another step closer to Big Henry. "Call me a freelancer, if you will."

"Freelancer? Oh, you gots all kinds of schoolteacher words. Me and the rest of Chicken's men you see, that's what we are, too. Freelancers, though some call us other things."

Some of the men chuckled at that.

"How much for her?" Big Henry asked after the men quieted

back down. "How much do you want for the woman?"

"She's not for sale."

"Come on now. Give me a price. How's twenty dollars sound? When I'm through with her I might rent her out to the rest of the men and make some of my money back. Or maybe I would sell her back to you if you was insistent that way."

"Thanks for the offer, but I believe I'll pass."

"Thirty dollars."

"Answer's the same."

Big Henry leaned back against the rock wall behind him and studied Dunn intently. Only after the longest of pauses did he finally show a white-toothed smile. "Sure, sure. Finders, keepers, ain't that what they say?"

"I believe so."

Big Henry pointed to the skinned carcass of a deer hanging from the limb of a pine tree on the other side of the fire. "Help yourself to the groceries, but I hope you boys brought some of your own. Beans and flour ran out two days ago, and we drank the last of the coffee this morning."

"That's kindly of you, Big Henry," Injun Joe said. "We don't have much ourselves, but we've got coffee and flour and salt for a few days. Happy to share."

Henry seemed to lose interest in the newcomers then. He stayed where he was on his high perch above them, and busied himself wiping his Winchester down with a rag, only occasionally glancing at what was going on around the fire.

Budge Love cut one hindquarter off the deer carcass and deboned it and cut the muscles up into small chunks while John Rabbit took a cast-iron Dutch oven from beside the fire and set it on a thin bed of coals. The meal they prepared consisted of the meat, some wild onions, and a couple handfuls of flour to make a sort of venison gravy.

Dunn loaded an enamelware plate with the concoction and

carried it and a canteen of water to Rebecca McAlester. She took the food from him without looking at him, and began to feed the boy.

Dunn remained standing over them. The boy was dressed in a navy-blue sailor's suit with brass buttons on the jacket and a pair of knickerbockers that ended above his knees. He opened his mouth like a hungry little bird each time she held out the spoon for him, and never took his eyes off Dunn.

"How old is he?" Dunn asked.

"He'll be three this June," she answered.

"I see you've already got him wearing breeches. My mother didn't breech me till I was five."

She didn't answer, instead feeding the boy another spoonful of the gravy.

"A boy big enough to wear pants ought to be able to feed himself," he added.

She took the bottom hem of her dress and dabbed at the boy's mouth with it.

"When I speak to you, I expect an answer." He started to strike her, but changed his mind. "I'm beginning to think you're one of those that likes being hit."

She finally looked up at him. "You'll hit me no matter what I say, so why talk?"

Her defiance continued to surprise him. Even then, in her miserable state, she risked angering him.

"You stay where I can see you," Dunn said.

The gray clouds overhead were thickening and becoming darker, and threatened another rain. Dunn left Rebecca McAlester with her child and headed to the cave to check it out.

"Only level ground in there is at the back," Big Henry called down to him as he passed before him. "Careful you don't step on Abner."

One side of the interior of the cave was taken up by a solid slab of stone running down to the cave floor at a forty-five-degree angle, and providing no place to spread a bedroll. The narrow passage between the foot of the slab and the other cave wall ran with a steady trickle of water. He followed it further into the cave until it became so dark he could barely see.

The floor of the cave flattened and dried out at the very back of it, and there were a few bedrolls spread out there. Among them he could make out the dim form of a man lying there on a blanket. His shirt was off, and a crude bandage crusted with dried blood was wrapped around his middle.

"That you, Henry?" the man asked.

Dunn turned and left without answering him. It was drizzling rain again by the time he came out of the cave. He looked to the McAlester woman.

"Go on in there and get out of the rain," he said to her.

He didn't wait to see if she did as she was told, and went to gather his bedroll and saddlebags. He was almost to where he had left them when Big Henry called out to him again.

"Take that bucket over yonder and go fetch us some water before you settle in," Big Henry said.

Dunn took up his saddlebags and bedroll and turned to where he could see Big Henry.

Big Henry stroked the barrel of his Winchester with the rag while he stared at him. "Everybody here takes a turn doing the chores. You ain't above doing your part, are you?"

Dunn glanced at the wooden water bucket near him. "That bucket's three quarters full."

"Why don't you go get us some more, anyway? That there's just rainwater from last night and has probably gone sour."

Dunn looked down the ridge towards the creek. Big Henry was trying to put him in his place again, and wanted everyone to see him taking orders and carrying water for the big man in camp.

Injun Joe walked over and picked up the bucket. "I'll do it."

"I asked the dude," Big Henry said.

Injun Joe sloshed the water in the bucket out on the ground and started down the path through the rocks. "I don't mind. Was going down to the creek to wash out my socks, anyway."

"You going to wash socks in the rain?" Big Henry asked.

"Barely drizzling," Joe said as he started down the mountain with the bucket.

Big Henry frowned at Joe's retreating back, but said nothing else, willing to let the matter drop.

Dunn followed Rebecca McAlester and her child into the cave, and when they reached the back of it, he handed her a blanket from his bedroll to go with the one she already carried. "For you and the boy."

"You murder men, steal me and my child. Beat me and threaten me, and now you're suddenly concerned for my well-being?" she said.

"Only protecting my merchandise."

The wounded man lying on his blanket moaned.

"What's the matter with that man?" she asked.

"Gutshot, I'm guessing."

He moved back into the better light closer to the cave entrance and took off his caped coat and spread it out on the sloping rock where he could sit on it. From his position he, could see the lower half of Big Henry's body, but the outlaw couldn't see him.

Injun Joe came back with a fresh bucket of water, and he came to Dunn after he had set it down.

"Big Henry wants the woman bad," Joe whispered.

"His tough luck."

"He'll try to take her if you won't sell. He's bad medicine. They say he's killed more men than the pox."

"You let me worry about that."

"Chicken will be back soon, and that won't be any good if he decides to side with Henry. You watch him when he gets here. Used to ride with Bloody Bill Anderson up in Missouri. And that one with his arm in a sling you saw out there. He's been with Chicken since the war. He's slick with a pistol, and they say he might be the best since Deacon Fischer gave up the ghost. The best unless it's Morgan Clyde or maybe Virgil Beck."

"Clyde?"

"That marshal, the one that used to work for the railroad."

"Clyde isn't so good."

"If you say so," Joe said. "Be best if we ride out of here as soon as we've had time to rest a little, but I don't think Henry'll let us. Not with the woman."

Dunn took his hat off and set it beside him. He took a comb from his vest pocket and began to comb his hair, taking great care to make sure the part in it was exactly down the middle. "Tell the Love brothers and John Rabbit that I want to talk with them. Tell them not to come all at once. Make it look like they're only checking out this cave, or bored and restless and wandering around."

"What you got in mind?"

"Sideways," Dunn said.

"What's that?"

"Sideways, Joe. Sometimes you've got to think sideways when head-on won't do."

"What's that supposed to mean?"

"Means Big Henry's big, but he's stupid. I'm not stupid, Joe."

"There you go again," Joe said. "I never said nothing about stupid."

Dunn stared at the Choctaw out of his narrow-set, odd eyes. "The question isn't if I'm stupid, it's how smart are you?"

Chapter Twelve

Instead of loading their horses on a railcar and taking the Katy south to Canadian Station, Morgan led his posse east on the road to North Fork Town, an old trading settlement that had been all but abandoned when the Katy laid its rails and the merchants moved to the new town of Eufaula a few miles to the west.

"I'm not questioning your sense of direction, but ain't we going the wrong way?" Cumsey asked after they had traveled out of sight of Eufaula.

"Got a stop to make first," Morgan said.

Ben Clyde stared at Morgan's back, but didn't say anything. He hadn't spoken to any of them since they had left Eufaula.

They soon came to a stretch of rocky shoals on the North Canadian River. That natural fording place was the reason the road struck the river where it did, and in normal weather the water usually ran only fetlock deep on a horse. However, although the river level had fallen, it was up to their horses' bellies and they barely managed to cross, their horses pushing hard against the current and scrambling to keep a foothold.

Once across, they rode out onto a flat expanse of bottom ground. A little farther on they came in sight of a small log cabin with a shake roof and a stone chimney on one end of it.

The farm looked better than the last time Morgan had been there, and it was obvious a lot of hard work had gone into improving it. The cabin logs had been whitewashed, a few new cedar shakes showed where the swaybacked roof had been patched, and there were flower boxes to either side of the door that were new. However, it was still a run-down, rawhide affair.

The walls of the rickety old barn behind the house leaned permanently from whatever windstorm had almost blown it over in the past. Two recently plowed and planted fields lay in front of the cabin, but most of that acreage had flooded and was standing ankle deep in water. The majority of the planted corn hadn't sprouted or had drowned soon after it did. Several whitetail deer were standing in one of the cornfields grazing on the tender new corn plants that had somehow managed to survive.

A tall, lanky man wearing an old Confederate forage cap ran out of the cabin with a double-barreled shotgun in his hands. He threw the shotgun to his shoulder and fired both barrels at the deer in the field.

"Get out of here!" he shouted.

The range was far too great for a shotgun, and the deer bounded across the field unharmed and jumped the split-rail fence on the far side.

The man with the shotgun only then noticed the four riders sitting their horses in the lane leading to his house. He looked them over, his gaze landing last on Morgan.

"Can't keep'em out of my corn." His accent was pure Alabama, lazy and thick as sorghum molasses or the slow bubbling of peanuts boiling in pot. "I run'em off, and the next time I look they're back again."

"Bad as that corn's looking, I believe I'd let them have it," Morgan said. "You've got to be the worst farmer I know."

The man with the shotgun gave him a wry look. "What would you know about farming? I'm cursed is what I am. Last year the drought got me, and now it won't quit raining."

"Well, you could always eat the deer."

"I've ate deer meat 'til it's running out my ears. I was counting on a bumper crop to catch me up this year. Ain't too late to break that ground again and replant if it would only stop raining."

Morgan twisted in his saddle and gestured at the three men with him. "You remember Cumsey Bowlegs?"

"I remember him."

"That man beside him is John Moshulatubee, Choctaw Lighthorse. The other is Lieutenant Clyde from Fort Gibson."

The farmer's gaze lingered longest on Ben Clyde, but he held back whatever he thought about saying. "Glad to meet you."

"This ugly galoot with the shotgun is Dixie Rayburn," Morgan said. "Used to work for me when I was packing a badge for the Katy."

Dixie scowled at Morgan and rubbed absentmindedly at where the lobe of his left ear was missing, a leftover from his days as a soldier. "What do you want, Morgan? You didn't come here to give me farming tips."

"Need you to ride with me."

"I can't seem to get it through to you that I'm done with peace officer work." Dixie tucked the empty shotgun under one arm and tried to tuck in a part of the tail of his shirt that was flapping.

"I'm asking you, because I need your help."

"What's happened this time?"

"Somebody abducted a woman. Killed the two men with her, and then ran off with her."

"You don't say? Who's the woman?"

"J.J. McAlester's wife."

"Well, then, there'll be plenty out looking for her. You don't need my help."

"This is a bad bunch we're after."

"All the more reason for me not to go. Besides, I got this

farm to tend to."

"They took her baby boy when they got her."

Dixie winced, but shook his head. "You still aren't listening. I told you I'm done."

"Hate to hear that." Morgan gathered his bridle reins as if to go.

"You come all this way, no sense in you leaving without getting a bite to eat." Dixie turned towards the cabin and waved at them to follow him. "Besides, the Missus wouldn't let me hear the end of it if she found out you were here and I didn't tell her."

"Don't you think we ought to be going instead of dawdling about?" Ben asked Morgan when he saw that Morgan intended to take Dixie up on the offer for lunch.

Morgan gave Ben a look. "Dawdling?"

"That's what I said."

"Well, whether you like it or not, *Lieutenant,* you aren't running this show," Morgan said. "Now come on and eat, or sit here on your horse while we do. I intend to make up for the breakfast I missed this morning."

Morgan turned his back on Ben and motioned at the cabin. All of them, including Ben, followed Dixie beneath a large oak shade tree beside the cabin, and tied their horses to a pair of hitching rails there. A team of young mules was tied there, also, still in harness and hooked to a heavy stone sled. They acted green and more than half flighty, and Morgan gave them plenty of room. Besides the team harnessed to the sled, he could see more mules and several horses in a peeled pole corral built off one side of the barn.

Morgan pointed at the pair of mules and the stone sled. "Breaking in a new team?"

"Yeah. Been doing a little trading to make ends meet. Mostly it's work teams, but I sold a good string of green-broke saddle horses up at Coffeyville last fall."

"Never took you for a bronc buster."

Dixie gave him a half-amused scowl. "I see you're still riding that zebra dun."

"He suits me fine."

Dixie grunted. "Seeing that horse reminds me of why I'm not going with you. My old rib bones never did mend like they should have, and every time they grind and creak or get a bit achy when the cold comes, I think about the bullet that horse's former owner put in me."

The zebra dun gelding had once belonged to the Arkansas Traveler, a crazed former Confederate sniper and hired assassin that had mistaken Dixie for Morgan and put a bullet in him from ambush. The Traveler was dead, but neither Morgan nor Dixie were liable to ever forget him, horse or not.

"The horse had nothing to do with it," Morgan said.

"Sure, but a lot to do with why I might live to see my hair turn gray and you won't," Dixie said. "This old farm ain't much, but I don't wake up worrying about getting shot or stabbed."

"I understand."

Dixie turned to the others with Morgan. "Come on to the house and light and set. We'll have us a bite to eat, and while we're at it you can fill me in on the latest gossip."

Morgan laughed to himself at that. In addition to being a worrier, Dixie had always been as gossipy as they came, and because of it he was as good of a source for every rumor in the territory as there was.

Dixie let Ben, Cumsey, and the Lighthorse officer get ahead of them, purposely falling back beside Morgan. He pointed at Ben Clyde's back. "You and him patching things up between you?"

"Not hardly."

"Says something that he's riding with you."

"He isn't here because of me. Until this morning, I haven't laid eyes on him since we were all in Eufaula last year and he was first assigned to Fort Gibson," Morgan said. "I think his mother's got him convinced that he's going to be a power in the territory one day, and he believes getting McAlester's wife back is a good way to build a name."

"Might be he's out to show you he's every bit the man his daddy is."

"No, he's made it plain how little he thinks of me."

"Give it time. Some wounds take longer to heal than others."

"I've wanted to talk to him for years, but I finally get the chance and now I'm wishing he'd stayed back in Eufaula. Business like this is no place for a wet-behind-the-ears kid."

"Me and you fought a war when we weren't any older than him," Dixie said. "And that horse thief with you isn't any older than your boy."

"Yeah."

"You're worried about this one, aren't you?"

"No more than usual, except for making sure he doesn't do something stupid."

"I imagine he'll do fine."

Morgan nodded grimly. "I suppose so. I only wish he wasn't so hardheaded. I'd feel better if I thought he would listen to me when I need him to."

"Comes by it honest."

Morgan scowled at Dixie, but didn't say anything.

Dixie pointed at the cabin when they neared the front door. "Don't say anything to her about trying to get me to go with you."

As if on cue, another voice called out to them before Morgan had a chance to answer him. When he looked towards the cabin, he saw a woman standing in the open doorway. Her mane of thick red hair was bundled up carelessly atop her head, and instead of the fine dresses she had once worn, she wore a plain work dress with muddy patches at her knees as if she might have recently been in the garden.

Her arms were crossed at her chest, and the look on her face wasn't a happy one. She might have been mad at Dixie, but most of her wrath seemed aimed at Morgan.

"What do you want, Morgan?" she asked. "And don't try and tell me you've come by here only to visit."

"Molly," Morgan said with mocked hurt.

"Save your blarney for the lasses young enough and dumb enough to believe you. What are you trying to get him to do this time?" Molly's Irish brogue had never truly left her, even after all her years in the States, and it came back the heaviest when she was upset.

"I need his help."

"He's not going anywhere with you. Not if he wants a wife to come back home to."

Morgan stopped where he was, willing to wait out whatever else she had to say. Molly's bark was always worse than her bite, unless she was really mad. And he could tell her temper hadn't got the best of her yet, for she wasn't throwing things or taking a swing at him.

Waiting out her verbal tongue-lashing gave him time to see how different she looked. She was still pretty, but there was no denying that she wasn't the same woman he had known back in his days marshaling Sedalia and Baxter Springs. Back then, there were men who fought over Red Molly O'Flanagan. The queen of the railroad they called her, with hair like fire, and a saucy laugh like the ringing of brass bells. She had always been a big-framed, buxom woman with curves no kind of dress could hide, but he guessed she had lost at least twenty pounds since he had last seen her. Her eyes, once flashing and taunting, were dull and the skin beneath them marked with black half circles.

Molly was pushing forty, just like he and Dixie, but someone who didn't know her would have thought her older than that. It was as if she had aged ten years all at once.

Molly must have seen how he was looking at her, for she patted at her hair and tried to brush some of the mud from her dress. "You'll have to excuse me. I would have cleaned up if I had known I was going to have company."

"Ah, Molly, you're as pretty as ever," Dixie said.

"Well come on, the lot of you, and quit standing there gawking. I'll see what I can warm up on the stove. I'll see no man at my door without feeding him proper." She waved them inside.

The men took a seat at the table while Molly fussed over her cookstove with her back turned to them. Dixie and Cumsey were doing most of the talking, and Morgan's attention drifted away from whatever story they were telling. He watched Molly and wondered how advanced her sickness had gotten.

As if to answer his question, she quickly ducked into another room and out of sight. He heard the faint sound of her coughing, and she looked pale and flushed when she returned, even though she tried to keep her face turned from them. And he also saw that her hands were shaking.

Molly was a lunger, although she had managed to keep her disease a secret from her friends for a time until it became too advanced to hide it any longer. He had hoped that she would get better, but she seemed worse, instead. He wondered how much of that was the tuberculosis and how much of it was to be attributed to another problem she also tried to keep hidden.

It was a sad thing, seeing her like that, slowly falling to pieces. There were those that would have branded her as nothing but a woman of ill repute, but Molly was made of good stuff beneath the tough shell she tried to protect herself with. Once a whore, yes, but even in those days she was better than the profession she chose. He remembered her once nursing him back to health when an outbreak of cholera had almost killed him in Kansas. It had been Molly who had remained behind to help the doctors with the afflicted when almost everyone who could fled town. And there were other times when she had been there for him, and he wasn't one to forget that. Still, Molly could be difficult to get along with. To say she was a complicated, stubborn woman was an understatement.

She served them a leftover pan of cornbread, some pork steaks, and turnip greens warmed up on her stove. She took a chair beside Dixie at the head of the table and watched them eat, paying particular attention to Ben.

Cumsey took the last bite from his plate and nodded at her. "Red Molly . . . er, I mean Mrs. Rayburn, that was what my mama used to call larrupin'. Haven't had a meal that good in a long while."

John Moshulatubee nodded his agreement. "Thank you kindly, ma'am."

Molly gave them a smile that revealed a little of her former magic, and seeing her taking such pride in men enjoying her cooking was a side of her Morgan had never thought to see. Who could have imagined Red Molly keeping house and fussing around the kitchen like a mother hen? But then again, her marrying Dixie was equally surprising. He watched the interaction between them—the way she rested one arm on the back of his chair, the subtle touch of her hand on top of his, or the way he smiled at her over the least little thing—and he was glad they had found each other and somehow felt as if he were intruding into something fragile and private that wasn't meant for his eyes.

"You set an exquisite table, ma'am," Ben said.

Molly arched one eyebrow at him, and then shifted her gaze to Morgan. "Such fine manners."

"Simply giving credit where credit's due," Ben said.

"I've seen what they feed you soldier boys at those forts," Molly said. "And I'll take your thanks with a grain of salt."

"I admit, army chow leaves a lot to be desired," Ben said with a laugh.

"You favor your mother some around the eyes, but other than that you're the spitting image of your father when I first met him after the war," she said.

Ben stiffened, and the look on his face showed that he was trying to think of something to say that wouldn't give offense or come off awkward, but he eventually ducked his face back to his food.

Morgan chose the same tactic and looked at the carbine hanging over the front door on pegs and said to Dixie, "I see you've still got your Spencer."

Dixie glanced at the gun, and then back to Morgan. "I've traded that Yankee carbine off two or three times over the years, and I always go get it back. Don't know why, but I guess it suits me."

Molly frowned at them both, and then said to Morgan, "He's not going with you, and that's that."

"No worries, Molly. He's already turned me down," Morgan answered.

Molly went on like she hadn't heard him. "I won't have him brought back to me carried on a wagon tailgate."

She started to say something else, but stopped short and put a hand to her chest. He could hear the rasp of air as she tried to suck in a breath. She stood quickly and ducked into her bedroom again and slammed the door behind her. All of them at the table rose without a word and went outside, embarrassed, either by her outburst or because of the coughing coming from the bedroom.

Dixie followed Morgan to his horse. "You know she didn't

mean it. She's only upset and letting her tongue get the best of her."

Morgan tightened the cinch on his dun. "No hard feelings. You two take care of each other."

"She worries, that's all. You know what she's been through," Dixie added. "And I promised her I wouldn't pack a gun for pay anymore when I married her."

"Man ought to keep his word."

Dixie hitched up his pants and adjusted one of his suspenders while he let out a heavy exhale. He looked at the sky as if trying to calculate the coming weather, or simply thinking of something to say. "You ever consider how odd it is that we ended up friends?"

Morgan knew what Dixie meant—two men who had not only fought on opposite sides of a war, but who had also fired shots in a few of the same battles. One of them could have fired a bullet to kill the other as easily as they could have met later.

"I guess life's funny like that," Morgan said.

Dixie scuffed at the mud with the toe of one boot. "It bothered me that you didn't come to our wedding."

"Didn't know you two had gotten married until yesterday."

"I paid that Moon boy two dollars to ride to Fort Smith and leave you a letter inviting you," Dixie said.

"Never got it."

"Figures. I bet that fool boy spent that money with the first whiskey peddler he came across and never got more'n a few miles down the trail. Lying little cuss."

Morgan swung up in the saddle. The men with him were already riding away, but he lingered. "You used to poke fun of farmers, but maybe you'll make a go of this place yet."

Dixie shook his head. "I doubt it. We've been talking about maybe moving back to Eufaula. Fellow there has offered to sell me the livery barn, and we're considering it if we can scrape up the money he's asking."

"You've put a lot of work in here. Might be hard to leave."

"Only person making money off this farm is that crafty Creek that leased it to me," Dixie said. "Everybody likes to laugh at the lazy Indians letting the white men rent their ground, and using it to point out that this whole territory is going to waste when there's plenty needing land. Well, you go take a look at my landlord. He's got him a couple of cabin spots in the hills. Just loafs around from one to another, hunting and fishing as it pleases him while I work like a slave to make him a dollar. Doesn't work unless it suits him. Takes a nap when he wants to. Doesn't want much and doesn't need much. Only him and his hounds and nothing to disturb his peace. Now who's the fool in this situation?"

"Don't envy him too much. They'll lose this territory in time."

"Ain't it a shame? Guess I'd better get back to working these mules if I'm going to keep this place afloat. No lying around on the porch with the hound dogs for me." Dixie turned away and went to the mules and began checking their harnesses. One of them kicked at him, but he dodged and paid it little mind other than to give it a gentle cussing under his breath and rub it on the shoulder to calm it.

"One last thing," Morgan said. "McAlester has put a reward out for the return of his wife and child."

Dixie looked back at him. "How much?"

"A thousand dollars, plus two hundred apiece for the men that did it."

Dixie let out a low whistle. "That's a lot of skully."

Iskulli was the Choctaw word for money, and the version of it Dixie used had become common slang in the territory.

"Thought you might like to know." Morgan felt ashamed, but it was too late to take it back.

Dixie untied the mules, took up his driving lines, and started them towards the barn, walking beside the sled they dragged. The young mules were skittish and stopped and started and jerked at the trace chains, unsure about the sled, but Dixie coaxed them along. He looked back once at Morgan, but no more after that.

Morgan was about to leave when he saw Molly appear in the cabin's open doorway. She was slightly slumped, as if suddenly exhausted, and there was a white handkerchief clutched in one of her hands.

"Leave him be," she said. "I never asked you for anything, but you grant me that much."

He was close enough to her that he saw the blood spots on the handkerchief. "I can get this done without him."

"Then why did you ask him?"

"Because I trust him."

"And because you know the power you hold over him. He wouldn't admit it, but he won't sleep tonight thinking he let you down."

"If I had known you were . . ." Morgan stopped what he was about to say.

"If I was what?"

"Like you are," Morgan said. "If I had known, I wouldn't have asked him."

She gave a bitter chuckle. "Like I am? Are you saying all the dew has dried on the rose?"

"I didn't mean anything by it," he said. "You're sick. Simple as that, and nothing you can do about it but to try and get well."

"Sometimes you can actually act like you care." She coughed once, a wet, rattling cough, and immediately put the handkerchief up to cover her mouth.

"I always did, only not the way you wanted," he said.

She smiled a weary smile. "That water's long gone down the

brook. It's him I worry about."

"I won't come back if that's what you think best."

Her eyes were tear damp as she stared at him. "I do."

She went back inside and closed the door, and he turned and rode down the lane. He trotted the zebra dun to catch up with the others.

"That Molly is something else," Cumsey said as Morgan joined them.

"Good cook, but I never did care for a hot-tempered, bossy woman," John Moshulatubee said

Cumsey turned his head and cocked it to show his surprise that the Lighthorse officer was engaging in some frivolous banter for once. "She ought to scare you. Don't let her looks fool you. Maybe you don't know it, but Red Molly's a regular pistoleer like our Marshal Clyde here."

Morgan frowned at Cumsey, but the young horse thief either didn't notice or acted like he didn't.

"How many notches has she got on her gun?" Cumsey went on. "Two, three? Reckon it might have been more if the consumption hadn't gotten her while she was still in her prime. She damned sure ain't afraid to pull a trigger. I heard she busted one while he was sitting in an outhouse. Put a whole cylinder in his chest, and you could cover the bullet holes in him with the palm of your hand. Regular Wild Bill, except she's got better tits."

Morgan pulled his horse up in the road, and the look on his face was tight and hard. When he spoke, it was in a tone that neither of them had heard out of him before. "Cumsey, you ought to quit talking."

Cumsey took measure of the way Morgan was looking at him, and nodded. "Reckon I was talking a little loose. No offense meant."

Moshulatubee was the first to start his horse down the road

again, followed by Ben, and Cumsey put in alongside them. Morgan trailed a little distance behind them.

After a while, Cumsey leaned from the saddle closer to Moshulatubee and Ben and whispered. "He doesn't mean anything by it. Got to have his space sometimes. All those shooters are like that. Touchy and hair-triggered as their pistol guns."

Morgan heard him, whether or not Cumsey thought he didn't. But he let it slide, his composure returned to him and his mood thoughtful.

It stung some, but Cumsey was right. He'd become hair-triggered over the years. Shoot first, think about it later, words and decisions flying out like bullets, apt to strike friends as well as foes. You told yourself that living on that edge was the price to stay alive, but what was it Red Molly had once told him? Something about a thin line and how easy it was to cross and how hard to get back.

Chapter Thirteen

Molly was sitting at their kitchen table with a single lamp burning when Dixie came back to the house a little before sundown. There was a tear in one of his shirtsleeves, and a bright red welt could be seen on the skin of his exposed upper arm.

"What happened?" she asked as she rose and went to the stove to pour him a cup of coffee.

"One of those young Johns bit me. Got a snap like a steel trap, that one does." He plopped down in a chair and let out a heavy breath.

"You need to be careful," she said as she brought two mugs of coffee to the table and set one in front of him.

"Oh, I imagine they'll be better tomorrow. Was thinking I might use them to break up that west field as soon as the ground's dry enough. Time enough yet to try and replant if the weather will break in our favor."

She watched as he gave her his usual optimistic smile, one that was meant to let her know that everything was going to be all right, even if he didn't truly believe that himself. "Want me to warm you up something to eat?"

"Too tired to eat." He motioned her to sit with him.

She sat down across the table from him, took out a brown bottle from a pocket on her work dress, and poured a dolt of clear liquid from it into her coffee. "I don't think the rain is over yet."

"March's always a wet, muddy month in these parts." He

noticed the slightly glazed shine of her eyes and pointed at the laudanum bottle on the table while she stirred her coffee with a spoon. "That bottle was more'n half full yesterday."

"Don't do this," she answered.

"Worried about you, is all."

She sat her coffee mug down after a sip. "I can't have you accusing me all the time. You knew how it was before I married you, and never once have I hid it from you."

"Doctor said you needed try to wean yourself off of it, and then maybe you might get rid of it altogether."

"I'm doing better, but some days it's worse," she said.

He saw that her temper was rising the way it did any time he mentioned the poppy water, and decided to let it go like he had so many times.

"Noticed you're coughing today. More blood this time?"

She nodded.

"Maybe we ought to take a trip up to Muskogee and have Doc Chillingsworth see you again."

"Nothing he can do."

"You don't know that."

"I've been to doctors."

They sat in silence for a long time, with the only sounds the occasional thump of a coffee mug on the tabletop and the constant tick-tock of the clock he had bought her as a wedding present.

"What are you thinking?" she finally asked. "I can tell when something's bothering you."

"You still love him, don't you?" he asked. "That's why you're so hard on him."

"First you're checking my medicine bottles and now you're accusing me of being untrue?" she said. "I'll remind you one more time of what you promised. Remember the night before we got married and I told you that you could ask anything about me, but you were never to ask me again?"

"I remember."

"Morgan Clyde isn't the only man that knew me before you did, and he won't be the last to come around and remind you of what I was," she said.

He reached a hand across the table and laid it on top of one of hers. "Didn't mean it like that. I trust you and I know you love me, but I think there's a part of you that might still have feelings for him."

"I never took you for the jealous type."

"I'm not jealous. I knew how you felt about him from the get-go, and I made my peace with that. And I know I've got most of you, and that's more than I ever thought a man like me could have."

"A man like you?"

"I know I'm not handsome. Not a smooth talker, and no smarter than most. Can't give you the things you ought to have, and can't do what I'd like to do for you. You should have better. Far better."

"You fool man. You're the only one who would marry a woman like me and think you don't deserve me," she said. "Well, you don't deserve me, and you don't deserve my problems. That's the reason I turned you down the first two times you asked me."

"I thought it was because my cowlick wouldn't stay down flat on my head," he said with a grin. "You know how much hair tonic it took to grease that down when I came courting you?"

She laughed and put her other hand on top of his. "Don't ruin the good thing we've got going here. Keep telling me how young and pretty I still look. Keep picking flowers and leaving them where I'll find them, and all the other silly stuff you do to remind me how much you care. Sit with me like this and let's listen to the frogs and the crickets singing outside and maybe tell me one of your funny stories to make me laugh. And when we're through you take me to our bed and I'll snuggle up with you and we'll do it all again tomorrow. Because you know what? That's real. More real than anything I've ever known since I was a little girl."

"I'm glad you feel that way." He smiled his smile again, but it was obvious there was something still bothering him. He pulled his hand from hers and took his empty coffee mug to the stove.

"Go ahead, say it," she said. "I know what's bothering you."

He poured his coffee but didn't turn around. "He said there's a thousand-dollar reward for the return of the woman and her child. Two hundred more apiece for them that took her."

"No."

"My posse pay, plus my cut of that reward money would pay the lease. And it would maybe give us enough to go ahead and buy the livery in town."

"I said *no.* We'll get by."

"The corn drowning out will break our backs."

"You're not like him."

"You don't mean that. Morgan's got his ways, but he's as good as they come."

"Aye, he's my friend, too, but you know as well as I do, he's always been a man with the Devil nipping at his heels. Pray for him, but don't think you have to go with him."

"We need the money."

She rose and went into the bedroom. He followed her, but she shut the door in his face.

He leaned and put his face close to the door. "I won't go if you don't want me to."

"Liar!"

He went back to the table, and was sitting there an hour later when she opened the door. The lamp wick had burned down to a point it only gave off a feeble glow, and neither of them could see each other's faces in the dark.

"You leave me a gun," she said. "I'm not staying here by myself without one."

"I'll leave the shotgun for you."

"I don't know how to load it."

"You got your little nickel-plated Smith & Wesson."

"It's too small. I saw a big red wolf at the edge of the woods the last time you were gone overnight."

"I doubt that wolf will come back, but I reckon that .32 would tend to him if you hit him right."

"I want a big gun."

"I'll load the shotgun before I leave."

She stood there without speaking, and he could hear her breathing.

"I'll fix you something to take with you in the morning. Be like you to go off and forget to take something to eat," she said after a long wait. "You get any skinnier and people will go to talking about what a poor cook I am."

"I'll be back home before the week's out," he said.

"Let's don't talk about it anymore. I knew you were going with him the moment I saw him sitting his horse in the yard."

"I'm sorry, Molly."

"Are you coming to bed or are you going to sit at the table all night?"

"I didn't know if you'd let me."

"Shut up and put out that lamp."

Chapter Fourteen

The clouds thinned and the sun showed itself by late afternoon, and every man at the caves took advantage of it by laying out his things to dry. Gear and clothes and other random items were strewn about the rocks, and someone had even rigged an improvised clothesline by stringing a lariat rope between two trees. Enjoying the first warm rays of sunshine in days, the men stood about the fire, some of them in various states of undress, and told stories while more of the deer meat was cooked. Only the woman and her child and the wounded man stayed in the cave.

Charlie Dunn, apart from the others, spread his oilcloth coat on a flat rock in front of the cave. He took off his sack coat and brushed it as clean as he could with a brush he carried in his bags for that purpose. He removed his tie from his collar, and folded both it and the coat neatly and laid them on the oilcloth. Last, he removed his double shoulder holster rig and hung the weapons on the limb of a bush close at hand. He was as gentle and meticulous with them as he was with his clothes.

The pistols were a matching pair of .45-caliber Colt single-actions with short, three-and-a-half-inch barrels, what some called a Shopkeeper Model. Some of the custom work had been done in Colt's shop in Hartford, Connecticut, and the rest specifically for him by the Kansas City gunsmith he had purchased them from. The original grip frames were swapped with longer ones taken from a pair of 1860 Colt Army Models, and the grips themselves were burled walnut with a high gloss finish instead of the hard rubber, gutta-percha panels found on most Colts. The color case hardening and blued steel of the fancy revolvers was almost entirely engraved with scrollwork, and the front sights were made of thin blades of bone.

He brushed his bowler hat clean with the same brush he had used on his sack coat, and then hung the hat with the guns. After rolling up his sleeves, he opened one pouch on his saddlebags and took out a small leather bag containing his shaving kit. Along with it, he pulled out a sharpening strop and unfolded it.

He hooked the ring end of the strop on the same bush where he hung his guns and hat, and held the other end in his hand to keep it taut. He took the ivory-handled straight razor, not from the shaving kit bag, but from where he carried it in a slit pocket in his vest. He folded the razor open and passed the blade back and forth on the strop in a steady rhythm. After a while, he tested the razor's edge on the back of his forearm and was satisfied when he saw it effortlessly shaved a patch of hair there.

Injun Joe walked past him on his way to the fire and saw him testing the razor. "You know how to put an edge on a blade."

"My father was a barber, and always a stickler for a sharp razor and a clean shave," Dunn said.

"Henry's talking to the others and working his self up to trouble," Joe said in a quieter voice.

"Maybe I can win him over," Dunn said a strange grin.

Injun Joe moved on. Dunn put away the strop, knelt on the oilcloth, and propped a little mirror in front of him where he could see himself in it. He was dabbing shaving cream on his face when he saw the new man come into camp behind him. He watched him in the mirror while he continued to lather his face.

The newcomer was an older man wearing a floppy brimmed

hat and a red wool Mexican poncho, and with the gray chin whiskers of his long beard braided down to his chest. From the way the men deferred to him, Dunn assumed he was the Chicken Whitehead he had been told about.

Big Henry was one of the outlaws that immediately went to Chicken's side, and Dunn used the mirror to watch the two of them talking, although he couldn't hear what they were saying. But he did see Big Henry point at him.

Dunn took up his razor and scraped it down one cheek. He wiped the blade clean on a towel before he looked behind him in the mirror again. Big Henry was coming his way.

Big Henry stopped a few feet behind him, so close that only his chest was visible in the mirror. "Ain't right for you to bring a woman here and keep her to yourself. Stingy is what it is."

Dunn moved the razor carefully along his other cheek, keeping watch on Big Henry's reflection and giving no response.

"I'm fixing to go in there and have me a round with her," Big Henry said. "Unless you figure to stop me."

Dunn glanced at his pistols hanging on the bush in their holsters. They were close, but still beyond his reach. It was something he knew that Big Henry had noticed, also, and timed his approach accordingly.

"The woman belongs to me," Dunn said in a mild, unconcerned tone with the razor paused against his chin.

"I'll break you in half before you lay hold of those pistols," Big Henry said.

The razor made a scraping pass over the short whisker stubble on Dunn's chin. Dunn wiped the blade clean and turned his face from one side to the other in the mirror, inspecting it as if to decide where to shave next. "A gentleman should always maintain a well-trimmed appearance, don't you think?"

"You cocky little shit." Big Henry lunged forward and grabbed Dunn by the left shoulder.

Instead of trying to pull away, Dunn gave with the tug and used it to start his counterattack. His balance was that of an acrobat, and he spun toward Big Henry and leaped high at the same time with the razor blade flashing at the end of his right arm. Big Henry's right fist was drawn back, but instead of delivering a mighty blow, he staggered back a step clutching at his throat with both hands. Blood was already squirting out from between his fingers.

Dunn followed the leaping slash to Big Henry's throat with a backhanded swipe to his hamstring a little above his knee. Both cuts were fast enough to appear as one continuous motion.

Big Henry fell to the ground, and his body jerked and his legs convulsed. Dunn was standing over him by then, the bloody razor hanging limply in his hand. The giant black outlaw tried to say something, but whatever it was came out as only a choking gargle. And then Big Henry died, bled out in a matter of seconds.

Dunn looked down at the bloodstains freckling his white shirt, and then went to the bush and began putting on his pistol rig. Both the guns and his bowler hat were back in place by the time he turned back around to face the outlaws near the campfire. All of them were staring at him.

Dunn saw that Injun Joe was sitting on a rock off to one side of the rest. And he saw the Winchester rifle half-hidden behind the Choctaw. The Love brothers were both by the fire. He locked eyes with them for a brief instant, and thought he saw Jesco give him a slight nod. That was good. He hadn't been sure about them.

John Rabbit stood beside the outlaw with the bad arm. That was how Dunn had guessed it. If there was a fink in the bunch it was going to be John Rabbit.

Dunn focused his attention on Chicken Whitehead and his men, taking special care to watch for any of the guards that might appear on the rocks above him.

He turned his neck this way and that in a peculiar motion, as if stretching the muscles in it. "Injun Joe taught me a new word not too long ago, *Na hullo.* He said that means asshole."

One of the Indians in Whitehead's gang laughed at that.

Dunn gave them an impish grin. "Well, which one of you *na hullos* is going to show me how upset you are about Big Henry?"

No one said anything to that. Dunn waited and let the audacity of his dare settle in on them. Such men pounced upon weakness like cats on mice, and understood nothing but raw, mindless strength and bloody cunning. It was a gamble how they would take it, but he plunged ahead, too far gone to stop now.

It was Chicken Whitehead who answered him. "That was a neat bit of work with that razor, but you've got more gall than you've got sense."

Dunn ignored the old bandit and kept his speech aimed at the other men. "Personally, I think I likely did some of you a favor getting rid of Big Henry. Man like that can get bothersome."

"I reckon Henry asked for it, but you're about to get yourself in a worse kind of trouble if you don't quit running that mouth," Chicken said.

Dunn ignored the outlaw leader. "What about it, boys? Are you happy robbing pissant banks with old Chicken here and getting shot up for a few dollars, or are you ready to make some real money?"

Chicken's voice was harder and his speech more clipped than it had been before. "You and the others get your stuff and leave. Take the woman and her kid with you. Nobody will stop you."

"I'm not going anywhere, old man," Dunn said.

Chicken's right arm was half hidden by the front of his Mexican poncho, and Dunn guessed that the outlaw leader already had a hold on a pistol or was close to it. The wounded outlaw to one side of him had turned to face Dunn, and there was something peculiar about the way he positioned his bad arm in the sling that supported it.

"If I didn't know better, I'd say you were trying to pick a personal fight with me," Chicken said. "That what you're trying?"

"Hey, Jesco. How is it you cowboys say it?" Dunn asked. "Hooking bull, right?"

"Don't you drag me into this," Jesco said from over where he and his brother, Budge, stood.

"I said a hooking bull. Right?"

"Yeah, that's right. Hooking bull gets his way in the herd," Jesco answered.

"And you want to be the hooking bull of my bunch?" Chicken asked.

"Now that you mention it." Dunn gave his smart-ass grin again. His nerves were twitching so that he wondered if it showed to the others, like quivering snakes slithering and writhing beneath his skin.

"You talk too damned much." Chicken went for the pistol under his poncho as he spoke.

The old bandit had fast hands for his age, but not fast enough. Dunn drew not one pistol from its shoulder holster, but both of them. Chicken's pistol had barely come out from under the poncho when Dunn's first bullet struck him low down in the belly and doubled him over. Dunn held both of his Colts at arm's length, and walked towards the old outlaw firing first one revolver, and then the other—cocking and firing, cocking and firing. His second bullet took Chicken in the shoulder, half spinning him, and the third busted a kneecap and knocked that leg from under him. The fourth bullet caught him in the chin as he was falling.

Chicken had barely hit the ground when the outlaw beside

him swung his crippled arm towards Dunn. The four-barreled .32 Sharps Pepperbox pocket pistol hidden in that sling popped once, and a bullet whipped past Dunn's face.

Dunn squatted and pivoted on the balls of his feet with his right-hand Colt swinging towards the man with the derringer. But John Rabbit stabbed a big, antler-handled sheath knife into the man's ribs, and then a rifle roared and a lead .44 bullet tore off the top of the same man's head before Dunn had a chance to fire. Dunn jerked his head to where the shot had come from and saw Injun Joe holding a smoking Winchester.

The shooting stopped as quickly as it had started. Both of the Love brothers had their pistols out, but so did a few of Chicken's men. They were all faced off in a mixed-up bunch. Some were slowly backing away from each other, and some were holding their ground. Nobody wanting to risk dying by shooting first, and at the same time afraid to lose the advantage of the weapons they had ready.

It was Dunn who lowered his guns first. He holstered one and began to eject the empty cases out of the other while he watched the men before him. His ears were ringing from the gunfire, and there was a sudden tremor that ran through his body, as if the rush of excitement and fear and adrenaline were only then peaking. The feeling was better than anything he knew, and he wanted to laugh or scream with the thrill of it.

He held his composure and gestured with a nod of his head at the dead man in the arm sling. "I wasn't looking for trouble. That was between me and Chicken and that one there."

Slowly, those of the Whitehead gang left standing put away their weapons. There was nothing friendly in the way they looked at him, nor was there a sense of peace, but he definitely had their attention.

"That woman Big Henry offered me thirty dollars for is worth a whole lot more. About four thousand more."

"Who's going to give that for a woman? I don't care whose wife she is." One of the guards said that from up on the rocks. Dunn hadn't heard him arrive, but Injun Joe had a watch on him and still held his Winchester propped on one hip.

"You throw in with me and I'll show you," Dunn said.

"Even if you're telling the truth, four thousand doesn't split to much with so many of us," another man said.

"You ask yourself, when's the last time you boys made a haul like I'm talking about?"

"Chicken was always square with us." Still another said.

"Square enough to bleed over? Nobody wins if we all start shooting again. It's likely not a one of us would leave here in one piece."

"Even split?" the same man asked.

"Twenty-five percent for me. You men split the rest even among yourselves."

"That's steep on your end."

"Hmm, let me see. How best to explain this?" Dunn gave a cluck of his tongue. "You see, in every business there is management, and then there are the workers. I guess you could say I'm management material, and you're not."

"Who says?"

Dunn pointed at Big Henry's body, and then at the other two dead men. "Call that my bona fides."

"Count me in," another of the men said. "Chicken said that Denton bank was going to be ripe, but all we got was three hundred dollars and our asses full of lead."

Some of the others mumbled their agreement. John Rabbit swiped away some of the splattered gore from his face with one hand, and then bent over and pulled his knife free and wiped the blood from the blade on his victim's pant leg. He and one of the new men took the dead man by the heels and drug him away. Other men were doing the same for Chicken and Big Henry.

Injun Joe came close to Dunn. The Choctaw was still keeping a close watch on the others. "Nobody cares about Big Henry, but what you did to Chicken won't set well with some of them."

Dunn finished reloading one pistol and shifted to the other. "It wouldn't surprise me if one or two of them slip off tonight, but I think most of them are going to stay."

"What do you want more men for? That man was right. Money splits too thin."

"You've got to think bigger, Joe. I say we change the rules."

"I don't know. How much are you talking about?"

"All of it. I'm talking about all of it . . . the whole territory."

Chapter Fifteen

Morgan and his posse crossed the South Canadian by means of a boat they found pulled up on its north bank, loading their saddles and gear in it and letting the horses swim alongside. After that, they made seven more miles, keeping their horses to a trot over muddy trails before they finally made camp in the timber on top of a little mountain southeast of Canadian Station.

Cumsey sat with his saddle for a backrest and his legs outstretched before him. He was whittling on a stick with his bone-handled Barlow pocketknife and staring contentedly at their campfire. Morgan stood not far from him with his back to the flames.

"You ought not stare at the fire like that," Morgan said.

"He's right," John Moshulatubee said from where he knelt on the other side of the flames frying salt pork in a skillet. "A man has got two sets of eyes, nighttime eyes and daytime eyes. The old warriors, if they were going to raid at night, used to always wait awhile in the dark to find their nighttime eyes."

Ben glanced at Morgan from where he sat on the trunk of a fallen, windblown tree, but Morgan gave him a subtle shake of the head. Morgan had once heard an army surgeon explain how a human's pupils dilated or contracted, depending on the amount of light, but the Choctaw peace officer's explanation made the same point.

"Well, say what you want to, but what's the good in having a fire if you can't watch it?" Cumsey asked.

"You do what you want to," Morgan said.

"You really think about not looking at fires and stuff like that?" Cumsey asked.

"Pays to be cautious."

Cumsey paused his whittling and pointed at Morgan with the blade of his pocketknife. "Come to think of it, best as I can recollect, I ain't never seen you sit in a room without your back to a wall, and even now you're holding that cup of coffee with your left hand so you can keep your gun hand free. Must wear on you, always worrying like that."

"Habit, I guess," Morgan answered.

"What other habits you got?"

Morgan shrugged. "I don't know. Rules a man comes by to help him stay alive. Ways a man keeps his edge. Most of it's common sense."

"How many of those tricks did you learn the hard way?"

"Those are the ones you remember the most," Morgan said.

"Well, count me out. Whatever they pay you ain't enough. I prefer my peace of mind and not a worry in the world. Free and easy, that's how I like it."

Morgan gave him a wry look. "Now listen to you. Peace of mind? You've been ducking and dodging the law since I first came to the territory."

Cumsey waved a dismissive hand. "Ah, that was only fun and games. Kicking up my heels a little, you know? Never put much thought to it."

"Oh, yeah. Fast as greased lightning and twice as slippery, isn't that how you like to tell it?" Morgan pulled out a fresh cigar and grinned at Moshulatubee before he lit the stogie with a burning stick from the fire.

Moshulatubee laughed.

"Laugh all you want to, the both of you," Cumsey said. "I

admit, you lucked out and caught me once, Clyde, but . . ."

"I caught you twice."

"And I got away without so much as breaking a sweat. And you, Mr. Lighthorse, how long have you boys been after me? And you ain't never come close enough to get so much as a whiff of me, much less arrest me. Outrunning and outfoxing you fellows is child's play."

Morgan shook out the burning stick and drew on his cigar until the burning end of it lit his face in red. "Seems like I recall finding a young fellow a lot like you hanging by his neck in a thicket. As I remember it, that fellow didn't look like he was having much fun at the time."

"I was off my game that day," Cumsey mumbled.

"Sure you were."

Morgan remembered the day well, the time he first met Cumsey. He had found Cumsey hanging by his neck from a tree at the end of a sagging rope, left there for dead by a trio of marshals with a grudge against him and a notion to administer some vigilante justice. It would have been the last of Cumsey if those marshals had paid a little more attention to their work, and if Morgan hadn't chanced by and cut him down before he strangled. That time, Cumsey had pulled a sneak gun on Morgan later in the day to make his escape. Not only did the half-breed horse thief have a knack for being hard to catch, he was equally hard to keep hold of if you caught him.

But say what you wanted to about Cumsey. He might be full of brag, but he had plenty of grit. He had been right there in the middle of the fight when those same marshals that hanged him had later cornered Morgan in Eufaula. Granted, after it was all over, he had made a point of getting gone during the confusion following the gunfight, escaping Morgan's custody for the second time in the matter of a few days.

"You think McAlester will pay up? That's a lot of money,"

Cumsey said.

"I suppose he meant it," Morgan replied. "He's lost his wife and his son, and he's like a man falling out of a tree and grabbing at every limb on his way down."

"Guess that boy ought to be glad he's got a rich daddy," Cumsey said. "There will be plenty out trying to find him so they can collect on that reward."

John Moshulatubee turned over a piece of salt pork in the skillet with his fork and deftly dodged the splattering of hot grease it caused. He glanced at Cumsey. "Bowlegs? You kin to those Bowlegs over around Wewoka and Sasakwa? Know a few of them. Good people."

Cumsey grinned. "That depends on who you believe."

"What do you mean?"

"Depends on whether you believed my mama or not," Cumsey said with another grin. "She belonged to John Jumper until after the war. Her mama was a slave, too, and came here from Florida with his band back in the old days."

Cumsey cut a curly shaving from his stick and watched it flick into the fire before he continued. "Mama never jumped the broom with no man I know of, but lots of slave girls ended up with a little biscuit in the oven and no husband after the baking. Just the way it was. Hard times for sure. But that might not have been how it happened, either, because my mama, God rest her soul, liked men about as much as I like horses, even after she was a freed woman.

"She always claimed my daddy was old Billy Bowlegs, the Alligator chief himself. Said he was the love of her life, and that he died before she could convince him to claim me. That's how come she gave me his name. Maybe he really did take a fancy to her for a time, but she was always trying to make things sound better than they really were."

Moshulatubee grimaced and gave Cumsey an apologetic look.

Cumsey waved a dismissive hand at him. "Doesn't matter. Whether it was him or some other fellow that sired me, I was a woods colt for sure."

Moshulatubee obviously still felt uncomfortable about bringing up the matter, and made a point of studying the cooking pork, as if it had suddenly become the most interesting thing in the world, and to avoid having to look at Cumsey. Ben, too, was busying himself like he was looking for something in his saddlebags.

Cumsey put away his pocketknife and stood. "Think I'll go take the feed bags off the horses and then take them down to that creek and water them."

Morgan looked to the other side of the fire past John Moshulatubee. The horses were tied to trees barely out of the firelight.

"You want some help?" Morgan asked.

"I got it. Enjoy your cigar."

"Hey, Cumsey," Morgan said before Cumsey had taken a step towards the horses. "A fellow good at getting out of tight spots like yourself might be thinking how easy it would be to get on his horse once he got down there to the creek and never come back."

"Ah, now, Marshal. I agreed to help you, didn't I?"

"I didn't give you much choice," Morgan answered.

"No, you didn't."

"Cumsey, I give you my word when this is over, I'll make sure Judge Parker and District Attorney Clayton know how you helped. No guarantees it will do you any good, but I'll try. Maybe you getting on the right side of things will go well towards showing that you're really reformed of your old ways."

"Appreciate it," Cumsey said. "But just so you know, I'm not going with you to Fort Smith after this is over. You talk with the court folks all you want, but nobody's locking me up. And that goes for you, too, Lighthorse. You damned Choctaws ain't going to tie me to no whipping post."

Morgan clenched his cigar in his teeth. "Guess we'll have to cross that bridge when we get to it."

"Guess so."

Ben looked at Morgan after Cumsey disappeared into the night. "Am I given to understand that he is a known thief?"

"You're bothered by that?" Morgan asked.

"I am."

Morgan nodded his head thoughtfully, as if considering the matter, before he answered. "As I understand it, your great-grandfather Vanderwagen served two years in a Prussian prison for stabbing a border guard before he came to America, yet that didn't stop your grandfather from hanging his portrait over the fireplace, did it?"

"He was never in prison."

"Why? Because Adolphus said so? Because the Vanderwagens would never stoop to having a criminal in their lineage?" Morgan asked.

"He fought the British beside Washington at Saratoga. He commanded a battery of artillery. He was a hero."

Morgan blew out a puff of tobacco smoke and waited for the cloud of it to float away before his answered. "His wife, your great-grandmother, was still alive when I married your mother. She tended to talk when she drank too much brandy, and I recall she once told me that he was a Hessian mercenary who swapped sides and joined the Continental Army after one of his officers had him whipped for insubordination."

"I don't believe that."

Morgan's eyebrows lifted. "You don't believe your great-grandmother spent most evenings of her elderly years quite tipsy and giggling and whispering salacious stories, or that your great-grandfather was a once a criminal and a turncoat?"

Ben lunged to his feet and pointed a finger at Morgan. "Do you think I don't know how you despise Mother's family? I think you are trying to twist the matter to conceal your own questionable behavior."

Morgan took the cigar from his mouth and flicked the ashes from the end of it. His expression was mild when he looked back at Ben. "What questionable behavior would that be?"

"Meaning I find it highly unusual, if not downright illegal and unprofessional, to have a wanted felon serving in a posse. Not to mention that we are known by the company we keep."

"Whatever your great-grandfather's failings were, they didn't stop him from being one hell of a soldier. Sometimes scoundrels make the best fighters."

"I'll hear no more of this."

"Suit yourself, but I happen to think Cumsey is one of those who simply got off in life on the wrong foot," Morgan said. "And no matter what Cumsey's done, there might come a time when you're damned glad he came along."

Ben gave a grunt and turned his back to Morgan to end the argument.

Moshulatubee looked at Morgan. "You think Cumsey'll stick?"

"We'll see."

Later that night, after they were all in their bedrolls, Morgan woke from his sleep. Instead of moving, he lay still and listened to the sound of a horse moving somewhere close. And then he glanced at where Cumsey had lain down. His first thought was that Cumsey was sneaking away from their camp, but the horse thief was still there in his bedroll.

Morgan slid his Colt out from under his blanket and rose to his knees facing towards the sound of the walking horse. The fire had burned down to coals, and there was only its dim light to see by. In that red glow he saw that Moshulatubee was awake and staring at him. And then Cumsey moved under his blanket.

"Somebody's coming," Cumsey whispered as if they all didn't hear the noise.

"Wake up, Ben," Morgan hissed.

"I'm awake," Ben hissed back at him. "I heard it while you were still snoring."

Moshulatubee rose without a sound and took his rifle and moved towards where their horses were tied. Morgan stayed where he was and waited. Whoever was out there was coming closer. The sound of Cumsey cocking his Winchester carried loudly in the tense silence.

"Who do you think it is?" Ben was standing by then, his Springfield rifle in his hands.

"Keep down, or get behind some cover," Morgan said to him.

"I'd appreciate it if you fellows didn't shoot me," a voice called out to them.

It was Dixie Rayburn's voice, and Morgan could barely make out the dark shape of a man sitting on a horse in the timber only a few yards away from him.

"Come on in," Morgan said.

Cumsey was adding firewood to the coals by the time Dixie dismounted and led his mount to them. Instead of a horse, it was a mule he brought to the fire at the end of one bridle rein.

"Changed your mind?" Morgan asked.

"Figured somebody ought to go with you and play nursemaid. You Yankee boys never did know your ass from a hole in the ground when it comes to riding the roughs." Dixie led his mule past the fire and tied it to one of the trees near their horses. It was a big sorrel John with a chug head and a pair of ears bigger than any Morgan had ever seen on a mule.

"I remember a time when you would have had sense enough not to go on a manhunt riding a mule. Comes to a chase you might as well be riding in a wagon," Morgan said.

Dixie dragged his saddle and blanket off the mule's back and gave it a rub on the neck. "Only thing I had on the place that was fresh shod and fit for a hunt. And don't you underestimate Sodom here. He's green and he's still got a lot to learn, but he'll do. And he's faster than he looks."

"Sodom?"

"Used to have another to go with him. Matched pair. Hardest set of mules I ever broke. Tougher'n wang leather. Kick, bite, sull, spook, you name it. Sinful they were with every nasty trick in the book. Make a preacher cuss they were so bad, so I named them Sodom and Gomorrah. But Gomorrah choked on a horse apple last fall and I lost him. Now there's only old Sodom here to try my patience."

"How long have you been wondering around in the dark trying to find us?" Morgan asked.

"Lost your trail after you crossed the river. Surprised me when I saw your fire. Figured you'd already be to McElhaney's Store by now, or laid up at Canadian Station waiting to get an early start in the morning."

"We're not going there," Morgan said.

Moshulatubee had rejoined them at the fire, and he and Cumsey gave each other surprised looks. Ben's expression by the firelight was stoic and reserved, and perhaps there was still a touch of anger in it after he and Morgan's argument.

"If you don't intend on trailing those killers, I assume you must have a pretty good idea where they're going," Dixie said.

"By now there's been no telling how many people worrying over the ground where the woman and boy were taken. What tracks there were will be rubbed out or washed out by the rain," Morgan answered. "Every hour we waste cold trailing them is an hour they get further away from us and the less chance we have of running them down."

"And you think they're headed where?"

"Don't have a clue."

"What do you mean you don't have a clue?" Cumsey asked. "I'm counting on you to tell me where they're headed."

"How would I know?"

"You said they were headed southeast after they left McElhaney's."

"Doesn't mean they kept going that way."

"Let's say they did. Half the reason I wanted you with us is because you likely know every hideout this side of the territory. Where would you go?"

Cumsey rubbed at his eyes and glanced back and forth from the fire to Morgan several times. "They could be headed anywhere. We'll play hell finding them if they're headed down into the Kiamichi Mountains or the Winding Stairs."

"I asked you to give me your best guess."

"Might be they're headed to the caves. The more I think about it, the more I think that's where they might be going."

"Keep talking."

"No telling who's liable to be at the caves. Good place to wait things out if you're on the scout. And some of the boys trade horses there," Cumsey said. "Lots of big rocks, kind of a natural fort, good water, and plenty of trails in and out."

"How far away is it?"

"Less than a day's ride if we hustle. Not so far, but it's rough, woods country."

"That settles it then," Morgan said.

"And what if they aren't there?" Ben asked.

"Then we look somewhere else." Morgan shifted his attention to Dixie. "Hate to do it to you, but I want to be riding in another hour or so. Means you won't get much sleep."

"I'll get by," Dixie said.

Morgan went back to his bedroll and got under his blanket.

Dixie made his own bed nearby, but the other three men remained by the fire, waiting for Morgan to say something else.

"That all you got to say?" Cumsey asked.

"You heard the man," Dixie said. "Get you some sleep. Could be a long day tomorrow."

"So we're going to the caves?" Ben asked.

Morgan lifted his hat from where he had rested it down over his face to block the firelight. "That's the plan."

"I told you there's no telling who's liable to be there," Cumsey said. "I've seen twenty or thirty men there at a time if you catch it right. And you ain't never seen the place, or you wouldn't be so willing to ride in there."

Morgan dropped his hat back over his face and said nothing else. Moshulatubee and Ben took that as their cue, and went to their own blankets. Cumsey was left alone by the fire.

"You hearing me?" Cumsey asked. "I'd rather crawl buck naked in a rattlesnake den than go in that place looking for a fight."

"Welcome to law enforcement, son," Dixie said. "Ain't it grand?"

Chapter Sixteen

"Bledsoe should have been back by now," Dunn said as he paced back and forth in front of the men lounging about in front of the cave. "Be like that fool to get lost."

Joe looked up from the card game he was playing on a blanket with two of the other men. "Long ride to Canadian Station and back. Doubt he'll be here before dark."

"He better be."

"You worried something happened to him?"

"I don't give a rat's ass about him. What I'm worried about is whether he delivered my message or not."

"Simple enough job. I imagine your letter got where it was going."

"Joe, find me two men to put on guard," Dunn said.

Injun Joe looked up from the handful of playing cards he was studying. "Already got two lookouts. You want to change them out?"

"No, I want two more," Dunn said. "More than that if you think we need it. I want a man watching every trail in and out of here."

"You think the law will show up? None of them have ever come here before."

"That's because they didn't want to bad enough."

Injun Joe got up from the game and motioned at John Rabbit and one of Whitehead's gang to follow him. The three of them ducked down into a narrow corridor between the rocks and disappeared.

"And no more hunting," Dunn said to those remaining. "A gunshot carries a long ways."

"We'll run out of meat before too long," one of the outlaws said. "What's left of that deer is all the fixin's we got left besides what you got and the supplies Chicken brought over from Briartown."

"Go fishing or something," Dunn said. "I imagine there's fish in that creek down below."

"Got no hooks."

"Then jump in the damned water and catch them in your teeth if you want to. Hell, I don't know!" Dunn turned away, angry and feeling that he had made a fool of himself. He had never fished or hunted in his life, or been any kind of outdoorsman. And it bothered him that he hadn't thought of bringing more supplies to the hideout. Of course, he hadn't planned on being so long at the caves when they had originally set out after the woman, nor had he so many men with him then. Still, he was pleased with how it all was going, given his change in plans and considering how he was making it up as he went. Better than he had hoped, in fact.

The woman and her kid had found a place a little away from the men in a patch of sunlight filtering down through the treetops. The boy was playing around her, ducking and dodging in and out of the rocks and giggling. When Dunn came closer to them, he saw that the boy held a pistol somebody had carved for him out of a stick of wood. It was a crude carving, but it was plain enough that the toy was meant to be a pistol.

The boy turned at the sound of Dunn's footsteps behind him and pointed the toy at him and made a gunshot sound. Pow! Pow! As soon as he recognized it was Dunn his eyes went wider and he scampered to his mother's side.

Dunn stopped in front of them and looked again at the toy pistol the boy held. He wondered which of the outlaws had whittled it for the kid.

He knelt before the boy and motioned to him. "Come here, boy."

The boy clutched his mother's side and refused to come forward.

Dunn pointed at the toy pistol. "You like guns?"

Still, the boy didn't answer.

Dunn made a pistol shape with his fingers, pointed it at a tree beside them, and mimicked the boy's earlier imitation of pistol shots. "Pow! Pow!"

The boy gave him a hesitant smile.

"Come here," Dunn said. "I won't hurt you."

The boy took a hesitant step, but his mother took hold of him and stopped him.

"Let him go," Dunn said.

"He's done nothing to you," she said.

"I said I won't hurt him. Let him come."

The boy took another two steps closer to Dunn. He was big enough to run, but still young enough that his stride held a hint of the tottering, wobbly motion of a small child.

Dunn pointed at the boy's toy pistol. "You like guns?"

The boy nodded.

Dunn drew one of his pistols and held it out for the boy to see. The woman gasped, but stayed where she was.

"Please," she said.

Dunn ignored her and maintained eye contact with the boy. "Do you know the wonderful thing about guns?"

The boy shook his head solemnly.

Dunn hefted his pistol up and down to draw the boy's attention back to it. "Some say God created men, but Sam Colt made them equal. Because, you see, with one of these, the biggest man can be knocked down by the smallest."

"Wike David and Gowiath?" the boy asked. His speech was so heavily tainted with baby talk that he was hard to understand. "Mama say David knocked that giant in the head with a wock," the boy said.

It dawned on Dunn what the boy was speaking of, and he nodded. "Exactly like David and Goliath, only better than a rock. If a man practices enough with one of these, and if he has the necessary will, he can be as big as a giant. Even a boy like you. You would like that, wouldn't you?"

Again, the boy nodded.

"And when they know you can best them, they will respect you," Dunn said. "All the smarts in the world won't make them listen to you unless they first respect you."

The boy never took his eyes off Dunn's revolver.

"Dunn held out his pistol to the boy. "You want to hold a real gun?"

"No," the boy's mother said.

Dunn placed the Colt in the boy's hand, but didn't relinquish his own hold on the weapon. "Feels good, doesn't it?"

"My poppa has a big gun," the boy said.

"This one is made to wear under my coat. A gentleman always keeps his pistol concealed."

"Can I shoot it?"

Dunn's gaze flicked to the mother, then back to the boy. "No, it is a man's gun, and you are only a baby."

"I'm no baby. I big."

"If you want to be a man you must first learn to talk like a man. No more baby talk."

The boy's mother grabbed at him, and Dunn took the pistol back. She pulled the child to her, putting a little more distance between them and Dunn than there had been before.

"Leave him alone," she said.

"You do him no favor by coddling him."

"He's a child."

"My mother would never have allowed me to talk like that at his age."

"Such a fine man you are," she said with a bitter, disgusted bite. "Your mother must be really proud of you."

"My mother sank to the bottom of Lake Michigan with the *Lady Elgin* and three hundred other souls when I was barely older than him," Dunn said. "And I would suggest you never, ever mention her again. You do, and I'll sew your filthy mouth shut."

He lunged to his feet and paced twice back and forth in front of her. His Colt revolver was still in his hand, and his face was flushed red. The woman pressed the boy's face to her chest.

"What kind of man is your husband?" Dunn asked when he finally stopped pacing.

"What do you mean?" she answered with a quaver in her voice.

"I mean, will he do like he's told?"

"Are you asking if he'll pay to get us back?"

"You better hope he pays. You better hope that man loves you and your boy dearly."

"And then you'll let us go?"

He waved a dismissive hand and turned his back. "I'll keep my word if he holds up his end."

"And if he doesn't do as you ask?"

Dunn scowled at her over his shoulder, and then looked away again.

"What kind of man can do what you're doing?" she asked. "I've heard you call yourself a gentleman, and yet, you do this."

He turned slowly to face her. "You don't think your husband has his sins? All that money, and no nasty little secrets? What about the Vanderbilts and Goulds and the Fisks and Carnegies?

I guarantee you, every one of them stepped on somebody else to get where they are. Why, I bet you with all the throats they've cut, you couldn't fit the bodies in a whole train of boxcars. That's the price to pay if you want it all."

"All? I've heard your men talking. You'll risk hanging for four thousand dollars? Sell your soul?"

"Easy for you to say. You wiggled that little brown ass of yours and latched onto a rich white man, eh? Me? I never had anything, except for a father who's only wisdom came at the receiving end of his razor strop, and the promise that when I grew up, I could work in the slaughterhouses or the canning factory for the rest of my life like all the other miserable suckers around me." His anger was such that little flecks of spittle flew from his mouth as he spoke. His motions and gestures became wilder the more he talked.

"But I got out. I went uptown and saw all those finely dressed people passing along Dearborn Street in their fancy carriages without a care in the world, and I told myself how grand it would be to live like that. I read my books every night, kept myself clean, and made sure to mind my manners. And then one day I got myself a job at the Tremont Hotel. I studied them and imitated their ways right down to the last detail. I was going to show all the boys back in Packingtown that I was really something. I was going to be somebody. One of them."

Dunn spun on his heel and paced away from her. He cocked and uncocked the pistol he held, a nervous tic, a habit like some people drum their fingers on a tabletop or fidget and squirm when they are thinking or when they are nervous or irritated.

"And what happened?" she asked.

He turned back to her. "I'll tell you what happened. You can be the smartest person in the world, work harder than anyone, be a damned saint in a suit, and it doesn't matter one bit. *Ladies and gentlemen,* what those words really mean is *money* and *power.* The only way you get into that world is to buy your way in, or they'll sniff you out and sneer and curl their noses like you're something somebody dragged off the gut pile."

"Was this in Chicago?"

He eared the pistol hammer back again with a clack and used the weapon's barrel to point at her. "What do you know about Chicago? You don't know anything."

She looked away from the pistol bore staring at her and tilted her head down and kissed the top of the boy's head. Her words, when they came, were muffled by the press of her mouth against his hair. "No, I guess I don't."

"Doesn't matter," Dunn said. "Thought Kansas City was the place for me. I heard you could go out west and things were different. Plenty of opportunity for a man with a little drive to him. Only I was too late getting to Kansas City. Things there weren't much different than Chicago, so I moved on. Got a chance to come to the territory. And you know what? I've finally found it. Oh, the fat cats are already here and they've got the money to back their play, but for once, a man like me has got an equal start with them. Everything's wide open for the taking. They know, and I know it."

"And how do you intend to beat their money?" she asked.

He shook the pistol in front of her. "This is my buy-in. Do you understand me? This is my ante in the game. Damn them all, and damn you too if you get in my way. They may not know it yet, but they're going to know my name, one way or the other."

The boy was crying by then; there was a tear rolling down her cheek, too. Again she spoke without looking up at him. "Please don't hurt us, Mr. Dunn."

"That's right. Mr. Dunn. I like the sound of that," he said with the volume of his voice rising. Some of the outlaws at the cave mouth had come to their feet and were staring at him.

He held his arms wide and spun in a slow circle looking up at the patch of sky revealed through the treetops. "You hear me, world? Chew me up and spit me out if you want to, but get ready because I'm coming for you!"

Chapter Seventeen

Morgan woke his posse two hours before dawn, and by early morning they struck a wagon road following the course of Gaines Creek and followed it southward down the upper end of Reams Valley. The creek was lined with timber, but the valley itself was dotted with small prairies already lush with spring grass. The farther south they went, the more the valley opened up. They passed two small homesteads belonging to Choctaw farmers, and a few other places where foundation stones or a few blackened bits of lumber or logs sticking out of the grass and weeds showed where other cabins and barns had once stood.

"Damn fine country," Morgan said after they had ridden most of the last three hours in silence. He and Dixie rode at the front of their cavalcade, with Cumsey and Ben side by side behind them, and Moshulatubee bringing up the rear.

"Used to be lots of cattle in this valley," Cumsey said. "Some Creeks had them a little village over there in the timber."

"What happened?" Morgan asked.

"Burned out during the war. First the Confederates run those Creeks off to Kansas, and then later the Union boys came down from Fort Gibson and set fire to everything between North Fork Town and Perryville."

Morgan nodded grimly. It was more than ten years since the war, but the territory was still in the process of recovering. The civilized tribes had been no different than their white counterparts when it came to choosing sides and taking up arms. While the Choctaws and Chickasaws sided almost exclusively with the Confederacy, the loyalties and passion of the Cherokees, Creeks, and Seminoles were split almost down the middle between the Blue and the Gray. Those that couldn't fight or wouldn't and tried to sit it out fared no better, for they, like everyone else, were caught in the middle of a storm that didn't recognize noncombatants. In addition to the Indian regiments that were formed, armies out of Texas, Kansas, Missouri, and Arkansas marched into the territory. And as if the regular forces weren't enough, partisan and guerrilla fighters raided through the countryside killing and stealing indiscriminately. Crops were burned or left unattended, homes razed, livestock driven off, and the families torn asunder. Two years into the war, and the eastern half of the territory became a ghost country with all its former inhabitants either hiding, dead, or having fled to Texas or Kansas to get away from the famine and desolation.

Morgan was still thinking about the war when he noticed that Dixie had stopped his mule at the crest of the hill they were ascending, and had one hand held up to shield his eyes against the sun while he stared into the distance. They all reined up and waited.

"What do you see?" Morgan asked.

"Didn't see anything," Dixie said. "Thought I heard singing."

Morgan rode to the top of the hill and stopped at a point where he could see beyond it, but without skylining himself or his horse, the same thing Dixie had done. He looked to where the road they followed crossed a wide open flat and then disappeared into the timbered line of a creek some three hundred yards to the south. Not only did he not see anything to warrant concern or interest, he also didn't hear anything.

"What's the holdup?" Ben asked.

"Dixie thought he heard somebody singing." Morgan shed his jacket and tied it behind his saddle with his bedroll.

"Singing?" Ben asked.

"Yeah, singing," Dixie growled. He moved his horse over the hilltop without saying anything else. The rest of them followed him.

Before long, they all heard what had caught Dixie's attention. The closer they rode to the tree line in the distance, the plainer the sound was. And it wasn't somebody singing. It was several somebodies singing.

"Sounds like church," Dixie said.

By the time they reached the timber, the notes of a hymn were clear, several voices singing in harmony with no musical instruments to accompany them. The melody was familiar, yet Morgan couldn't understand the words, for they were being sung in another language.

The road dipped down to the creek crossing. The creek was only twenty yards wide from bank to bank, and the road struck it at a rocky shoal. Parked there were several wagons, and there were saddle horses tied here and there in the trees.

Twenty or thirty people were standing solemnly at the edge of the water beyond the wagons, men and women and children, all of them Indians. Some were dressed in white men clothing, and others wore shirts or dresses made of bright cloth decorated with strips of silk or printed fabrics or beadwork.

An Indian man stood waist-deep in the water with the sleeves of his white shirt rolled up to his elbows, and facing the crowd with a black Bible held high overhead in one hand. His free hand was on the shoulder of another man standing in the water beside him.

"It's a baptism," Moshulatubee said when the posse stopped their horses in the road behind the Indian church congregation.

"Is that 'Rock of Ages' they're singing?" Morgan asked.

"They're singing it in Choctaw," Moshulatubee answered.

Several of the Indians glanced over their shoulders at the

posse, but their attention went back to the preacher in the water leading the singing. The preacher did not have a good voice, but he sang with passion, and his deep baritone reverberated along the creek bed. It blended well in some strange way with the higher voices of the women in the crowd.

The singing ended, and the preacher standing in the creek began to preach in his native tongue, still brandishing the Bible high overhead. The man beside him leaned back against the preacher's other hand until the preacher lowered his head gently underwater. All the Indians on the creek bank clapped their hands when the baptized man's head reemerged from under the water, and then they all began to sing again, a different song this time.

"Who's that?" Ben asked.

Morgan thought Ben was asking about the man in the creek still sputtering the water out of his nose and mouth, but then he noticed that Ben was pointing elsewhere. A white man was riding his horse across the shoal a little ways upstream from where the church congregation was gathered.

At a glance, he was a young, skinny man wearing a floppy cap. He saw the posse behind the church congregation at the same time they saw him, and immediately lashed his horse across the hip with the tail of his bridle reins. The horse lunged forward in a surge of water spray, and the rider whipped him again.

"Hold up there!" Morgan shouted.

His answer was that the rider drew a pistol and twisted in the saddle and fired at them. Somebody in the church crowd screamed, and by the time Morgan had drawn his own pistol the Indians were shouting and running through the posse back towards their wagons.

Morgan tried to maneuver his horse through the panicked Indians without riding over them. A woman dragging a young girl by her arm was coming right at Morgan. Before he could rein the dun in to keep from running them down, a pistol cracked again. The girl fell to the ground and the woman screamed. Morgan barely had a chance to glance down at the wounded child and the woman kneeling over her before the dun was past them.

By the time Morgan was clear of the crowd, the rider doing the shooting was coming out on the far creek bank. His horse's iron-shod hooves scrambled on the slick creek stones. Somehow, Ben and John Moshulatubee were already charging across the shoal after the man. Ben had his pistol out, and shouted something that caused the man across the creek to shoot at him. Morgan watched helplessly as Ben's horse reared high, front legs and hooves pawing the air and its mouth gaped open against Ben's hold on his bridle reins.

Morgan spurred the zebra dun into the water and splashed his way towards Ben. Something hissed past him, and then a burp of water erupted behind him where the bullet that missed him had struck. Ben had gotten his horse back under control by the time Morgan reached him and charged towards their attacker.

The man firing on them was having his own horse problems, as his frightened mount tried to bolt and spun in a scrambling circle and almost lost its footing. A rifle boomed from somewhere behind Morgan, and the horse staggered sideways. It was Dixie who had fired that shot, but before he could lever a fresh round into his Spencer carbine the rider across the creek whipped his horse into the tangle of growth behind him. Moshulatubee and Ben were right on his heels.

Morgan spurred the zebra dun to go after them. The gelding was chest deep by then and gathered its hindquarters under it and lunged high. Before it had made two such lunging strides it struck a pothole of deeper water and all but the tips of its ears and its nostrils went under. Morgan slipped from its back and hung on to his saddle horn with one hand while his other tried to hold his pistol above the water. After a maddening few seconds, the dun found its footing again and fought its way to the far bank dragging Morgan alongside it.

Once again on dry land, Morgan swung back into the saddle. Cumsey came out of the creek beside him, and his horse sprayed them both as it shook the water from its hide. Dixie wasn't far behind Cumsey, and the three of them listened to the sound of gunshots from somewhere in the timber before them.

Morgan noticed that the creek stones above the water's edge were spattered with blood, and Dixie saw the same thing.

"I'm pretty sure I put one in his horse," Dixie said. "Don't think he'll go far."

Morgan spurred into the timber with Dixie and Cumsey coming behind. They struck a narrow path through the thick growth, nothing more than a muddy trail beaten down by cattle coming to the creek to drink. That cow trail passed through the middle of a switch cane patch growing too high and too thickly to see anything around them, but another gunshot ahead of them told them they were going the right way.

They burst out of the canebrake at a run, ducking and dodging tree limbs, vines, and greenbriers that tried to tear them from their saddles and holding up an arm across their faces to fend off the lash of those they couldn't avoid. Suddenly, the woods opened up before them, and not far beyond, they could see daylight through the scattered timber where it looked like the terrain gave way to prairie once more. And Morgan could make out the forms of two horsemen silhouetted against that sunlit backdrop.

A dead sorrel horse belonging to the man they chased lay between them and those ahead of them with a bullet hole in its belly. They went around the fallen horse without slowing down.

By then, Morgan saw that Ben was down off his mount and standing over somebody sitting with his back to a tree. Ben had his pistol held to the man's head. Moshulatubee was still on his horse, but had his Winchester out with the business end of it pointed at the same man.

They reined their horses to a hard stop, and Morgan swung down from the saddle on the fly. His horse's momentum shot him forward and he was beside Ben in two long running strides.

"You all right?" Morgan asked.

Ben was breathing hard and only nodded.

Morgan glanced at the blood on Ben's jacket, but tore his eyes away and looked down at the man sitting on the ground against the trunk of the tree. He was younger than Morgan had guessed, barely more than a kid. His cap was gone, and a tangled mess of long blond hair hung over most of one side of his face. Raw red acne patches showed on the one cheek that Morgan could see, and the kid's eye not covered by his hair swapped wildly back and forth between Morgan and Ben's pistol barrel. The sharp knot of his Adam's apple bobbed up and down as he swallowed.

One of the kid's legs was bloody. Morgan could see an exit wound half the size of his fist on the inside of that leg where Dixie had busted him with the Spencer round. It looked like Dixie's shot had gotten the kid and the kid's horse in one go, the heavy .52-caliber lead bullet passing through the kid's leg and then into the horse.

"I'm bleeding like a stuck hog!" The kid's voice was high-pitched and frantic with pain. "Damn it, help me wrap something around it!"

The leg wound was bleeding badly. Morgan saw the empty pistol holster on the kid's belt, and there were no other weapons in sight on the kid's person other than a sheath knife. He pushed Ben's pistol barrel aside carefully and then knelt and jerked the knife from the kid's belt. Removing his neckerchief, he wrapped it around the kid's thigh, knotted the ends, and then twisted the knife into it until the improvised tourniquet was tight. The blood pumping out of the bullet wound slowed to a seep.

"Thank you kindly, mister," the kid said through clenched teeth.

"Hold that tight." Morgan let go of his hold on the knife.

The kid grabbed at his tourniquet while Morgan stood again. Ben held out an old LeMat pistol for Morgan to see. The French made cap-and-ball revolver model had once been issued in small numbers to Confederate cavalry troopers during the war, but Morgan hadn't seen one of them since. It was a large, cumbersome weapon, and one few men favored when they had the choice of other sidearms. In addition to the nine .42-caliber round balls it could carry in its cylinder, there was a second barrel underneath the main one. That second barrel was a 20-gauge smoothbore that loaded from the muzzle and could be charged with either shot or slug. Nine pistol shots and then a single shotgun charge to go with those—it was nothing short of a hand cannon.

Morgan looked at Moshulatubee, and the Lighthorseman pointed at the LeMat pistol. "He shot himself empty, or he might have done for the lieutenant."

Morgan shifted his attention back to Ben. "I asked how bad you're hurt."

Ben pulled down at his shirt collar until Morgan could see a tiny, bloody hole in the flesh above his collarbone. There were two more such blood dots on Ben's left shoulder where other pellets from the LeMat's shotgun charge had pierced his flesh.

"Peppered me a little, but I'll be all right," Ben said.

The kid on the ground moaned.

"What's your name?" Morgan asked him.

"Jimmy Bledsoe," the kid answered.

"How come you shot at us?"

"Thought you was after me. Ah, I'm hurting. Hurting bad."

"Why would we be after you? Seems like you've got a guilty conscience."

Bledsoe slung his head back to shake the hair off his face and looked at the badge Morgan was wearing. "I didn't know you was the law. I thought you were going to rob me."

"I think you're on the scout."

"Not me."

"Where do you live?"

Bledsoe jerked his head in a southerly direction.

"I asked you where you live," Morgan said.

"Near Edwards Store. Over at Red Oak, you know."

"That's thirty, forty miles from here and you're pointing in the wrong direction." Morgan looked at Cumsey. "Do you recognize him?"

"Told you I didn't get a good look at any of them," Cumsey said.

"What's he talking about?" Bledsoe gave Cumsey a frantic look, and then swiveled his head back to Morgan.

Morgan squatted back down at the end of Bledsoe's outstretched legs. "You weren't west of Canadian Station two days ago, were you?"

A wave of pain came over Bledsoe, and he gritted his teeth again and his whole body tensed until it subsided. "No, I never."

"Somebody ambushed and killed two men over that way. Stole a woman and her child."

"I don't know nothing about such as that."

"Where are you coming from?" Morgan asked.

"Ain't coming from nowhere except home," Bledsoe answered. "I was on my way to McAlester to get my horse shod."

"You're riding all the way from Red Oak to get a horse shod?" Morgan asked. "You know what, kid? You're a bald-faced liar."

Dixie had gotten off his horse. He walked to them and stood over Bledsoe with his Spencer cradled in the crook of his left elbow. He tore a hunk off of a black plug of chewing tobacco with his teeth and worked the chaw around in his cheek.

"You better come clean quick." Dixie shook his head at the wounded outlaw in a concerned way. "You've already got yourself in a heap of trouble. Might go easier on you if you tell us why you're dodging the law."

"I'm telling the truth."

"Like hell you are." Morgan sat down and pulled off his boots. He glared at Bledsoe while he poured the water out of them.

"Do you know you fired on a federal marshal, not to mention you wounded an officer in the United States Army?" Dixie asked, still shaking his head. "Soon as we get you to Fort Smith it won't take the Hanging Judge but about two ticks on his pocket watch to order your sorry ass hanged."

"I told you I don't know anything about no woman being taken," Bledsoe pleaded. "I'm always nervous about getting robbed. You know how it is. Lots of bad folks on the roads. I saw you boys and thought you meant me harm."

Morgan took off his socks and wrung the water out of them before he spoke again. "Is there a warrant for your arrest?"

"No, sir."

Morgan and Dixie shared a look between them.

"Kid, you'll start talking if you know what's good for you," Dixie said. "Fess up and tell us why you fired on us. Maybe you didn't have anything to do with stealing the McAlester woman, but you might have seen those who did it on your way. How about it? Six men, white and Indian, with a woman and little-bitty boy with them?"

"I ain't seen nobody since I left home until I run across you." Bledsoe leaned over and threw up with his lank, greasy hair hanging down over his face and his thin body heaving. When he straightened again there was a cold sweat on his face and a string of vomit hanging from his bottom lip.

Morgan had a hard time pulling his wet boots back on his feet. While he was wrestling with his footwear, Cumsey left them and rode back to the dead horse. When he returned, he was holding a Remington Rolling Block rifle across his saddle swells.

"That horse of his ain't wearing a new shoe job," Cumsey said.

"That's cause I ain't had him shod yet," Bledsoe said. "I said I was on my way to see the blacksmith, but I run on to you fellows first."

Cumsey nodded down at the rifle when he spoke again. "One of the men that took the McAlester woman was shooting a big bore rifle. Could have been a .50-70 like this one."

"Ain't you been listening to me?" Bledsoe asked.

Morgan stood and reached down and yanked the knife holding the tourniquet free. He flung the knife in into the woods.

"What are you doing?" Bledsoe howled.

"Tried to tell you, kid," Dixie said, shaking his head. "Now you've done pissed him off."

Chapter Eighteen

With the removal of the tourniquet, Bledsoe's wound started bleeding profusely again.

"Put it back or I'll bleed to death," Bledsoe said.

"How long you think it will take?" Morgan asked Dixie.

Dixie shrugged. "A man's body has a sight of blood in it. Gallon or two I'd guess."

Bledsoe tried to twist the tourniquet tight with his hand. "I'm sorry I shot at you. I'm sorry."

"Talk, kid," Dixie said.

"Give him the knife back or a stick or something," Ben said. "He's going to bleed out if you don't."

"Stay out of this," Morgan answered.

"You're killing him," Ben said.

"His choice," Morgan said. "What's it going to be, kid? You're losing a lot of blood."

Bledsoe's body had begun to shake. "I never would have helped steal that woman, but Dunn said her man would pay a whole lot of money for her."

"Who's Dunn?" Morgan asked.

"Charlie Dunn," Bledsoe said. "Little fellow. Dude from Chicago or somewhere up north. I never knew him until Injun Joe put me on to him."

"Who else is with Dunn?" Morgan asked.

Bledsoe moaned through gritted teeth. "Oh God, I feel bad. Give me something to twist this tight!" Bledsoe shouted. "Give it here and I'll talk!"

Ben shoved past Morgan, cast around at the foot of the tree, and found a stick that he broke to a short length. He handed it to Bledsoe, and the outlaw twisted it into the bandanna. Once the bleeding slowed again, he leaned his head back against the tree and closed his eyes.

"He needs a doctor," Ben said.

Morgan ignored him and squatted in front of Bledsoe again. "Talk."

"Are you going to get me to a doctor?" Bledsoe asked without opening his eyes.

"We'll tend to you. Now talk."

"John Rabbit was with us. He's the only one I know besides Injun Joe," Bledsoe said in a voice so quiet Morgan had to lean over him to hear. "Two others, Texas cowboys. Brothers."

"Who?"

"Budge and Jesco Love."

"How come you aren't with them?"

"Dunn sent me to Canadian Station to deliver a letter for him."

"Deliver it to who?"

"Never seen the man before. Fellow wearing checkered pants."

"White fellow?"

"Yeah. I handed it over and never so much as talked to him. I was headed back when I ran across you boys."

"Where are the rest of them?"

Bledsoe's Adam's apple bobbed in his throat again. "He'll kill me for telling you."

"Dunn?"

"He doesn't look like much, but that man scares me. The others don't see it, but I do," Bledsoe said and sighed. "He ain't right in the head. Crazy eyes like there ain't nothing behind them. You know, on the inside of him?"

"You've got worse troubles right now," Morgan said. "Are the woman and her child still alive?"

"Were the last time I saw them. Ah, damn I'm feeling bad."

"Where is Dunn hiding out?"

"I was supposed to meet them at the caves. Get me to a doctor. I don't want to lose my leg."

Morgan stood and walked a little ways off from Bledsoe and stood with his back to him. Dixie followed him, and so did Moshulatubee.

"What do you make of that?" Morgan asked in a quiet voice.

"Nothing except I'd say we've got a chance now to run them down," Dixie answered.

"Seems like little Charlie Dunn has gone outlaw."

"I figure he was born that way, only nobody looked close enough at him to tell it."

"That prissy little runt?"

"Oh, he's prissy, but you'll do well not to underestimate him," Dixie said. "Things have changed since you were in these parts last, and Charlie Dunn is a mean, nasty little cuss."

"All right."

"I don't get to Eufaula much lately, but I've heard some talk. Folks there say you listen most evenings and you'll hear him out at the edge of town banging away with those pistols of his and practicing. Dunn's itching to make a name for himself in the worst way."

Morgan considered what Dixie had said. There had always been something off about Charlie Dunn back when he was still checking in customers and carrying luggage up and down the Vanderwagen Hotel stairs—not only in the way he looked at you, but also the way he talked. Before, Morgan had simply thought Dunn nothing but a squirrelly kid.

"We ran across each other back in Fort Smith, and he

informed me he wasn't working for Helvina anymore," Morgan said.

Dixie grunted. "You know he killed Sergeant Harjo, don't you? Killed him in a pistol fight."

Morgan perked up at the mention of an old friend. Jim Harjo had ridden for the Creek Lighthorse. "How'd it happen?"

"The two of them got in an argument over a pretty little Creek girl that lives up on Elk Creek."

"How come the Lighthorse didn't arrest him and hand him over to us, or let the marshal's office know?"

"Dunn claims that Sergeant Harjo pulled a pistol on him, and the only witness was the girl and John Rabbit. I guess the Creeks believed him."

"Rabbit? Is he the same one our prisoner mentioned?" Morgan jerked his head back at Bledsoe behind them.

"Same one. Rabbit's Choctaw. Only reason I know who he is, is because he was working for the sawmill up at Muskogee when I went there to get some lumber. I noticed the men there were giving him extra room, and when I asked, I got the impression he's got a reputation as some sort of bad man. Can't tell you more than that."

"And the girl that was the other witness to Harjo's killing?"

"She backed Dunn's story. Said Harjo was drunk and mean and pulled on Dunn first. Self-defense."

"Harjo wouldn't touch a drop of liquor."

"Doesn't surprise me."

"He was good with a gun. Damned good."

"Not good enough, or else he didn't keep a close enough watch on Dunn."

"What about the Love brothers that kid mentioned?"

"Never heard of them, or that Injun Joe, either."

"What about you?" Morgan asked Moshulatubee.

"Don't know John Rabbit or the Love brothers, but I know

Injun Joe," Moshulatubee said. "His real name's Joe Jackson. Tribal court gave him twenty lashes across his back with a hickory switch for stealing hogs a couple of years ago."

"Well, he ain't stealing hogs anymore," Dixie said.

"No, he ain't," Moshulatubee answered.

The sound of several riders coming through the trees from the creek drew their attention. It was a few of the Indian men from the baptism.

"Talk some more to Bledsoe and find out what else you can," Morgan said to Dixie.

Dixie went back to the wounded prisoner while Morgan and Moshulatubee waited for the new arrivals. There were four of the Choctaw men, and they were all well-armed. One of them was the preacher. Moshulatubee conversed with him in Choctaw, and Morgan waited for the Lighthorseman to translate.

Moshulatubee looked back at him and tipped his head at the preacher. "Marshal, I'd like you to meet Benny Ludlow. Benny's one of the Lighthorsemen for Tobucksy County when he ain't preaching the gospel."

Morgan nodded at the man. "Glad to meet you."

The two Lighthorsemen shared a few more words in their native tongue, and the preacher's voice was gaining volume. Moshulatubee looked again at Morgan, this time with a grimace. "He says a girl child back at the creek got hit by one of Bledsoe's stray bullets. She'll live, but she might lose her arm."

Morgan remembered the little girl going down in front of his horse. At that time, he hoped she had only tripped and fell. He studied the hard faces of the Choctaws staring back at him while he let that news soak in. "Tell them I'm sorry."

"They want to ride to Fort Smith with us to make sure we get Bledsoe to the jail, and so they can tell their side of the matter to the authorities," Moshulatubee said.

"Tell them we aren't going to Fort Smith," Morgan said. "At least not right now."

"Already did," Moshulatubee said. "But they're mad and not listening real good."

"Tell them to wait." Morgan turned away from them and went back to Bledsoe.

The blond-headed outlaw looked worse than he had only moments before. In truth, the wound in his leg was a bad one, and not only due to the blood loss. There were tiny bone chips in the wound, and Morgan guessed it likely that the leg was shattered. Bledsoe opened his eyes and looked up at Morgan, but didn't say anything.

"Get on your horses and let's go," Morgan said to Dixie and Ben.

"What are we going to do with him?" Ben pointed at Bledsoe.

"I'm leaving him with those men," Morgan answered.

Ben looked at the Choctaws sitting their horses where Moshulatubee stood. "Do they have a doctor among them?"

"No, but the preacher is a Lighthorseman. He'll see to the prisoner," Morgan answered.

"You can't give me to those Indians," Bledsoe said in a weak voice. "They got no say over me. Not over a white man. I know the law. You take me to Fort Smith where I can have my day in court and plead my case."

Morgan gestured at Bledsoe and said to Ben, "One of his pistol shots hit a little girl back there on the creek bank. They say she might lose an arm."

"I never meant to hit any girl," Bledsoe said. "You leave me with those Indians and no telling what they'll do to me."

Morgan never took his eyes off Ben. "We've got a chance to get Mrs. McAlester back, but it's a small window. We ride now or we could lose our chance."

Dixie was already up on his mule, and Morgan went to the zebra dun and mounted. Ben waited a moment, but finally got on his own horse.

Morgan looked down at Bledsoe from the saddle. "I'm leaving you in their custody while I go after the McAlester woman and her child. We'll come back for you after we're through."

Morgan reined around and led them off. Cumsey and Moshulatubee fell in behind them as they headed back toward the creek and the road they had left. Morgan glanced back at Bledsoe once before they rode out of sight of him. The four Choctaw men were around the tree where Bledsoe sat and getting off their horses. Bledsoe was begging and pleading again.

When Morgan turned back around in the saddle, he caught Ben watching him.

"You're going to ride away and leave a prisoner with the friends of his victim?" Ben asked. "I know good and well you felt the same thing as I did back there. If that didn't feel like a lynch mob, I don't know what does."

"I left a wounded prisoner in the temporary care and custody of a duly appointed tribal lawman and his gentle church congregation while I continued my diligent and duty-bound pursuit of a gang of murderers and kidnappers," Morgan said while looking straight ahead. "That's what I'll say if anybody asks."

"Your job is to apprehend criminals, not to be judge, jury, and executioner," Ben said. "That man should stand before the court and not be left to the passions of an inflamed mob."

Morgan tapped the zebra dun with his spurs and trotted ahead of Ben. They soon reached the creek crossing. The rest of the Choctaws there were gathered against the side of one of the wagons underneath the shade of the spreading limbs of a giant water oak tree. The wounded girl lay on a blanket. She couldn't have been more than five or six years old. The pretty blue dress her mother had dressed her in was soaked in bloodstains, and a pair of women were wrapping her wounded arm in strips of white linen and tending to her as best they could. The Indians stared at the posse as they passed, but no one said anything.

Dixie rode alongside Ben when they were back on the road and headed south once more. "Shake it off, Lieutenant. Best thing is to try not to think about it."

Ben stared at Morgan's back ahead of them. "He knows what those Indians are liable to do to Bledsoe."

"We just left a little girl with her arm blown half off, and you're thinking about that pimple-faced little killer?"

"I feel as bad about that little girl getting hit as anyone. But no matter how repulsive the man and his crimes are, leaving him with those men makes us little better than vigilantes ourselves. I fear they will hang him."

"You fear?" Dixie gave a short bark of scoffing laughter. "Likely they will, or they might simply shoot his sorry ass to save the trouble of knotting a noose to fit his neck. I never took pleasure in seeing a man executed, but I might make an exception for him."

"That is no kind of justice I'm acquainted with."

"Back where you come from?"

"Anywhere."

Dixie leaned from the saddle and spat a stream of brown tobacco juice into the brush. "Why don't you ride back to that little girl and look her in the eye and explain justice to her?"

"I'm an officer in the United States Army and you are a sworn member of a federal posse. We are duty bound to uphold the process of the law."

"You ever read the Good Book?"

"The Bible?"

"That's the one," Dixie said. "I recall some words that might apply to this situation. Now I can't quote them verbatim, but that preacher back there likely could. You ask him if you're going back there."

"What words are those?"

Dixie leaned from the saddle and spat again. The sun was striking him in the side of the face, and he squinted slightly and cocked his head like a bird when he looked at Ben. "You reap what you sow."

"That's nothing but a convenient excuse," Ben said.

"Your daddy . . ."

"I will ask you one time not to refer to him as my daddy again," Ben said. "And I will also remind you to keep your tone polite. I have given you nothing but respect, and I expect the same."

Dixie squinted harder at the lieutenant. "All right then, your *paterfamilias*, your long-lost begetter, your alleged progenitor or whatever. Those words big enough to suit you, West Point? You see, I read me a few books, too. There's no denying that man yonder sired you, whether you claim him or not, and you could do worse than owning up to that. If you pay attention you might find out he ain't half the devil you think he is. Might be you could learn a thing or two from him."

"I will only warn you once more, or there will be trouble between us."

"Trouble? Having to whip your young ass is the least of my problems right now. If you don't want to be talked down to, ride a taller horse or you start making some sense."

Ben stopped his horse and his face was flushed with anger. "You insist on forcing my hand. Stop and get off that mule and give me satisfaction."

Dixie kept riding. "Save it for the schoolyard, sonny boy. You can come with us, or you can babysit that killer you're so concerned about."

"I . . ." Ben started.

Dixie cut him off. "Your choice. Simple as that. You want to ride with a posse in the Indian Nations, you better grow some bark on you."

"Stop, I said!" Ben called out.

Morgan twisted in the saddle and looked back at them, wondering what the raised voices were about. Cumsey and Moshulatubee behind them had stopped to give the bickering pair room.

Dixie didn't pull up his mule. In fact, he kicked it up to a rocking chair lope.

"What's going on?" Morgan asked as Dixie went past him.

Instead of answering Morgan, Dixie began to sing a song from the war. Those who knew him knew he was a man with a love of music, and the song was always a particular favorite of his, if not one that was acceptable in some company. "O, I'm a good old Rebel, now that's just what I am. For this 'Fair Land of Freedom' I do not care at all."

"Come back here!" Ben shouted.

Dixie kept riding. His voice was surprisingly good, and it carried well. The rhythm and the cadence of the song somehow matched the easy stride of the mule and the rock of the saddle beneath him. "I'm glad I fit against it, I only wish we'd won. And I don't want no pardon for anything I done."

Ben was still sitting his horse in the road glaring at Dixie's back. The others behind him moved on again, and passed him by without looking at him. Only Morgan held back.

"That man is incorrigible," Ben said.

"True, but there's no one I'd rather ride with."

"Why doesn't that surprise me?"

"Mind telling me what your problem with Dixie is?"

"The same problem I have with all of you. The further we go, the more I'm sure of it."

"Sure of what?"

"There are places where all of you would be little more than outlaws, yet you don't even realize that. You've been out here too long," Ben said. "Look at your posse. You pinned a badge on a horse thief, and that unreconstructed Rebel farmer you are so fond of may be worse. You tortured that man back there, and none of your chosen men did a thing to stop you. In fact, Dixie all but cheered you on."

"You didn't stop me, either, so that means you came to the same decision I did. Is that what's really bothering you?"

"That's right. I'm ashamed I didn't stop you. What would you have done to make him talk?"

Morgan closed his eyes for a moment and rubbed a hand across the whisker stubble on his chin. He opened his eyes and his exhale might have been a sigh. "It's not like you thought it was going to be, and that bothers your sensibilities, doesn't it?"

"It does."

"We're the good guys today because we wear the badges that say that's so." Morgan tapped the badge on his chest. "We're the good guys because there's a woman and her child stolen and suffering who knows what right now, and we're the ones going after her. That's as clear as I can make it for you."

"A man does not have to stoop to the level of a criminal to apprehend a criminal. If you won't stand for the letter of the law, who will?"

"And all of civilization will fall apart because I bend the rules? Because I give more credence to a victim instead of those who victimize them." There was a slight uptick at the corner of Morgan's mouth. "I know a certain judge who you might get along with."

"Don't patronize me."

Morgan pointed at the rest of the posse moving down the road and leaving them. "Every one of those men knows we're in the right, not only because of what I just said, but because they know the kind of men we're after. You've been in the territory long enough now that you should understand that, same as they do. Sometimes the law out here is simply the best that can be done at the time."

"So it doesn't matter what we do to get Mrs. McAlester back?" Ben spat back at him. "Fight fire with fire. No-holds-barred, the ends justify the means, and all of that."

"You're damned right."

"How far will you go?"

"What?"

"If that's the case, how far would you go to do it?"

"Every man draws lines that he won't cross."

"You're dodging my question," Ben said. "Say we catch up to them. Get the drop on them in an ambush or sneak up on them and find them in their bedrolls one night. Would you shoot them all in their sleep? Tell me the truth."

Morgan paused ever so slightly before he answered. "I'd kill every man jack of them. Never bat an eye if that's what I thought it required, or if I thought it would save the woman and child or any of you."

"Listen to yourself. Those are the words of an assassin, not a peace officer."

Morgan cleared his throat. "Ben, maybe you ought to go back."

"Go back?"

"You could go back to where we left Bledsoe. See to it that he gets a doctor, or take him on to Fort Smith or somewhere else and hand him over if that will ease your conscience. You're right. It's an ugly business, and not everybody's cut out for it."

"You're trying to get rid of me because I dare challenge you? The great Morgan Clyde, who all the people tip their hats to or step out of his way when he goes down the street. Did it ever occur to you that it's not respect you've earned in this depraved territory, but rather that everyone fears you?"

The patient, placid calm disappeared from Morgan's face. "You don't like it that I left that outlaw with those Choctaws, then here's your chance to do something about it. Go now. I respect a man who sticks to his convictions, even if I don't agree with them."

"I'm not quitting," Ben said. "And I'm not going to keep quiet when you're wrong."

"Suit yourself. I'll tell the others to stop. Seeing the way you're wincing and the way you're sitting in the saddle makes me think that shotgun charge you took did more than pepper you."

"I'm fine."

"Still, it won't hurt for one of us to take a look at it."

"You know," Ben said. "There was a time when I was a boy that I imagined what a fine man you must be, and made all kinds of excuses for you. Closed my ears to the bad things said about you."

"And now here I am in the flesh, with all my ugly warts. Maybe given time both of us will understand the other better. Find what common ground we share."

"You don't understand. I despise you," Ben said. "And I see that everything Mother and Grandpa said about you was true. You're no good. You've thrown off what little of decency you ever possessed."

"I hate to hear you say that." Morgan put the dun down the road after the rest of the posse.

Chapter Nineteen

The man in the checkered pants arrived in Eufaula on a morning train right at daylight. He didn't enter the Vanderwagen Hotel through the front doors. Instead, he used the back door that led through the kitchen. He passed through the long hallway that led from the kitchen and stopped at a door halfway to the lobby. He knocked gently on the door, and after a delay he heard someone stirring inside the room.

Helvina Vanderwagen heard the rapping on her door, but her head was foggy with sleep, her feather mattress felt unusually luxurious, and she was reluctant to rise. She rolled onto her side facing the sunlight streaming through a crack in her curtains. She had kicked her covers off sometime during her slumber, and the sunshine felt good on her bare skin, so good that she yawned and stretched both arms wide as if she could absorb more of it.

She rubbed the sleep from her eyes, batted them a few times to clear her vision, and frowned at the form of the man beside her and with his back turned to her. He was wrapped in her sheet, all but the top of his head hidden. And he was snoring loudly. She gave him a hard shove in the back to wake him, but he only snorted like a pig and wallowed his body deeper into her mattress and pillows.

"Wake up and get dressed," she said as she swung her legs over the edge of the mattress and put her bare feet on the Persian rug on the floor. "And keep quiet until they're gone.

The gossips already have enough to say about me."

The man in her bed did not answer her, nor did he stir. He simply groaned and pulled the sheet over his head.

"You heard me," she said.

She ran a hand through the tangle of her blond hair, then rose from the bed and went to the full-length mirror on the far side of the room. She stood before it naked and gazed at her reflection, turning slightly to provide different angles, and cocking her legs this way and that and striking different poses. Placing both hands under her breasts, she lifted them slightly and frowned critically.

The man in the bed behind her was sitting up and smiling. "Now, there's a sight."

She looked in the mirror and frowned once more. "I look old."

"You could pass for twenty."

"I've already let you in my bed, so you can stop the flattery. I can see with my own eyes how my body is falling apart."

"I like those little dimples in your butt," he said.

"There are no dimples in my butt." She turned in the mirror and looked back at her posterior's reflection.

"None in the front either," he said.

"Turn away and quit looking at me. At least allow me that much modesty."

"You like me looking at you. That's why you're standing there."

"Try for once to act like a gentleman."

"I much prefer my current behavior."

She gave him a look that was intended to be severe, but couldn't fight back the naughty grin that replaced it. She ran a hand over her belly and watched herself in the mirror. It was a thing that she was most proud of—that she had borne two children, yet her stomach was almost as flat and taut as it had been in her girlhood. Almost. Despite her constant attention to what she ate and dedication to some sort of daily exercise, she had put on a few pounds over the last two or three years. Furthermore, Newton's Law of Gravity was starting to show its effect, and things were sagging slightly instead of staying in their rightful, pert places.

The knock on her door sounded for a second time, still only a light rapping, but more insistent. She went to the dress form in one corner of the room where one of her girls had hung a freshly laundered and pressed dress for her, along with a clean chemise, bloomers, multiple petticoats, and a corset. On another form beside the dress was a steel-hooped crinoline.

"I always wondered how you ladies tolerated having to wear all of that," the man on the bed said.

"The appearance of beauty has its price," she answered.

"I much prefer you without all of that."

"I told you to quit watching me," she said. "It's not for a man to witness the mysterious rituals of a woman's dressing."

"Whoever's at your door will have either given up and left, or will have beaten your door down and woke everyone in the hotel by the time you cinch that rig on," he said.

She took one last look in the mirror and gave a little sigh. "I suppose you're right. I wonder who could be so rude as to awaken me at this hour?"

She slipped a thin cotton nightgown over her head, let it fall in place, then picked up a robe off the floor and put it on and belted it loosely closed. Next, she took a brush from her dressing table and worked it through her hair. By that time, the knocking on her door came a third time.

"Remind me never to come calling when I'm in a hurry to see you," he said.

"Keep quiet and stay in here until they're gone." She went into the little parlor that made up the only other room in her apartment and closed her bedroom door behind her. The knocking came again.

She crossed her sitting room in three strides and unlocked the doorknob and cracked the door open. The man in the checkered pants standing in the hallway cleared his throat and gathered in preparation for what he was about to say. He was a tall, dark-skinned man with a thick black handlebar mustache and a short-brimmed hat.

"I suppose you have a perfectly good explanation for waking me before ten," she asked before he could say anything.

"You said you wanted the message from him as soon as it came," the man in the checkered pants replied.

She opened the door a little wider and stuck her head out in the hallway and peered down it both ways, and then she stuck a hand out to him. "Well, give it here."

He handed her the brown paper envelope.

"Did he deliver it himself?" she asked while she tore open the envelope.

"No, he sent a man in his place."

"Very well, then. You may go now."

She shut the door in his face and went and sat upon her parlor couch with her feet drawn up under her. She pulled forth the letter from the envelope, unfolded it, and read the message. It was written in a neat, painstaking cursive hand. She threw the letter across the room the instant she finished reading it.

She lunged from the couch and yanked her door open again. The man in the checkered pants was almost back to the kitchen, but the sound of the door made him look back.

"How many men can you get together?" she asked.

He considered that for a moment before answering. "Three, maybe four at best. More if you give me time."

"Get them."

"Where do you want them?"

"Close."

"All right." The man in the checkered pants tipped his hat to her and went into the kitchen and out the back door.

Helvina heard the shuffle of feet and turned to see one of the hotel maids coming from the other end of the hallway. The Indian girl ducked her head once she saw her employer.

"Don't stare at your feet," Helvina said. "I want you to go get Mr. McAlester from his room."

"He's already in the dining room eating his breakfast."

"Good. Give me fifteen minutes and then tell him I would like to speak with him in my quarters."

"In your quarters, ma'am?" The girl cut her eyes up once, but looked away again.

"Yes, my quarters. And keep your gossipy little mouth shut about this. One word of this leaks out and you're fired."

"Yes, ma'am."

"Do like I told you. Scat!"

The maid gathered her skirt in both hands and turned and went back to the lobby at a trot. Helvina closed her door, picked up the letter from the floor, and went back into her bedroom. The man in her bed had fallen asleep again. She ignored him and dressed and groomed herself.

"Get up," she said to him when she was finished. "J.J. McAlester will be here soon."

"What?" he asked and threw the sheets off of him.

"I received confirmation that Charlie has Mrs. McAlester and her child in hiding."

The man wiped at his face and fumbled for his clothes on the floor. "That's good."

"Not all good. I should have known he would try something like this. He's always been too ambitious."

"I take it you're talking about your man. Dunn, is it?" He found his pants and pulled them on. "I thought you said he could be trusted to do like he was told."

"Oh, he did exactly like he was supposed to up to a point."

"But?"

"Read the letter he sent us." She threw it at him.

He caught the piece of paper and read it quickly, then gave her a displeased look. "It seems you're right. Young Mr. Dunn is very ambitious."

"How dare he!" she said pacing about the room. "The fool is going to ruin everything!"

"It could be worse." The man dropped the letter on the bed and continued dressing.

"How could it be worse? My agreement with him was that we would pay him to deliver the woman and child into our hands or hold her until needed, depending on the instructions we gave him once he had her. And now the pompous little villain has the audacity to inform us he expects a ten percent ownership or he will kill them both and ruin the whole setup."

"Maybe we should wash our hands of the whole matter."

"I've put too much into this, and so have you. And what if he were to be captured, or threatens to tell of our involvement?" she asked. "What will Mr. Gould and Mr. Bond say when he finds out you tried to strong-arm one of his business partners?"

"Mr. Gould may not approve of my methods, but I think he will be well pleased with the results if all goes as planned."

"Haven't you been listening? It isn't going as planned."

The man pulled on his shirt and spent the time buttoning it in deep thought. He was pulling his suspenders over his shoulders when he finally spoke again. "My job is the least of my concerns if this gets out, but the more I think about it, the more it becomes clear that nothing has really changed."

"What do you mean it hasn't changed?" she asked.

"I wouldn't have slept another sound night knowing that there was even the slightest risk that your Mr. Dunn might talk after this was over. I say we pretend to play along with him, and then remove him at our convenience."

"You mean have him killed?"

"Don't try to play demure with me. I think what we like about each other is that we can drop such false pretenses when we're alone," he said. "There are men who will do such for a small fee. I have a few in my employ, as I'm sure you have."

"How exactly would you handle this?"

"Let Mr. Dunn continue to help us in our venture, and then we will dispose of him. The fact that he suggests what he does shows that he has no concept of who and what he is dealing with and that he can't be trusted. I'm sure you have already considered such a contingency, perhaps even before Mr. Dunn showed his true colors."

"You will handle his disposal?" she asked.

"*Disposal,* I like that word, but I prefer to refer to the matter as *liquidating an asset.* Sounds much more businesslike, wouldn't you say?"

A slight pout formed on her mouth.

"You don't agree with my decision?" he asked. "I'm beginning to think you have some attachment to this Mr. Dunn."

"No, I'm in full agreement, but I must admit to some regret."

"I have a good memory for names. I recall a boy that worked here in the hotel with that same last name."

"I gave him a chance. Practically took him under my wing. To say I have a lot of time invested in him is an understatement."

"How about your bed? Did you let him there, too?"

She tried to slap him, but he caught her wrist and stopped her palm inches from his face. "Such temper. Perhaps what I speak hits too close to the truth. Perhaps it bothers you that your charms aren't as powerful as you think they are, and that your little boy lover was working you while you thought you were working him."

"You think me such a stupid slut?"

"I think you are a woman who will do whatever it takes to get what she wants. I see that easily in you, for I possess the same quality." He gave her a grim smile to try and soothe her anger, but did not release her wrist.

"Do you think I let you bed me as a business arrangement?" she asked.

"Could be, or maybe it was simply for sport. It was fun, wasn't it? You are an especially noisy and enthusiastic lover, and I judge from that you either had a good time or you are a very superb actress."

"You bastard."

He clucked his tongue and shook his head. "Such language out of a lady."

"It will be a cold day in hell before you ever crawl into my bed again."

Again, he shook his head. "Either way, I don't care. What I do care about is that things go as planned. I expect within the week to inform the board that I have made a new purchase for a nominal price. For that accomplishment, I also expect to receive a very large bonus or maybe even a small shareholding such as Mr. Dunn is foolishly trying to acquire."

"You can let go of my hand now," she said.

"Not until you tell me more about Mr. Dunn."

"There's nothing to tell. I found him working in a hotel in Kansas City while I was staying there. He had some awkward crush on me or something, and was always making excuses to be around me when he could. After some time, I judged him smart enough to be useful and hired him as my valet. He wanted to come with me when I moved my business to the territory."

He let go of her arm and sat back on the edge of the bed to pull on his shoes. "You trusted him with too many details. Who else knows?"

"I told him we wanted McAlester's wife taken and what the job paid. Nothing more."

"That makes him smart and nosy. I don't like either quality in anyone but myself."

There came another knock on the door that interrupted their conversation.

"That will be J.J.," she said.

"Did he request this meeting, or did you invite him here? Meaning had you already decided to liquidate your Dunn and go ahead with it before you showed me the letter?"

She patted at her hair and checked herself in the mirror once more before she answered him. "You're not the only one with a brain."

The outfit she had chosen was a navy-blue riding habit with a white ruffled blouse underneath the tight-waisted jacket. The skirt, like the jacket, was of a tighter cut and showed off her long, sleek figure instead of hiding it beneath hoops and petticoats.

"How do I look?" she asked.

"Simply ravishing, my dear. Even your fangs do not show."

"Don't come out unless I call for you," she said. "I think it best that we break it to him gently."

The man sitting on her bed waved his hand at the door in a grand and mocking gesture. "You have the first play. Make it a good one."

Chapter Twenty

The posse left the road and went overland for four miles before they stopped in a pine thicket at the foot of the San Bois Mountains. They didn't unsaddle their mounts, but the men started gathering fuel for a fire so that they could cook a meal.

"No fire," Morgan said, and then looked at Cumsey. "How far from the caves are we?"

"Hour or two's ride, maybe," Cumsey said.

"Then we won't put up smoke. I don't particularly care to advertise our arrival."

John Moshulatubee must have been already thinking the same thing, for he produced a sack of cornbread and several tins of canned oysters and beef from his saddlebags. Cumsey took one of them and began cutting the top of the can open with the blade of his pocketknife.

"Don't think I'll ever get used to this tinned food," Cumsey said. "Man can cut his hand off opening one of these. Feel like I need a hammer and a chisel."

Moshulatubee offered one of the cans to Dixie to open, but Dixie held up a palm to fend him off. "Not me. I snatched me a can of Yankee oysters after the fight at Harpers Ferry. Those oysters must have been spoiled, 'cause I was sick for three days. Never have trusted that tinned meat since. Just give me a piece of that cornbread and I'll make do."

Ben was the last to get off of his horse, and Morgan noticed. "Let's have a look at your shoulder."

"I told you I'm fine," Ben answered.

"I'm going to look at it, or you can have one of the others do it," Morgan said.

Ben began to strip out of his jacket and shirt, mumbling his complaints under his breath. He motioned at Moshulatubee, and when he was stripped to the waist, he took a seat on a ledge of rock. All of them could see the dried blood caked on his shoulder and upper chest.

The Lighthorseman leaned over him and probed at his wounds for a while. "You're lucky. You were far enough away that the buckshot didn't do much more than bust your hide, except for that one by your neck."

Moshulatubee slipped a knife from a sheath on his belt.

"What are you doing?" Ben leaned away from him and held up a hand to keep the knife away.

"Quit complaining," Moshulatubee said. "You want me to dig that shot out, or do you want it to fester?"

"I worry that what you'll do with that knife will be worse than getting shot."

"Anybody got any whiskey?" Moshulatubee asked. "Those young doctors that the council sent to college back East have been teaching how we ought to use a clean knife."

"Stick it in the fire," Cumsey said.

"Don't want to ruin the temper in my blade. Those doctors said liquor works."

Dixie went to his mule, dug in one of his saddlebags, and came back carrying a pint bottle of whiskey. He gave Morgan an apologetic look. "For medicinal purposes."

Morgan couldn't quite hold back a hint of a smile and nodded. "Medicinal purposes."

Moshulatubee sloshed some of the clear alcohol over the blade, then gave it another splash for good measure. Done with that, he put the neck of the bottle to his lips and swallowed a jolt.

"What was that for?" Ben asked him.

"Steadies my hand," Moshulatubee replied. "Now hold still. That pellet is barely beneath your skin and I can see the top of it."

Ben bent his neck and craned his head over to one side. He locked eyes with Morgan while the Lighthorseman probed with the tip of his knife. He didn't flinch, but all of them could see how his teeth were clenched against the pain, even if he wasn't going to admit it hurt.

"There. You'll be stiff and sore for a while, but I'm pretty sure you'll live." Moshulatubee held up a bloody, single lead buckshot pellet between his thumb and forefinger for Ben to see.

"That's all?" Ben asked.

"Here." Moshulatubee handed Ben the buckshot. "Keep it for a souvenir of your first manhunt in the territory."

Ben was still examining the chunk of lead when the Lighthorseman sloshed some of the whiskey on his wounds. He flinched and gave a howl of pain. "What was that for?"

Moshulatubee shrugged and took another drink from the bottle. "If it cleans a knife, then it might do some good on your wounds. You might want to rig some kind of bandage over that."

Dixie took the bottle back, had a drink, and then handed it to Cumsey. The young horse thief also took a healthy pull from the bottle. Both of them were watching Morgan out of the corners of their eyes.

When Cumsey was finished he grinned and held out the bottle to Morgan. "Who knows? Might be we all get killed and this might be our last drink."

Morgan held the bottle at arm's length, contemplating it. "Medicinal purposes?"

All of them grinned, especially Cumsey. "That's right."

Morgan turned up the bottle and swallowed a slug of whiskey. He grimaced when he lowered the bottle and wiped at his mouth with the back of one forearm. He nodded at Dixie. "Next time, bring better whiskey."

Cumsey reached for the bottle, but Morgan pulled it out of his reach. "No more. I've had the displeasure of riding with a drunken posse, and don't care to do it again."

"Now, Marshal . . ." Cumsey said.

Morgan shoved the stopper back in the bottle and shook his head. He made as if to throw the bottle into the woods.

"Hold on there," Dixie said to stop him. "There ain't but a drop or two left. As a leader of men, you should understand company morale."

"What about the lieutenant?" Cumsey asked. "Maybe he would care for a dose of courage."

"No thanks," Ben said while he was putting on his shirt.

"Too good to drink with us?" Cumsey asked.

"Like the marshal said, I don't think intoxicating spirits go with this kind of work." Ben took up his jacket and walked away into the trees.

"Ben . . ." Morgan called after him.

"I don't think he cares too much for us," Cumsey said. "I was only picking at him."

Morgan threw the whiskey in the brush. "He's touchy like his mother."

"Well, say what you want about him, but he's determined," Moshulatubee said. "He ran that fellow down this morning and tackled him off his horse on the fly. Nice bit of riding."

"Young Lieutenant Brass-Ass there is too spit and polish to suit me, but it sounds like he's got guts," Dixie said.

"It was a damned fool stunt," Morgan said. "He's lucky he didn't get himself killed."

"I recall another fellow I know who might be accused of being foolhardy when he's on the fight." Dixie made a point of not looking directly at Morgan when he said that.

Morgan scowled at him. "Sometimes I wonder why I keep getting you to help me."

"Could be because of my sunny disposition and wise council? Or is it because I'm the only man you could find riding such a stylish mule as that one yonder. Kind of give this posse some shine, don't he?"

They all laughed, even Morgan.

"I'm thinking we lay up here until dark. Catch us some shut-eye," Morgan said.

"And what if they're gone by the time we get there?" Dixie asked.

"Then we'll keep after them. But I prefer to come on those caves in the dark."

"I shoot a rifle better in the daylight."

"That goes both ways. Cumsey says they'll likely have lookouts posted if they're there. We'll wait until tonight and see if we can get close."

"You want me to ride on a ways and scout?" Moshulatubee asked.

"No. We bust that covey of quail and no telling how far they'll fly before they light again," Morgan said.

He went to his horse and untied his bedroll from behind his saddle. The others followed his lead and did the same.

"I don't mind telling you I could use some sleep," Dixie said. "And besides, maybe those outlaws we're after will catch wind that we're after them and get scared and send that woman and kid down the mountain and go to waving the white flag."

Morgan unrolled his bed and spread it out on the ground near the horses and underneath the shade of a pine tree. He unloaded his guns and sat on the blanket and wiped them down with a can of oil and a rag. None of them said anything else to him, for it was clear that he was deep in thought about something.

The other men laid out their own bedrolls, each choosing their spots in a scattered fashion. Ben Clyde came walking up through the timber at the time they were all laying down their bedrolls.

Cumsey propped himself up on one elbow. "Better catch you a nap, Lieutenant."

"I thought we were close," Ben said.

"Marshal wants to wait 'til dark."

"I cannot agree. We have already lost enough precious time."

None of them answered him, and John Moshulatubee appeared to be already asleep.

"If you're going to keep tromping around out there in the woods you better watch out for snakes," Cumsey said. "There's some big old rattlers around these parts. Take old John Moshulatubee there with you. I bet he's a fine snake hunter. Why, he could keep one eye on the snake and being looking for a stick to kill it with his other eye."

Apparently, Moshulatubee wasn't sound enough asleep to not hear what Cumsey said for he stirred and answered, "I heard that, Cumsey. I promise you, when this is over, I'm going pay special attention to you."

"Now, you're being as touchy as the lieutenant. No call for that."

"Do you recall a good roan saddle horse you stole two years ago down near the Lenox Mission?" the Lighthorseman asked.

"Allegedly," Cumsey said. "People are always blaming me every time a good-looking bit of horseflesh or a pretty woman goes missing."

"That roan horse belonged to my uncle," Moshulatubee added. "The more you talk, the more I keep thinking about how much I like my uncle."

Cumsey flopped on his back with a big grin and stared up through the treetops. "Get you some sleep, boys. We ride at sundown. Damn it to hell! I always wanted to say that."

Chapter Twenty-One

Helvina Vanderwagen sat on her parlor couch and stared at J.J. McAlester sitting in a chair across from her. The tick-tock of the ornate brass clock on the table beside her seemed especially loud in the silence. For once, she was at a loss for words and unsure how to start such a conversation with the man.

"Why did you bring me here?" he asked, a hint of irritation in his voice.

"I needed to speak with you in private."

"I assumed that." He straightened the knot of his tie and shrugged his shoulders inside of his suit coat.

"I asked you here so that I could speak with you about your missing wife and son."

McAlester stiffened in his chair so suddenly that his carefully combed and parted hair fell down across his forehead. He swiped his hair back in place. "What do you know of them? Have you some word of them?"

"Your wife and son are fine as of this moment," she said.

"And how do you know this? Speak up."

"That is what I brought you here to discuss."

McAlester's expression changed. "I never have trusted you, and I'm beginning to feel that my gut hunch was correct."

"I have word that your wife and son can be returned to you if you cooperate."

McAlester came up out of his chair. "I'm going to find a peace officer, and when I return, we shall continue this talk."

"You walk out that door and your family is dead."

He paused halfway to her door. "Woman or not, you'll hang for this."

She dabbed at a drop of sweat on her neck with a lace handkerchief. "There is no need for me to hang, nor for your wife and dear child not to be returned to you as safe and sound as they were the last time you saw them."

"You conniving witch!" he snapped at her. "What game are you playing? I'll be damned if you will threaten me or my family."

"I assure you, J.J., I am not bluffing. If you want to see your wife and child again alive, then you will sit back in that chair and hear me out. Should you go to a peace officer with this or tell anyone, or should you refuse what I'm about to offer you, the men that hold your family will not hesitate to murder them in a most unpleasant manner."

"Men. You mean your men?" he said as he sat back in the chair.

"I did not say that, but what I will say is that those men await confirmation from me that you will cooperate. If they do not have such confirmation from me by tomorrow morning, they will assume you are not cooperative and take action accordingly. That's something I'm sure you do not wish to happen."

"So this is why you talked me into coming to your little party, isn't it?" he asked.

"Every minute you spend insulting me puts you closer to what neither of us wants to happen." She pointed at a folder on the coffee table between them. "You will find there the paperwork signing over your coal claims in the Indian Territory, both those you have already developed and those undeveloped, including your portion of those which you own in partnership with the MK&T. Also, it is a bill of sale for your store, hotel, and other businesses in McAlester, plus all property holdings and realty you own within the boundaries of the Indian Territory. You will sign those documents, and when you do, you will be paid a purchase price for your trouble and your family will be returned to you."

"So that's what this is about?"

"You should breathe, J.J. Your face is turning red."

"You have some nerve. I will never sign anything."

"You will sign those papers, or your wife and child are lost to you forever. I can only imagine what a load that would be on your conscience."

"You are a fool if you think you can muscle me out of what's mine."

"There will be no negotiation, no haggling as you western men call it. Make up your mind." She leaned forward and poured herself a cup of hot tea from the teapot before her. She lifted the cup and saucer before her and looked at McAlester through the rising steam. "Would you care for a cup of tea? I'm guessing you're a man who likes a lump of sugar."

He reached for the folder on the table and opened it and browsed its contents. "You call this a purchase price? What you're offering is a pittance!"

"That amount should be more than enough to see you and your family out of the territory, and to give you a new start somewhere else. I am sure a man of your capability and industrious nature will make a go of it elsewhere."

"The money is so you can make this look legal afterward."

"That is my concern, not yours."

"Suppose I were to sign this. How can you even imagine that's going to hold up in any court? You must be mad."

"I'm quite sane, and I assure you I have given this much thought."

He grunted and shook his head at her. "I admit that I'm surprised you would try this with me, but have you any idea who else you're bucking?"

"You mean the MK&T? I feared your partnership with Mr. Gould would cause some stubbornness on your part," she said. "Am I correct that you assume Mr. Gould's money and power will protect you, or somehow the force of his might will make all this go away even if you sign those papers?"

"You cross Gould, and he'll squash you under his heel like a bug," McAlester threw back at her. "You're playing a game above your ability. I will give you a chance now to return my family to me. If you do so by the morning, I give you my word I will consider the matter settled and refrain from relating your crimes to the authorities. We'll both go our separate ways and forget we ever met."

She turned her head towards the door to her bedroom. "Bert, I assume you have been eavesdropping. Will you be so good as to come sit with us and show J.J. that it is he who is playing a game above his ability?"

MK&T Superintendent, Bert Huffman came out of her bedroom, and gave a bow to McAlester. "I'm sure this is a shock to you, J.J. Business matters can be so unpleasant sometimes, can't they?"

"You rat bastard. This is your doing. You're trying to run me out."

"In a nutshell, you are exactly correct. The MK&T has long wished to establish complete control of the coal that powers our railroad, though we knew you would never sell willingly."

"You're offering me a measly twenty thousand dollars for everything I have worked to build."

"I offer you your wife and child back."

McAlester sighed and sagged in his chair. Both Helvina and the railroad superintendent could see that he was done.

"Bert, would you be so kind as to bring J.J. that pen and inkwell over there?" Helvina said.

McAlester lifted his head enough to look at them through his shaggy eyebrows when Huffman brought the writing utensils. "And how can I trust you to give me back my wife and son? How do I even know you'll let me out of this room alive?"

Helvina shared a look with Huffman, and when she looked back at McAlester her expression was as coy as ever. "Why, J.J., I suppose you'll simply have to trust us."

Chapter Twenty-Two

There was a dull rumbling in the distance, faint and so far away as to be barely heard. Charlie Dunn hunkered beside their campfire and studied the darkening evening sky with uncertainty. "Was that thunder?"

Injun Joe nodded. "Clouding up. Looks like it might come another storm."

"That's great, more rain," Dunn said.

"Maybe it won't make it here," Joe answered.

"We ride for Briartown tomorrow. Can you guide us there?" Dunn asked.

Injun Joe nodded.

"Somebody's supposed to meet us there if nothing has changed," Dunn added. "If they don't show or things don't look right, then we get rid of the woman and that kid and find another place to lay low until things cool off."

"You think it might go bad?"

"I never said it was going to be easy, and Bledsoe should have been back by now."

"What if we go to Briartown and get the message you're waiting for and everything looks good?"

"Then we get paid."

Injun Joe went quiet for a while, and his uneasiness was apparent when he finally spoke again. "I never killed a woman or a kid."

"Do you want to leave witnesses if this goes bad?" Dunn asked.

"No, but if it comes to that, let Rabbit do it. He won't mind."

Dunn looked over to where the smaller Choctaw sat on a rock sharpening his antler-handled knife on a whetstone. It was a large blade, but crudely made. It looked to be forged from some old scrap of reclaimed metal. The steel had never been polished and was almost black, with the hammer dimples and strike marks still showing. Rabbit passed the blade back and forth along the whetstone resting on his thigh.

Rabbit looked up and caught Dunn watching him. His eyes were deep set in their sockets, round and dark and unreadable beneath the downturned brim of his hat. His long hair was gathered in a single braid and tucked inside the collar of his shirt. He broke eye contact and went back to sharpening his knife.

Dunn initially thought Rabbit incompetent and the least trustworthy of the men with him. But the shifty Choctaw had managed to guide them to the caves in the dark of night, and then had backed him in the fight to take over Chicken Whitehead's men when Dunn expected him to do the opposite. Perhaps it was time to reconsider Rabbit and find ways to make him more useful.

Budge Love came down through the rocks from above the cave with a clank of spurs and the scrape of boot soles. He shoved his hat back on his head, squatted by the fire, and laid his Winchester across his thighs so that he could free his hands to pluck a chunk of meat from the simmering pot beside the flames. He bounced the hot piece of venison around from hand to hand and blew on it before he tossed it in his mouth. He wiped his fingers on one knee of his fringed leather shotgun chaps and looked at Dunn.

"Thought you were on guard duty," Dunn said.

"Jesco done relieved me," Budge said. "He's up there watching now."

"Get somebody else to stand for Jesco," Dunn said. "I want you and him to ride to Briartown and scout things out. If everything's on the up and up, you lay over there for the night and wait for us. If something doesn't look right, you let me know."

Budge glanced at the sky to the west before he answered. "Suits me. Might be a good night to have a roof over my head."

Dunn dismissed the outlaw cowboys from his mind and shifted his attention to Rebecca McAlester and her son a little distance away. Both she and the child were kneeling with their heads bowed and their hands clasped together in front of them.

"Somebody ought to tell that woman that if God listened to her she wouldn't be here with us," Budge said.

"My mama used to make us kneel when we said our prayers," one of the new men said from the other side of the fire.

"She's one of those fussy mothers like your mama must've been," Budge said. "Seen her holding school this morning with that boy. Making him say his alphabet and count his numbers. She was reading to him from some old newspaper that somebody must have left in the cave."

Dunn got up and went inside the cave where he had stowed some of his belongings. When he came back out, he was carrying something in one hand, but it was hard to make out what it was in the failing light. He walked straight to where the woman and child were praying and stood in front of them.

"Quit that and look at me," he said to her.

Rebecca McAlester opened her eyes, but remained kneeling with her hands clasped. The boy ducked behind her and peered at Dunn around her side.

"What do you want?" she asked Dunn.

"They tell me you can read and write," he said.

"I can."

"Where did you learn that?"

"At the Bloomfield Academy when I was a girl."

"Thought those Indian schools only taught you red heathens how to sew clothes and cook real food."

She hesitated, her expression bearing one of caution. "They taught us sewing and culinary skills, as you say, but they also taught reading, arithmetic, and natural philosophy, as well as Scripture. What school did you attend?"

"Don't you act uppity with me, Squaw." He pitched a small notebook and Dixon pencil on the ground in front of her. "Show me how smart you are. Write me a note saying you're unharmed and in good condition."

She picked up the notebook and pencil and got to her feet. "Is that all?"

"I think it would be good for both of us if you beg and plead with your husband to comply with any demands I make of him."

"And what demands are those?"

"Nothing you need to know. Do like I said and sign your name to it," he said. "And I want a small personal item from both you and the boy. One that your husband will recognize."

Before she could answer him, he reached down and grabbed the boy by the arm. She grabbed at her child, but Dunn pushed her in the chest and knocked her down. He reached inside his vest pocket, and the razor blade was in his hand when it reappeared.

"No!" she screamed.

He yanked the squirming boy to him and smirked at the mother. "I think a thumb or maybe an ear will do quite well to prove possession, don't you?"

"Mama!" the boy cried.

The razor blade made a quick slash, and she screamed again. Dunn caught something in his hand and held it up before him.

It was a brass button from the boy's sailor coat. He dropped the boy to the ground, and she immediately scooped the child up in her arms, sobbing.

He held the razor blade before her. "And what shall I cut from you? That blue dress might do the trick."

She tore at something at her neck and held it out to him. It was a tiny gold locket on a chain necklace. He pocketed the necklace while he stared at her.

"I expect that will do," he finally said, then turned to look towards the campfire. "Hey, Rabbit. Come over here."

Rabbit rose, tucked his knife into it sheath, and walked over to them. His approach was cautious, like some kind of wild animal that sensed it was walking into a trap. His eyes flicked between the kneeling woman and Dunn.

"Rabbit, from here on out Mrs. McAlester is your personal responsibility," Dunn said. "We'll be moving again tomorrow morning. Maybe we get her and the kid sold back to her people, or maybe not. Either way, things are liable to get dicey, and I can't watch her all of the time. I want you to stick to her like glue. She's not to get out of your sight."

"I'll watch her good," Rabbit answered.

"If she tries to run, you stop her. If she opens that mouth of hers when I've told her to be quiet, you shut her up. Your job is to make sure she does like she's told. I would have one of the other men tend to her, but I don't trust them not to go soft on her. You aren't soft, are you, Rabbit? You'll put her in her place if you need to?"

The tip of Rabbit's tongue unconsciously slipped out of his mouth and licked at his lips while he studied her. "She will do like I say."

"Understand this, also." Dunn was speaking to Rabbit, but his gaze was on the woman. The intent of his words meant as much for her as it was the Choctaw. "If things go bad . . . if we get cornered or if everything's gone to hell in a handbasket . . . if I give you the nod, you kill her and the boy. No questions asked. No hesitation. You kill'em."

"All right."

"I like your attitude today, Rabbit," Dunn said. "You keep it up and I'm going to start liking you."

Dunn went back to the fire and left Rabbit standing over the woman and child. Injun Joe looked up at him and nodded at Rabbit's back.

"What was that all about?" Joe asked.

"I told Rabbit his new job is to guard the woman," Dunn answered.

"He don't like women. His head ain't right." Joe made a circling motion with one hand held beside his head and he widened his eyes. "He'll do bad things if he thinks he can."

"I'm counting on Mrs. McAlester recognizing Rabbit's tendencies. She'll be on her best behavior because of it," Dunn replied.

Joe looked past Dunn at Rabbit's back again. The woman and the child were getting to their feet. He noticed that the woman held her right arm tight to her hip, and guessed she was hiding something in her hand and behind her dress. Rabbit pointed at the cave and said something that Joe couldn't hear well enough to make out. The woman pushed the child in front of her and started into the cave with Rabbit following a few steps behind them. For an instant, Joe thought he saw the bright gleam of some shiny bit of metal not quite covered by her hand, but he didn't mention it to Dunn.

"She's a proud, stubborn woman," Joe said.

"Rabbit will keep her in line."

Joe kept his face expressionless and said nothing else. He

simply watched the woman disappear into the cave carrying whatever weapon she had managed to gather on the sly.

Inside the cave, Rebecca McAlester clutched her son to one leg and looked back at the half circle of daylight that marked the entrance. Rabbit was silhouetted there facing them. Without words, and by his positioning, he was telling her that she was to stay in the cave and go no farther than where he stood without his permission. She was simply relieved that he did not follow her to the back of the cave. She had seen the way he looked at her even before Dunn had assigned him to guard her. Since she was first a captive, every time she looked his way, she caught him staring at her. The touch of his eyes upon her made her skin crawl. All of her captors were evil men, but she knew without being told that Rabbit was worse than any of them, even Dunn himself.

She led the boy to their blanket and they sat down and watched Rabbit standing in the cave mouth. The boy soon climbed onto her lap.

"Mama," the boy said after a while, "I don't hear that man breathing anymore."

It took her a moment to understand what the boy was referring to. He was talking about the wounded man with whom they shared the back of the cave. In the gloom, she could only make out his general form, lying flat on his back on a pad of blankets. Her son was right. All through the previous night they had listened to the slow, heavy breathing of the wounded outlaw. More than once, he had woken them gasping for air, as if the bullet the other outlaws claimed he had taken in his guts had also damaged his lungs. But now, his breathing was so quiet that it couldn't be heard at all.

She left her son on their blankets and crawled towards the wounded outlaw. She smelled him before she reached him. It was a bad smell, some mix of feces, vomit, and some other putrid scent like something slowly rotting. She still could not hear him breathing.

She reached out a hand and laid it on his chest and couldn't feel him breathing. She shook him gently, and his body felt strangely rigid. What was his name? What had she heard them call him? Abner, that was it.

"Mr. Abner?" she whispered. "Mr. Abner?"

He did not answer her because he was dead and had been for some time.

"I think this man is dead," she called out to Rabbit or anyone else who might hear her. "Do you hear me? He's dead."

Rabbit did not answer her, nor did he come to confirm what she said. Instead, he remained standing and looking her way, as if his rat-like little eyes could pierce the darkness and make her out as clearly as if she stood in sunlight. He stood that way for a long time, and then he sat down with his back to the cave and took out his knife and began sharpening it again. She felt the grate of the steel's passing on the whetstone in her teeth the way some people were sickened by the sound of fingernails scraping a blackboard.

She crawled back to her son and hugged him to her. Without thinking, she began to rock back and forth. She thought she heard thunder somewhere in the distance, but it was hard to tell if it was really thunder or some groaning coming from deep inside the mountain. And it was hard to think at all with Rabbit's knife scraping the whetstone as steadily and repeatedly as the ticking of a clock. She tried to close her ears and her mind to it all and find some shred of peace inside her, but it was a futile attempt. All she could do was rock.

No one came to tend to the dead man, not for a long time. When they finally did come, the light at the mouth of the cave was only a dim gray eye and they were nothing more than brief shadows passing through it. She heard boots scuffing on the rocks, their grunts of exertion, and the sound of the dead man's body sliding over the floor of the cave as they drug him away. Later, she heard rocks clacking together as if they might have thrown him in a crevasse and were now covering his remains. The passing of one of their friends meant nothing to them, and she knew her own life meant even less.

Rabbit put away his knife and whetstone, and she suddenly found the silence even worse than the sound of his sharpening. She wanted to scream at them all. She wanted to scream to remind herself she was still alive. She wanted to scream because it was all she could think to do. But she did not utter a sound, rocking still, clutching her child even tighter to her. He had fallen asleep in her arms, but the press of him against her was enough to make her feel less alone.

She glanced at the place where the dead man had lain, wiped the tears from her cheeks with her hand, and then reached down and felt of the stone floor next to her until her hand found what she had laid there. The cold steel of it pressed against her palm. It was only an eating fork she had stolen during her last meal. A pitiful weapon, yes, but she gripped it like a sword.

Chapter Twenty-Three

Morgan's posse broke camp at dusk. Ben was the first on his horse, and he watched the others checking gear, tightening saddle cinches, and all the other thousand things men did to occupy their hands and minds when they were worried. The young officer's impatience was not lost on the others.

Morgan got up on his horse, but instead of leading them off, he turned to face them. "We go easy and we go quiet. Cumsey, you're the only one of us who has ever been to the caves, so I want you to scout in front of us."

Cumsey nodded. "I'll do my best, but I hope you know what you're getting into."

Morgan shifted his attention to the others, but they all noticed that his words seemed particularly aimed at Ben. "Pay attention. Speak up if something doesn't feel right. Trust your gut and keep your cool, no matter what."

"Is that all?" Ben partially turned his horse to face up the mountain as if to go.

"You don't have a clue what we might be riding into, do ya?" Dixie asked him.

"All of you," Morgan said in a flat, hard voice, "when's the last time you heard about a woman being taken and her menfolk gunned down in broad daylight? Cumsey says men that did it never so much as called out a warning or tried to stop Mrs. McAlester and those with her. They just opened up and went to killing."

"That's right," Cumsey mumbled.

"I've seen about every kind of crime imaginable, things that don't make you sleep good at night, but nothing like this since the war," Morgan said.

"They're bad ones, I reckon," Dixie said. "Bad as bad gets."

"All the more reason to quit stalling and get it done," Ben said. "I'm sure we all would like this to be over and to return the woman and her child to her family tomorrow. With a little good fortune, maybe that's what we'll do."

Morgan continued like he hadn't heard Ben, and shook his head slowly and grimaced. "Have you ever seen dogs run off from their owners and go feral? I'm talking about gentle old Shep and Rover and Spot one day wagging their tales and begging to be petted, and the next packed together and maiming and mangling everything they can run down. Kill crazy, not because they're hungry, but simply because they get a taste for blood."

It was Cumsey that nodded his head. "When I was a boy there was a pack of dogs like that on Sand Creek, and I had an old cur that ran off and got with them. That bunch of mutts raised hell for a while killing stock, until they finally tore into John Jumper's hog pen one night. John wasn't home, but his nephew, young kid ten or eleven maybe, heard those shoats squealing and all the barking and ran outside the cabin and tried to put a stop to it. Those dogs, must have been twenty of them, attacked him and tore him up so bad he almost died. I went with some of the men the next day hunting that pack, and I remember John Jumper telling me not to think about them as dogs when it came time to kill them. Said they had forgotten what they were and become something else worse than any wild critter. Worse than wolves or a hydrophoby skunk."

"And if you don't already know it, a man can go wild, just like a dog," Morgan added. "These men we're after have got the taste for blood, and there's nothing to expect but the worst from them."

"You figure you can arrest that kind of men?" Cumsey asked.

Morgan's eyes were always a cold shade of blue, but in that moment they turned as icy as any man's were capable of turning. "Never known a bloody bunch like we're talking about to go down peaceful. If they won't, then we put a bullet in them the same as that John Jumper told you about that pack of dogs. Put'em down because that's usually all you can do with their kind to end the killing. If any one of you has got no stomach for that, then it's best you go back to Eufaula right now."

All of them nodded at him grimly, a mix of nervous energy and determination showing in the tight set of their faces. Morgan's gaze shifted and landed on Ben. The two of them locked eyes for a moment.

"Are you good with that, Lieutenant?" Morgan asked. "We'll arrest them if we can, but my intent, first and foremost, is to free Mrs. McAlester and her son. Anyone that gets in the way of that gets put down. No questions asked, no quarter given."

"Perhaps it won't come to that," Ben said.

Morgan gave him one last look and then turned his horse and started it up the mountain. Moshulatubee kicked his horse to a trot in his wake.

Dixie delayed and looked at Ben. "What he's trying to tell you is not to think too much. You do, and you're liable to get that woman and her kid killed, not to mention yourself or one of us."

Ben started to reply, but Dixie put his mule after Morgan. Only Cumsey and the young lieutenant were left at the foot of the slope.

"I suppose you have something to say, as well?" Ben said. "By all means, don't hold back."

The last of the sun was just then sinking behind the

mountaintop above them, and Cumsey wrinkled his nose and squinted into the last light. "I was only thinking. That's all."

"Thinking about what? Are you scared?"

"You mean going after those killers if they're really at the caves?"

"That's exactly what I mean."

"Oh, I'm scared a little, and don't mind admitting it. A man would be a fool not to be," Cumsey said. "But that wasn't what I was thinking."

"Care to enlighten me?"

"I was thinking about Hannah. She's one of the schoolteachers over at the Ashbury Mission," Cumsey said. "Pretty as they come, and smart as a whip, too. Maybe too smart sometimes. A man can't get nothing past her. Said I wasn't to come see her again unless I was serious and ready to make an honest woman out of her."

"I'm sure she's quite the woman to have you speak of her so. I suspect many a man has thought about a sweetheart on the eve of battle."

Cumsey sighed. "Sure wish I had a chance to see her before Marshal Clyde drug me off with him."

"I imagine you will see her again once this is over."

"Suppose so." Cumsey sighed again, replaced his serious look with one of his devilish grins, and pointed up the mountain after the others. "What are you waiting for, Lieutenant? Thought you were ready to get your name in the papers. Be as famous in the territory as your Pa Clyde up there."

"I would as soon there be as little association with my name and his as possible," Ben said. "The best thing about this coming to a conclusion is that I will never have to see him again with any luck."

They put their horses after the others, and soon all five men were going single file up the narrow steep trail that wound its way up the mountain. It wasn't much of a trail, and in places was no trail at all, but Cumsey took the lead and seemed confident he could navigate with or without a clearly defined course. At times he rode ahead and would be gone out of sight for a while, and then he would come back and talk with Morgan before he left again. Before long, they were cloaked in darkness. Nobody spoke, each man lost to his own thoughts.

They traveled that way for the better part of two hours, up and over one mountain and then a long, gradual climb up another. They wound through dense stands of pine and hardwood timber, picked their way over rocky outcroppings and ledges, and forded several streams before they topped out on a point of mountain overlooking a vast swath of country to the southeast. The moon popped out briefly from behind a patch of clouds, and they could see where the shadowed folding of several little mountains marking the headwaters of where Fourche Maline Creek slowly gave way to the lighter highlight of a long, narrow valley several miles away and below them.

Cumsey pointed at a place about halfway between their position and the valley. "The caves are down there across that big draw and up on the other side. I say we come on them from the top. Harder to pick our way in the dark, but we'll make less noise than rattling around the rocks and climbing out of that canyon."

"Sounds good to me," Morgan said. "Lead the way and let me know when we're close. We'll go in on foot."

Dixie's saddle creaked, followed by the flopping of his mule's ears as it shook its head. He looked up at the clouds blotting out the moon again, and then turned his face to the breeze.

"Looks like it might blow up another storm," he said.

"Might help us if it does," Morgan said, eyeing the same dark wall of clouds to the west. "Bad weather will likely have them hunkered down and let us get close in enough to do what needs doing."

Cumsey led them off again. They stuck to the mountaintop and passed above the head of the deep canyon he had pointed out earlier. In another half hour Cumsey stopped them again. By then the occasional gentle breeze had increased to harder gusts that rustled the tree limbs.

"This is about as far as we can go without risk of them hearing us," Cumsey whispered.

Morgan was the first to get down from his horse, and he said in a hushed voice, "We leave the horses here. Lieutenant, I'd appreciate it if you stood guard here. I need Cumsey to take us in the rest of the way. Bring our mounts when we call for them."

"Not a chance. I'm going in with you," Ben answered. "Have someone else stay back if you think it necessary."

"Well then, I guess we better not spook them," Morgan said, and then coughed into his hand.

"Are you coming down sick? I heard you coughing more than once today," Dixie said as he stepped down from his mule.

"It's nothing. Got a cough, that's all. Touch of the croup if I don't miss my guess. Must be all this damp weather."

"I don't mind telling you that this one worries me," Dixie said.

Morgan tied the dun to a tree and shucked his Winchester from his scabbard. "I don't like it any more than you do. From what Cumsey tells me there's no way to get on them except for crawling in blind and hoping we don't get noticed. No way to get a look at them and make a plan. We'll have to make it up as we go."

"That's what I was afraid of."

"We've done it before, and you're still among the living."

"Barely."

"Barely counts."

"Yeah, but Molly will kill us both if I get shot again."

Morgan couldn't laugh, but there was a hint of it in his answer. "We're after a pack of stone-cold killers, and you're worried about what she'll do to you?"

"You know her. Those outlaws we're after are child's play compared to that woman when she's on the prod. I'd rather get shot and mutilated seven times over by them than have her mad at me."

"You love her, don't you?"

"More than anything."

"I'm happy for you. Happy for both of you."

"Let's get this done. You getting all mushy on me is bothering me." Dixie turned away from Morgan and rubbed his mule's neck. "Now, Sodom, you stay here and be a good boy. You've done me proud so far, so don't you be braying and pawing 'cause I'm leaving you tied up. Keep quiet and I'll be back to fetch you in a bit, and then we'll go home and I'll make it up to Molly and you can have a bait of corn in your feed trough."

Morgan eyed the sky one more time, and then the shadows of his men. "Take care that you don't hit the woman or the child if this comes to a shooting."

"We don't even know if they're at the caves," Ben said.

"Well, we're about to see. Aren't we? Lead the way, Cumsey."

Chapter Twenty-Four

The posse moved through the timber in a widely scattered line with Morgan, Cumsey, and John Moshulatubee in the center, and with Dixie and Ben on the ends. They moved slowly and as quietly as they could. The mountaintop was mostly pine timber, and the carpet of damp pine needles softened their footfalls so that they made almost no noise at all.

They crossed over the head of the draw that turned into a canyon somewhere below them, and they ghosted another hundred yards or so down the point of the mountain before Moshulatubee put a hand on Morgan's shoulder to get his attention. Morgan froze, and the rest of the posse did the same when they noticed he had stopped.

The clouds had completely blocked out the moon by then, and Morgan could barely make out Moshulatubee's form beside him. He thought the Lighthorseman was pointing at something ahead of them and tried to see what it was. And then Morgan saw a shadowed flicker of movement not fifty or sixty yards ahead of them. A gust of wind whipped through the pines.

"Guard," Moshulatubee leaned his head close to Morgan's ear and whispered under the cover of the wind.

Morgan moved left, circling around the man ahead of them. The woods began to open up, the trees becoming more scattered and the ground more rocky. The guard they had passed stood on the lip of a bare rock shelf. Below him the mountain fell off into the jumble of exposed sandstone that Cumsey said held the outlaw hideout.

They found a steep eroded channel between two rock slabs and passed down it and huddled at the bottom. The labyrinth of giant boulders and ledges and the cloud-dark night made it hard to determine a course.

"Where would they have the horses?" Morgan whispered.

"Could be picketed somewhere up on the mountaintop, but we always used the stone corral," Cumsey said.

"You take Moshulatubee and get where you can cut them off from their horses," Morgan said. "Dixie, you and Ben come with me. Where's the cave?"

Cumsey hunkered close to Morgan and pointed him on a side-hilling path that led along the foot of the highest series of ledges. "The big cave is over there. Smaller one down below the stone corral."

Morgan took off through the rocks with Dixie and Ben following him. In places, the going was easy; in others it was a case of trial and error. The exposed sandstone was arranged like stair steps leading down the mountain, as if the mountain benches had worn away and left only the jagged remains of their core. And there were many places where those great slabs of rock appeared to have slid apart or where water had cuts channels between them. Those cracks ran like hallways in a crazy house, often turning at right angles around some boulder or passing down through an entire ledge or bluff from top to bottom.

They worked their way through that maze slowly until Dixie hissed at Morgan. But Morgan had already spied what Dixie was warning him about. Ahead of them he could see the glow of a fire.

Without being told, Dixie began to climb the rocky slope above Morgan to gain higher ground. Ben followed Dixie's example and began to work his way down among the rocks below Morgan, no doubt intending to encircle the fire from the opposite side as Dixie. Morgan moved a little closer to the fire. From his new vantage point he could see the flame shadows flickering and dancing on the smooth face of the bluff above it.

He waited to give Dixie and Ben a chance to get into position before he moved again. The slope angling up to the foot of the bluff where the fire was burning seemed to open up somewhat. The black shape of a twisted and gnarled pine tree rose up from the foot of a horse-high rock, and he moved to the tree and half-climbed the rock and bellied down on it. From that elevated vantage point he could see the outlaws' campfire.

The fire was stacked high with wood and burning hot and heavy in the strengthening gusts of wind. Four men stood or lounged around it. The firelight was bright enough that Morgan could barely make out the dark maw of a big cave opening not far beyond the fire along the foot of the bluff.

Morgan second-guessed his decision to go into the hideout in the dark. Cornering anybody in such a place was going to be hit and miss. But without fifty men to encircle the place there was no way to handle the job in the daylight, and he didn't have fifty men. Plus, Cumsey had sworn they could never get close to the hideout without being spotted in the daylight.

Morgan hoped Cumsey and the Lighthorseman had the outlaws' horses found, and that Dixie and Ben had found good positions. He settled in behind the top of the rock he lay on to use it as a bulwark and put his Winchester to his shoulder. Gunsights were useless in the dark, but the outlaws' fire was so big that Morgan could faintly make out a hint of the front blade on his rifle. He moved it until it covered the men at the fire.

"Federal marshals!" he called out. "Throw up your hands!"

Those found in such a place were no doubt desperate men, but apparently some were more desperate than others. While some of the men at the fire were momentarily frozen, either yet to register what was happening or their startled minds still trying to make a decision, others broke and ran.

One of the men was running for the cave. His pistol blossomed fire and a bullet smacked against the rocks well wide of where Morgan lay. Morgan fired two rapid shots at the running man just as he disappeared out of the firelight and thought he heard the man fall. Another gun boomed, and it sounded like Dixie's Spencer.

"I've got twenty marshals with me!" Morgan shouted against the wind. "Throw down your guns and surrender!"

He expected somebody to shoot his way again, but no more gunshots came. He could still hear men scrambling through the rocks.

"Who the hell is out there?" A man's voice called out.

"This is Marshal Clyde," Morgan called back. "I'm going to give you about a minute to send Mrs. McAlester and her son out to me, and to hand yourselves over."

"We don't have a woman or a kid with us," the voice answered.

"Give them over or we're going to start shooting in that cave," Morgan said.

Morgan had no idea who was in the cave or how many, or if the outlaws were using it at all. But most of the men at the fire had run in that direction.

"We'll smoke you out or burn you down. What's it going to be?" he said.

Another bullet clipped the pine tree close to Morgan, and then men were running out of the cave mouth. Gunshots reverberated off the rocks in a sound that all mixed together in one continuous roar. Somebody up at the top of the big bluff fired, and Morgan hoped it was Ben taking out the guard they had passed by on their way down the mountain.

But the outlaws coming out of the cave weren't rushing for

the mountaintop. They were filtering down through the rocks in the direction where Cumsey had said the horse corral was.

Morgan raised up on his knees to get a better view of things. Several men were passing below him going down a path between the boulders. They were barely ten yards away, and he fanned the lever on the Winchester and sent three fast shots amongst them. There was no fine aiming, only point and shoot. Somebody cried out, either hit or startled, and then another gun flamed below Morgan.

A bullet hit the boulder at Morgan's knees and showered him with thin, sharp-edged flakes that stung his face. He fell back behind the top of the boulder, took a deep breath, then thumbed fresh cartridges into the Winchester's loading gate while he shifted his position slightly down the mountain.

He was coming over a rockslide when he saw another group scampering in front of him. The Winchester jumped to his shoulder, but he held his fire. In the split second before he squeezed the trigger his mind registered the pale flash of clothing. His immediate thought was that it was a woman's dress.

Someone shouted something from down the mountain that Morgan couldn't understand, and then more guns opened up. Morgan was working his way after what he thought was the woman when he heard the clamor of shod horse hooves.

He ducked down a crack between two rocks, made a sharp turn, and ran into someone. He and the man he had crashed into both staggered back, trying to get their rifles into play.

"Damn, I almost killed you," John Moshulatubee said.

Morgan eased his hammer down. "Did you see the woman?"

"No."

"I thought I saw her coming this way."

"Cumsey's down."

"How bad is he hurt?"

"Don't know," the Lighthorseman said. "We scattered some

of their horses down to the creek, but they came on us and the shooting got too heavy and we had to pull back in the rocks."

"We can't let them get away with the woman and the boy."

Moshulatubee started down through the rocks with Morgan on his heels. They came to the edge of the high ledge that was one wall of the horse corral. Men and horses were scrambling below them.

A woman screamed.

His rifle came up again, but there were no clear targets. He caught the flash of the woman's dress as he had earlier.

"Don't hit the woman," Morgan hissed.

A horse passed beneath him with her on its back, and then two more horses ran after the one carrying her. One of the outlaws spotted them up on the lip of the bluff and the gunfight started again. Moshulatubee fired once, and then disappeared.

One last horse and rider charged out of the corral a good deal behind the others. The rider fired once at Morgan as he passed underneath him. Morgan leaned out over the edge of the bluff and fired almost straight down. The horse and rider kept going. Sparks flew off the iron horseshoes of their mounts as they charged down the mountain and into the canyon below the hideout.

Morgan was too intent on listening to the sound of their retreat and didn't pay enough attention to the horse corral. Apparently Ben and Cumsey had managed to drive off enough of the horses to put most of the gang on foot, and they were still in the corral. A shot cracked and a bullet ricocheted off the rocks above and behind him. By the time he could duck there were five or six men shooting at him.

"Get the son of a bitch!" somebody shouted.

Morgan climbed higher up the mountain, back towards the caves. All around him, bullets struck the rocks. Some bits of debris hit him in his left eye, and he pawed at it with the back of one hand. Blind in one eye and fighting the dark with the good one left to him, he stumbled and fell twice. He had no clue if Moshulatubee had gone down, or where Ben and Dixie were. He could hear the outlaws behind him coming up to him. They had somehow sensed that the posse was small in number and were out to take their revenge. The table had turned, and the hunted were now the hunters.

He fired one shot behind him in the general direction of those who pursued him. He didn't aim, and his only intention was to slow them down and to buy time. No more shots came his way. His bad eye was still watering but felt better.

He came suddenly to the foot of a high rock bluff farther down towards the canyon and away from the cave where the fight had started. He looked up at the sheer face of stone and searched for a way to the top. No way showed itself, so he moved along the foot of the bluff until he came to a scattering of boulders spilled down from above. Crouching there, he faced downhill and scanned the darkness for signs of attack.

The first gust of wind on the storm front was a big one, swaying the treetops as it rolled over the mountaintop. There was a crack of thunder and a dazzle of jagged lightning, and for an instant, he could see the mountain below him with some clarity.

And then he saw them, ghosting shadows moving up through the maze of rocks. There were four of them, and maybe more, spread out in a wide, loose skirmish line. He shifted his position slightly until he stopped against the fat trunk of an ancient, gnarled pine tree growing straight up the face of the bluff.

There came the sound of a turkey's gobble, but it was no turkey making that sound. It was a war cry and a taunt. He pointed his rifle down the mountain and waited for the next bolt of lightning to light the world again.

"Hey, lawman!" A voice shouted at him from somewhere

down the mountain and spaced wide of the turkey caller.

"Clyde!" the same voice called out his name. "Come out and fight, you son of a bitch!"

And then came that turkey gobble war cry again. They thought they had him cornered and alone, and they were right.

When the next bolt of lightning came, they were even closer to him, and his Winchester cracked hellfire of its own and the storm of lead and lightning swallowed everything.

Chapter Twenty-Five

Red Molly walked to her cabin door and opened it to look outside. It was the third time she had done that, and the ugly sky building to the west and south bothered her as much as it had the first time she had peered out that evening.

The territory was known for the frequency and fierceness of its storms, especially tornados, or twisters as some called them. When she was younger, she had survived such a windstorm when a funnel cloud had dropped down out of the sky with no warning and savaged a Pacific Railroad camp outside Sedalia, Missouri. Her flight out of the path of the tornado had been so wild and frantic that she remembered little except for the sound, a monstrous roaring like the gates of perdition had opened wide. When it was over, ten men were dead or missing, and not a tent in the camp was left standing. Lumber and timbers were turned to splinters, horses and mules were found in the tops of trees or impaled with debris, and a swath of ground a quarter of a mile wide was chewed and torn like some giant beast had raked it apart with its claws. And she had been near or seen the remains of other such twisters since then, and those experiences had left an impression on her, mainly a healthy fear of dark, springtime wall clouds.

But the dark clouds to the west and the threat of a twister weren't what had her so worried. True, she feared being alone in a storm, but it was another fear that kept making her rise from her table and go look out the door. Throughout the day, her anxiety grew, and the more she dwelled on it, the more she was sure that something had happened to Dixie or was going to happen. It wasn't exactly a premonition, but rather a deep sense of dread that she couldn't shake.

If Dixie were home, he would assure her he was more than capable of taking care of himself, but she knew that bad things happened no matter how careful you were and no matter how hard you tried to avoid them. That was the one lesson life had taught her first and foremost, and that point had never ceased to be driven home.

She closed the door and went back to the table and finished the rest of her mug of coffee, scolding herself for her worries. She had known little but hardship since her girlhood in County Kerry. Orphaned at the age of twelve during the Potato Famine, she had thought to solve her problems by going to America, but from the moment she stepped off the sailing ship in the New World she had found that you couldn't outrun your woes. The new start she had hoped for was only the same old battle for survival that she had known in Ireland.

She looked around her at the inside of the little cabin and considered how good it made her feel. A humble and poor abode, yes, but cozy and solid and not so different from the thatch-roofed cottage she had known as a child. And there was her garden, which she loved.

Despite the years of hard and reckless living, she had somehow come to a point in life she would never have guessed. After all the years of whoring, all the boomtowns and sin cities and railroad camps, it was as if she had come full circle. And although things in no way matched the images of her girlhood flights of fancy as to how she would one day live her life, like the cabin she sat in, she had somehow become comfortable. And despite Dixie's constant worries about their finances, she felt safer than she ever had before.

Like the farm, Dixie was something she had never guessed she needed. No, he didn't stir the same fire in her as some men once had. Not like her first husband, a devilishly handsome gambler with a charm and a line of blarney to match his looks. Instead of being a red warning flag, the sense of danger about him had made her want him all the more. Remembering what a fool she had been over him was like sharing the memories of another woman she barely recognized.

The infatuation between them was as thin and short-lived as a quick romp between the bedsheets. A run of bad luck at the card tables and a growing penchant for booze on his part, and what she thought then was the love of her life became a nightmare. The fool had broken her in a hundred ways, and not just financially, before he picked a fight with the wrong man and got himself killed.

And then there had been Morgan. Why was it that she had been drawn to such men? Morgan wasn't weak or dishonest like the gambler had been, but bad for her in other ways. She recognized that half the allure of him had been knowing that there was something in him that wouldn't let him be had, something broken inside him the same as in her. It was as if she purposely went looking for those who would break her heart. What she wanted always getting in the way of what she needed.

And then Dixie came along. Never in a million years would she have guessed he was the man for her. There was none of the challenge and none of the danger about him, yet the more she came to know him the more he made her laugh. And with him she slowly learned to let down some of her guard. For the first time in her life she felt like she could truly be herself. Red Molly could step into the background, and she could be someone else. She could be nothing more than Molly O'Flanagan, a country girl from County Kerry with mud on her dress and a pair of Dixie's cast-off brogan work shoes on her feet. Puttering around in her garden or watching her chickens scratch around the yard while she hummed old Irish tunes that she hadn't thought of in a lifetime.

That someone else wasn't tough or brazen. Sometimes it was all right to be weak and to need a shoulder to lean on, or someone to wrap you in their arms and to tell you it was going to be all right. Dixie was what she needed before she knew what she needed. The love she felt for him was deeper and different from anything she had known before, and it grew stronger every day. She didn't deserve what he gave her, and knowing that made the fear of losing him even greater.

She eyed the bottle of laudanum sitting on the table next to her coffee mug, then shoved it away from her and glared at it. All the years it had taken her to find what she had found, and there she sat a wreck. Sick with tuberculosis and unable to shake loose from what had started as some kind of crutch and had wound up an addiction as heavy as chains. Why couldn't she have had more sense when she was younger and healthier?

Thunder boomed in the distance and the flash of lightning momentarily lit her windowpanes. Maybe it was silly to worry about him when he hadn't been gone but a day, but she couldn't help it. There wasn't an hour a day when she didn't look around her at least once and wonder when it was going to end. Good things rarely lasted. Life was full of nasty surprises that came out of nowhere with a suddenness to match that bolt of lightning.

She poured herself another cup of coffee, avoided the laudanum, and thought about the farm. The more she thought about it the more she decided she liked it. Dixie was bound and determined to buy the livery and move to Eufaula, but why couldn't they stay right where they were at? Yes, it was hard to make a living, but they were getting by. They had made a good start and it would be a shame to throw it away.

Whether he would admit it or not, he was a good farmer and knew everything there was to know about it. And she could learn and help him more. He was always reminding her that they only leased the land and could never own it, but who was to say that wouldn't change? Everyone she heard talk about the subject thought it was only a matter of time before the Indians lost their land. Maybe it wasn't fair or right, but she could see the signs of that for herself. Already it seemed like there were more white people in the territory than Indians, all of them looking to take hold of something. She felt she had hold of something and wasn't about to let go of it.

If only Dixie hadn't gone with Morgan. If he was home with her, she could tell him what she was thinking and they could make new plans. It was all going to be all right.

She eyed the laudanum bottle again, and vowed that she was going to cut back her doses like the doctor said. Even if she didn't, and even if her lungs got no better, well then, she was still twice the woman most were. Maybe she had put away Red Molly when it suited her, but that wench was still there when she was needed. Ask anyone and they would tell you, Red Molly had her faults, but nobody ever said she wouldn't fight to keep what was hers.

She rose from the table and went to her bedroom where she packed a small traveling bag. She stuffed her nickel-plated pistol inside the bag, along with a change of clothes and a few other items. Then she put out the lamp and went to bed.

She didn't sleep well, and was back up again before dawn. She put on her good pair of shoes and a clean dress, nothing fancy but nice enough she wouldn't be ashamed to be seen in it. After a quick cup of coffee, she went to the barn and fed the horses and mules Dixie had left penned. Once they were through eating their corn, she caught one of the horses. It was a little red roan mare that she remembered Dixie saying he had ridden several times. She never had learned to ride very well, for the only horse her father had owned back in Ireland had been an overgrown, plodding plow horse, and when most people in County Kerry wanted to go somewhere, they went there on their own leg bones.

She saddled the roan filly under lantern light. The saddle was a man's saddle, a high-backed, high-swelled, heavy thing with a brass horn, but the only one left on the place. No matter, the few times she had ridden in her life had all been astride, usually riding her father's old plow horse bareback. Maybe there were places where folks would look askance at a grown woman riding like a man instead of on a sidesaddle, but she had never been one to care what people thought. Besides, it wasn't like anybody was going to mistake her for a lady. Anybody that had been around very long knew what she had been before she married Dixie.

She led the mare to the house and wrapped one bridle rein around her front door latch while she went inside and retrieved her bag. She hung the handles of the bag over the saddle horn, and then went to where Dixie's double-barreled shotgun leaned in one corner of the front room. She frowned at it and debated on whether or not to take it with her. It was an old muzzle-loader, complicated to load and too long and cumbersome to suit her tastes. In the end, she decided against it and left it behind.

The roan filly, although still only green broke, seemed gentle enough and stood docilely while Molly tried to get in the saddle, but it was hard to get a foot in the stirrup wearing a dress. Finally, she took the washtub leaning against the front wall of the house and set it upside down on the ground beside the horse. Using it for a mounting block, she was able to get in the saddle easily.

"There, that wasn't so bad," Molly said as much to herself as she did to the filly. "Now you be a good lass and don't jump out from under me."

She adjusted her bridle reins, then nudged the filly with her heels. The roan proved to be a brisk walker and headed out down the driveway towards the road like she was glad to be going, ears perked forward and hooves clip-clopping.

"Such a bonny lass you are." Molly leaned forward in the saddle and rubbed the mare on the neck.

The sky was barely lightening when she struck the road running from old North Fork Town to Eufaula. Regardless of the booming thunder from the evening before, there had only come a light shower, and the river crossing was low enough to barely wet the mare above the ankles.

By the time true sunup came Molly was on the edge of Eufaula. The town was quiet and sleepy so early in the morning. Her intention was to ask if there was any word from the posse, and she was in no mood to wait. She would wake someone if she had to.

And if there was no word . . . well, then, she would just go and find Dixie.

Chapter Twenty-Six

Morgan lay on his belly atop the high bluff with his Colt revolver resting on one forearm. He had been lying that way for a long time, despite the cold rain pouring down on him. Nothing moved below him on the mountain, but still he remained where he was, watching and waiting.

It had been a close call, climbing up to the top of the bluff under fire. His Winchester lay somewhere down in the rocks where it had been shot from his hand, and he was bleeding in several places. He was stung and scraped and cut and his left knee was already swelling where he had struck it on a rock, but somehow he had avoided getting shot, despite the hail of gunfire aimed his way. And he had given as good as he got. He had put one of them down before he made a run for it.

He waited longer, and the bitterness of a failure nagged at him worse than his aches and pains. Most of the gang had gotten away, and the woman and child with them. And he had no idea where the rest of his posse was or if any of them were still alive. Anything could happen during a fight in the dark, but his attempt to rescue the woman and child was nothing short of a train wreck. He replayed in his mind all the things he should have done differently.

The outlaws below him had either given up the fight, or they were playing possum and trying to make him think they were gone. He hadn't heard or seen any sign of them since a couple of them had tried to climb up with him not long after he had taken that position. He had pelted them well with his Colt for their trouble, and since then all was quiet.

The coughing spell he had been fighting off for some time finally got the best of him, and he winced and expected the sound to draw gunfire. Nothing happened, despite all the noise he was making.

He scooted back on his belly from the edge of the cliff. When he rose to his feet, he stayed crouched, and when he walked away, he went in the direction he thought led back to the cave and the outlaws' campfire. Another fit of coughing overcame him, and he was startled to hear that his dry cough had turned into something farther down in his chest. He was barely halfway back when a quiet voice called out to him followed by the clack of a cocking gun.

"I'm thinking that's you, Morgan, but you better say so in a hurry," Dixie said.

"It's me."

"Are you all right? Heard all that shooting and I started working my way down to you as soon as I could."

"You took your sweet time."

"Cumsey's shot and somebody had to tend to him, and we got the boy."

"You got him?"

"The lieutenant did. One of those outlaws had the kid up in the saddle, but they dropped him. The lieutenant was close enough to snatch him."

"Well, that's at least one bit of good news."

"What about you?" Dixie asked. "You get any of them?"

"Got one back down there, and maybe another when we first came on them by their fire. Might have clipped one or two more, or maybe not."

"Yeah, you got that one by the fire. He's lying up there right now where he fell, paroled to Jesus."

"What about you?" Morgan asked.

"I think I winged one when they were running out of that cave, but it's always hard to tell in that kind of fight," Dixie answered. "I heard those horses and was coming hot and heavy to help you, but then I come across Ben and the boy."

"What about Moshulatubee?"

"He's up there at the cave. Come on." Dixie turned and went back up the mountain, picking his way along a winding path that he had somehow found through the rocks.

The rain had slackened to a steady drizzle by the time they came to the cave. Cumsey or Ben weren't to be seen, but Moshulatubee had built the fire back up and was standing by it. The Choctaw lawman nodded at Morgan. In the firelight Morgan could see that there was a nasty cut on one side of his face.

"Looks like that one came close," Morgan said and pointed at Moshulatubee's face.

"Nothing but a cut. Bullet knocked my bootheel from under me and pitched me on my face," Moshulatubee answered.

"What about Cumsey? How bad is he hurt?" Morgan asked.

"Took a bullet in the hip. He's in the cave out of the rain with the boy and Lieutenant Clyde."

A sudden shiver crawled across Morgan's skin, and he moved closer to the fire. Dixie came to stand across the flames from him.

"We botched this one bad," Dixie said.

Morgan squinted at him through the stream of water running off his hat brim. "Yeah, we did."

"At least we got the boy," Moshulatubee offered.

"It's a wonder we didn't get him killed," Morgan said. "Both him and his mother. I should have opened right up on them when we came on them at first. Then we might have stood a chance pinning them in the cave and waiting them out."

"I expected you to. You let that son of yours get in your head," Dixie said.

"Wouldn't have mattered," Moshulatubee said. "They weren't all in the caves. Me and Cumsey were expecting only a guard or two to be watching their horses, but we ran on to a half dozen of them. I think they were getting ready to ride out."

Morgan glanced at the body of a dead man lying between the fire and the mouth of the cave. Dixie noticed him looking and walked over and toed the dead man over on his back with his boot. Morgan and the Lighthorseman joined him. Moshulatubee knelt beside the body and struck a wad of matches and held them over the body.

"Recognize him?" Morgan asked.

"Nope," Moshulatubee answered.

"I do," said Dixie. "That's John Rabbit I was telling you about."

Morgan's rifle bullet had struck the Indian in one side and come out the other. Moshulatubee bent down and began to go over the body. After he had searched the man's coat pockets, he pulled back the dead Indian's long hair from one side of his head and moved to where both Morgan and Dixie could see what he was looking at. One of the Indian's ears had been cut off some time in the past, and all that was left was an ugly, scarred hole.

"Rapist," Moshulatubee said. "Must have got caught."

"You cut off a rapist's ear?" Dixie asked.

"Fifty lashes with a hickory switch across his back and an ear for the first offense. Second offense gets a man a hundred lashes and his other ear cut off," Moshulatubee said. "Third offense and he gets to stand in front of a Lighthorse firing squad. Cherokees do the same."

"You tell that to Lieutenant Clyde and you'll get to hear one of his lectures," Dixie said. "He'll have you looking for that man's long-lost ear to try and sew it back on."

"Did Ben make it through the fight in one piece?" Morgan asked.

"Not a scratch on him that I could tell," Dixie said. "Maybe you ought to go in the cave with him and get out of the rain. You look all tuckered out."

"I am all tuckered out." Morgan turned away and hobbled toward the cave.

Chapter Twenty-Seven

Charlie Dunn pulled his horse up at the foot of the mountain, breathing hard after their charge down through the rocks, and the wound in his neck aching fiercely. Injun Joe was the next to catch up to him. The big Choctaw had the woman up in the saddle in front of him.

"Anybody else make it?" Dunn asked him.

"A couple, I think, but I don't know where they went," Injun Joe said.

Rebecca McAlester was still squirming and fighting to get free, but Injun Joe's arms held her pinned. Dunn rode alongside Joe's horse and slapped her hard across the face. She moaned with the pain of the blow.

Dunn put his hand to the wound in his neck and was surprised to feel something sticking out of it. He took hold of the cold steel protruding from the wound and yanked it free. It was too dark to see, but he knew what he held by the feel of it. It was an eating fork.

"You see that?" Dunn said. "It's a damned fork. The stupid bitch stuck me with a fork."

"That why you dropped the boy?" Joe asked, whether or not he could see the fork in the dark.

"You were supposed to have her under control," Dunn snapped at him. "I'd cut her ass in a thousand pieces if she weren't worth so damned much."

He slung the fork away, and then he put a hand back to the

bloody puncture holes in his neck. And he could also feel the stinging lines of claw marks tracing down one side of his face. He tried to hold down his building rage and to think clearly.

The fight from the cave down to the horse corral had been hot and heavy, and in the ensuing madness, he hadn't paid enough attention to the McAlester woman. Injun Joe was dragging her along while he carried the kid to the horses. He had barely thrown the kid up on his saddle when he heard the woman shriek. Before he could turn around, she had broken free from Joe's hold and stabbed him in the neck, and then proceeded to try and claw his face off. He flung her off his back, but in doing so he lost hold of the boy and the little devil either fell or jumped off the far side of his horse.

There had been no time to hunt for the kid, not with Clyde and his damned posse shooting down into the horse corral. Joe had grabbed hold of the woman again, got her up in the saddle with him, and they had charged out of the corral and down through the rocks.

"That damned Clyde. I promise you I'm going to kill that bastard," Dunn said.

"I don't think any of the rest of the boys are coming," Joe said.

At that same moment gunfire erupted on the slope above them.

"Somebody's catching hell," Joe said.

"Yeah."

"I don't think there was no twenty marshals that hit us."

"Well, however many there were, maybe the rest of the boys are thinning them out a little," Dunn answered.

"I don't like stopping," Joe said. "Anybody that makes it out of this can meet us at Hoyt's," Joe said.

Dunn cocked his head and listened to the sound of gunfire in the distance. He hadn't expected his kidnapping to necessarily go off without a hitch, but he also hadn't expected the law to find him so quickly. Nor had he expected to be attacked in the middle of the night. His assumption had been that any party of lawmen would be too worried about the woman and child to engage in a fight with him, or to storm a stronghold like the caves. And then the woman had stabbed him.

"We'd best get going," Joe said.

Dunn hesitated. He had no idea in which direction he should head. Joe must have sensed his confusion, for he put the spurs to his horse and splashed across the creek with the woman reeling in front of him in the saddle. Dunn took one last look back towards the cave and then set out after him.

Chapter Twenty-Eight

Morgan came out of the cave with a wool blanket wrapped over his shoulders and went and sat on a rock beside the campfire. The rain had quit sometime in the night, and the clouds were thin enough overhead that they were letting a little sunlight show through them. Dixie came up from the rocks below the cave. He was carrying two extra rifles over one shoulder and had two gun belts looped over the other shoulder.

Morgan was ashamed to have slept so long. Dixie had obviously been up for a long time, if he had slept at all.

"Any sign of them?" Morgan asked in a hoarse voice.

Dixie shook his head. "Moshulatubee is out scouting for sign. I found two more dead men this morning. One down by the corral, and the other about halfway between there and here. And some blood on the rocks where we might have winged another one."

Morgan coughed, and the rattle in his chest was worse than it had been.

"That cough of yours is starting to sound bad," Dixie said.

"It's nothing. I've been fighting off the croup. It'll pass."

"I think you're coming down with a little more than the croup."

As if to prove Dixie's point, Morgan's teeth started to chatter. He clenched his jaw tight and fought against the shivers wracking his body. He had woke that morning in a clammy sweat, and now the flush of fever was shifting once again to a chill.

"Found something else peculiar down below," Dixie said.

"What's that?"

"Found four more bodies stuffed in a crevasse with some rocks piled in over them," Dixie said. "Not the three we did for. They've been dead for a while, but not long. Bodies just starting to bloat."

"Oh?"

"Body on top was gutshot. Old wound. Somebody had bandaged him," Dixie said. "Two other fellows were shot to pieces. The last one was a big black fellow with nothing but a strip of hair down the top of his head like some of them Osage or Ponca Injuns sport."

"Did the one with the Mohawk have a bad eye?" Morgan asked.

"That's him."

"Henry Buck," Morgan said. "Went by the name of Big Henry. Chicken Whitehead's right-hand man. We've been looking for Henry for a long time."

"Well, you don't have to chase after him anymore," Dixie said. "Somebody fixed his wagon. Not shot like the others, but cut up. Whoever took a blade to him like to have cut his head off."

"I got word in Fort Smith from the Rangers that Chicken's gang tried to rob a bank in Denton, Texas. The wire said they might be headed into the territory."

"So what do you figure?" Dixie asked. "Chicken's gang was already here, and then Dunn's boys rode in and they had a disagreement?"

Morgan coughed again, fought another one off, and then nodded. "Could be."

"That would explain why there were so many," Dixie said.

"Not one gang but two. Cumsey said there was no telling who we might scare up here."

"Speaking of Cumsey, how's he doing this morning?"

"I'm as right as rain," Cumsey said. He was hobbling down from the cave to them with a decided limp.

"Ain't nothing right about the rain we've been getting, nor the way you're walking," Dixie threw back at him. "How's that backside of yours? A little tender? Turn around and show the marshal your badge of honor."

"Go jump in the creek," Cumsey growled.

"Young Cumsey here got himself shot in the ass," Dixie said. "Maybe you ought to tell him he'll do better if he's facing who he's fighting."

"It's nothing, just a scratch," Cumsey said.

"You're lucky somebody in that bunch was shooting a peashooter or you'd have no ass left at all. Bored a hole in one cheek as it is. Morgan, you should have heard him squalling last night when Moshulatubee checked to make sure the bullet had passed through clean. You would have if you hadn't been sleeping like a dead man."

"You'd squall, too, if somebody was poking a knife in your tender parts," Cumsey said.

"Go ahead, take you a seat beside the marshal."

"Believe I'll stand."

"I bet you will. What I want to see is you ride down off this mountain. Imagine your saddle's going to smart a bit."

Whatever Cumsey was about to say was interrupted by the appearance of Ben Clyde and the McAlester boy from the cave. The young lieutenant was leading the boy by the hand to them.

"After that fracas last night, I don't know which we look more like, a hospital or a nursery," Dixie said.

Morgan pulled his blanket tighter about his neck and eyed the child. While filthy and sporting a black eye incurred during his fall from the horse and escape from the outlaws' clutches, the boy looked little worse for wear, especially considering everything else he had been through. But in Morgan's experience children were often much more resilient than adults. Perhaps they were so inexperienced and naïve that they lived in the moment, rather than thinking of all the dire possibilities and ramifications that went with adversity. No doubt the boy was still scared and traumatized, as timid and cautious as a rabbit right then, but he seemed to have latched on to Ben as a source of perceived protection and refuge. He clutched Ben's hand, hid partially behind his leg, and peeked out at Morgan with big eyes, unable to fight off curiosity.

"Well there, who are you?" Morgan asked.

The boy ducked his face behind Ben's leg, but peered out again after a while.

"I bet you're the very boy we've been looking for," Morgan said. "Your father sent us all the way here to get you and bring you home."

"Papa?" the boy asked.

"That's right. I guess the lieutenant has already told you who we are."

The boy rubbed a grubby hand at his nose. "I want my mama."

Morgan glanced at Ben, then shifted back to the boy. "We won't quit until we get her, too."

"I want my mama. Where is she?"

"Some of the men that took you got away with her."

"Mama said to wun. Wun weal fast and hide."

"You're a brave boy. You got away from some very bad men."

"That's what Wieutenant said."

Ben let go of the boy's hand, gave him a look to make sure it was all right, and then began putting together some breakfast from the supplies the outlaws had left behind in their flight.

Dixie took a seat beside Morgan.

At first the boy stuck close to Ben, but the longer he watched the others the more he seemed to relax. He was especially curious to watch Dixie wiping down his guns and oiling them.

"Mr. Dunn had a big gun wike that," the boy said.

"Did he now?" Dixie asked.

The boy nodded. "I don't wike him. Mama said he was bad. He hits Mama, and he shot some other bad men. Shot them with his pistol gun. Mama said I wasn't to wook, but I saw it."

"Mr. Dunn won't bother you anymore, so forget about him," Dixie said.

The boy shook his head. "He said if I ever tried to wun from him, he'd cut off my ears and throw me down in that big hole over there."

Dixie pointed at Morgan. "You see that man right there?"

Again, the boy nodded with wide eyes. For some reason, he seemed more leery of Morgan than the others.

"That man there is Marshal Clyde. He's meaner and tougher than Mr. Dunn by a long shot. That's why Mr. Dunn ran away, 'cause if he comes back, Marshal Clyde will throw him down that hole."

"You got a big gun?" the boy asked Morgan.

Morgan tried to smile at the boy. "You're safe, boy. Soon as we get you fed, we'll take you home."

"What about Mama?"

Morgan got up and left the fire, and Dixie followed him. They stopped out of earshot of the boy.

"Are we going to go after her with that boy in tow, or are we taking him back to his daddy?" Dixie asked.

"We could drop him off some place safe on the way."

"McAlester ain't any farther away than Eufaula. We could take the boy back home and find a doctor to work on Cumsey. Ben, too. And you look like you could use some doctoring yourself. In case you haven't noticed, we aren't the spry, healthy bunch we used to be. Me and that Lighthorseman are the only ones left that ain't ailing."

Morgan coughed again, a hard, hacking cough. Even when he wasn't coughing, Dixie could hear the wheeze in his chest when he breathed.

"Maybe you could take Cumsey and the boy. Ride for the Katy tracks. Ben, too, if you can get him to go," Morgan said. "Send a wire to the boy's father. Catch a train to McAlester or wherever J.J.'s at now. Me and Moshulatubee will keep after them."

"Listen to yourself," Dixie answered. "You're barely on your feet and getting worse."

"I'll be fine."

"You're as white as a bedsheet and sweating like a whore in church, even though you're hugging that blanket like you think it will blow away."

"If we don't go after them now, the woman is likely lost for good, if we didn't get her killed already."

"Hard as it is to say, maybe we call it quits until we can get patched up and outfitted for a longer chase."

"You wouldn't quit if that was Molly they had."

"I don't like it any better than you do. I'm only telling you what you already know, but won't admit. We're licked for now."

"I should have gone after them the instant the fight was over."

"You're sick, and I don't care who you are. A man can only do so much, even you, Morgan Clyde."

"They're liable to kill her and stash her body. Unless somebody squeals on their identity, there's no proof who did it."

"We know Dunn is leading them."

"On the word of an outlaw who's likely dead by now."

"The boy can identify Dunn."

"She'll slow them down. They'll kill her for that if nothing else."

"Or maybe Dunn is thinking the woman might be his only protection for the time being. And have you asked yourself why he stole her and the kid? There are plenty of women to steal, so why her? He's out for some kind of payday."

"You mean he kidnapped her to sell her back?"

Dixie took out his pipe and his tobacco sack. "That's the only reason I can think of, and it sounds like you have been thinking the same thing. If it was a simple case of woman snatching, then why did they take the kid along?"

"Could be a matter of revenge. Maybe he and J.J. had some kind of falling out."

Dixie's mouth formed a puzzled frown. "Could be, but it doesn't smell right. And ask yourself who those men were who got gunned down riding with her buggy."

"I recall J.J. saying they were his employees, like they were just men who worked for him and happened to be escorting her to join him at Eufaula."

Dixie loaded his pipe and scratched a match on a rock beside him and lit the tobacco. He squinted at Morgan through the pipe smoke. "A man like J.J. didn't make his money paying men to stand around a business meeting. Cumsey said they were armed to the teeth. Sounds like they were guards to me. Might be that old J.J. was worried somebody might bother his family."

"Why?"

Dixie waved the match out and flung it away. "I'd say you ought to ask him that."

Morgan adjusted his hat on his head and rubbed thoughtfully at his mustache. "I'm sticking after them. You can take the boy in. Spread the word that we've flushed Dunn and his gang and have them on the run."

"You're as hardheaded as my wife. Arguing with you is like

arguing with a fence post."

They both heard a horse coming over the rocks above the cave. John Moshulatubee soon appeared on the ledge above them. He was leading the posse's horses.

"I trailed the ones that managed to get horseback," the Lighthorseman said. "They crossed the creek and went over the mountain headed north."

"What about the others?" Morgan asked.

"Some of them managed to catch a few of the horses we scattered. They struck out south with some riding double and some on foot."

"I saw the woman up on a horse with somebody when they made a break for it out of the corral," Morgan said to Dixie.

"Sounds like they're headed north with her, then," Dixie replied.

Morgan turned to the fire. "Get that breakfast wolfed down and saddle your horses. Time to go."

Less than a half hour later they had gathered their things, along with some stuff left behind by the outlaws. They carried that gear to the top of the bluff where Moshulatubee waited with their horses.

Cumsey and Morgan were the slowest to make the climb. Cumsey stopped the instant he made the summit, panting and wincing. Dixie and Moshulatubee were already busy rolling some of the outlaws' rifles in a bedroll to secure that bundle behind one of their saddles.

Cumsey stayed where he was, trying to catch his breath and waiting for the pain to subside. Dixie hung a pair of gun belts on his saddle horn and noticed Cumsey standing there.

"You ain't so talkative when you're shot," Dixie said.

"Why is it that the only two times I've ever been shot, or so much as scratched, has been when I'm with you, Clyde?" Cumsey asked.

"You know, I've said the same thing a time or two," Dixie said, throwing a look over his shoulder at Morgan.

Whether he had heard them or not, Morgan didn't pay them any attention. He readied the dun, taking longer than usual and pausing often to lean against the horse. When he was finally up in the saddle, he sat with his back to them, slumped and staring haggardly down the mountain. He was normally a man who never slouched in the saddle, either out of pride or good posture and training, but they could all see how sick he was.

Ben put the boy up on his horse and swung up behind him. Dixie was up next, leaving only Cumsey still on foot. The horse thief had saddled his bay, but was reluctant to mount.

"Waiting won't make that saddle feel any softer," Dixie said. "Are you going to ride, or are we going to have to build a litter to drag you along?"

"I get the sense you think something about this is funny," Cumsey said as he gritted his teeth and lifted a boot for his near stirrup.

"Man's gotta find his fun where he can," Dixie said.

Cumsey settled into his saddle seat with a groan. "I'll be sure to remember that if you ever get shot."

"I quit showing my ass years ago," Dixie said as he reined around and set his horse off after Morgan and the rest of them.

After some time, Ben rode alongside Dixie. The McAlester boy was asleep in his arms.

Ben nodded at Morgan's back ahead of them. "He's quiet this morning."

"He's always quiet," Dixie answered.

"I mean quieter than usual."

"Morgan's sick, plus he doesn't like to admit he's beat," Dixie said. "Admitting that would be the same as admitting he's not invincible."

"We could have surrounded them if he had brought more men."

"Right or wrong, he does things his own way. Take it as a compliment that he wanted you to come along. Means he thinks something of you, and he don't cotton to many."

"He didn't ask me to come."

"And he didn't say no, either. Whether you know it or not, that man there would do anything for you."

"That man abandoned me. Ran off and left me and my mother when I was eight years old," Ben said. "Bet you didn't know that, did you?"

"Oh, I don't know the all of it, but I know some," Dixie said and took out his pipe again. "I know he's talked more than once about how long he looked for you when he got back from the war, and how your mama and your grandpa did everything they could to keep him from finding you."

"That's a lie."

"Lieutenant, be careful what kind of insults you throw around. I don't know how it is back East, but out here there are a lot of us that don't have much to hang our hats on but our reputations and our word. Brand a man a liar or a coward and he's liable to fight you over it to prove he ain't."

"My apology. I did not mean to insult you," Ben said. "It's only that you are misinformed and have heard only one side of the story."

"I might say the same thing about you." Dixie tapped his pipe on his saddle horn to knock the old ashes from it, then scraped at the inside of the bowl with his pocketknife blade before he spoke again. "It's every man's right to determine on his own what's the truth and what's not, but did you know your grandpa sicced the Pinkertons on Morgan? They roughed him up some to try to make him quit looking for you."

"Is that the kind of preposterous stories he tells to cover up his failings?" Ben asked.

"Have you wondered how he got that busted hand?" Dixie asked. "And he had him another run-in with the Pinkertons not too many years ago when I first came to know him. He had to knock a few heads and Lord knows what else to settle that matter, and I gathered it had a lot to do with what they did to him back before he came West."

"Nothing could be farther from the truth."

"Like I said. Every man finds his own truths." Dixie put his knife away and began to pack fresh tobacco in his pipe.

"He had his chance," Ben said.

"If he thought so little of his family, then how come I knew about you before I ever met you the other day?" Dixie asked with his pipestem paused before his mouth. "How come he used to talk to me about you and your sister?"

"What do you know of my sister?"

"Not much, but I gather she died of the fever when she was a little thing."

"And where was he?"

"I think he regrets that more than anything. Man like him is harder on himself than whatever you can throw at him." Dixie tucked the pipestem in one corner of his mouth and struck a match with his thumbnail and lit the tobacco. When he spoke again it was between puffs on the pipe and clouds of smoke that floated up around his face. "There'll come a time when you'll look back and have your own regrets. All of us do."

"Did he put you up to this?" Ben asked.

"To what?"

"To speaking for him."

"No, I expect he'd be madder than tarnation if he knew."

"I hate him."

Dixie took that statement with the same calm expression he had borne throughout their conversation. "Those are strong words, and there might be a day when saying such is one of those regrets I was talking about."

"Do you make a habit of butting into other people's business?"

"Just talking, that's all. You take that boy there's daddy." Dixie pointed at the McAlester boy. "I doubt old J.J. McAlester wears angel wings, but you ask that boy when he wakes up and I bet you anything he sets store by him though he might not can say why. My own daddy was a lazy ne'er-do-well and the worst farmer and advice giver you ever knew. But you know what? I'd give anything if he were still alive and me and him could set and talk a spell. Maybe he wasn't perfect, but he was my daddy. And we only get one of those."

"I never had the privilege of a father, good or bad, and there's no getting around that."

"I'd say that's up to you." Dixie tapped his mule with his heels and put it ahead of the lieutenant.

Ben stared after Dixie, an irritated frown on his face. Before he could think on what the farmer had said to him, Morgan stopped his horse and the Lighthorseman pulled up with him. The two of them held a conversation that was too quiet for Ben to hear, but when they were finished Morgan swung his horse around to face the rest of them.

"Moshulatubee says we're not so far behind them as we thought. The sign's fresh and he found where they stopped once to rest their horses. There are two men with the woman, and he thinks they might be headed for Briartown or somewhere else on the river. Might be they're aiming to cross the river at Hoyt's Ferry."

"How far is that from here?" Ben asked.

"We can be there by nightfall if we hustle."

"You're so sick you can barely ride."

"They're likely to camp tonight, and maybe that will let us

catch up to them."

Ben opened his mouth to say something else, but Morgan reined his horse around and started through the woods, stopping the conversation. Moshulatubee and Cumsey immediately took off after him.

"Come on, Lieutenant," Dixie said as he rode past Ben. "You heard the man."

"He's a fool."

"Maybe, but he's the kind of fool I wouldn't want chasing after me if I were Charlie Dunn. Also the kind of fool I reckon that McAlester woman would appreciate, considering we're likely her last hope."

Chapter Twenty-Nine

The man in the checkered pants and three other men sat their horses and waited at the back of the Vanderwagen Hotel. At a little past daylight Helvina Vanderwagen came out the back door.

"Where's my horse?" she asked.

"Your horse?" the man in the checkered pants asked.

"That's what I said, wasn't it?" Helvina snapped.

She was wearing the same dark blue riding habit she had worn the day before, only this time she was wearing a hat. Not the feathered, stylish kind of hat that she was often prone to wearing, but a plain, broad-brimmed gray felt. A wrist purse hung from her left hand.

"You're not coming with us, are you?" the man in the checkered pants asked. He was a wide, strong-looking man, made even more so by his square-cut, jutting jaw and the close-cropped black beard he wore beneath a round-topped bowler hat.

"I was of a mind to send you by yourself, but I'm constantly reminded that if you want something done right you better do it yourself," she said. "Now go down to the livery and get my horse."

The door behind Helvina opened and Adolphus Vanderwagen came to stand with her. The man in the checkered pants gave Adolphus an appraising look, then jerked his head at the other two men with him. The trio rode away towards the livery barn.

"I want to get to Briartown before Mr. Dunn," Helvina said to her father.

"Are you sure that is enough men?" Adolphus asked. "My own men should arrive here on the evening train. We could wait until then."

"I'm sure my plans are sufficient to see this matter through to fruition," she said.

"My, aren't we a bit testy this morning?" Adolphus replied.

"First Bert Huffman, and now you," she said. "Men trying to tell me what to do and how I should do it when none of you thought of this. It was my idea. Mine and mine alone, but you all seem to have conveniently forgotten that."

"I haven't forgotten, nor am I surprised that you are smart, conniving, and ruthless to exceptional levels," he said. "You are my daughter, after all, and we Vanderwagens have always bred true."

"Even now, you must find some way to give yourself credit."

"And it's exactly like you not to admit that you need my help."

"I could do this without you. In fact, I'm doing this without you."

"Is that why you asked me here? So you can show me what a big girl you've become? To rub my nose in your success?"

Helvina gave a soft, snorting exhale to show her disdain. "I admit that I thought you might prove useful. The scope and scale of my business interests are about to expand greatly, and I shall need someone I can trust. Certainly, Mr. Dunn hasn't proved trustworthy."

Adolphus took out his pocket watch, glanced at the time, then tucked it away again. "Although this scheme of yours has come far closer to success than I ever thought it would, you still aren't done, yet. Not until you have ownership of McAlester's holdings in your hands and all the loose ends tied up."

She turned to face the hotel and looked up at one of the second story windows. "He's up there in his room right now, ready and waiting to sign the papers."

"I thought your intention was to have him sign them before you gave him his family back."

"Mr. Huffman and I almost got him to sign the paperwork, but the old goat is stubborn. He will only sign when he sees his wife and child."

Adolphus tilted his head back slightly and tapped the tip of his walking cane on the ground. "Ah, Superintendent Huffman. I take it you fully trust him."

"Do you know something about Huffman that I don't, or do you simply dislike him?" she asked.

"On the contrary, from what little I gather, he is a man with whom I share much in common . . . a man after my own heart if you will," Adolphus said. "And that's exactly the reason I wouldn't trust him."

She waved a dismissive hand at him. "You worry too much."

"Remember, dear, the bigger the prize, the nastier the players. Believe me, I know. Don't let your ambitions blind you to possible knives aimed at your own back. Jay Gould did not get where he is by sharing with those weaker and smaller than he is. Careful that you don't draw too much of his attention."

"Huffman has assured me that Gould has no idea about the . . . hmmm, the McAlester acquisition."

"Don't be so sure, Daughter. And if he isn't aware of you now, he soon will be."

"Is there any other condescending advice you wish to give me?"

"Now that you mention it, I suggest that if you won't wait for reinforcements, then you let your men handle this and you stay here. It's always best to keep oneself removed from these matters. Deniability, you know, if worse comes to worse."

"Are you going with me, or not?"

"As much as I don't look forward to a horseback ride, what kind of father would I be if I didn't accompany you?" he asked. "But then again, who is trustworthy enough to stay here and make sure Mr. McAlester doesn't get cold feet and decide to talk to the authorities?"

"That's exactly the kind of father you are," she said. "Very well, stay here and keep an eye on McAlester."

"Is there any word of Ben?" Adolphus asked.

"No," she answered with a worried look.

He patted her on the shoulder. "No worries. He has not even been gone three days. I'm sure he is at this moment wandering around the countryside making a big show of putting out the valiant effort and learning in the meantime what a fool his father is."

"I don't guess it will hurt for Ben to be gone a little longer. The last thing we need is Morgan showing up here."

"Yes, that is a concern. The man is quite good at blundering into things and making a muck of them," Adolphus said. "I thought I had him out of the picture once and for all back in Fort Smith, but alas, he has always been a thorn hard to remove."

Helvina whirled on him. "You did what?"

"Oh, it was nothing, really. At least nothing that he can ever trace back to me. I saw an opportunity, and simply tried to take advantage of it."

"I asked you what you did."

"I offered your Mr. Dunn two hundred dollars to remove Morgan from the playing field. But Mr. Dunn proved no more dependable in that endeavor than he has in yours."

"You fool."

"What would you have me do? Morgan has made no qualms about his hatred of me, and frankly, I have some scores that have long needed to be settled. A Vanderwagen, once crossed, does not forget."

"It has taken me years to get to this point, years on my own. And you do something like that without talking to me first?" Helvina's face was flushed red.

"He has no idea. The dumb brute may be skillful when it comes to a brawl, but his cunning only goes so far."

"Morgan is not the same man you once knew. He's . . . he's harder. Much harder. Have you any clue how many men he's killed?"

"Am I wrong to think that hint of care in your voice is not for your dear father's well-being?" he asked. "After everything, something in you still clings to that man?"

"I have nothing left for him. Nothing."

Adolphus smirked. "You have always been drawn to the rakish, scandalous sorts. Your mother was the same way, like an alley cat in heat when it came to such men."

Helvina stiffened and glared at him. "All these years and you still can't let her memory rest in peace. I wonder if she was truly the wicked thing you have always made her out to be."

"Haven't I always been there for you?"

"Oh, yes, you are always there. But in whose interest does your presence benefit? The older I get the more I realize you look out for yourself first and foremost."

Adolphus cleared his throat and straightened his coat front. "Let's not fight. It does no good."

"Leave Morgan alone. Do you hear me? This is not the time. I won't have you adding complications to what is already a difficult matter."

"I . . ."

"Promise me," she cut him off before he could finish.

"Dear . . ." he stammered.

"Your word."

"Very well then. What's between he and I can wait until a more opportune time."

Her men came back leading her horse, a beautiful bay mare with a hide as sleek and shiny as a seal. The mare had been cooped up in her stall too long, and pranced on nimble hooves, each flick of her legs nimble and graceful.

The man in the checkered pants led the mare alongside the mounting block near the back door. He dismounted and held the mare by the bit shank while Helvina climbed to the top step and mounted her sidesaddle.

"Take care, Daughter," Adolphus said.

"Keep a close watch on J.J.," she said while she hooked the back of one knee around the sidesaddle post and arranged the drape of her dress so that it hung properly. "I should be back this evening, but you can send a rider to me if something should go wrong."

"Rest assured, I can handle my end."

Helvina started to ride away, but hesitated. "If Morgan and his posse should return, I expect you to remember our talk. No trouble, hear me?"

Adolphus waited until she was too far away to hear him before he answered her. "No trouble, dear. Morgan will be no trouble at all."

Chapter Thirty

Red Molly rode to the barbershop and tied her horse in front of it, even though Noodles wouldn't be open for another two hours. She had a hand lifted to knock on the door when she noticed Helvina Vanderwagen and the men with her gathered behind the hotel. No sooner than Molly spied them, Helvina mounted her horse and she and three of the men rode down the street past her.

Helvina gave Molly a cool, haughty look, but said nothing in passing. Molly spat in the street and scowled at Helvina's back.

"I should have given you a mouth full of me fist a long time ago. Riding down the street like you're the queen of Egypt," Molly said under her breath.

There never had been any love lost between her and Helvina Vanderwagen, not since Helvina had first arrived in Eufaula, or what was then the construction camp of Ironhead Station. Back then, even though Helvina was nothing more than the pampered mistress of the crooked railroad construction superintendent who had eventually gotten himself hanged, she had acted like she was better than anyone else and caused more than her share of trouble. For the thousandth time, Molly wondered what Morgan had ever seen in such a woman, or what any man would. Oh, she was a looker, but she was like bad fruit that was shiny on the outside and rotten at the core.

Helvina and her party turned off on the road to North Fork Town, headed west. Molly was still watching them when the door behind her opened. When she turned, she saw Noodles standing there rubbing the sleep out of his eyes.

"I think I hear someone out here," he said.

"Who's that with Helvina?" Molly asked.

Noodles blinked once, rubbed his eyes again, and stared down the road at the riders. "That one in the checkered pants, he has been around for a week or so. And then I see him yesterday morning going in the back of the hotel. He acted like he didn't want to be seen."

"Does he work for her?"

"I think he is friends with Signor Dunn."

"That little pimp that used to work at the hotel?"

Noodles nodded. "I see him talking with Signor Dunn, and then again the evening before Signor Dunn left town with those Indians."

"Indians? Charlie Dunn never struck me as the kind to keep company with Indians. Not his style."

"Two Indians and some cowboys, I think. I went back inside the shop before I could look good, because they . . . how do you say? They look like the *mafie* men in Sicily. Lots of guns, and the look on their faces, you know. Men who would do bad things."

Molly looked back at the hotel in time to see the man Helvina had left behind going back inside. "Who's the fancy gent?"

"That is Signora Vanderwagen's *patri.*"

"Her what? Speak English."

"Her father. The papa, you know."

"What's he doing here?"

"I see him yesterday at the train depot, but he no friendly. I try to talk with him to practice my English like you always say, but he busy. I hear him ask when the train will run today, and I think he is waiting for someone to come."

"One Vanderwagen was more than enough, and now there

are two," Molly said with a frown.

"Everybody have no time to talk. Many new people since Signor McAlester's woman was taken. Signor McAlester came for a haircut yesterday, but he wouldn't talk, either. I understand he worries, so I don't bother him."

"Is McAlester still here?"

"He is at the hotel, I think. The big chief with the tall hat left yesterday, and I see some others get on the train with him. The railroad men, I don't know."

"You see a lot, don't you?" Molly gave Noodles a look like she was reappraising him, which was something she had done several times since she had known him. At times the Sicilian could seem the sort to stumble and bumble through life, timid and unsure, but she had long since learned that Noodles had his own kind of mettle and was foxier than he appeared at first glance.

"I watch and I listen," Noodles said.

"And nobody pays much attention to you, do they?"

Noodles shrugged. "If you come for the rent, I have it ready for you."

"Your rent's not due for another week," Molly said.

"Yes, but I pay you now." Noodles stepped aside and held the door open for her.

Molly glanced one more time at Helvina and the other riders going down the road. Something about the sight of them bothered her, and it wasn't only the fact that she didn't like Helvina. Those men riding with Helvina had left her with the same impression that Noodles had gotten from those he saw with Charlie Dunn. What had he called them in his Sicilian gibberish? Mafie men? Although the word was new to her, she knew the kind well from her years working the saloons and bawdy houses, badmen and toughs, and what one of the Mexican girls she had once worked for had referred to as *mal hombres.* Ireland had their kind too, as well as everywhere else in the world, she assumed. The bad feeling that had been plaguing her grew worse.

"Helvina's up to something," Molly said as she stepped inside the barbershop. "But then again, that woman's always up to something."

Noodles motioned her to take one of the chairs as he closed the door behind her. "Where is Signor Dixie? Did he come with you?"

Instead of sitting, she turned her back to him and stared out the front window. She was chewing on her lower lip the way she did when she was worried. "No, he's gone off with Marshal Clyde."

"Signor Clyde, I cut his hair before he left. It was good to see him after so long."

"Morgan used to scare the dickens out of you."

Noodles gave a thoughtful frown. "Yes, he scares me sometimes, but I think him a man who I want to be my friend. The *mafiosos* in Sicily weren't always men who steal and burn. Not in *mi patri*'s time and long before. They were the brave men in the beginning, the angry men who would fight to make things right. The men who would fight for the little ones and the old ones, and those who were not brave or strong. I think Signor Clyde is like that."

"You say you were at the depot yesterday. Has there been any word from Morgan and the posse?" she asked, her mind too much on her worries to fully register what Noodles had said. "A telegram? News?"

"No. You worry about Signor Dixie?" Noodles asked.

"I'm going to find him and bring him home," she said.

"I would not worry. More men went to find Signor McAlester's family. A posse? Is that how you say it? They left the evening after Signor Clyde left with his men. I hear some say

Signor Clyde wouldn't let them go with him, but they all want the money Signor McAlester say he will pay to have his *famigghia* back."

"How many went?"

Noodles shrugged. "Many, but some of them were very drunk."

"Sounds like a mob. Had to work their courage up, I guess."

"Are you hungry? You can eat with my family. The children are always happy to see you."

Molly could hear the sounds of Noodles's family stirring in the back room, and the noise of rattling pots and pans made my Noodles's wife preparing breakfast. "Didn't you hear me? I said I've got to find Dixie. I've already spent too much time here as it is."

Noodles followed her outside and watched her ready herself to ride. The roan filly, despite having been ridden several miles already, was more fractious than before and wouldn't stand still for her to get a foot in the stirrup. She finally managed to get the mare standing alongside the boardwalk in front of the barbershop to help her mount.

"You should get a gentler horse," Noodles said.

His mentioning of the horse angered her, especially since it sounded like one of Dixie's laconic observations. Why was it that men were always assuming what she could and couldn't do? Granted, the mare was green and still needed a lot of training, but it was her choice if she wanted to ride it. Men thought they were so powerful simply because they might be able to ride an unruly horse or lift something heavy, but she had always been an uncommonly strong girl and more than capable of doing what needed doing. Maybe not as strong as a man, but a stubborn mind could be almost as good as muscles, not to mention that most men she had known didn't have a lick of sense.

She waved goodbye to Noodles and started her horse down

the street to the south towards Canadian Station. She looked for a last time down the road to North Fork Town as she passed by it, but Helvina and the others were already out of sight. Still, the uneasy feeling wouldn't leave her.

Chapter Thirty-One

The tracks made by Dunn and Injun Joe led Morgan's posse out of the mountains and down into a long narrow valley. In the midst of that valley they struck a faint wagon trace. By then, Morgan's illness had worsened. Fever sweat dotted his forehead and his chest rattled with every breath.

He stopped them in the middle of the wagon trace and spat a wad of phlegm onto the ground. He looked up at them with haggard eyes. "Dixie, take the boy and Cumsey to McAlester. Follow this road west and you strike the Texas Road not far from where we turned off it."

"I've been to McAlester," Dixie said. "You're so sick you can't think straight."

"It's hot today, that's all."

"Only thing hot is that fever of yours. If anybody's going to McAlester it ought to be you."

Moshulatubee had ridden ahead, tracking the outlaws, but he came loping out of the timber on the far side of the valley, headed back to them.

"Beats me how that crooked-eyed Choctaw can track like he can," Cumsey said, but cut off whatever else he intended to say when he moved wrong in the saddle. He winced, sucked in a quick breath, and cocked his bad side out of the saddle seat.

"They're still headed north," Moshulatubee said when he reached them.

"How far ahead of us are they?" Morgan asked.

"About the same. Sign's hot, but I'd say we haven't gained on them much," the Lighthorseman replied.

Morgan straightened his back and wiped at the fever sweat on his face. "Ben, it'd be best if you went with Dixie and Cumsey."

"No, I'm sticking to the pursuit," Ben said.

"That goes for me, too, Marshal. I ain't so bad off I can't ride," Cumsey added.

"You need to have that wound tended." Morgan had listened to him cursing most of the way down the mountain, and knew he was in pain.

"Reckon this little old bullet hole can wait another day. I'll stick with you, same as the lieutenant."

"You've done your part."

"It ain't finished."

"You've been complaining and poking fun of riding with us ever since we started."

"That woman they've got, she could belong to anyone of us. I'd like to think if she was my wife or my sister or something . . . well, I'd like to think if somebody had a chance to get her back that they wouldn't quit," Cumsey replied, and then pointed at the boy riding in front of Ben. "My mama wasn't much, but even so, I set store by her. Reckon that boy there does, too. Boy ought to have his mama."

Morgan started coughing again, and it was Dixie who spoke, instead. "Well now, Cumsey Bowlegs, you're starting to sound like a regular law abider. Careful, now. Word gets out and you'll ruin your poor reputation."

"We'd best be moving," Moshulatubee said.

Dixie rode his mule beside Ben Clyde's horse and took the McAlester boy from him. "You invalids go ahead and ride yourselves into the ground. I can take the boy in to town by myself."

Dixie had barely gotten the boy on his mule with him when a rifle shot cracked over the valley. The bullet that went with the sound knocked a dirt clod loose in front of Morgan's horse, and it reared high on its back legs and spun and tried to bolt. Morgan barely had time to get hold of the dun before more shots came their way. Their mounts danced and milled in the trail in the initial moment of confusion. The leather of Moshulatubee's saddle scabbard hissed as he fought his horse under control and snaked out his Winchester carbine. Morgan already had his Colt clenched in his fist.

Cumsey was the first of them to put the spurs to his horse, and the rest followed him back towards the timber at the foot of the mountain they had just descended. It wasn't a far run, but it was mostly open ground. A ragged volley of gunshots was aimed their way, and bullets cut the air around them.

"Back there in those trees," Moshulatubee shouted and pointed behind him across the valley with the barrel of his rifle as they raced over uneven ground.

Another gunshot sounded and a tiny cloud of powder smoke blossomed where Moshulatubee had pointed some two hundred yards from them among the copse of trees clumped on top of a hill. They hadn't covered twenty yards before Ben's horse grunted and went down. Ben launched himself from the saddle, and the violence and momentum of the horse's fall propelled him through the air. He hit the ground rolling.

The zebra dun had a fine handle, and even at a dead run, the gelding dropped its hindquarters into the ground and skidded to a stop when Morgan asked. He rolled the dun back over its hocks and raced back to Ben. One more stop and another rollback, and Ben was leaping behind his saddle. Riding double, they charged after the rest of the posse for the cover of the tree line. The rest of the posse was already off their mounts and taking cover by the time they made it to the timber. Cumsey threw his Winchester to his shoulder and fired two rapid shots back across the valley just as Morgan and Ben bailed from the dun's back and scrambled to find cover.

"How many of them are there?" Morgan asked.

"How the hell should I know?" Cumsey threw back at him. "I thought I saw powder smoke, so I figured to take some of the starch out of them."

"Can't make anything out, but I'd say there's a passel of them," Dixie muttered. He was down behind a fallen pine tree's trunk with his Spencer resting across it.

"Where's the boy?" Morgan asked.

Dixie jerked his head back behind him at the thick trunk of another pine amidst a cluster of rocks. "Boy, you stay behind that tree. Hear me? Don't you come out 'til I tell you to."

"Ben, stick with the kid. Make sure he keeps his head down," Morgan said.

Ben nodded and moved towards the McAlester boy. He was limping from his fall and had lost his army hat, but he had his pistol out and seemed little worse for his tumble other than a slight limp.

The gunfire aimed at them ceased almost as quickly as it had begun.

"Maybe I got lucky and peppered them some," Cumsey said.

Morgan scrambled towards Cumsey and Dixie, keeping as low as he could and behind cover. He dropped to a knee beside Dixie. "They'll play hell getting at us across open ground."

Dixie licked a thumb and reached up and wiped his front carbine sight with it. He tucked in behind his rifle stock and aimed across the valley with a grim expression. "First one to try is going to wish he hadn't."

In the distance, Morgan could make out movement, as if whoever had attacked them was adjusting their position or scattering out. "Dixie, you and Ben take the boy. Keep to the woods and make for the Texas Road."

"Maybe later. They ain't got us treed, yet."

"You never were worth a damn at taking orders."

"My third-grade teacher used to say the same thing," Dixie replied.

Cumsey moved to the cover of another tree, closer to the two of them. "I guess there's a dozen of them or more."

"Could be, or there could be half that many," Moshulatubee said. "No way of telling, but I think there's only two or three of them doing the shooting."

"This is my fault," Morgan said. "I didn't expect Dunn to double back on us."

"Hand the boy over! Turn him loose!" Someone shouted to them across the valley. "Ya'll hear me?"

"Sounds like he's drunk," Dixie said.

Morgan agreed. Whoever it was did sound like he was drunk. A different voice across the valley said something they couldn't make out, followed by ribald laughter and catcalls from a few other men. Another gunshot boomed, but the round struck nowhere near the posse.

"Quit shooting! You'll hit the boy," one of the voices across the valley shouted.

"I don't think that's Dunn's bunch," Dixie said. "Nope, I think we've had the bad luck to run across another kind of trouble entirely."

"Throw down your guns and come out where we can see you!" The same man as before shouted.

"Come and get us!" Cumsey yelled back at him.

"Surrender or we'll kill every man jack of you where you stand!" came the reply.

"You tell him, John!" A different man among their attackers encouraged the first. "We've got'em. They ain't going nowhere. Nothing but meat in the pot."

Somebody whooped, followed by laughter, and a bullet rattled the tree limbs over the posse's head.

"I know that voice," Dixie said. "I'd swear that's old John Decker the brickmaker doing most of the talking."

"Who the hell are you?" Cumsey shouted at them.

"We're the law, you child-stealing sons-a-bitches!" was the answering call.

Dixie set aside his Spencer and rolled on his back and began to cut a chaw of tobacco from a plug he carried. Morgan was fond of cigars, but he had never seen a man more in love with tobacco than Dixie. One moment he was smoking a pipe and the next he had a chaw of chewing tobacco packed in his cheek.

Dixie caught Morgan watching him, and it was as if he read Morgan's mind. "I chew when I'm working, and smoke when I've got time to contemplate."

"How about you contemplate on how to get us out of this?" Morgan asked.

Dixie shook his head. "No, those boys over there are poor shooters, but one of them might get lucky and hit my pipe and it's the only one I've got."

Morgan peered over the log and across the valley. "You out there, this is Marshal Clyde. You're firing on a duly sworn federal posse."

No answer came and the valley went quiet. No more laughter and no more gunshots.

"I think you got their attention," Dixie said.

"How do we know you ain't lying?" asked the man across the valley after a while.

"Don't you fire another shot," Morgan yelled. "We've got the McAlester boy back and are taking him home."

Cumsey lowered his rifle and looked Morgan's way. "Dixie's right. That's John Decker's voice. I bet him and those with him are out after the reward money."

"They're moving." Dixie took up his rifle and readied himself behind the log.

They could see riders moving among the trees on the other side of the wagon trail. Three riders appeared, riding their way, but the others were riding in the opposite direction and trying to keep out of sight. Morgan stood up from behind the log, but Dixie and Cumsey stayed behind cover.

"You make a fine target standing up like that," Dixie said.

Morgan didn't respond, for he was too intent on watching the three men coming their way. Moshulatubee came and knelt between Morgan and Dixie.

"Looks like most of them are leaving," the Lighthorseman said. "And they're making a point not to let us see who they are."

Morgan didn't hear them. He stepped over the log and started walking toward the trio of riders when they were within a hundred yards. He was standing out in the open with his pistol hanging at the end of his arm. A gust of wind rippled the waist-high grass around him.

"Damned fool," Dixie said.

"Best we stay here and cover him," Cumsey said.

"It ain't Morgan I'm worried about," Dixie said while he kept walking.

The one in the center of the three riders was a portly man with outsized forearms and hands, and a belly to match. He rolled in the saddle like a sailor on a swaying ship.

"That's Decker the brickmaker like I thought," Dixie half mumbled to Morgan. "He's so drunk he can barely ride. Don't recognize the other two."

"I recognize that one on the right," Cumsey called from behind them. "Don't know his name, but he's partnered up in that new store at Eufaula."

The riders' horses' legs hissed through the tall grass, and in a moment, they were pulling up a couple of yards in front of Morgan and Dixie. Cumsey shifted his position slightly and rested his Winchester's barrel on the side of a tree.

"You can quit pointing that rifle at us," the storekeeper on the right said to Cumsey. "I'm afraid this has all been a bad misunderstanding."

"Believe I'll keep a bead on you," Cumsey replied.

Dixie waited for Morgan to speak, but it didn't come. Morgan only stared at them.

"You shot at a posse, you bunch of fools," Dixie said. "Not to mention you damn near killed an army officer."

The storekeeper and the man on the opposite end passed a glance between them, and if their bearing was already uneasy, they suddenly looked ready to flee. Only the brickmaker seemed like that news didn't upset him too much. But then again, the whiskey smell on him was strong enough to carry to where Dixie and Morgan stood.

"How were we supposed to know you were lawmen?" the brickmaker slurred. "We're out after the McAlesters, same as you."

"Shut up, Decker," the storekeeper said.

"I don't see a single badge on them, even now," the brickmaker continued. He had a Winchester laid across his lap. The other two men had made it a point to sheath their rifles, but not him.

"You ought to do like that man says and shut up while you can," Dixie said.

"To hell with you, Rayburn," the brickmaker answered. "What're you doing out here? Thought you'd be laid up with your whore."

The brickmaker leaned out from his saddle. It was unclear if he was leaning out to spit or vomit, or maybe to get down from his horse. Or maybe he simply was so drunk that he swayed that far. Either way, he made it easy for Morgan.

Morgan charged forward in three long strides and hit the brickmaker in the face with the barrel of his Colt. The sound of the impact was like a ripe watermelon being struck. The brickmaker toppled from his saddle and landed in a sloppy heap. Morgan kicked him twice as soon as he hit the ground. The brickmaker's horse ran away, and the action caused the other two riders' mounts to shy and dance around.

"I'd hold still if I was you," Cumsey said while he squinted down his rifle sights at the two still on their horses. Dixie also had them covered with his Spencer.

The brickmaker groaned and tried to get up. Morgan let him get to his knees before he kicked him in the chin. Bits of teeth flew out of the brickmaker's mouth. He rolled once, and managed to get on his hands and knees. He was cursing and spitting blood, but instead of trying to fight he groped for his lost hat in the grass. Or maybe it was his rifle he was looking for. Morgan took him by the hair and yanked him back to his knees.

"Morgan," Dixie called out.

Morgan held the brickmaker's face up to the sun and pressed his revolver's barrel between the brickmaker's eyes.

"He's had enough," Dixie said more loudly, and charged toward Morgan.

He hit Morgan with his shoulder, and at the same time he pushed the pistol away from the brickmaker's head. Morgan staggered a few steps, righted himself, and swung the pistol in a backhanded blow aimed for Dixie's head.

Dixie barely managed to duck and avoid being hit. He stood between Morgan and the brickmaker and held up a hand to fend off another attack. "It's me, Morgan! Stop it, now! He's had enough."

Morgan brought his Colt up and pointed it at Dixie's face. He was breathing in ragged gasps, and the wild look in his eyes told that in his fury he was blind to anything and everyone.

"Damn it! It's me!" Dixie shouted.

Morgan blinked slowly and lowered the pistol. After a few breaths, some of the madness left his face. He nodded at Dixie, then turned his attention to the other two men still up on their horses.

"I ought to kill you here and now," Morgan said.

The storekeeper backed his horse a step. "I told him and the others not to shoot, but they wouldn't listen. I should have gone back home as soon as they started drinking. To tell the truth, I guess some of them were likely drinking before we left town. Never was my intention for this to happen. Had I known it was going to be like this . . . only wanted to get McAlester's family back, and maybe a piece of that reward he promised."

Morgan appeared calmer, but his stare was still an ugly thing.

"Let it go, Morgan," Dixie said.

"We're sorry, Marshal. It was an accident," the other rider said. "That's what we came over here to tell you instead of going straight back to town. Thought we might help anybody that was hurt."

"I want to know the name of every man jack that was with you. You hear me?" Morgan acted as if he was going to say more, but started coughing again so hard that it bent him over at the waist. He was still coughing when he turned and went back into the trees.

Dixie watched him go, then turned back to face the town men. The brickmaker was still down.

"I thought he was going to kill us all," the storekeeper said.

"Marshal Clyde is bad sick and not himself. And that lieutenant you boys like to have shot is his son."

"We told you we didn't do any shooting. It was Decker and some of the others."

"You better ride out of here while you can."

"Is he going to come hunting us?"

"Go on home."

"What about him?" The storekeeper nodded at the brick-maker who was lying flat in the grass and not moving.

"He's under arrest. We'll bring him along," Dixie said.

"I've never been arrested in my life. I'm a deacon at the Methodist church. I got a family."

"Go home like I said."

The two town men turned their horses and rode away. Dixie glanced at the bloody heap lying in the grass. The brickmaker looked bad enough to be dead, but he wasn't. His painful moans testified that he was still among the living.

"You picked a bad day to play the fool, Decker," Dixie said.

Cumsey went to catch the brickmaker's horse. Dixie picked up the brickmaker's rifle and jerked his pistol out of his holster. Lieutenant Clyde and the McAlester boy came to the edge of the grass and stared at the downed man. Morgan had gone to stand beside his horse, leaning against it with his back to them.

"He would have killed that man if you hadn't stopped him," Ben said looking back over his shoulder at Morgan.

"Maybe or maybe not," Dixie said.

"He's crazy," Ben added.

"No, he's not crazy," Dixie answered in a quiet voice. "He's just sick and tired, and he's scared."

"Scared? I don't think he's scared of anything."

Dixie shook his head. "He's scared all right. Scared that he's failed and won't finish what he set out to do, but mostly I reckon he thinks he almost got you killed and that scares him worse even than failing."

"He . . ." Ben started.

"You can pick your friends, Lieutenant, but you don't get to pick your family. Whether you like it or not, that man yonder loves you and he'd send a thousand Deckers to hell with his bare hands and damn his own soul to perdition if it meant not losing the one good thing he thinks he ever did. You."

"He almost killed you when you tried to stop him, and yet you still defend him," Ben said.

"I defend him because I know him, and because he's my friend. He means well, even if he doesn't always handle things the way he should and has a hard time admitting he's wrong. He gives you his word, then that's the way it's going to be. He can't stand what doesn't seem right or just, and he hates a liar and a sneak and a backbiter worse than anything. You know his measure because of that. And if ever I was to get myself in a jam where nobody else in the world would help me, I know he would, come hell or high water, same as I would for him. No questions asked. Same as he pulled your fat out of the fire. He's that kind of a man, and if you ain't figured it out by now, that's a rare damned breed."

Ben was staring at Dixie trying to muster what he was going to say next when Moshulatubee came by him carrying a hatchet.

"Come on, Lieutenant," the Lighthorseman said. "Marshal Clyde says we're going. Help me cut some poles so we can rig a travois to drag that sorry drunk's carcass to town."

"It's been nothing but bad luck since we left," Dixie said. "Can't remember a worse manhunt."

"Oh, I've been on worse," Moshulatubee answered. "All of us are still standing."

"True."

They chopped down two tall, slender pine saplings and lashed them together to form a triangle-shaped frame with the point of it secured to the brickmaker's saddle horn and a blanket stretched across the base. It was a crude version of the type of travois that the plains Indians used to carry their camp belongings from place to place.

The brickmaker was still lying where he had fallen. He was

conscious, but his head wound from where he had been struck with the pistol barrel still had him groggy and unable to stand. He also claimed he was blind in one eye and that the nerves in his broken teeth were paining him fiercely. It took three of them to get him on the travois. They tossed him on it unceremoniously, ignoring his complaints and assurances that they were killing him and that he was going to have them all hung for their mistreatment of him.

Dixie put the McAlester boy back up on his mule, and the lieutenant rode the brickmaker's horse, riding between the travois poles. Morgan was the last to mount, and scowled at them all when he saw them watching him as if there was some debate as to whether he could manage the feat. He led them out, slumped over in the saddle and his body periodically wracked and shuddering when another coughing spell overwhelmed him. The rest of them fell in behind him.

"Thought we were going to McAlester," Dixie said when they crossed the road going north instead of turning onto it.

"No, he said we're going to Eufaula," Cumsey answered.

"I can't believe he's quitting the hunt, even as sick as he is."

"I don't reckon he figures we can catch Dunn now, what with having to drag that tub of guts along," Cumsey jerked his head at the brickmaker, "and the lieutenant losing his horse."

"Maybe some of the others out on the hunt will get the McAlester woman back," Dixie said, but there was something in his voice that sounded like he didn't believe his own suggestion.

"There's no way we were going to run down that hotel fellow now, no matter what Clyde decided. You reckon she's still alive?"

"I don't know. That's the thing about manhunting I don't like."

"What don't you like?"

Dixie squinted at the horizon. "Well, besides being a general pain in the backside, the consequences are what I don't like most. All kinds of consequences."

Chapter Thirty-Two

The Love brothers met Dunn and Injun Joe on the outskirts of Briartown two hours after sundown. The two outlaw cowboys appeared ahead of them as if by magic, ghosting out of the dark with nothing more than a creak of saddle leather and slow-moving shadows. Dunn's hand went to one of his pistol butts before his groggy mind and bloodshot eyes realized who it was in the road. It had been a hard, fast trip from the caves, and the lack of sleep and the miles were wearing on both he and Injun Joe. He and the surly Choctaw hadn't said two words between them in the last several hours, and the McAlester woman was slumped limply in front of Joe in such a state that Dunn couldn't tell if she was asleep or simply so worn out that her spine had lost the ability to support her.

"Where's the kid?" Jesco Love asked.

Injun Joe was giving the two cowboys a rundown of what had happened back at the caves when Dunn interrupted him.

"None of that matters," Dunn said. "Is anybody waiting for us in Briartown?"

"Wasn't nobody there when we left," Budge Love answered.

Dunn considered that news in silence for some time, but finally nodded his head. "That's probably best. We can lay up and get first look at whoever is coming to meet us. Get an idea of how things stand."

They rode along a narrow road following the north bank of the river. It was so overhung with tree limbs and mats of greenbriers that it was more like riding down a dark tunnel. Briartown itself was hardly a town, and in fact no town at all. Instead, it was a scattering of a few houses and cabins surrounding a small store and trading post on the edge of a flat expanse of river bottom and scattered prairies. A lamp burning in one of the store windows was the only sign of life in the settlement, but their arrival didn't go totally unnoticed. A pair of mongrel dogs barked at them and growled and scratched a half circle around them as they passed.

"The storekeeper let us sleep in his hay barn last night," Jesco Love said. "It's not much, but it's dry and that loft door makes a fair place to watch the road from."

"Knock on his door and tell him we're going to use it again," Dunn said.

Jesco spurred his horse through the dogs, cursing them, and rode to the store. Dunn could hear him talking to someone, and then he came back to them.

"He says it's all right," Jesco said.

Dunn detected a note of irritation in Jesco's voice. "What's the matter?"

"That storekeeper acted about half cagey this time," Jesco answered.

"I told you that you pissed him off griping about the price of that Choc beer he makes," Budge said.

"Man thinks too highly of his beer," Budge mumbled. "Never could stand a sassy merchant. I ought to go back over there and line him out. Teach him a little respect for his betters."

"Leave him be. We've got more important matters to attend to," Dunn said. He could only imagine what the storekeeper had endured at the hands of the Love brothers, and wasn't surprised that they might have already worn out their welcome.

The barn mentioned was a tall-sided structure made of poles set in the ground and framed over with rough-sawn board-and-bat oak boards. The roof of it was round and held a hayloft with a little door above the big one at ground level, and with a haymow hanging in front of it.

They rode inside and Dunn dismounted along with the others. Budge Love was already closing the barn door behind them. Though dark inside, there were places where the lumber siding and bats had shrunk enough to form cracks, and narrow spikes of moonlight shone through. Dunn could barely make out the shadowed forms of a pair of wagons, and thought he could see what was a milk cow stanchion and a pair of horse stalls.

Jesco produced a lantern from somewhere and lit it.

"Our daddy would whip our asses with a plowline if he ever caught us burning a lantern in his hay barn," Budge said. "That's how Uncle Rufus burned his down, and Daddy never forgot it. Why he . . ."

"Shut up, Budge," Dunn's voice was hard and clipped, and there was a warning in it.

"Damn, but you're testy tonight," Budge said. "You and Joe crawl up there in that loft and get you some sleep and you'll feel better in the morning. Both of you look like you've been rode hard and put up wet. Give me some money and I'll go buy some more of that overpriced Injun beer. That ought to put that storekeeper in a better mood."

"Shut up, Budge." It was Jesco who said that this time, and there was the same sharp warning in his voice.

"He does tend to chatter on, doesn't he?" a new voice said, a woman's voice.

Budge lifted the lantern higher and shifted it to reveal what the others had already seen. There in edge of the weak pool of light was Helvina Vanderwagen leaning against a wagon wearing a fancy dress, and there were four men split to either side of her. Every one of those four men held a gun pointed at them, and there was a smirk playing on her mouth.

The man in checkered pants standing closest to Helvina stepped forward and pushed the shotgun in his hands a little closer towards Injun Joe's belly. "You'll keep your hands away from that pistol if you know what's good for you. And that goes for the rest of you."

Two of Helvina's men moved behind them, and one of them put the barrel of his rifle up against Budge Love's spine. Dunn could feel the other man hovering behind him, no doubt with a similar weapon pointed at his back.

"Helvina, to what do I owe this honor?" Dunn said. His demeanor was calm and flippant, but he kept his hands well away from the pistols hanging under his armpits. "I wouldn't have thought you would come yourself. You flatter me."

"Cut the cocksure act, you little runt," Helvina threw back at him.

"Why, Helvina, are we cross? Truly, you hurt me." The grin had never left Dunn's face.

She gave him a hateful glance, then looked past him to Rebecca McAlester who had plopped on the barn floor the instant she was taken off Joe's horse. She sat sprawled with her legs before her, hands in her lap. Her attention darted from one of them to the other, and the one eye visible through the tangled hair hanging over most of her face was wide and full of fear.

"You fool," Helvina said. "Look at her."

"She's still in one piece," Dunn answered.

"Barely," Helvina countered. "Where's her son?"

"Marshals hit us. We barely escaped with her as it was."

"I asked you where the boy is."

"Maybe those marshals have got him, or maybe he's dead. There wasn't time to doddle."

"I gave you clear instructions. I've promised her husband that both she and the boy will be returned no worse for wear."

"I imagine McAlester will deal just the same for the woman.

It's half the leverage, but should still be enough."

"What if the boy is dead? What if he isn't and he tells what he knows to the marshals?"

"The boy doesn't know anything except that I took him, and that's my worry and not yours. Trade her back to her husband. If the boy is still alive and with the law, then so much the better. McAlester gets his family safe and sound and we get what we want. Not like we planned, but it will still work," Dunn said.

"Like *we* planned? *We?*" Helvina asked. "Lately you seem to have a very grandiose opinion of yourself."

Dunn's answer was another grin, but his eyes flicked between the guns pointed at him and the woman taunting him.

"Don't you grin at me," she said. "I got your letter. Do you really think you can bargain with me after the fact? That you could blackmail me?"

"I merely suggested an alternative business proposition to be considered among equals." There was a faint hint of tension suddenly to be heard in Dunn's voice.

"Equals?" She straightened from the wagon and took a step closer to him and more fully into the lantern light. "You work for me. What little you are, you owe to me and me alone. I made you. Gave you every chance to better yourself, and yet you speak to me of equals? Oh, sweet Charlie, you were always a little crazy, but I'm afraid you've truly lost your mind."

"Made me?" Dunn's shoulders jerked as if he had been physically struck, and his left eyelid had started to spasm. Up until then he had been able to keep up his smirking, cocksure act in order to buy time and as a means to fend off Helvina's insults, but the thin veneer wore through, and he glared at her with smoldering hatred and barely controlled madness.

Helvina's laughter was shrill to him in the confines of the barn walls. "You thought you could muscle yourself into a partnership with me?"

"I don't think what you offered is commensurate with the risk I'm taking." Dunn's voice was strained and almost quavering.

"We're all taking risks, Charlie. What is it you chance? A couple of suits and a traveling case I bought you? Your combs and your little razor and the mirror you preen yourself in while you douse yourself in that cheap cologne you're so fond of? Those fancy pistols of yours? Oh, you risk so much," Helvina said while she waved a paper fan back and forth in front of her face. "What is it you said? You so like to throw around big words. Oh, yes, I think the four thousand dollars you were offered was more than *commensurate* with your risk."

"I want a cut of the action," Dunn said through his teeth. "Maybe not exactly what I suggested in my letter, but a real cut. If not, I'll bring the whole thing down."

Helvina continued to fan herself and paced back and forth in front of him, oblivious to his rage or enjoying it. "What did you intend by coming here? Did you plan to threaten to reveal my involvement, or are you even a bigger fool than that? Did you entertain notions of removing me and trying to deal with J.J. yourself?"

"I . . ."

Helvina laughed again. "That's it, isn't it? Such a greedy, bloody boy, aren't you? But did you ever ask yourself how you could keep J.J. from taking the matter to the law even if you could have pushed me out of the way?"

"I . . ." Dunn started again.

"You didn't think of that, did you? What, were you the brightest boy in your class? The prodigal in some country bumpkin schoolhouse where you beat all the other kids in the spelling bee? You see, you're trying to play games you have no aptitude for. Stealing the woman and the child was never the most difficult thing. There are lots of men I could hire who could handle that task, and for far less than I offered to pay you," she said. "Nor was it getting J.J. to sign over his holdings. No, it was being able to keep them once the deed was done. You have no clue how long I've worked to create the necessary alliances and backing to pull this off. But you wouldn't understand that, would you?"

"I don't like how you're talking to me," Dunn said.

"Then how's this?" Helvina said. "I think you are a twisted, ungrateful, two-bit street urchin, probably sired by some poor miscreant no doubt like yourself. Why, I could probably trace a whole line of such dysfunctional trash all the way from you through a hundred generations. Petty little men fighting for scraps and thinking to themselves that they deserved better if only someone would give them a fair play. Well, you know what? There's no such thing as fair play. Not in this life. And you know what else?"

Dunn took an unconscious step toward her.

"Take another step and I'll blow your sorry ass to kingdom come," the man in the checkered pants said. "Go ahead."

Helvina arched an eyebrow at the shotgun the man held leveled on Dunn's head, and then looked back at Dunn. "Charlie, Charlie, you untrustworthy, devious boy. When will you ever learn? Being smart doesn't make you special, and you aren't nearly as smart as you think you are."

She brushed past Dunn and bent over Rebecca McAlester. "Come with me, dear, and we'll get you cleaned up and a nice comfy bed. I'm so sorry for the way Charlie has treated you."

She took Rebecca by one arm and helped her to her feet. The pair of them moved slowly towards the barn door.

"What about them?" the man in the checkered pants asked and gestured at Dunn with the shotgun.

Helvina paused in the open barn door and looked back at

them. She flipped a hand in the air, waving it as if she were brushing off something. "You have my blessing. Go ahead."

Chapter Thirty-Three

Several things happened the instant Helvina Vanderwagen and Rebecca McAlester disappeared out the barn door, most of them too fast to comprehend, and all of them bloody and chaotic. First, the Love brothers simultaneously went for their pistols. The man in the checkered pants had no doubt intended to shoot Dunn in the guts, but the Love brothers drew his attention and he let off both barrels in their direction, instead. One of the loads of buckshot struck Jesco about belt-high three feet away and he staggered back, bent over at the waist like he was cut in two. He was dead on his feet and with the shock of it written all over his twisted face. The other shotgun load missed Budge entirely and knocked a nasty chunk out of one of the barn posts. One of Helvina's men about to shoot Budge in the back screamed and grabbed at the six-inch splinter of wood suddenly lodged in one of his eyes.

And at the same time, Charlie Dunn ran for the nearest dark corner. One of his pistols was in his hand and he thumbed two fast shots behind him without looking or aiming. By some miracle or stroke of incomprehensible fate, one of those bullets hit the lantern in midair just as Budge Love dropped it in order to grapple with one of Helvina's men. Both Budge and the man he was fighting burst into flames.

Dunn finally looked back when he ran against the far wall, and he did so in time to see the two human torches rolling on the barn floor. Budge had somehow held on to his pistol, despite the burning of his flesh, and he pressed the barrel into his adversary's torso and shot him repeatedly while both of them screamed their pain.

Horses milled among the men, and one of them knocked somebody down on its way out of the barn. The others followed it, and for a brief moment the gunfire slowed as men dodged the frantic animals.

With the horses out of the way, Dunn intended to shoot the man in the checkered pants, but the one with the splinter in his eye staggered between them just as he pulled the trigger and took the bullet, instead. Dunn shot him again, and then a third time before he finally fell, and by then Injun Joe was lunging at the man in the checkered pants with a knife. The man in the checkered pants swung his shotgun like a club and knocked the big Choctaw down to one knee, but barely dodged a slash across the chest in the process. He backed away clawing for the pistol on his hip. Joe scrambled towards him but didn't make it halfway there before he crashed into the fourth of Helvina's men. They both went to the ground punching and gouging.

Dunn snapped a hurried shot at the man in checkered pants, missed, and ducked low behind one of the wagons to avoid the pistol shot sent back his way. It smacked the wall behind him and went on through the planking, barely missing his head.

Dunn shifted position, duckwalked the length of the wagon, and peered around the end of it. Injun Joe and the man he had been fighting with were both sitting on the seat of their pants barely six feet apart from each other, Joe with his back against a wagon wheel, and the other man with his back against one of the middle barn posts. Both had their pistols out and leveled, but Joe got off the first shot. He pulled his trigger and kept on pulling it. His victim managed a single shot of his own before he slumped over dead, and Joe grunted and jerked at the impact of a chunk of soft lead boring through his thick body.

By then, the two human torches and the light they provided were burning low and the flames only cast the dimmest of flickering red light. Budge Love, with his hair singed almost entirely off his head and one side of his face blistered and burned past recognition, used the last of the life left in him and crawled across the floor and groped at the ankles of the man in the checkered pants. He could have been still trying to fight, even in his last throes of life, but it looked to Dunn more like Budge was begging to be put out of his misery. The man in the checkered pants obliged, and fired the last round from his pistol into Budge's upturned, snarling face.

The other burning man, already dead, lay off to one side, still smoldering, and the last flames flickering on one of his shirtsleeves had set fire to the layer of loose hay and powdery manure fluff coating the floor of the barn. In seconds, the flames went from nothing to a blaze.

Injun Joe swung his revolver in line with the man in the checkered pants, cocked it, and fired, but his hammer snapped on an empty chamber. The man in the checkered pants, also with an empty gun, threw his pistol at Joe and snatched up a Winchester off the floor. He fired once at Joe and pivoted on the balls of his feet and shot at Dunn from the hip. He worked the Winchester's lever fast and wild, and the shots came in one continuous roar. A bullet hit the wagon near Dunn's face, and a second one struck the ground at his feet, stinging him with dirt and debris. He scrambled back behind the cover of the wagon while he groped for his second pistol. More bullets knocked chunks from the wagon or hit the walls. The fusillade of lead was so hot and heavy that Dunn could do no more than lift one pistol up over the wagon top and fire blindly at the man in the checkered pants.

The Winchester's magazine finally ran dry, and at the same time Injun Joe lunged to his feet and lumbered by the man in the checkered pants, who was frantically looking for another weapon. Joe went past the wagon that Dunn was hidden behind and crashed against the wall like a wild bull, all three hundred pounds of him thrown into his charge. Wood splintered and loosened nails screeched, and then he bounced back and hit it again with his shoulder. His second effort was enough to bust a hole in the wall half the width of him, and he clawed at the edges of it and ripped loose another plank until he could get through the opening.

Dunn fired one more blind shot, then dove out the hole in the wall behind Injun Joe, tearing his shirt and scraping his belly on the busted lumber in the process. He ran fifty yards across open ground before he looked back at the barn, and saw the man in checkered pants coming out of the blazing doorway of the barn brandishing the rifle. A bullet cracked through the tree limbs beside Dunn, and then he was running again.

His line of retreat took him into a dense thicket of trees and tangled brambles, and he tripped and fell headlong to the ground. He was scratched and cut and panting by the time he had covered another fifty yards and crashed into Injun Joe.

The big Indian leaned against a tree, and his breath was coming in ragged heaves. "We played hell."

"How hard you hit?" Dunn asked.

Joe groaned and Dunn took that as affirmation that Joe's wound was a bad one.

"Do you think that was all of them?" Dunn asked.

"I don't know. Maybe," Joe replied.

The sound of running horses on the road drew their attention. There was more than one rider, but it was impossible to tell how many.

"That fellow in the checkered pants might have been the Devil himself," Joe said.

"Who was he?" Dunn asked.

"Never laid eyes on him before."

"Whoever he was, I owe him one."

Dunn rose and began to slip through the tree back towards the store.

"Where are you going?" Joe asked.

"I'm going to see if I can find our horses."

"They'll kill you for sure."

"Come help me."

"I'm hit bad."

"Suit yourself." Dunn moved through the darkness, and the fear and adrenaline had him jumpy and his senses tightly wound to the point he was pointing his pistols at every shadow and at every sound.

After half an hour he came back leading a pair of saddle horses. One of the horses had belonged to Jesco Love, and the other one was Joe's.

"Are they gone?" Joe asked.

"They're gone, but that storekeeper is forted up and so is somebody in the house across from the store. I had to be careful they didn't take a shot at me," Dunn said.

"Lucky they didn't. Probably think we're trying to burn them out."

"Think you can ride?" Dunn asked as he got up on Jesco's horse.

"Where are you going?"

"I'm going to kill that fellow in the checkered pants, and that bitch that put him on us," Dunn said. "And when I'm through I'm going to find Morgan Clyde and do the same for him."

"You're biting off a pretty big chunk."

"Are you coming with me? I'd think you'd want to get even."

"I don't know if I can get on a horse."

"Stay here and bleed, then." Dunn reined his horse around and put him to a walk.

Joe did get on his horse, and the pair of them skirted the settlement under the orange glow of the burning barn. When they were far enough away from the settlement they found the road again and struck out on it going west towards Eufaula. Behind them, a column of embers rose into the sky like lightning bugs and drifted across the face of the moon.

Chapter Thirty-Four

Townspeople stopped what they were doing and lined the street to watch when Morgan and his posse arrived back in Eufaula in the late afternoon of the following day. Most of them noticed that there seemed to be something wrong with Marshal Clyde and that some of the other posse members bore wounds, but most of their attention landed and stayed on the body of their local brickmaker riding on the travois. Whispered speculation was soon going through the ranks of those gathered.

There was no jail in Eufaula, but there was a doctor in town, a young man who had only recently hung his shingle out along the railroad tracks claiming his prowess in all things medical. They left the brickmaker under his care, for the man was in no shape to be a flight risk, whether it be a jail or a doctor's office, either one.

The doctor also gained two other patients. Both Lieutenant Clyde and Cumsey turned themselves over to him to have their wounds examined.

"This new sawbones ought to be paying us a commission for bringing him so much business," Dixie said.

Morgan barely glanced at him. Dixie thought he looked a cold, clammy kind of pale.

"Old Doc Chillingsworth never had a sign that fancy," Dixie said looking at the doctor's shingle hanging out over the street from the roof of the porch in front of his office.

"That's because Chillingsworth was drunk when he painted

his," Morgan said.

"You ought to go in there and have him take a look at you before you come down with the pneumonia."

Morgan only shook his head and rode on to the livery barn. Dixie noticed how slowly he dismounted.

"Why don't you let me put your horse up?" Dixie asked. "I reckon your stubborn pride can let me do that much for you."

To Dixie's surprise, Morgan nodded at that and handed him one of the zebra dun's bridle reins. He walked away without speaking a word.

"Where's he going?" Dixie asked.

"Same place I am," Moshulatubee said over the back of his horse he was unsaddling. "A good soft hotel bed sounds mighty fetching right now. Soon as I send a few telegrams at the depot house, I'm going to rent me one and have a nice long sleep."

Dixie was intent on watching Morgan walking to the hotel, and almost didn't notice Cumsey come riding by the front of the livery. "And where are you going? Thought you were getting your backside patched back together."

Cumsey grinned and pulled his horse up. "Oh, that doctor poked and prodded me enough to make it hurt, then he told me that my wound was already healing closed and all it needed was a little time and rest. Slapped a little salve and a fresh bandage on it and charged me two bits."

"Are you hunting a feather mattress, too?"

"You boys have your feather mattresses. Me, I got a pretty gal to see," Cumsey said. "You figuring on stopping me?"

"Morgan's trying to do you a good turn. I wouldn't run on him," Dixie said.

Cumsey frowned over that. "You tell him he can find me over by the Ashbury schoolhouse if he needs me."

Mention of Cumsey's sweetheart made Dixie think of Molly. He was still thinking of her after Cumsey was long gone and he had finished stabling his and Morgan's mounts. By then, he had decided that he would tell Morgan he was going home to be with Molly. Furthermore, he would tell Morgan that he wouldn't be going back out after Dunn if that's what Morgan intended to do once he was over his illness. He had barely left the livery barn when Noodles came out of his barbershop and crossed the street to meet him.

"Did Signora Molly find you?" Noodles asked.

"Find me?"

"She come here this morning looking for you. She say she is going to find you."

"She walked all the way to town?"

"No, she ride a horse."

"What horse? What color?"

"A red one with lots of white hairs."

Dixie slapped his leg in frustration. "That roan filly is barely broke to saddle, and half flighty to boot. I don't know which is worse, her riding that roan or being out on the roads the way things are lately."

"I think she will be all right."

"That's what McAlester's woman probably thought, too, before she got taken. Which way did she go?" Dixie asked.

Noodles pointed down the street to the south. "I think she say she go to Canadian Station."

"You got a horse I can borrow?" Dixie asked. "My mule's wore out."

Noodles shook his head. "No. Horses cost much and I am a poor man."

Dixie forgot about Noodles and was soon lost in his own thoughts. The Sicilian barber understood that it was best to leave him alone and went back to the barbershop.

What are you up to this time, Molly?

Dixie so fully dwelled on his worries that he didn't notice

Helvina Vanderwagen until she was almost right on top of him. She was riding a horse and leading two others towards the livery barn.

"Out for a ride?" he asked with a bend of his hat brim as a matter of politeness and good manners.

"Of a sort," Helvina said without stopping.

"Go far?" Dixie asked more out of a loss of something to say than because he was curious. Helvina Vanderwagen had always made him uncomfortable and out of sorts when he was around her.

"Not far. Just out to tend to a little business matter."

"You're usually fond of traveling in your buggy. Can't say I've ever seen you horseback," Dixie said.

"One must do whatever it takes to succeed."

"Well, I hope it works out like you want." Dixie didn't like the sound of his own words, but he couldn't seem to stop himself from saying foolish things. Helvina cared as little about what he thought of her dealings as she did the three-legged, tick-ridden stray dog that she was always threatening and scolding away from her hotel porch.

"I'd say it went fine," Helvina replied as she rode on to the barn, almost riding over the top of him in the process.

He dodged out of her way, and it didn't come to him until then to wonder why she was leading two spare saddled horses. For a moment, that struck him as odd, but he didn't spend much time dwelling on such an observation before he went back to thinking about Molly. Mostly, he was worried that if Helvina had rented three of the livery's horses, then there would be none left for him to go find Molly.

Damn, Molly, why couldn't you stay home?

Maybe Morgan or the Lighthorseman knew somebody who would loan him a horse. At least his recent troubles were over, and the risks of posse work behind him. Morgan's manhunt was as good as done, whether he would admit it or not. Since leaving his home, Dixie had feared that something might happen to him that would leave Molly alone on the farm for good. However, he had come through the hunt unhurt, and now whatever was left of Dunn's gang was far and gone from him. Now he could focus on finding her and talking her out of whatever foolishness she had thought up this time. She was awfully stubborn and often became determined to do the strangest things, like riding a green broke filly that he could barely ride himself just because she wanted to or to prove to herself that she could.

He started towards the hotel, hoping that Morgan and Moshulatubee weren't asleep yet, and his back was barely turned when Charlie Dunn and Injun Joe topped Cemetery Hill and stopped their horses to look over the town.

The cemetery was far enough away that nobody noticed the outlaws' arrival except for Hank Bickford. He was working under the roof of his blacksmith shed, trying to heat a broken wagon axle so that he could hammer weld it, when he looked up and spied the two badmen sitting their horses at the edge of Clyde's Orchard. The overgrown fence around the cemetery almost hid them, but there they were plain as day from his angle. Hank was a peaceful man, but he had lived long in the territory. Long enough to go through all kinds of trouble, and long enough that he knew men on the scout when he saw them. He had also seen Morgan's and the posse's arrival back in town, and considered how their coming and the two outlaws up on the hill might go together. He came to no concrete conclusions, but some of the general inferences he came to set the hair on the back of his neck to sticking out like porcupine quills and a shiver of warning ran down his spine.

"What are you looking at?" his wife, Lottie, said as she

pumped the leather bellows to add some air to the coal flames in his forge basin.

Hank set his hammer, tongs, and the red-hot axle on the anvil and walked to the edge of the shed and took one more look up the hill. Then he turned back to her. "I think I'll quit this for now and go to work in the woodshop."

"You just got that axle hot enough to hammer," his wife said with her hands on her hips and a put-out look on her face. Lottie was a big woman with a temper almost as bad as Red Molly's, and a disdain for things that didn't make sense. And she had no compunction about letting her husband know when she thought he was making bad decisions.

"It can wait," Hank said. "Why don't you go on to the house."

"I could help you in the woodshop."

"I can manage it myself, and I'm sure you have your own work to tend to."

"You want me to bring you some lunch?" Lottie was still frowning.

"I'm not hungry."

"I suppose you'll skip supper, too."

"I expect I'll work late tonight."

Lottie gave him one last look, grunted her displeasure mostly to remind him that she was, indeed, displeased with his reticence, and then stomped off towards their house nearby.

"Oh," Hank called after her.

She stopped and looked back. "You changed your mind about lunch?"

"No, I was just trying to remember where I put my pistol."

"It's in the chest at the top of our closet."

"Get it for me, will you? Leave it on the kitchen table for when I get home. I imagine it needs a cleaning."

"You're acting like you've lost your mind. That axle fixed would have put two dollars in our can, but you quit to go to the woodshop and piddle around at what suits you. And now you're talking about cleaning that rusty old gun when you haven't carried it in so long that you don't even know where you put it. What in the Sam Hill has come over you?"

"Never you mind."

"Don't you tell me *never you mind.* If I knew any more, I'd fix that axle myself."

"The blacksmith shop can wait," Hank said.

She saw where he was looking, and shaded her eyes with her hand and had her own look at the men up by the cemetery. "Isn't that Charlie Dunn?"

Hank nodded, impatient for her to leave him alone.

"I never have liked Charlie," she said. "There's something about him that's not right. Wouldn't turn my back on him for nothing. And that Indian with him doesn't look any better."

"No he doesn't."

"Hmph," she said.

"Couldn't have said it any better myself," Hank muttered to himself as he went inside his woodshop.

Lottie could scold him all she wanted. She might not know it yet, but he was pretty sure that his town was about to be in greater need of coffins than it was wagon axles. And he had sold his last good cedar box the day before.

Chapter Thirty-Five

Red Molly was almost to Canadian Station when she met the posse that had ambushed her husband on the road. One of them waved his hand in greeting, and the roan filly beneath her was startled at the movement and shied sideways so hard that Molly almost fell from the saddle.

She righted herself through some minor miracle and got the filly back under control. The last few miles of her journey were causing her to rethink her choice of mounts. The filly was prone to spooking at the most mundane things along the roadside. A weed stalk waving in the wind might appear to the filly as some monster about to eat her. Molly had assumed that the horse's antics would cease once they had traveled far enough to cut some of the edge off her, but it had gotten no better, regardless of the sheen of sweat darkening the filly's hair coat. And it had taken her half an hour to coax the filly on to the ferryboat to cross the river, getting herself dragged and jerked around at the end of a bridle rein in the process when the filly repeatedly tried to wheel and flee.

But she had seen Dixie handle far more cantankerous horses, and the filly was a pretty thing with an especially smooth trot. When behaving, the filly was a pleasure to ride. She vowed that the spirited young animal wasn't going to get the best of her. She also swore that she would ride the filly every day once she had found Dixie and returned home. And maybe she could help him exercise a few more of the horses as they needed it. It would be a way to pull her weight on the farm and help him, and that fit with her newfound determination to talk him out of moving to town. She had always been a little scared of horses, but she had to admit that riding down the byways on a fancy-stepping steed to be an enjoyable feeling.

She expected some of the men to laugh at her for almost falling off the filly, but none of them did. She recognized several of the men in the group; one of Eufaula's storekeepers was among them, as well as one of Preacher Pickins's deacons down at the Methodist church, and another man who worked on one of the Katy's railroad crews and who used to frequently enjoy a drink in the back of her shop. It was obvious that the party had been traveling overland for some time, for they were grimy and their horses caked with dried sweat and road splatter. She wondered what had so many of them away from town and journeying together.

"Hello, Molly," the railroad worker said. "Long time, no see."

Molly gave him a smile, waved, and considered other things she detected about the group of men. Most of them had a hangdog air about them, and she had a strong suspicion that several of them had been drinking and were now suffering hangovers.

"What has you out on the road?" Molly asked as she brought the filly to a stop.

Several of the men passed uneasy looks between them. It was obvious that something had recently gone wrong for them.

"Oh, we've been out trying to help get J.J. McAlester's family back to him," one of the men said.

"I take it you didn't have any success."

Again, the men passed odd looks between them, and a few of them made as if to ride on to the river and end the conversation. There was something off about them, but she didn't know what it was. She had been around vigilantes and noose parties in more than one boomtown, but the posse didn't have that hard air or the bloodthirsty edge about them. Most of them weren't the type. She thought they ought to consider themselves lucky that they hadn't caught up to the outlaws that had taken McAlester's family, for most of them would have likely gotten themselves hurt or worse.

"You didn't happen to run across Marshal Clyde's posse, did you?" she asked the men as they began to file past her.

She received no answer, but caught one of them giving her a strange look. He averted his eyes and ducked his head as soon as she looked at him.

"Did you see Marshal Clyde or any of the men riding with him?" she asked again.

The storekeeper and the church deacon held back and waited for the others to move on. The sense of dread and the premonition of impending danger that had driven her to go look for her husband came back stronger than ever when it became apparent they didn't relish saying whatever it was that they were about to say.

"What is it? Spit it out," she said.

"Ma'am," the storekeeper replied, "I have some bad news."

"Don't tell me something has happened to my husband."

"Your husband's with Marshal Clyde's posse?" the deacon asked.

"He is. Now tell me why you are all acting so strange."

The two of them shared a look similar to what the others had done earlier. The deacon wouldn't look her in the eyes, but maybe that was because he knew the kind of woman she had once been, as if giving her the courtesy of looking at her during a conversation might somehow taint him.

"Ma'am, I'm afraid . . ." The storekeeper hesitated.

"If something happened to Dixie, you had better tell me now." She felt the red rush up her neck and into her face.

"We came across Marshal Clyde's posse. They had the McAlester boy and we mistook them for the outlaws who took him. Some of the men accidentally shot at the posse."

"What? Was anyone hurt?"

The storekeeper shook his head. "Nobody was hurt, at least I don't think so."

The deacon gave a scoffing exhale. "Tell that to Decker if he's still alive."

"Are you sure? What about my husband, Dixie Rayburn?" Molly asked with her voice rising.

"He was with Clyde," the storekeeper answered. "And he wasn't hurt."

"But you said somebody named Decker might die. Are you sure that Dixie wasn't injured?"

"I know your husband, or at least he has come into my store on a few occasions. Decker that we mention was one of the men with us. Once we realized our mistake, we called a parley with Clyde and rode over to set things right and apologize. Clyde pistol-whipped Decker and beat him half to death. Granted, Decker was drunk and so were some of the others. That's the main reason the fiasco went as far as it did, but there was no call to try and kill him. It was a bad day all around, and I'm ashamed to have been a part of it. We both are."

"That's right," the deacon said. "Now if you don't mind, we'll move on."

They left Molly sitting her horse in the road with her mind spinning in a thousand directions at once. Although they had assured her that Dixie had come through the ordeal unscathed, she couldn't help feeling that they might be mistaken. After all, they had admitted to drunkenness and confusion leading to their attacking the lawmen. Who knew what else they might have got wrong?

"Where's Marshal Clyde's posse?" she called after the men.

The storekeeper twisted at the waist and looked back at her. "We saw the marshal's posse set out to the north before we went our own way. My guess is they were headed back to Eufaula, same as we are. That's what has most of us so nervous. Who's to say Marshal Clyde won't come for us like he did Decker?"

Molly didn't catch any of his words past the revelation that Morgan's posse was likely on its way back to Eufaula. She turned the filly back towards the river, and kicked her hard with both heels. When the filly was too slow to get up to speed, she used the tail of her bridle reins to whip her across the hindquarters. Startled, the filly shot forward like a runaway train, almost unseating Molly. When she passed the men farther up the road the filly was in a dead run, and several of them scowled at her as she showered them with mud splashed from wagon ruts still half full of rainwater.

She threw a glance over her shoulder back at them, but paid them no mind after that. A little mud on them was the last of their concerns. And it wasn't Morgan Clyde they should be worried about, either. Morgan was child's play compared to her if they had hurt her Dixie.

Chapter Thirty-Six

Three more new arrivals got off the evening train in Eufaula, and Adolphus Vanderwagen met them at the depot. Lieutenant Ben Clyde was on his way from the doctor's office to the hotel when he encountered his grandfather and the three strangers in the street. He gave the three men with Adolphus a careful study, for they were the type to draw a second look from almost anyone. All of them had a sullen air about them, and all wore town suits and narrow brimmed hats in the latest dapper fashion. One of the men was carrying a leather rifle case in addition to his valise.

"Good to see you back," Adolphus said as if he didn't notice his grandson's cautious survey of the men with him. "Your mother can stop worrying about you now. That's all I've heard since you've been gone. Come now, let's go up to the hotel and you can tell us of your latest adventures roughing it in the wilds."

Ben was still looking at the men with Adolphus. When those three went on ahead of them, Ben nodded at their backs and looked a question at his grandfather.

Adolphus shrugged. "I've decided to move my business here."

"And those men?" Ben asked.

"They are also relocating in order to maintain their employment with me."

In Ben's youth, Adolphus had often hinted at various business interests or boldly spoken of some new enterprise sure to make him a windfall, although Ben had never been quite sure how the old man actually made his money. There had been a time when he thought his grandfather lived on some inherited wealth and wise investments, but he had long since learned that the family coffers were filled with more pretense and pride than coin. He was tempted to question Adolphus about what business would require him to have three men in his employ, much less three men willing to relocate from New York, but decided against it.

There was no telling what pie-in-the-sky dreams Adolphus was pursuing, and Ben was too tired to care, not to mention that the doctor's probing had set his wound to aching. Days in the saddle and the other physical ardors of the manhunt had worn on him. And now, with his mother's hotel in sight, he couldn't keep his mind focused on anything very long except for the possibility of a hot bath and getting some well-needed rest.

His mother must have seen him coming, for the hotel's door swung open and she came across the porch in a swish of dress and with her arms open wide before he had even made it halfway up the steps. Her face was flushed and her smile was radiant as she hugged him, then leaned back to make a show of looking him over from head to toes.

"When I heard you were wounded, I positively wanted to die," Helvina said. "I was just on my way to the doctor's office to check on you."

"I'm fine, Mother."

"How badly are you hurt?" She reached for the bit of bandage protruding from inside his shirt collar.

"It's only a scratch," he said as he leaned away from her hand.

She was about to say something else when J.J. McAlester came charging out of the hotel lobby, almost crashing into them. He glanced among them, and his gaze landed last on Ben.

"You were with Marshal Clyde's posse, weren't you?" McAlester asked.

"I was."

"I'm told you brought back my son."

"He's with the doctor."

"Is he hurt?"

"The boy had a rough go of it, but he's all right. The doctor simply thought it best to examine him to make sure."

McAlester gave Helvina an odd look.

"I'm so happy for you," Helvina said. "I can only pray your ordeal is almost over, and that your wife, too, is soon rejoined with you."

McAlester grunted, looked away from her and then back again before he went down the steps and along the street at a jog.

"Poor man," Helvina said.

Adolphus joined them on the porch and nudged Ben's elbow. "Were you fortunate enough to arrest some of the scoundrels who stole that man's family?"

"No arrests, but we gave them a fight," Ben said almost absentmindedly while he stared with bleary eyes into the hotel lobby.

"Oh, dear," Helvina said with her hand raised to her mouth. "I told you not to go. I told you it wouldn't be how you imagined it."

Ben kept looking into the hotel lobby. "No, it wasn't anything like I thought it would be."

"What about Mrs. McAlester?" Adolphus asked.

"They got away with her." Ben's head turned slowly to gaze at his mother. "I was surprised to learn that the leader of those outlaws was once in your employ. Charles Dunn, I believe is his name."

"Charlie?" Helvina's eyes widened and her hand remained at

her chin. "Oh, that is a nasty surprise."

"So, he did work for you?"

"For a time. I must admit I sensed something wrong about him. That's the reason I let him go, though I never suspected such as this from him."

"Well, your feeling was correct. That's a bad bunch he's leading. Hard to believe men like that even exist," Ben said.

"That's what you did not understand. It's why I tried to keep you from going."

"I told you, Mother, I'm still in one piece."

"So you are, but it's still best to keep oneself somewhat removed from such . . . events . . . away from the taint and distaste of those kind of men."

"Keep away? That could have been you who was stolen. What would you have me do then? Leave you to your fate so that I don't have to deal with the unseemly?"

"I saw how it brought your father down, and I won't have that happen to you."

"What brought him down, Mother?"

She waved a hand at him, only a quick, lazy flick of her wrist and her fingers, as if to dismiss his question as something less than it was. He started to go inside the hotel.

She put a hand on his chest to stop him. "Don't be mad. You know I only worry about you."

Adolphus cleared his throat. "Why such gloomy conversation? How about we share the good news with him."

"Ah, yes," she answered. "How would it strike you to hear that your mother's business is about to greatly expand?"

Ben's voice was flat. "Is it now?"

"Good fortune has dropped an excellent opportunity in my lap, and your grandfather and I were only this morning discussing who would be best to oversee the management of the business."

Ben's gaze shifted between them. "I suppose you mean me."

"Exactly."

"All right then." He leaned slightly against her hand still pressing against his chest.

"You're not the least bit excited?" she asked.

"I just want some sleep. We can talk about it later." He gently pushed her hand down and started past her.

"Here I tell you that I'm about to make you one of the richest men in the territory, and you won't even give me the time of day!" she threw at his back. "Sometimes, Ben, you floor me. How can you ever hope to be respected if you don't even respect your own mother? I do my best to give you everything I can . . . to make sure you . . ."

He paused in the doorway and looked back at her over his shoulder. "I'm perfectly capable of earning my own way, Mother."

"But . . ."

"Do you think the men I command respect me because of my rank? Oh, they obey because they have to, but they only respect you when you earn their respect. You never liked me being a soldier, but it has taught me that much."

"Well . . ." she gasped.

He disappeared into the hotel without another word, leaving Helvina and Adolphus on the porch.

"The boy grows more stubborn every day," Adolphus said. "That troubles you, doesn't it?"

"He's always been stubborn, just like his father, but he'll understand once I get a chance to explain things to him."

Adolphus tapped the tip of his walking cane on the end of one porch board and then looked up at her. "How much do you intend to explain to him? As much as I love him, I'm afraid our Benjamin lacks that certain mettle that it sometimes requires to turn ambitions into reality. How would he take it if he knew the extent of your machinations?"

"Perhaps no better than he would if he learned of yours," she answered.

"True, true. I guess we will have to continue looking after him and keeping our efforts towards his well-being to ourselves."

Helvina frowned at him and then cast a critical eye at the three men waiting on the edge of the street just off the porch. She pointed a finger at them. "Yours?"

Adolphus nodded. "As you said to Benjamin, it appears that the Vanderwagen holdings are about to greatly expand. As such, I thought to provide additional manpower."

She arched an eyebrow at him. "For the Vanderwagen name? For Benjamin?"

"But of course."

She gave a grunt of disdain. "You mean you intend to try and horn in on my hard work in whatever fashion you can."

"Ah, Daughter, you hurt me. Truly, you do."

She gave him a frown so like his earlier one that neither could have denied their family relation. "Go be a good father for once and find Bert Huffman for me. I need to talk to him."

"I don't know where he is."

"Find him."

Adolphus sighed. "No rest for the wicked. Isn't that what they say?"

Chapter Thirty-Seven

Charlie Dunn ducked under the low tree limbs and wove his way through the tangle of greenbriers and undergrowth with the nimbleness and ease of a rabbit. In the midst of the thicket he came to a small clearing where two horses stood unsaddled and tied to a cedar tree at the center. He could barely make out the form of Injun Joe lying on a blanket underneath the same shadowed canopy in the fading light of dusk.

The big Choctaw scooted back against the tree trunk until he was sitting upright and gathered his Winchester rifle across his lap. "That you, Dunn?"

"It's me," Dunn said as he hunkered down at Joe's feet.

Joe readjusted his position slightly, and grunted and grimaced at the pain the movement caused him. There was blood, both dried and wet, all over the Choctaw's shirtfront, and two blue-bodied blowflies were buzzing around him.

"Where you been?" Joe asked. "Thought you had run off."

"I took a look around town."

"Anybody see you?" One of the blowflies had landed on Joe's cheek, but he didn't bother to swipe it away.

Dunn shook his head and then looked back over his shoulder at the thicket that lay between their hideout and town. "Nobody saw me."

"What are we going to do?" Joe asked in a voice that was short of breath. He laid the Winchester on the ground alongside his right leg.

"I found that bastard in the checkered pants." Dunn adjusted the pistol under one of his armpits and craned his head one way and then the other, as if the muscles in his neck were tight and bothering him. "He and McAlester's wife are hid out in a little shack at the edge of town."

"I got a hole in my guts," Joe said. "I need a doctor."

Dunn went on as if he hadn't heard Joe. "Figure I'll go back into town tonight."

Joe groaned and it sounded to Dunn like nothing so much as the sighing exhale of an exhausted horse. He remembered as a boy seeing an overworked cart horse buckle its knees and go down in the cobbled street, unable or unwilling to pull the load hitched to it another inch. No matter how the horse's owner had whipped and cursed it, it wouldn't get back up. And it had made that same, groaning sigh as it quit.

"I got to get to a doctor," Joe said. "You've got to help me."

"You want to get yourself hung?"

"It's not you that's shot. You ain't dying."

"Who says you're dying? And who ever said I'm supposed to be your keeper?"

"My guts are torn to pieces. I can smell it."

"That's only fat meat and blood you're smelling," Dunn said. "You'd be dead already if you were gutshot."

"I heard a hoot owl over there in those trees before you came back," Joe said. "He hooted three different times."

"What in the hell is that supposed to mean?"

"My grandma said that if you hear an owl hoot three times it means somebody's going to die before daylight."

"That's the stupidest thing I ever heard. If somebody died every time an owl hooted in these woods, we'd all be dead. There wouldn't be a person left alive in the whole territory."

"You believe what you want, but my people know things you white men will never know," Joe replied.

"You ain't dying, you damn fool Indian."

"You don't know. You got to get me to a doctor." One of Joe's hands darted out and grasped Dunn's shirtfront, jerking the smaller man to him. Joe's other hand lifted the barrel of his Winchester and pressed the muzzle against Dunn's jaw. "You hear me?"

Their faces were only inches apart. Even in his weakened state, Joe held the rifle effortlessly one-handed. The steel of the rifle barrel pressing against Dunn's flesh was like a ring of ice, even on a warm, humid evening.

Dunn's eyes blinked rapidly, and between one of those blinks his straight razor appeared in his right hand. He put the blade to Joe's neck.

They stared at each other for a matter of a few heartbeats, and Dunn's eyelids flickered like the batting of moth wings. Joe lifted his chin higher, but his eyes never wavered from Dunn's wild stare.

The Choctaw's great chest rose and fell like a set of deflated blacksmith bellows and the wildness in his dark eyes dimmed. Slowly, Joe hooked his thumb over the Winchester's hammer and let it down. The rifle fell away and so did Joe's hold on Dunn's shirtfront.

"All right, so you're dying," Dunn hissed. "Nothing you can do about it. But what you can do, is die like a man. Hear me? Answer me, damn you!"

Joe nodded his chin the tiniest fraction, and even so little of a movement caused the razor stinging his flesh to draw another few drops of blood.

Dunn pulled the razor away from Joe's neck. "Before too long you can drag that fat ass of yours and that rifle to that shack I told you about and help me get us a little payback."

"I . . ." Joe started.

"Give hurt for hurt," Dunn said. "Don't sit here crying in the woods. Take one or two of those sons-of-bitches with you when you go. Make them remember Injun Joe and all that warrior stuff you're always talking about."

Dunn folded the razor closed with a snap. All the while, he never quit staring at the suffering Indian.

"Warriors," Joe said in what was barely a whisper.

Dunn nodded. "They're going to remember us, Joe. One way or the other, everybody in the whole territory is going to know who we are. If we can't beat them, we'll lay them out hip deep in the street. They'll think God's own plague has come down among them, blood and fire."

Chapter Thirty-Eight

Molly thought she was going to lose consciousness, but somehow she didn't. She thought she would scream but couldn't. She closed her eyes against the pain running like a tremor through her body from head to toe, and her back arched and her feet thrashed as she struggled to suck in a breath of air. That first breath came after a panicked eternity, a wheezing gasp that felt like shards of glass piercing her lungs and chest from the inside out. Air, precious air.

The hard road felt even harder between her shoulders where it had struck her, and she rolled onto her belly and tried to get her hands under her while she wheezed and the tears ran from her eyes. Only a part of her mind registered the sound of the roan filly's fading hoofbeats.

It had all happened so fast. One moment she was on the filly's back, and the next she was lying on the ground. She rose to her feet, and by then the filly had already run out of sight.

Her recrossing of the South Canadian on her way back to Eufaula had taken far too long. And waiting for the ferry and then riding out its slow drag across the muddy brown waters was almost more than her impatience could tolerate. She didn't wait for the filly's hooves to touch dry ground. As soon as the ferryman dropped the gate on the north bank she was up on the filly's back and whipping and kicking, leaping the frightened horse off the ferry in a thump of hooves. The ferryman barely managed to get out of her way, and threw some choice words after her as she and her horse charged up the steep riverbank and disappeared over it in a cloud of sprayed sand.

It was only a few miles from the river to Eufaula, and she let the filly run. Accordingly, they veritably flew down the tree-lined wagon road. Her red hair became unbound and it flew behind her. Those flaming tresses flapping behind her in the wind and the fierce look on her face could have passed her for some wild Celtic warrior or priestess.

Not long into the filly's sprint Molly had spied something lying across the road in front of her. It was some kind of snake, and a big snake at that. Its length nearly stretched from one edge of the road to the other.

She barely had time for what she was seeing to register before the filly was almost on top of the snake. Like Molly, the flighty filly also saw the serpent at the last second. Instead of scotching to a stop, the filly made a wild, twisting leap over it. Falling from the saddle during that leap was the last thing Molly remembered.

Remembering the snake made Molly cast a fearful glance around her, but it was nowhere to be seen. With her breathing coming a little easier, she examined herself. Nothing seemed broken, and other than a scrape on the heel of one of her palms, she was uninjured. But her head was already aching, and her entire body hurt and felt as if none of her joints were put together as they had been before her fall.

She straightened her dress about her, swiped a strand of her hair out of her face, and started up the road after the fleeing roan filly. She hoped she didn't have to go too far on foot, because the more she walked the more she began to wonder if she wasn't hurt worse than she thought.

She walked almost a mile, and by then her head was hurting so badly that she was nauseated. And there was still no sign of her horse. It was at that point that she decided she needed to sit down for a while and gather herself. She would go on into town after a little rest.

She found a suitable tree growing close to the road edge and sat down on the ground with her back to its trunk. She was sitting there when she fell asleep.

Chapter Thirty-Nine

Morgan woke up in a tangle of sweat-clammy sheets. The night's fever had left him drained and thirsty, and he lay there for a while before he could summon the energy to swing his legs over the edge of the bed and place the soles of his bare feet on the hardwood floor. Morning light was showing through the curtains. There was an enamelware pitcher on the dresser near the window, and he rose and went to it. The floorboards creaked under his weight, and he thought that sound could have very well come from his bones.

There was no water in the pitcher, but he stood there staring into its hollow volume, as if by staring he could will the emptiness into something to quench his thirst. He was standing like that when he heard the voices on the street.

He set the water pitcher aside and waved back one of the curtains to where he could see down to the street below. He was watching the group of townsmen gathered near the Katy depot house when he began to cough. When he was through, he opened the window and spat a wad of phlegm out of it. That action caused one of the men at the depot to look his way and point at him in the window. Morgan couldn't hear what they were saying, but that accusing finger pointed his way and their hard stares told him who they were talking about. He left the window open and went back to his bed.

It was an hour later when he woke again to the sound of an arriving train. He felt no better than he had before, and his sheets were sour and the entire room was choking him. He dressed quickly and went down to the lobby. The first person he saw was Helvina sitting at one of the tables in the dining area. He stopped before her.

"You look awful," she said between sips of coffee. "Are you sick?"

"Where's Ben?" he asked in a hoarse voice.

"You sound as bad as you look. He's still asleep."

"Is J.J. McAlester still staying here? I need to talk to him, too."

"He is, but I believe he and his son are taking lunch over at the café. I hear it was quite a touching moment when they were reunited."

Morgan started to say more, but had to cough.

"I'd say you ought to go back to bed, or maybe go see the doctor," she said.

"I'll be fine."

"I guess that's a matter of opinion, but you might want to check to see if you still have a job before you start making plans." The look she gave him was both coy and satisfied.

"Say what you mean," he said.

"You haven't heard the news, have you?" she asked.

"What news?"

"You've made the people here mad, real mad. There is a crowd gathered at Reverend Pickins's church right at this moment. I'm surprised your ears aren't burning."

"What's good old Useless Pickins spreading about me this time?" Morgan asked at the mention of the Methodist preacher who had been a thorn in his side more than once.

"Euless," she answered. "I believe his name is Euless."

"What's that skinny hypocrite whining about now?"

"You beat that brickmaker half to death, and everybody knows it. They've wired Judge Parker demanding he fire you and that charges be filed against you for assault and attempted murder. I'll be surprised if they don't come for you with torches and pitchforks next."

"That brickmaker almost got our son killed."

She set her coffee mug down on the table so hard that a good dose of it slopped over the rim. "*You* almost got our son killed. *You.* I told you not to take him with you."

He started towards the door.

"What?" She called after him. "Are you going to go out there and hunt down everyone that's talking bad about you? Beat them, too? I suggest you start with the preacher. That will really be a good look for you."

He didn't stop or look back at her, but he did let the door slam closed behind him as he went out on the porch. When he was gone, she rose and went to the front desk. There she took up a quill pen and two pieces of paper.

Adolphus came down from his room upstairs while she was finishing writing on the second piece of paper. He looked at what she had written and frowned over what he read.

Helvina pretended not to notice his presence, and called for one of her hotel staff. Shortly, one of the young Indian girls appeared.

"Take this over to the depot and tell the telegraph operator I want these messages wired right now," Helvina said to the girl. "Tell him to immediately bring me any replies to my telegrams."

"Yes, ma'am," the girl said, and then she was gone out the door.

Adolphus stared at his daughter.

"What are you looking at?" Helvina asked.

"A U.S. senator and the Creek chief? The connections you make never cease to impress me," Adolphus said. "I take it you think Judge Parker and the U.S. marshal are not immune to political pressure?"

"I'm told that brickmaker is married to a Creek woman. That makes him a member of the tribe, and perhaps the good senator and the chief would both like to know that a federal deputy marshal has attacked a poor Indian."

"Ah, and poor Morgan has no clue what you set against him," Adolphus said.

"I simply want him out of the way for a time."

"You play dirty, Daughter."

"I play to win."

He gave her a thin smirk. "Is there any other way to play?"

She smoothed the front of her dress and dabbed at her hair before she started for the door.

"And where are you going?" he asked.

"I'm going to talk to J.J.," she said. "He's been holding out on me, but he's going to sign my papers this evening, one way or the other. The longer this goes, the riskier it gets."

Adolphus gave her his thin smile again. "Risk, yes, but think of the prize, Daughter, the prize."

Morgan moved across the street to the boardwalk alongside the depot. Moshulatubee was waiting for him there. They both stood there for a while in silence, watching the trainmen unloading some goods out of a boxcar.

"You look like hell," the Lighthorseman said.

"That's what people keep telling me," Morgan answered. "Where's Dixie?"

"Last I saw he was down the other side of the barbershop."

"Just like him to be gone when I need him."

"You've got worse problems," Moshulatubee said with a wry tone.

Morgan gave him a look. "Did that brickmaker die?"

"No, he's going to pull through. That ain't the problem I'm talking about." The Lighthorseman leaned out past Morgan in order to be able to see down the street. He nodded in that direction.

Morgan turned. The wagon had no tailgate, and when it rounded a corner before it reached them and pulled up in front of the livery, Morgan could see the blanket-covered body lying inside the wagon bed.

Everybody else on the streets must have seen the same thing, for a crowd was soon gathered around the wagon. Morgan and Moshulatubee moved to the back of the crowd. The driver got down as the crowd threw questions at him.

"Who's that in the wagon?" was the loudest of those questions.

"Don't know," the driver answered. "Found him hanging by his neck from a tree not far from Canadian Station."

Another man in the crowd reached into the wagon bed and pulled back the blanket from the body's face. "Don't recognize him."

"Me, neither," another replied.

But Morgan and Moshulatubee did recognize the body. It was the kid they had captured at the Indian baptism days before.

"You say you found him hung?" one of the crowd asked the driver.

The driver nodded. "Strung up from a high limb with his hands tied behind his back and a good manila rope around his neck. Pull that blanket back farther and see where somebody shot him before they hung him."

Two women in the crowd gasped as more of the dead outlaw's body was revealed. More people pressed closer to the wagon. Morgan and the Lighthorseman took that moment to leave.

"There's a bunch up at the church already clamoring for your arrest," Moshulatubee said as they walked. "They find out you turned over that kid outlaw to a bunch of Indian vigilantes and they will really start howling."

Morgan stopped and whirled on the Choctaw lawman. His face was livid with anger.

Moshulatubee held up both palms and took a step back from Morgan. "Easy. I'm on your side, and my fat's in the fire same as yours if they find out how that kid wound up with his neck stretched."

"Sorry," Morgan said. "I'm a little off my game."

"Yeah, you look a little shaky. No offense intended. Are we going after McAlester's woman?" Moshulatubee asked.

"We are. That's why I asked you about Dixie. And where's Cumsey?"

"Cumsey snuck off as soon as he got the chance."

"He's a damn fool," Morgan said.

Moshulatubee grinned. "Aren't we all?"

Morgan nodded. "Got me there. Why don't you go up to one of those stores and stock us up for another three or four days on the trail?"

"Already did. Figured you would go as soon as you had some rest," Moshulatubee answered. "But are you sure you're up to another hunt?"

"You're starting to sound like Dixie. I'll meet you back at the livery. I want to talk to McAlester before we leave."

"You aim to get us paid for bringing in the boy and those of Dunn's gang we put down?" Moshulatubee asked.

"I aim to find out why Dunn stole McAlester's family. Dixie said some things that put me to thinking, and the more I think, the more something about this whole affair doesn't set right."

"I gave up trying to figure out why men do the things they do a long time ago, especially you white men."

Morgan left the Lighthorseman and moved on down the street. He ducked into the first general store he came to, and was met in the doorway by a man in checkered pants going out as he was going in. They almost ran into each other. Morgan took a step back and gave way, but instead of passing through, the man in the checkered pants remained before him. Morgan noticed that the man held a wood box filled with miscellaneous groceries under one arm.

"Pardon me," Morgan rasped, expecting the man to move.

"You first, Marshal," the man said and stepped slightly out of the way and waved a hand to invite Morgan inside.

Morgan remained where he was. He got the sense the man was mocking him, though he didn't know why. "You seem to have me at a disadvantage. Don't believe I know you."

The man's face tightened slightly, as if what Morgan said somehow disappointed him, but he quickly recovered. "Virgil Beck, at your service."

Morgan made no move to offer a shaking of hands.

"People in the territory say you're hell on wheels, Clyde. Good to put a face to the reputation," Beck said after a moment of silence, and with that same trace of irritation.

"People say a lot of things." Morgan fought off the tickle in his chest and didn't cough.

Beck readjusted the load under his left arm. Morgan noticed the pistol holstered high on Beck's right hip, a Smith & Wesson No. 3 revolver. And there was the butt end of some kind of pocket pistol sticking out of Beck's vest pocket behind the chain of his pocket watch.

"What is it you do here in Eufaula?" Morgan asked.

"Oh, I'm only passing through."

"To where?"

"Now, Marshal, that's kind of rude. I seem to have somehow angered you. Perhaps you have mistaken me for someone else," Beck said. "I assure you there are no papers on me. No trouble here, and I'm sure that's just the way you like it."

Morgan's reply was only a nod.

Beck reached up and gave Morgan a tip of his hat brim.

"Only paying my respects, that's all."

Morgan put a fist to his mouth and coughed into it, and then he moved past Beck and on into the store. "I need to get some cigars."

Beck stood in the doorway and looked back inside. "Don't know if I would be smoking with a cough like that."

Morgan turned to reply, but Beck was already gone out the door and moving across the street. Moshulatubee came in the door right after he left.

The Lighthorseman looked back out the open doorway at Beck's retreating figure. "You know who that was?"

"Virgil Beck," Morgan replied.

"I was just outside the door and heard what he said. What I mean is, do you know who he is?"

Morgan nodded. "I've heard of him."

Other than the name, Morgan knew little more about Beck than the gossip told in barrooms and over campfires. Western men were prone to talking about bad men and pistol fighters, outlaws and lawmen, and soldiers and Indian wars the same way some back East talked about boxers and politicians.

Beck, it was said, had once ridden for the Royal Canadian Mounted Police. But it was after Beck left the Mounties that he made a name for himself as a pistoleer down in the States. A few years earlier, Beck had been the talk of the Kansas newspapers when he supposedly killed two soldiers in a pistol fight in a hog ranch saloon on the outskirts of Fort Hays. The rumor was that one of the soldiers had assumed a new name and joined the army to get away from a past murder he had committed. The family of his victim was wealthy enough to put a private bounty on the fugitive's head, and Beck tracked him down.

"What's he doing here?" Moshulatubee asked.

"Said he's passing through," Morgan answered.

"They say he's killed ten men."

"Do you know him?" Morgan asked.

"No, and I don't want to," Moshulatubee said. "You figure he's after that reward McAlester promised?"

Morgan shrugged. "Maybe so. I thought you were going over to the livery to get our horses ready."

"I was until I saw J.J. McAlester and his boy headed for the train. Thought you might want to know."

"Did they get on the train?" Morgan asked.

"Don't know."

"Damn, I wanted to talk to him."

Morgan hustled outside and started along the boardwalk with Moshulatubee on his heels. They hadn't gone a few steps when they met J.J. McAlester walking their way. Helvina was walking with him, but the McAlester boy was nowhere in sight. Morgan stopped and waited for the duo to come to him, while Moshulatubee went past them, headed on to the train.

"McAlester, I'd like to talk with you," Morgan said when McAlester and Helvina reached him.

"Ah, yes, I'm afraid I haven't gotten around to thanking you for the return of my son," McAlester said. "As you can imagine, this all has me in a tizzy, but you have my thanks."

"Just doing my job," Morgan said. "But I have some questions to ask you, if you don't mind."

"About what?"

"About your thoughts on why anyone would have reason to steal your family."

"How should I know?"

"You have no suspicions? No enemies you can think of? Nobody who might want to hurt you or your family?" The train was leaving the station, and the noise of it made Morgan look that way and frown. When he spoke again it was in a louder voice, which he could barely manage. "I know you and Chief Cole had a run-in a while back. Could it have had something to do with that? Is there anyone who might have a lawsuit against you or anyone you have brought suit against?"

Helvina leaned against McAlester and said, "Why, I can't imagine anyone with a grudge against J.J."

Morgan ignored her and kept his gaze on McAlester. "Think real hard, Mr. McAlester. I'm going to be frank with you. We were lucky to get your boy back. The men that took your wife are gaining on me by the minute, and I need every bit of help I can get if we stand a chance of recovering her."

"I can't think of anything offhand," McAlester answered. "And for your information, Chief Cole and I have patched up our differences."

"Are you sure there's nobody you can think of?" Morgan asked.

"I think I would know if I had angered someone to the point that they wanted this kind of revenge," McAlester said. "I treat everyone fairly and honestly. Ask anyone who knows me."

"Now, let's don't fight," Helvina said. "Surely, Morgan, you realize that J.J. has suffered a great deal in the last few days. I don't know what good harassing him with your questions will do."

Morgan frowned. "Perhaps he and I could speak alone."

"We're going to be late if we don't hurry," she said to McAlester.

"Oh, yes," McAlester stammered.

"You'll have to excuse us," Helvina said. "I have promised him a special meal at the hotel, and it is ready as we speak."

Morgan started to protest, but another bout of coughing overcame him. By the time he had recovered, the two of them were already past him. Morgan felt his temper rising, but was suddenly too weak to pursue them. He leaned against one of the posts supporting the boardwalk awning he stood under and waited for the moment to pass.

Moshulatubee came back from the depot. "McAlester put his boy on the train headed south with a nurse woman he hired."

Morgan considered that while he watched McAlester and Helvina walk towards the hotel. He couldn't help but notice the sway of her bustle and the way she clutched at McAlester's elbow.

Morgan felt the fever coming back over him, and it took too much effort to make his voice loud enough to be heard. "We'll round up Dixie and go. We know Dunn was headed north towards Briartown, so we'll see if we can pick up his trail there."

Moshulatubee held out a telegram folded in half. "You might want to read this first. Got it while I was at the depot."

The message was short and to the point. It was from U.S. Marshal Upham and informed him that he was to return to Fort Smith immediately to discuss his recent actions in the pursuit of the McAlester family's kidnappers and his arrest of the brickmaker. He was to consider himself suspended from duty upon receipt of the message. Morgan wadded the paper up and stuffed it in his vest pocket.

"What are you going to do about that?" the Lighthorseman asked.

"You read my personal correspondence?"

"Call me nosy if you want to. I may have a crooked eye, but I ain't blind and I can read," Moshulatubee said. "You haven't answered me. What now? That telegraph operator has a separate message that says the same thing, but that he's supposed to give Preacher Pickins's bunch. You ain't going to have a leg to stand on when the word gets out that your badge has been taken away from you."

"Do you want to cash in on all of McAlester's reward?" Morgan asked.

"Wouldn't mind that at all," Moshulatubee answered. "That, and there's a chance we can still get that woman back. It's a slim chance, but somebody needs to try."

"Are you going to pretend like you didn't read my telegram if anybody asks?"

"I won't lie, but what's between you and your white court doesn't interest me in the least."

Morgan stood away from the porch and his head swam and he felt woozier than he had before.

"You all right?" Moshulatubee asked. "Maybe you ought to give it one more day. Lay up here while I go over to Briartown. If I cut Dunn's sign, I'll send you word."

Morgan shook his head and started to argue, but stopped himself. "All right, you ride over to Briartown. Maybe I'll see that sawbones, or maybe I'll just take a hot bath to try and break up this crud in my chest. Get a little rest. You come back here if you don't find anything. Send someone back for me if you cut Dunn's sign or hear of his whereabouts. Take Dixie with you. He's steady and he'll know what to do."

The Lighthorseman didn't give Morgan a chance to change his mind, and he took off in a fast walk towards the livery. Morgan went to the hotel, and by the time he had climbed the stairs and made it to his room his heart was beating like he had run the whole way. He leaned against his doorjamb for a while before he finally took his key and opened the door. It had been a long time since he felt so bad, not since he had almost died of the cholera many years before.

He managed to close the door behind him and get to his bed. There he sat down and took off his boots, but stalled again. He sat like that for several minutes telling himself he should get up and go with Moshulatubee, but he didn't get back up. Instead he reached for his vest pocket where he usually kept his cigars. It dawned on him then that he had forgotten to buy more cigars at the store, and all that was in his pocket was a single stub of hand-rolled tobacco barely as long as his thumb.

He jammed that cigar stub in one corner of his mouth. He didn't light it, and only sat there clenching it while he stared at his window. He was still sitting there when he heard the clip-clop of a trotting horse passing below that window and headed out of town. He thought it was likely the Lighthorseman's horse headed to Briartown, and Morgan whispered a string of profanity and flung the cigar stub across the room.

Chapter Forty

Earlier that morning, Dixie woke up in the livery barn. There had been no vacant rooms in the Vanderwagen Hotel, so he had gone back to the livery to spend the night on a hay pile. He slept fitfully and woke up often, not because the hay didn't make a comfortable bed or because he hadn't slept in such humble accommodations before, but because he couldn't quit worrying about Molly. He saddled his mule and started out of town at the same time Morgan was in the store across the street talking to the man in the checkered pants. Dixie was glad Morgan didn't see him, for he didn't want to talk to him right then. Morgan would only try and talk him into staying with the posse.

Dixie's intention was to ride south towards Canadian Station, the way Noodles had said Molly had gone, but he barely made it past the south end of town before he spied the roan filly. She was standing saddled outside a split rail corral near a small log house in a thick stand of trees. He would have missed seeing her if the white in her hair coat hadn't stood out so.

The cabin lay a good hundred yards off the road, and the front of it faced away from him. When he rode closer, he saw that the filly was tied to the corral. He dismounted, draped a bridle rein over the top rail of the corral, and eased up to the filly until he could put a hand on her neck. The young horse showed no signs of injury, but her hair underneath the saddle blanket's edges was coated in a crust of dried sweat and road grime, as if she had been worked hard sometime earlier.

He left the filly and moved towards the front of the cabin. At that same moment he heard a woman cry out. His first thought was that it was Molly, and he lunged around the corner. The first thing he saw was an Indian woman stumble out the front door. Right behind her came a man in checkered pants. That man kicked at the woman's ankles and tripped her before she was two steps beyond the doorway. She sprawled headfirst and landed on her belly.

"You'll quit if you know what's good for you, Squaw," the man in the checkered pants said.

"I think it's you who better quit," Dixie said from the corner of the cabin.

The man in the checkered pants turned to face him. The woman remained on her belly crying. Dixie saw then that her wrists were bound together.

"Who the hell are you?" the man in the checkered pants asked.

Dixie saw the pistol on the man's hip, and his own hand was already wrapped around the butt of the revolver in his own holster. "Keep your hand away from that hog leg and step away from her. Do it now."

The man in the checkered pants smirked and gave a shrug of his shoulders like he didn't give a damn while he lifted both hands wide and above his waist. "You're butting into something that's none of your business."

"Are you all right, ma'am?" Dixie asked the woman.

"Help me," she begged.

"Ma'am, you're going to have to get up yourself." Dixie didn't dare take his eyes off the man in the checkered pants.

He yanked his revolver free of his holster and clacked the hammer back to full cock to cover the man. He tried to watch the woman in his peripheral vision.

The man in the checkered pants looked down at the pistol

Dixie held pointed at him. "Now, that isn't friendly at all."

"Please help, me," the woman begged again. "My name is Rebecca McAlester. These men took me . . ."

Dixie felt the presence of someone behind him and heard the scuff of a boot sole on the ground before her words even had time to soak in on him.

"What have we got here?" a voice said.

There came the sound of a cocking firearm, and then another voice said, "This fellow bothering you, Beck?"

Dixie looked over his shoulder and saw three men standing at the corner of the cabin, having come from the corral side of the cabin the same as he had. One of the three had a Henry rifle pointed at the small of Dixie's back. Dixie let the hammer down on his pistol, and then lowered the weapon to hang alongside his leg.

"Go ahead and drop it," the man with the Henry rifle said.

Dixie dropped his pistol. The man in the checkered pants, Virgil Beck, went to the woman and jerked her to her feet. It was then that another man came around the corner. It was Adolphus Vanderwagen.

"What do you want us to do with him?" the man with the Henry asked Adolphus.

"Put him in the cabin with the woman for now," Adolphus said.

Beck shoved the woman into the cabin, then turned to stand face to face with Dixie. "You know who I am?"

"A woman-beating lowlife, I reckon," Dixie said.

Beck hit him in the jaw with a hard right fist. Dixie staggered against the cabin wall, shook off the pain, and straightened again.

"That's for pointing a pistol at me," Beck said.

"Get him inside before somebody sees us," Adolphus said. "And catch that mule before it gets away."

The man with the Henry gave Dixie a shove in the back with the barrel of the rifle, and Dixie followed Rebecca McAlester inside.

"How did you know she was here?" Adolphus asked when they were all inside and the door was closed behind them.

Dixie readjusted his Johnny Reb forage cap until it once more sat straight on his head and rubbed at his sore jaw. When he did finally look up at Adolphus, his face was grim and hard-set.

"Who the hell are you?" Dixie asked.

Beck punched Dixie again, this time so hard that it drove the back of Dixie's head against the wall. It took Dixie a while to recover, and he was still wobbly when he bent over and reached for his rebel cap that had been knocked from his head. Beck stepped on the cap before Dixie could take hold of it.

Dixie jerked the cap out from under Beck's boot and then looked at Adolphus and spat blood on the floor. "I don't know who you are, old man, but you better hope to hell you didn't hurt my Molly. You better shoot me now if you did, because I'm going to do everything I can to end your sorry ass."

Adolphus looked among his men. "What's he talking about? Who's Molly?"

"That's her horse out there," Dixie said. "Where is she?"

Adolphus gave his men a questioning look.

"Nobody's been here except me and the squaw," Beck said. "I went to the store to get something to eat, and when I came back that roan horse out there was standing by the corral. It had one bridle rein broke in two. I took a look around, but I'm guessing that horse was tied up and pulled loose or threw somebody and ran off."

"Half the territory is looking for her," Adolphus gestured at Rebecca McAlester, "and you leave her by herself? You couldn't wait until we got here to relieve you?"

"I tied her up before I left," Beck answered. "I was untying her after I got back when she kicked me. That's how she got out the door. And then this fellow showed up."

"We need to move her before anyone else finds this place," Adolphus said. "You must have lost your minds bringing her here. There's a posse in town looking for her right now."

Beck nodded. "I saw that marshal this morning while I was buying groceries. I don't think he'll give us much trouble. He looked half dead on his feet, like he was sick or something. Either way, he didn't impress me much."

"What do you want us to do with him, Mr. Vanderwagen?" One of the other men standing in the room asked and nodded his head in Dixie's direction.

Dixie's head jerked at the mention of Adolphus's last name, and Adolphus noticed the recognition. He watched Dixie and seemed to be considering his answer.

"Wait until tonight, but get rid of him," Adolphus said.

Three miles to the east, Cumsey tried to dress as quietly as possible in order not to wake the woman in the bed. But instead of pulling on his boots, he sat in a chair and watched her sleep. Her naked form was sleek and taut as a young deer, and her coffee-colored skin looked soft and inviting against the paleness of their bedsheets with the morning light spilling through the east window. Her full lips made him want to trace a finger along the pouting shape of them, to kiss them, yet he resisted.

Watching her caused a hunger in him and a mix of feelings he couldn't put to words. And he recalled the first time he had seen her, the recently widowed young black woman that turned more heads than his own when she walked down the streets of Eufaula. Her husband had been murdered in the trouble that took place when the Katy was building through the area, and for a time she had worked as a laundress before the administration at the Indian school had the good sense to put her Kansas education to use. Not only had they given her a job teaching the children, but they had also supplied her with a house in what remained of the nearby settlement of North Fork Town, almost a ghost town since most of its former inhabitants had moved over to Eufaula to be closer to the railroad.

After a time, she yawned and stretched, and partially opened one eye for a moment to see him sitting there. "What are you doing?"

"Watching you," he said. "I've always thought you were pretty, but it never hit me just how beautiful you are until now."

She cracked an eye open one more time, then pulled the sheet over her. "Come back to bed and quit looking at me like that."

He reached down and tugged on the first of his tall-topped boots. Both of her eyes came open at the sound, and she pushed her back up against the iron headboard and sat up in the bed.

"Where are you going?" she asked as she rubbed a hand across her face.

He tucked his pants leg into the boot top and reached for the other boot without looking up at her.

"I asked where you're going?"

He shook out the boot, still unwilling to meet her gaze.

"You're leaving, aren't you?"

"I'll come back after I'm done."

"If you go, then don't come back. I mean it."

"I . . ." he started.

"I told you. You either change and make an honest woman out of me, or you don't come around here anymore," she said. "I'm tired of your coming and going, prowling around like some old tomcat. I'm tired of you saying you're going to change when you never do."

"I reckon Marshal Clyde is wondering where I'm at," he said.

"You don't owe that man anything," she answered. "You're

only looking for another excuse to run off."

"He trusts me. Asked me to ride with him."

"And then he'll arrest you when it's over."

"He said he'd speak for me to the Fort Smith men, help me work out the charges against me."

"And who says they'll listen to him, even if he keeps his word? He's just using you."

"That McAlester woman might still be alive."

"Let the white men tend to their own problems."

"She's Indian."

"Then let her people get her back. Stay out of troubles that aren't your own."

"You don't mean that," he said. "Clyde is counting on me."

"Think you're going to get that poor woman back and everybody is going to throw you a parade? Pat you on the back and tell you that you're just as good as they are?"

"You know better. It's just that . . . that I've been thinking."

"What have you been thinking about, Cumsey Bowlegs? What? All I see is you being the same fool you've always been."

"This here territory isn't going to belong to the Indians much longer. Heck, the white folks already took it, the Indians just don't know it, yet." He grimaced and leaned back in the chair. "I see how dreamy you get talking about us making a home and settling down like normal folks. You know, grabbing hold of something we can call our own. But the only way we're ever going to grab hold of anything is if we figure out a way to be part of this."

"Part of what?"

"Times are changing. Don't you see? I was born here, but I ain't never had no place. I always been in between, not Indian, not black, not white, just whatever somebody said I was. I've been a fool, just like you said, but maybe I can change. Maybe I can find me a place. Find us a place where we belong. Maybe one day a boy of mine . . . the people they'll tell him that I was one of the men who got Mrs. McAlester back. They'll say I was one of the good men, and not say I was this or that. And he'll be proud and he'll know where he belongs, that he's got roots bought and paid for. I'll earn that for him, maybe."

She snorted. "You aren't going to change their minds. My Saul used to talk like you. Big talk, and what did it get him? They beat him to death."

Cumsey knew little about her first husband, for she had never before brought him up of her own accord, and he had always avoided questioning her. But people talked, and he had heard enough of that talk to know that the man had been a cook for the railroad construction crews, and that he had been killed by another man working for the railroad, a white man who was paid for his gun more than busting his back building tracks. And he knew that it was Morgan Clyde who had avenged her husband's murder, but he didn't say that.

"Ain't trying to prove nothing to nobody except myself," he said. "And what about you? You proud of a man that sits by while a woman's been stolen? What if that was you needing help?"

"Marshal Clyde will get her back if anybody can," she said.

"It's a bad bunch he's after."

"That man was killing people when you weren't anything but a boy. Leave him to what he's good at."

"I . . ."

"Do you love me, Cumsey?" she asked as she pushed away the sheet covering her and crawled across the mattress closer to him. "Do you love me like you said last night?"

"I do."

"Do you want me?"

"More than anything."

"Stay here then and make me believe you. Stay here and let

those troubles outside that door work their course, and let it just be me and you," she whispered.

"Ain't you been listening to me?" he asked in a voice almost as quiet as hers. The caress of her lips on his neck lingered after she pulled her lips away, and he wondered what kind of fool would willingly leave her for any reason.

"Let's not fight. Come back to bed, Cumsey," she said. "I've got another hour before I have to be at school."

He took one of her hands without thinking, and she pulled gently, insistently until he felt himself getting up out of the chair and leaning towards her. A rooster crowed somewhere outside, but he barely recognized the sound. He had almost forgotten even the four walls around them.

Chapter Forty-One

Red Molly came awake with a start, and there was the sudden panic of feeling lost. She had only intended to sit and rest awhile, but it threw her off to find herself curled up on her side in a little nest among the leaf bed and to see the sun rising. She vaguely remembered having woke up once or twice in the night, but had no clue why she hadn't gotten up.

She stood and dusted off her dress as well as she could, and then walked out on the road and looked it up and down. Her body ached from her fall and her headache was no better. She wished she had a drink of water, but it was only a mile or less into town.

Worse than her headache and her thirst was the need to take the bottle of laudanum out of her wrist purse. She tried to hold back the growing anxiousness she felt overcoming her, and the twitchy, fluttery hunger, but it wouldn't go away. Her arms and hands were already itching, and she scratched at them without knowing she did so. She hadn't had a sip from the bottle since the afternoon before, but she took it out and had a tug from it before she managed a dozen steps towards Eufaula. The guilt she felt was only short-lived, for it was an old and dear friend to her, and she shoved it down inside some dark cranny inside her and moved on. Another sip from the bottle and she felt her nerves settling.

She was barely in sight of town when she spied the roan filly standing with a mule in a corral back in the trees. There was a small log cabin there alongside the corral. Apparently the filly had run all the way to town, but at least someone had penned the horse for Molly.

She turned off onto a set of wagon ruts leading to the cabin. It wound through the grove of oaks that almost hid the cabin from the road. There was nobody in sight, and she was about to call out to announce her presence when she thought she heard Dixie's voice. It was muffled, but she was sure she had heard him talking somewhere nearby, perhaps from inside the cabin.

She moved closer, and it was then that Molly recognized the mule in the pen with the filly. It was the big sorrel John mule that Dixie called Sodom. Her saddle and other tack lay against the cabin wall, and Dixie's gear was there, as well.

Molly moved closer to the cabin wall. Again, she heard a voice coming from inside the cabin, only this time it didn't belong to Dixie. It was another man speaking.

There were no windows in the cabin at the back or on the wall she stood against. She moved around the corner to where she could see the front of the cabin. Between that corner and the front door was a window, a tiny, dirty square of four-paneled glass. Curtains hung haphazardly at both edges, but there was still a thin strip of opening between them. She stepped closer and peered through it and into the cabin.

At first, she could see nothing, but then she pressed her face closer to the glass. Dixie sat on the floor of the cabin next to the rock fireplace. His hands were tied together in front of him. A dirty-faced Indian woman in a torn dress sat on the floor beside him. Molly started to call out to him, but then a man holding a rifle stepped into view. He had his back to her, and his body totally blocked her view of her husband.

Molly couldn't make out all they were saying, but she caught enough of it to understand when the man with the rifle said something about killing Dixie and dumping him in the river.

She ducked away from the window when the man with the rifle turned toward it, and when she dared peer through the glass again, she saw not him, but a man in checkered wool pants. And there seemed to be another man just out of sight of the window. All she could see of him was one of his hands and the silver-handled walking cane it held.

Molly backed to the corner again. She had put her little pistol in one of her saddlebags, but somebody had taken them off her saddle.

She could hear people moving inside the cabin, and again guessed that there were more men inside than the two she had seen. She pressed one ear against the wall and thought she heard other voices.

Her mind raced to determine what she should do. Dixie had obviously got himself in some kind of fix, and if she didn't do something they were going to kill him. She had no weapon, and she looked around for something that would serve as one. She moved along the corral fence until she found a short length of tree limb that had fallen from one of the oaks. She tested it in her hands, but found that it was brittle and half rotten in places. Any good Irish girl knew how to pick a good stout club, but she could snap that pitiful stick between her hands. It would never do to club a grown man, much less more than one of them. She wished she had a pocketknife like Dixie always carried. It wouldn't be much, but it would be something. She despised feeling helpless.

It took everything she had to walk away from the cabin. She cast several glances behind her at it before she made it back to the road. She had decided to go for help, but leaving wasn't easy. They could kill Dixie before she could get back to him.

She gathered her dress in the grasp of one fist and hiked it clear of her ankles and ran for town.

★ ★ ★ ★ ★

Helvina opened her apartment door that led out into the hallway between the hotel lobby and its kitchen. She gave a seemingly casual glance up and down that passageway before she headed to the lobby in a swish of dress fabric and the crinoline petticoat under it. She carried a leather briefcase under one arm, and J.J. McAlester and the Katy Superintendent, Bert Huffman, followed her out of her room.

She stopped short of the lobby and checked that nobody was around to hear her before speaking. "J.J., I'll remind you to do exactly as you've been told. I have men who will be watching us the whole way, and those guarding your wife this very instant have instructions to kill her if they detect anything amiss on your part or signs of anyone following us. Do you understand me? There will be no second chance at this."

"I understand," McAlester said. "Let's get this over with."

"Very well then." Helvina turned back to the lobby and led them out of the hotel.

None of the three of them noticed Ben Clyde step out of the kitchen's open door into the hallway. The young lieutenant was munching on a piece of cold bread, and he had heard everything they said. He watched them leave the hotel with a faint frown on his face.

Out on the street, the trio moved past the barbershop, then the blacksmith shop and funeral home. They were only a little ways past the edge of town when they saw a woman running towards them. When she came closer to them, Helvina recognized that it was Molly O'Flanagan. The redhead only gave Helvina a moment's glare, and she passed them by without slowing.

Helvina looked over her shoulder to follow Molly. "Now where is that Irish trollop going in such a hurry?"

Chapter Forty-Two

Somebody was trying to beat down the hotel's walls, or at least that was Morgan's first thought before he realized that it was somebody knocking on his door. He had fallen across his bed and went to sleep, and the sound startled him so badly that he staggered upright and reached for the bedside table where he usually left his pistol. It wasn't there, and it took him a few more seconds to realize that he was still wearing his gun belt. The pounding on his door sounded again, and he stalked towards it on shaky, half-numb legs.

He opened the door just as the man beating on it cocked back his fist to hit it again. It was Preacher Pickins standing there, as thin and stoop-shouldered as ever. There were three other men in the hallway with him whom Morgan didn't recognize.

"What do you want?" Morgan asked.

Euless Pickins adjusted his wire-framed glasses on his nose and lifted his turtle chin a little higher before he replied. "We wish to speak with you."

"Well, speak."

The preacher's face went taut, and the sharp point of his Adam's apple bobbed beneath his white collar. "These men with me have volunteered to ride with you to Fort Smith."

Morgan was having a hard time focusing. "They volunteered for what?"

"They are to go with you to make sure you turn yourself over to Judge Parker's court," Pickins answered. "And they will testify to your crimes."

"Testify? Not a one of them was there when your good brickmaker shot at me."

"That is not how I understand the facts," Pickins said.

"Oh, you don't?"

"Consider this a citizen's arrest," Pickins said, "I hope you will go peacefully and not force us to . . . Well, don't make this harder on yourself than necessary. I assure you that you will be treated in a Christian fashion. We only wish justice to be served."

"You wouldn't know justice if it ran over you."

"I pity your soul," the preacher said with a shake of his head.

Morgan slammed the door closed.

He hadn't even turned back to his bed before the preacher knocked on the door again. The flush of anger welled up in Morgan hotter than the fever that was already burning his body. He jerked the door open again.

"I have a telegram that says . . ." the preacher started.

Morgan didn't let him finish. "You listen to me, Useless. You listen because I'm only going to tell you one time."

Pickins started to stammer something while the others with him backed down the hallway.

"You knock again, and you better have already got yourself right with the Lord," Morgan said. "You understand me?"

Morgan slammed the door shut again, locked it, and went back to bed. There was a little clock on the dresser across the room, and he was surprised that it was only eight-thirty in the morning, and that he had only slept less than an hour before Pickins woke him. He half expected the preacher and his minions to knock again, but they didn't. He took off his gun belt, laid it on the bedside table, and fell back asleep sometime later.

That sleep was restless. First he was hot and then he was

cold. When he did find some sort of slumber it was filled with crazy fever dreams. He dreamed of the war for the first time in more than a year, and he dreamed other things that either never were or were pieced together so crazily that he wasn't sure if they were memories or the imagination of a madman. Friends and enemies long since gone passed in and out of those dreams, and he felt like a ghost in someone else's patchwork nightmare. What seemed like an eternity was actually only another thirty-minute nap, and then came a knocking on his door again. He got out of bed cursing while he bumbled his way across the room. The knocking on the door didn't let up.

His teeth were chattering while he fumbled for the doorknob. He rubbed at his eyes and tried to clear his head of the crazy visions still fresh enough to seem real. His pistol was lost somewhere in his tangled bedding, and he cocked back a fist as he opened the door. Only it wasn't Useless Pickins standing there. It was Molly.

"Thought you were that preacher." He lowered his fist and gave her an apologetic look.

It wasn't until then that he noticed how nervous and fidgety Molly seemed. She could be that way when she needed the opium, but she seemed truly frightened. He could see it in her eyes and the way she kept glancing down the hallway back the way she had come.

"I need your help. They've got Dixie," she said.

"Who's got Dixie?"

"I don't know, some men," she answered. "They've got him tied up in a cabin between here and the river. I heard them talking about killing him."

"You got away from them?"

"They didn't even know I was around. It's pure luck that I even happened to go by there and find him."

Morgan opened the door wider and left it that way for her as he went to get dressed.

"And they've got an Indian woman, too," Molly added. "I think she might be McAlester's wife."

Morgan tugged on his boots, and then slung his gun belt around his waist and buckled it. He ran his hand through his thick black hair to slick it back, and put on his hat. His teeth were still chattering, but he didn't take the time to grab his jacket.

"You look awful," she said.

"I swear I'm going to kill the next person that says that to me."

Molly grunted at his reply, and then darted out of the room. He followed her down the stairs to the hotel lobby, tucking his shirt in as he went. She was walking fast, and even the little effort it took to keep up with her had his heart racing. She waited for him at the front door while he stopped and coughed until his eyes watered.

He glanced out the glass panes in one of the hotel doors when the worst of the coughing was finished, and saw that Preacher Pickins had a crowd gathered at the depot, likely still considering what they were going to do about him.

"That fool," Morgan rasped.

"Come on," Molly said.

Morgan stayed where he was. "Have you seen Cumsey?"

"No."

"Where's the cabin at? Tell me how to get there."

Her eyes widened and she shook her head. "I'm going with you."

"No, you're going to find us some help," Morgan said. "That's what I need you to do. Look for Cumsey. I think he's around here somewhere."

"Morgan, you can't stop me! Don't even try."

"Moshulatubee won't be back from Briartown, yet, but you

find Cumsey or whoever else you think can help," Morgan said, thinking out loud. "You tell them to come running."

Molly started out the door, but he grabbed her by the arm.

"I don't need to be worrying about you. If you want to save Dixie, then listen to me and do like I asked," he said.

She jerked away from him, but didn't flee. Her face was flushed, and he thought for a moment that she was going to hit him.

"Tell me where that cabin is," he said in a quieter, calmer voice,

She started to argue, but didn't. "It's about a hundred yards past the edge of town. Take the first set of wagon tracks to the right."

"How many men were there?"

"I didn't see but three," she answered.

"Know any of them?" he asked.

"I don't. I saw two real good, but the third one, I couldn't see anything of him other than his hand and a silver walking cane."

Morgan took that news with a grim nod and went past her and out onto the porch. He gave another brief glance at Reverend Pickins's crowd at the depot. One of the men over there shouted something at him, but he ignored it and started down the street in the opposite direction, going towards the river.

Behind him, Molly waited until he had walked a few yards before she darted across the street. She gave him one last mad and stubborn glance before she went inside the barbershop.

Chapter Forty-Three

Charlie Dunn was in a foul mood by the time he and Injun Joe made it to the cabin where the McAlester woman was held. Joe had to stop often, and his wound was bleeding again before they were halfway there. The big Indian was sweating profusely, even though the morning temperature was somewhat cool.

Dunn sniffed the air during one of their breaks. He had told Joe that he wasn't gutshot, but that wasn't true. Joe now smelled like nothing more than a pile of guts. It was the smell of death. Dunn only hoped the big, dumb bastard could live long enough to help him.

When they finally came close to the cabin, Dunn guided Joe to a hump of ground screened by dense thicket. He and Joe laid down behind an old rotten log and looked at the cabin's front door about sixty yards away. There was a man Dunn didn't recognize inside the corral unsaddling a red roan filly and a big sorrel mule. And there was no one else in sight.

Come to think of it, the filly and the mule hadn't been there, either, when Dunn had spied on the place last. He wondered how many people might be inside the cabin.

"Joe, I want you to stay here," Dunn said in a whisper. "Take you a good rest with your rifle, and if that fellow with the checkered pants shows himself, you shoot him."

"What if he ain't alone?" Joe asked.

"You don't worry about anybody else. You make sure you shoot him first. Make sure he's down for good."

Joe propped his Winchester's forearm on top of the log and squinted at the cabin. Dunn rose beside him and started walking off, bent low and trying to keep cover between himself and the man in the corral.

"Where are you going?" Joe hissed.

Dunn pointed at a large hackberry tree some fifty yards away. "I'll be right over there."

From behind the trunk of that tree he would have the same view of the cabin's door, but that position would place anyone coming outside in a cross fire. Joe nodded his understanding of the tactic.

It took Dunn several minutes to move into position without being seen by the man in the corral. The woods were thick around the cabin, and made such stealth possible. Dunn knelt on one knee behind the tree trunk and watched the man at the corral go back inside the cabin. Minutes passed. A swarm of gnats and several mosquitos flew around his head and tried to land on his face. He didn't want to swat at them for fear of being seen, but the flying insects were almost more than he could take. He despised them almost as much as he despised waiting.

A half hour passed by, and the bugs grew greater in number. He could hear them scurrying in the leaf bed, and they buzzed incessantly where they flew. A squirrel barked from the treetops somewhere behind him, and a number of crows started a noisy back-and-forth, cawing until he almost couldn't think. He looked over at Joe, and could only see the Indian's rifle barrel protruding over the log. He wondered if the fat fool had fallen asleep, or if he was dead.

The sound of someone coming towards the cabin jerked his attention away from Joe. He slid one of his Colt pistols out from its shoulder holster. He knew he had unusually fast hands, but his marksmanship was something that continually frustrated him. Although, he would have admitted that to no one. Pointing a pistol at a target and hitting it seemed like a simple thing, but no matter how hard he had practiced with his weapons, he hadn't been able to master any sort of fine accuracy. And he had chosen his short-barreled revolvers for their ease of concealment. Much like the razor blade he carried, they were fine for a belly-to-belly fight, but not well-suited for a country ambush. He considered moving closer to the cabin, but there was little cover to be found in front of him.

However, he was given no chance to change positions. Soon, he could catch his first glimpses of three people walking through the trees on the far side of the corral. As they came closer, he saw that one of them was Helvina, but the other two with her were men that he didn't recognize. He glanced Joe's way again, but still couldn't see if Joe was ready.

The cabin door opened and the man in the checkered pants appeared. He stepped outside and said something to Helvina. The two men with her disappeared into the cabin, but she and the man in the checkered pants remained outside the door discussing something.

Why didn't Joe shoot? Dunn prepared himself for the sound of the Indian's rifle crack, but it never came. Dunn aimed his pistol at the man in the checkered pants, but his front sight wouldn't be still and he knew he would miss.

Helvina and the man in the checkered pants went inside the cabin and closed the door. Dunn cursed under his breath and slapped at a mosquito that had latched itself on to his neck. He felt the smear of his own blood under his fingers.

Again, he glanced Joe's way. He could barely see the top of Joe's hat this time, and was now sure that Joe was alive and awake. Yet, Joe hadn't shot. Dunn hissed another string of profanity and swore he was going to cut Joe's throat.

Joe was known to be an exceptional rifle shot, but the stupid Choctaw couldn't even manage the one simple job given to him, and now there was still the man in the checkered pants to deal with, which complicated Dunn's plan, for he fully intended to kill Helvina Vanderwagen. He had sworn that above all, but unlike the man in the checkered pants, he didn't want her killed from afar. No, he wanted her to know it was him, and to savor that recognition and the fear in her eyes. Without knowing he did it, he put a hand to the vest pocket that held his straight razor, while his eyelids began to flick like the dance of the tiny insects moving through the sunlight.

And then his head snapped in the direction of the sound of someone else coming towards the cabin. Whoever was out there was moving through the woods towards him, avoiding the trail Helvina and the others had used, and on the end of the cabin opposite where the corral stood. And whoever was coming, they were trying to be quiet. He could barely make out the occasional crunch of dead leaves and catch a flicker of movement among the trees.

Dunn didn't try to get the big Choctaw's attention to alert him to the possible danger. He simply backed farther into the woods, and moved far enough that he was confident that the new arrivals would pass between he and the cabin, and where he could observe whatever was about to happen. His new position also gave him the opportunity to retreat, if necessary.

He had barely settled behind a new tree when he saw Morgan Clyde step to the edge of the more open ground close to the cabin. There was a pistol in the lawman's hand and he seemed to be alone.

Chapter Forty-Four

Noodles was sitting in his barber chair with a newspaper held open in front of him. It was the most recent edition of the *Indian Journal.* He folded the paper closed and smiled at her.

"Ah, good to see you," he said.

"Good to see you, too," Molly replied absentmindedly while her eyes searched the room.

"I see that you are back from your journey," he said. "Did you find Signor Dixie?"

Molly didn't answer him, wasn't even looking at him, in fact.

Noodles tapped the newspaper on his lap with one finger. "We have a newspaper now. They make it in Muskogee, but maybe we get one here, soon. I think this will be a good town before long."

"You can't even read," Molly said.

"I learn. What are you looking for? Did you come to get your rent?" He made as if to get up out of the chair. "I get your money now."

"Quit worrying about the rent and keep the money until the end of the month. Have you still got Pork Chop's shotgun?"

Pork Chop had been an old, washed-out faro dealer that had once occasionally worked for her and hung around even when he wasn't working. Like Noodles, he had become one of the few in her inner circle back when she had opened the barbershop. But Pork Chop had been murdered in the fighting with Judge Story's outlaw marshals, a fight that had nearly almost got she and Noodles killed, too.

Noodles said nothing, but gave her a questioning look.

"I want to borrow it," she explained.

He went into the back room and soon returned with a double-barrel Parker 12-gauge. It was a short, stubby shotgun with double hammers and barrels that barely extended past the forearm, what some called a coach gun.

He handed her the gun and a canvas sack of brass shotgun shells. "I keep it in the wall where Pork Chop hid it."

"I'll bring it back," she said.

"You can keep it. At first I think it is a good thing to have, but now I worry that my children will find it. Plus, I no good shoot."

"Not a good shot, that's how you say it."

Noodles shrugged. "You keep."

The curtain that divided the barbershop from the back room parted slightly and a face appeared there, then another. It was Noodles's daughters with their little faces framed in canvas. Usually, they were all over her, jabbering and giggling when she came to visit, but they stayed where they were and stared at Molly and the gun she held.

"You go on now!" Noodles said to the children and waved his hands at them.

The faces disappeared and she could hear them running across the floor in retreat. She cracked the double breeches open and shoved a cartridge down both chambers, a process much less complicated and quicker than trying to load Dixie's antique old muzzle-loading scattergun. When she finished, she looked up to find Noodles staring at her with a look on his face somewhere between fear and concern, the same look those beautiful, olive-skinned baby girls had given her.

"Why are you looking at me like that?" she asked.

"Why do you want that gun?"

"I need a gun because I need a gun," she snapped at him.

"You are in trouble. I see that," he said. "I come help you."

"No, you stay here," she said as she went out the door.

Noodles's wife came into the front room, her little girls hugged to her under each arm. She was a petite, pretty woman in high-button shoes and a dark dress with a tall collar. The worry lines at the corners of her eyes wrinkled as she watched the door slam closed in Molly's wake. She gave her husband a questioning look.

"Ah, Mama," Noodles said while he put an arm around his wife's shoulders. "I'm afraid *Signora Testa Russu,* she going to shoot somebody again."

Chapter Forty-Five

J.J. McAlester went immediately across the room and stooped to hug his wife, who immediately began to cry. Superintendent Huffman took Helvina's briefcase from her and went to the table next to the woodstove and began to lay out various papers and a pen and inkwell.

Helvina paid little attention to McAlester's tearful reunion, or to Huffman's preparations. She stood with both hands on her hips and frowned down at Dixie where he sat on the floor with his back against the cabin wall.

"What's he doing here?" she asked.

Virgil Beck nodded at Dixie. "Found him snooping around."

"No, I mean why is he still here?"

"Want me to get rid of him?" Beck asked.

"That's exactly what I mean."

Beck started to take hold of Dixie, but Helvina held up a hand to stop him. Her next words were aimed at Dixie. "Where's Morgan?"

Dixie didn't answer.

"One of you go outside and have a look around," she ordered the men standing around her.

"Do as she says," Adolphus said.

Helvina glared at her father. "Are you trying to mess this up like you do everything else?"

Before Adolphus could answer her, she turned back to Dixie,

then gestured at Mrs. McAlester. "How did you know she was here?"

"I didn't," Dixie said. "I saw my wife's horse here. I've been looking for her."

Beck gave Helvina a nod. "There's a horse out there that showed up this morning with no rider."

"And the rest of Morgan's posse might be hunting all over town for Mrs. McAlester right now."

"Nobody knows she's here," Beck said.

Helvina pointed at Dixie. "He found her, didn't he?"

"I think he's telling the truth about looking for his wife."

"You think?"

"Helvina . . ." Adolphus said in a placating voice.

She glared at her father, but her attention went right back to Dixie. "You're married to that redheaded whore, Molly, aren't you?"

Again, Dixie didn't answer her.

She recalled seeing Molly running down the road on their way to the cabin. "Maybe he is telling the truth."

"That's what I was trying to tell you," Beck said.

"At least I hope it's true," She pointed again at Dixie. "Make sure you put him where nobody will find him."

"I don't need to be told that," Beck said. "I'm no more anxious for a hanging than you are."

Beck and one of the other men took Dixie by the shoulders and jerked him to his feet. The man with the Henry rifle shoved Dixie toward the door.

"You want me to tend to him?" the man with the rifle asked.

"No, I'll handle it," Beck said.

Beck opened the door and put a pistol against the small of Dixie's back. "Get moving."

Dixie stumbled out the door. For a second it looked like he might try and make a break for freedom, but the pistol was pressed against his back once more.

"Don't give me any trouble and I promise you I'll kill you clean," Beck said.

"How much does she pay you for this kind of stuff?" Dixie asked as they moved through the timber towards the bank of a small creek that fed into the river a mile farther in the direction they were walking.

"Shut up and walk," Beck said. "Purely a matter of business. Don't take it personal."

"I just wondered how much it took to buy a sorry sack of shit like you," Dixie said.

"I don't work cheap," Beck replied.

"Low-down, back shooting, bastard," Dixie said. "Why don't you give me a gun and let's see how much you're really worth."

Beck chuckled. "I'm almost tempted."

"Try me."

"All you loud Americans, so full of big talk. I'd almost shoot you for free," Beck said while he gave Dixie a hard shove in the back.

Dixie used the separation created between them to turn and face Beck. He strained at the grass rope they had tied his wrists together with in an attempt to free his hands.

Beck raised the pistol and pointed it at Dixie's head. "You can keep walking, or I can kill you right here. Your choice, but I would much prefer not to have to carry your body to the river."

Dixie glanced over Beck's shoulder and his expression changed. Beck heard the footsteps behind him and spun towards that sound with his pistol ready. The first thing he saw was a red-haired woman, and the next thing was the shotgun she held.

CHAPTER FORTY-SIX

Molly ran as fast as she could towards the cabin, but her lungs failed her before she was halfway there. She stopped, bent over, heaving and coughing with the shotgun held across her thighs, and when she straightened again, there was blood on her mouth and chin. She still hadn't caught up to Morgan, yet, and wondered if he had detoured to get help, not realizing that every moment they delayed was a moment Dixie might be murdered.

She cursed the illness that had so weakened her, and cursed Morgan Clyde's stubborn soul. Poor Dixie. He had nothing but a lunger wife and a pneumonia-riddled marshal to come for him. He deserved better.

Straightening, she took her laudanum bottle from her wrist purse, pulled the cork stopper, and took a pull of the bitter concoction. She wanted more, but fought off the hunger. It wouldn't do for her to make herself stupid on the poppy with what she had to do.

She didn't wait to strike the faint, wheel-rutted trail that led to the cabin, but cut off diagonally through the woods before she got to it in an attempt to take a shortcut. Maybe she could catch up to Morgan that way.

The oak trees had left a thick deposit of dead leaves on the forest floor, but the recent rain had left them wet and quiet under her feet. She could see the cabin faintly through the tree limbs ahead, and it wasn't until then that she began to ask herself exactly what she was going to do when she got there.

Her answer came when she arrived in sight of the cabin's front just in time to see Dixie being marched away by a man with a gun. The man holding the pistol on Dixie was the man in checkered pants she had seen before when she spied through the cabin window.

In that instant she forgot all about Morgan Clyde. She walked faster with the shotgun held in both hands, and skirted a wide semicircle around the cabin in order to stay out of sight of its other occupants. The undergrowth was dense in places and snagged at her dress. It was in one of those thicket places that one of her feet became tangled in a greenbrier vine and almost tripped her. She was jerking that foot free of the thorns when she almost stepped on top of an Indian.

The Indian was lying on his back behind a deadfall log. At first she thought he was dead, but then he opened his eyes. She pointed the shotgun at him and took a few steps away from him.

"Help me," the Indian said, and one of his hands groped for the shotgun barrel almost like he was blind.

She backed away another step, still keeping the gun on him. And she noticed then the blood all over the Indian's belly. She took a few more backwards steps, then turned and went on. She looked back once, but the Indian wasn't making any attempt to reach for the rifle lying on the log above his head.

She didn't go far before she had lost her bearings. She wasn't even sure in which direction the cabin lay. Panic rose up in her, and she strained to hear any sound that indicated where Dixie and the man with him had gone.

A faint trail like the kind wildlife or cows make showed itself ahead of her, and she turned into it. She followed its course for a ways, but still didn't come into sight of Dixie. Again, she stopped and listened. She could hear men talking ahead of her.

She cocked one shotgun hammer and moved towards that sound.

She had the sudden feeling that she was too late, and she abandoned all caution and charged forward. The voices had sounded like they were farther away, so she was shocked when she burst out into a more open expanse of woodlands and saw Dixie not twenty yards ahead of her. He was facing her way, but the man in the checkered pants stood between them with his back to her. She couldn't see the pistol he held cocked and aimed at Dixie, but she sensed what he was about to do.

The more widely scattered trees allowed the sunlight to hit the ground, and a thin covering of grass lay between she and the men. Without hesitating, she moved in a beeline towards them, and the grass padded and quieted the sound of her approach. She was about to raise her shotgun when she saw Dixie's eyes widen in recognition of her presence, and then the man in the checkered pants whirled to face her.

She stopped not ten long steps from him. His pistol was pointed at her chest and her shotgun was leveled on him without her remembering doing it. And she also realized that her hands were shaking and that she was crying.

"What have we got here?" Beck asked. "Are you going to shoot me, lady?"

"Put down that gun and let him go." Her own words sounded far off and as if they belonged to someone else, and she couldn't seem to focus on anything but the pistol in his hand.

"Molly . . ." Dixie said.

"I never killed a woman, but don't think I won't," Beck said.

"I said leave him be!" Molly screamed at him.

Beck was about to shoot her. He was going to shoot her in the face and then he was going to turn around and do the same thing to Dixie. She couldn't say how she knew that, but it didn't matter. She was already pulling the shotgun's trigger.

The shotgun roared at the same time as his pistol flamed, and she was knocked to the ground. Her shoulder throbbed, and, at first, she thought he had shot her. She dug in her heels and scrambled backwards while she groped for another hold on her shotgun. She was cocking it to ready the second barrel when she realized that the man in the checkered pants was no longer standing.

She sat upright and pointed the shotgun at Beck's body where it lay in the thin grass. The badman's hat lay a few feet from him, and it was covered in blood and gore.

Dixie rose up from the ground where he had dove to one side to get out of the way of Molly's shotgun blast. "Are you all right?"

She never took her eyes off the downed gunman, nor did she lower the shotgun.

Dixie came past Beck's body, gave it a momentary glance, and then came to her and squatted down beside her. He gently pushed the shotgun's barrels down until they were pointed at the ground, and then he took the weapon from her and uncocked it.

"Is he dead?" she asked.

"He's dead," Dixie answered while he looked her over for wounds.

She pushed him aside so that she could look at the body again.

"You don't want to look," he said with his mouth close to her ear.

He helped her to her feet, and although he tried to block her view of her victim, she saw enough. Her shotgun charge had struck Beck in the face. She felt as if she were suddenly going to vomit.

Dixie turned her around so that she didn't have to look anymore. "You did what you had to. I'd be dead if you hadn't."

"I thought I missed him."

And then she looked down at her throbbing shoulder, expecting to see a wound where Beck's bullet had struck her. Only, there was no wound. It dawned on her then that she had simply not gotten the shotgun's butt stock pressed firmly against her shoulder before she fired, and the recoil of the twelve-gauge had knocked her off-balance. That, combined with the shock of an exploding pistol point-blank in her face, likely put her to the ground.

"I'm sorry," Dixie said as she leaned on him.

She dropped the shotgun and threw both arms around his neck. "You better be, and you better never go off and leave me again."

The instant they hugged a gunshot sounded from the cabin. And then there were more gunshots. Neither of them saw Charlie Dunn fleeing through the woods past them.

Chapter Forty-Seven

"Sign the papers," Helvina said to McAlester. "Get over here and sign them now."

"I hope you hang for this," McAlester said as he helped his wife get up from the floor.

Helvina didn't like looking at Rebecca McAlester, for the Indian woman was a pitiful sight. Filthy and all but in rags, and there was a bad bruised knot on one of her cheeks. Helvina had intended to clean her up before bringing her husband to her, but there hadn't been time.

One of Adolphus's new men, the one who had gone outside to look around, came back inside. "Nobody else out there that I could see."

"Go back and keep watch," she said.

He did as he was told, leaving her in the room with Adolphus's other two men, Huffman, and McAlester and his wife. She went to the table and sat down in one of the chairs. She pointed at the chair beside her.

"Sit down, J.J., and let's be done with this," she said. "You refused to sign over your holdings until we showed you your wife. Well, there she is."

McAlester let go of his wife and took a seat in the chair. "You can't actually think you're going to get away with this."

"That's my worry," Helvina replied.

Huffman pushed the stack of papers in front of McAlester, along with the pen and inkwell. "It's all relatively easy. Sign in the places I have marked for you, and then I will hand you a cashier's check for the agreed upon amount."

"And then you and your wife can go about your lives little worse for wear," Helvina said. "Everybody lives happily ever after."

"You intend to kill us as soon as I sign, don't you?" McAlester had the pen in his hand, but held it over the first signature place rather than signing it, stubbornly reluctant just as he had earlier back at the hotel.

"There is no need of that," she replied.

"I don't believe you."

"Tell him, Bert."

The railroad superintendent leaned back in his chair. "She's telling you straight, J.J. Should you reveal our involvement in holding your family hostage, or should you contest this transaction in any way, my company is prepared to testify that you expressed an interest in selling your business, we took you up on the offer, but you had second thoughts after the deal was finalized. Subsequently, you came up with the wild story that blames Helvina and I in order to try and nullify the deal."

"Nobody will believe that."

Huffman reached over and tapped at the stack of papers. "Look closely and you will notice that all of these documents are back-dated to a time over a month ago. I believe that will fit our alibi quite well."

McAlester kept the pen poised over the papers. "You say *your* company. Does Gould know what you're doing?"

"I made Mr. Gould aware of the purchase yesterday. To say he was quite pleased is understating his enthusiasm."

"And you told him how you acquired my holdings?" McAlester asked.

"I told him everything."

"I think you lie."

"That is your prerogative. But ask yourself, if you were Mr. Gould, would you quibble about such a win or how it came about?"

"I'm not a thief."

"Perhaps not, but you are a man who right now can sell out and save his wife," Huffman said. "You will be not only saving her life, but yours as well."

"You're both disgusting."

Helvina slammed the flat of one palm on the table. "Enough with this! Sign the papers!"

"Don't sign them and you kill us, or sign them and you kill us?" McAlester said with a sigh.

"J.J.," Huffman said, "we promise you that you and your wife will come to no harm. We will move you to a different location and keep you there until things have a chance to cool off. After a time, you and your wife will leave the state, and if anybody asks, you will tell them that your wife was returned to you by someone who found her by accident. She had escaped her captors by some miraculous event, and was lost and trying to find her way home. Of course, you will be evasive about the name of her rescuer and other difficult details. And you will tell anyone who asks that they should respect the trauma that your wife has suffered and leave her to her healing."

McAlester glared at him.

"And should you think all this too complicated or don't believe we'll keep our word, I will tell you now that I have a man riding on the same train as your son. That man is under instructions to kill that boy when the train reaches McAlester. That is, unless he receives a telegram from me upon arrival telling him to leave the boy alone."

McAlester's shoulders slumped, along with his entire body. Helvina couldn't help the growing excitement she felt. McAlester might not believe the lies Huffman was telling him, but he was going to sign the papers, no matter. He had no other choice. All that would be left to do would be to put that cashier's check into one of McAlester's bank accounts and get rid of him and his wife for good. She had a certain bank clerk who she had worked very hard to curry favor with, and he would make sure that check showed to have been deposited much earlier than it actually was.

She didn't consider herself especially ruthless, but McAlester recognized the same thing she did. Allowing he and his wife to walk away would be stupidly risky, and would never work if McAlester decided to buck them.

McAlester signed his name, then signed more times as Huffman flipped the pages. Helvina rose from her chair and a rush of triumph ran through her. She picked up the cashier's check from the table and started to leave.

McAlester noticed that, and his reaction surprised not only her, but Huffman and Adolphus's two men standing guard in the room. He stabbed the sharp point of the pen into the top of Huffman's hand resting on the table. Huffman cried out, but McAlester punched him in the face and cut off the sound of his outcry.

One of Adolphus's men lunged towards McAlester to take hold of him, but the old merchant had an adrenaline rush playing in his favor and giving him strength. He bulled into the guard and drove him back toward one cabin wall. The weight of their two bodies smashed into Helvina and knocked her to the side. Adolphus's other guard had his rifle ready, but couldn't shoot for fear of hitting her or the man McAlester was grappling with.

Helvina tried to run for the door, but something tripped her and she fell. She didn't even have time to get back up before McAlester's wife stepped on her back and jerked the door open.

"Get her!" Helvina screamed.

By the time Helvina got to her knees, McAlester was down on the floor and Adolphus's man was clubbing him with the butt of the rifle.

"I said get her!" Helvina screamed again.

Huffman was standing in one corner holding his bleeding hand. Adolphus was in another corner, but he got his wits about him enough to pull a pocket pistol out from the inside of his suit coat. He pointed it at McAlester to keep him down on the floor. Adolphus's two men barreled out the door after McAlester's wife. Huffman was right on their heels.

Helvina took one step towards the open door, and then a gunshot sounded somewhere in the distance. She stopped where she was, startled, and then more guns began roaring right outside the cabin.

Chapter Forty-Eight

Morgan was almost to one corner of the cabin and about to peer around it when he heard Molly's shotgun blast. He looked in that direction, and at the same time the cabin's front door flew open. An Indian woman ran out of it, and then three men came after her. All three were intent on catching the woman, but one of them must have seen Morgan out of the corner of his eye. That one skidded to a stop and swung his rifle in Morgan's direction.

Morgan's Colt was already in his hand, and he shot the man once in the chest before the rifle could come to bear. The man staggered backward and went down on one knee. Morgan was about to shoot him a second time when a bullet splintered one of the logs beside his head. He barely had time to register the other two men, now stopped in their pursuit of the woman and faced off against him. He ducked back around the corner of the cabin just as another bullet slammed into the logs.

He was about to step back out and chance another shot when he sensed something behind him. He turned partially in that direction and saw a man with a pistol already pointed at him. It was the guard Helvina had sent outside to keep a lookout.

Morgan started to turn to bring his own pistol around, knowing all the while that he was never going to be fast enough. But a rifle boomed from the woods, and the man behind Morgan went up on his tiptoes, then toppled on his face before he had a chance to even fire a single shot at Morgan.

Morgan pressed the flat of his back against the wall, and waited for one of his enemies to come around the corner from the front of the cabin. He was waiting there when Cumsey and Ben came out of the woods at a run, ducked low and firing their rifles as they came.

Morgan moved back to the front of the cabin just as Ben's Springfield cracked. Morgan barely had time to recognize Bert Huffman before the railroad superintendent went down under Ben's gun.

Morgan was usually quick, but before he could manage to handle his only remaining adversary, Cumsey stepped past him working the lever on his Winchester. He fired three shots rapidly, and all three of them struck his victim. Soon there was nothing but black powder smoke on the air and silence.

Morgan sagged against the cabin wall with his breath coming in ragged gasps. Cumsey put a hand on his shoulder to steady him.

"You're lucky we came along," Cumsey said with a grin. "I think you're getting too old for this line of work."

"Yeah, thanks," Morgan said, but his eyes were locked on his son standing not far away and staring back at him.

Morgan gestured at the cabin's open door. Cumsey and Ben came close to him, and they all listened for the sound of anyone that still might be inside.

"Anybody in there better come out!" Cumsey shouted.

Morgan was glad Cumsey did the yelling, because he didn't think he could manage it himself. He looked for the McAlester woman while they waited, but she seemed to have gotten away into the woods.

Somebody moved inside the cabin, and at the same time Dixie and Red Molly appeared in front of the cabin some fifty or sixty yards away. They had McAlester's wife with them.

"Throw down your guns and come out with your hands

up!" Cumsey shouted again while he moved past Morgan and closer to the open door.

Ben looked fiercely proud and determined in that moment, but his Springfield was strangely uncocked and pointed at the ground. Morgan was watching him when J.J. McAlester came out the door with his hands in the air.

"Don't shoot," McAlester said.

Cumsey motioned with his Winchester for McAlester to move out of the way of the door. McAlester nodded wildly, spotted his wife, and ran towards her.

"Who else is in there?" Cumsey said into the open doorway and from well back to one side of it.

"Come out, Mother," Ben said. "I know you're in there. Tell whoever else is with you to give it up. It's over."

Ben's words had barely had time to settle on Morgan before Helvina stepped out where they could all see her.

"Oh, thank God you found me!" she said. "I thought they were going to kill me!"

Injun Joe wasn't asleep, but he was in a sort of weakened, dying daze when the gunfight started. He rolled over onto his side and fumbled for his Winchester. By the time he had managed to get the rifle rested on the log and ready to shoot, the fighting in front of the cabin was already a bloodbath. He tried to find his rifle sights so that he could aim properly, but his vision was off. He rubbed his eyes with the back of one forearm and tried again.

By then, there were already three men down in the yard, and three more men were gathered against the cabin and preparing to storm it. Joe wiped at his eyes again. He didn't recognize any of the three survivors, but his eyesight was failing him so badly that he couldn't be sure. He debated on which one to shoot first, even though he wasn't sure he could hit one of them in his condition.

The man in the checkered pants, that's who he was supposed to kill. And not one of the three men left standing had on checkered pants, nor did any of the dead.

Injun Joe wished he had never agreed to go with Dunn and steal McAlester's woman and child. It was a bad thing, worse than anything Joe had ever done. Worse than stealing hogs or robbing people on the roads, all of which Joe had done at one time or another. J.J. McAlester had good sense to have picked a woman like that Chickasaw girl. It was no wonder that McAlester was so rich. She reminded Joe of his own mother.

He didn't get to think on the matter any more before somebody stepped out of the house. It took him several seconds to realize that it was the man in the checkered pants. He tried to find his aim, no matter how blurry his target appeared.

Joe felt bad, worse than ever before. He almost let his Winchester drop from his grip, but fought through the moment. He had no confidence that he could make the shot, but if he didn't shoot, that mean little man from Chicago would likely find him and cut his throat with that razor he carried.

Joe pulled the trigger and sent a .44-40 round straight and true into the man standing in the cabin's door. However, it wasn't the man in the checkered pants he shot, nor even a man at all. But Joe never knew that, for he died soon after he fired his last shot.

Chapter Forty-Nine

One moment Helvina was standing before Morgan in the doorway, and the next moment she was lying on the ground with blood all over the front of her dress. It happened that fast. Morgan heard Ben cry out, and then Ben was on his knees over her body.

Cumsey turned to face whatever new threat was upon them, yet he didn't fire his rifle. Morgan, too, scanned the edge of the woods for whomever had shot Helvina. And he was too tired and too numb to have the good sense to take cover or to warn the others that they should, also.

Dixie called out to them, although Morgan couldn't understand what he was shouting about. Dixie had left Molly and McAlester's wife where Morgan had seen them before, and he was waving his arms over his head near a deadfall log straight out in front of the cabin.

"I think he said it's all right," Cumsey said.

They watched Dixie bend down and pick up a rifle from in front of the log and pitch it away. Then he walked towards them without a look back.

"There's an Indian out there behind that log," Dixie said when he reached them. He must have seen the questioning looks they were giving him. "He's dead."

Morgan looked around him. He hadn't shot the Indian, nor had Cumsey or Ben.

"That Indian had an old gunshot wound in his belly. Only

thing I could see that might have killed him," Dixie added.

Cumsey turned and ducked inside the cabin with his rifle leading the way. Morgan saw him go, but couldn't find it in him to do anything to help. He moved to stand over Ben and Helvina.

He put a hand on Ben's shoulder. "She's gone, Son."

Ben looked up at him with wet eyes, and Morgan couldn't help but be reminded of a younger version of Ben on a day when Morgan had said his goodbyes to his family, the day he had gone off to war. Ben had looked at him the same way then, the same hurt written on his face.

"Why?" Ben asked in a voice barely loud enough to be heard.

"There was a time when I loved her dearly," Morgan answered. "I guess a part of me always will."

"I was coming to warn her. To take her away before it was too late," Ben said. "I thought I could talk her out of whatever crazy scheme she was working on."

Morgan nodded and studied Helvina's cold still face. And he noticed the dress she was wearing, a dress with black and white checks.

"She always did like a stylish dress," he mumbled.

Adolphus Vanderwagen came out of the cabin with Cumsey following him with his Winchester leveled on the old man.

"Is she dead?" Adolphus sounded almost bewildered, and his voice was flat and emotionless. He wouldn't look down at his daughter.

Morgan grabbed Adolphus by the shirtfront with one hand and reared back his other fist to strike him.

"Don't," Ben pleaded barely in time to stop Morgan.

Morgan took a deep, ragged breath and lowered his fist.

"Go ahead, hit an old man," Adolphus said, and even in such a moment, there was a bit of his old self coming back, a bit of that snobbish, conceited evil that Morgan had hated for so long.

Morgan grabbed Adolphus's walking cane and yanked it away

from him. He swung it and struck it against the log wall to one side of the doorjamb. He had to hit the wall with it a second time to break it.

He threw the two pieces of the cane away and turned to leave. But he only made it a few steps before he felt himself falling. Falling and falling endlessly. He didn't even notice when the hard ground rose up to meet him.

CHAPTER FIFTY

Morgan woke in his hotel bed once more. It was his third day bedridden, but only the first where he felt somewhat lucid and on the mend. Even before he opened his eyes, he was aware of voices around him.

He looked to the side of his bed and saw Molly sitting in a chair in front of the window. Dixie lay on a pallet on the floor.

"How do you feel?" Molly asked.

"Like a ton of coal fell on me," Morgan replied.

"Pneumonia, that's what the doctor said. Said you're lucky you aren't dead. You had a horrible fever. If he hadn't had the good sense to get some ice blocks off the train and put them in bed with you, I don't think you and I would be talking now."

"Well, I feel better now."

"You do seem to be breathing better."

"Chest still hurts some."

"You ought to thank the doctor when you see him."

"I plan on it," Morgan said. "But you sure seem enamored with him."

Dixie propped himself up on one elbow. "This youngster ain't so bad. He's got a new treatment he wants to try on Molly's lungs. Thinks it might help her."

Morgan looked from one to the other of them. "Have you two been here the whole time?"

"We took turns sleeping on this pallet," Dixie said. "Though you talked so much in your sleep we didn't get much rest."

Morgan nodded at that. "It's good to have friends. I never had many."

"Us old-timers have to stick together," Dixie said.

"Old-timers? Speak for yourself, though I don't exactly feel young right now."

Molly laughed, and it sounded good to Morgan.

Dixie laughed, too. "Whether you know it or not, we are the old-timers now. More and more new faces in the territory every time I look around me. Won't be long until things are so civilized they'll run the likes of you and me off and lock the gates so we can't get back in."

"You and Molly have done me more than one good turn," Morgan said, "and I'd like to pay back some of what I owe you."

"You don't owe me anything," Molly said.

Morgan continued like he hadn't heard her. "I've got a little money set by. If you'll let me, I'd like to invest in that farm of yours. Help you get it off the ground."

"That farm won't ever make enough profit for me and Molly, much less enough to make you anything," Dixie replied.

"I don't care about profit. I'd just like to see you grow that place. Maybe someday when I've had enough of wearing a badge, I would have a porch to sit on. Watch you work those stupid mules of yours."

Dixie and Molly shared a look between them that Morgan couldn't interpret. Dixie cleared his throat and sat up against the wall. "We are leaving the farm and buying the livery barn here in town. We've been thinking about it for a while. Molly can be closer to the doctor and I can do a little more horse trading. Noodles has offered to buy the barbershop, and with that and what we can make with the livery we ought to do just fine."

"Well then . . ." Morgan said and left it at that.

"This is a good place to settle down," Molly said. "I think for people like us there are places where you're coming from and places where you're going, but never anything in between. Never anything that feels just right. *Home,* sounds a little strange, doesn't it?"

"I'm happy for you, Molly," Morgan said. "Happy for you both."

Dixie and Molly smiled at each other.

Morgan cleared his throat. "Has anybody run down Charlie Dunn?"

Dixie shook his head. "No sign of him. Moshulatubee said that the Indian that shot . . . well, you know . . ."

"Go ahead," Morgan said.

"The one that likely shot Helvina was Joe Jackson. You know, the Injun Joe that Moshulatubee told us about that was with Dunn at the caves."

"Then Dunn was likely around here, but we missed him."

"Mrs. McAlester says Dunn was leading those that took her, but that he and Injun Joe and two others had a fight with Virgil Beck and some more of Helvina's men over at Briartown. She thought he might have been killed in that fracas."

"Beck was working for Helvina?" Morgan asked.

"Appears like it. And it appears like Dunn was, too. I know you don't like to hear that, Morgan."

"No, I don't, but it is what it is. Though I can't imagine why Helvina was after McAlester's family."

"As I understand it, it was something to do with trying to take over McAlester's coal mines."

Morgan nodded grimly.

"Even if Dunn is still alive, I suspect he's headed for the high country by now," Dixie added. "But there are lots out looking for him."

"I wish we had caught him," Morgan said.

"Well, they might catch him, yet. At least we got McAlester's family back," Dixie said. "Speaking of that, I've got your share of the reward money."

"McAlester paid?"

"He did. I already divvied it up and gave Cumsey and Moshulatubee their shares."

"Your cut ought to help you out with your livery business."

"It won't hurt."

"Speak of the devil," Molly said.

Cumsey came into the room. As usual he was smiling. "I see our patient is back among the living."

"You sound like you doubted me," Morgan said.

"Naw, I knew you were too mean to die."

"Where's Adolphus?" Morgan asked.

"Two more marshals showed up yesterday. They've got the old man."

"Send those marshals up here. I want to talk to them."

"I'd as soon stay out of their sight."

Morgan tried to sit up in bed. Molly saw that he was struggling, and helped him until he was sitting semi-upright against the headboard.

"There's some paper and a pencil in my saddlebags," Morgan said. "I don't suppose any of you brought them to my room for me, did you?"

Dixie went to the closet and pulled out the saddlebags. He dug around in them until he found the pencil and paper.

Morgan used the top of one of his thighs as a rest and began to write. When he was finished, he folded the paper and held it out to Cumsey.

"You give this to Judge Parker," Morgan said.

"I told you, I'm keeping shut of those marshals, and your judge, too," Cumsey answered.

"You do like I told you. I've explained your situation in that message you're holding, and I'm going to tell those marshals the same thing. I've staked my word on you," Morgan said. "You're going to go with them when they take Adolphus to Fort Smith, and then you're going to talk to Judge Parker."

"That old hanging judge won't listen to me."

"You might be surprised. I've suggested that as a way to pay for your past crimes you be allowed to serve as one of his deputy marshals. He's always short of men."

Cumsey didn't even attempt to hide his surprise. "Me?"

"I bragged about how you've helped me on multiple occasions, and what a fine lawman I think you'll make."

Cumsey tapped his chest. "Did I hear you right? Me?"

"I might have stretched the truth a little, but yes, you."

"I ain't cut out to be no lawman."

Morgan put a fist to his mouth to cover his coughing. When he was through, he gave Cumsey a hard look. "Here's your chance. You want to keep running from the law, or would you rather run with it?"

"You really think that judge will listen to you?"

"No guarantees, but he's a smart fellow. And he's fair."

"I don't know. There's somebody I need to talk to first."

"All right. Go talk to her."

Cumsey started to go, but turned back with a funny look on his face. "How'd you know it was a 'her'?"

" 'Cause the only thing you've ever been a fool about is horses and women, and I don't imagine you need to talk to a horse."

Cumsey laughed, and like Molly's laugh, it was a good thing.

Dixie pointed at the door when Cumsey was gone. "That's a good deed you're doing for that young fellow. Not many would."

Morgan waved a weak, dismissive hand at Dixie.

"People know what you did for him and they're going to say you're turning soft," Dixie said.

"What they don't know won't hurt them."

"Cumsey didn't say it, but those marshals are already wanting to talk to you," Dixie said. "They've been here twice already, but you were asleep. You might be in some trouble."

"Is it to do with the brickmaker?" Morgan asked.

Dixie nodded. "They want to ask you some questions about what happened with him."

"And I'll give them my answers when they come. Where's Ben? I want to talk to him."

Again, Dixie and Molly shared a private look.

"What's the matter?" Morgan asked.

"Ben's down at the funeral parlor with his mother," Molly said.

"Well, go get him." Morgan realized that his voice was raised, and brought it to a lower volume. "Please."

"We tried to get him to come up here last night," Molly said. "I don't think he wants to talk to you."

There was an awkward moment of silence before Morgan finally replied to her. "That's too bad."

Molly got up out of her chair and gave a jerk of her head at Dixie and towards the door. Dixie took the signal and got up off his pallet.

"I believe the hotel serves lunch about now," Molly said. "We'll leave you alone so you can get some rest."

"Yeah," Morgan said while he stared at the ceiling. "I'm feeling sort of tired."

Chapter Fifty-One

Charlie Dunn spent two days and nights alone in the woods near the river, and was constantly on the alert for anyone who might be looking for him. Every bit of the feral instincts and the selfish cunning that had helped him survive his boyhood on the mean streets of Packingtown warned him to get as far away from Eufaula as he could, and as fast as he could. The game was over, and there was no reason to stay except to get himself hanged. Yet, he remained in the woods, dirty and bug-bitten to the point he was half covered in whelps and rashes, hungry and sleeping without a fire. Part of it was that he was not confident that he could strike out overland without getting lost, and wasn't going to risk traveling the main roads with lawmen liable to be hunting him. The other reason that he stayed close to Eufaula was that he couldn't stop thinking about Morgan Clyde.

Twice, Clyde had stymied his plans. The man just wouldn't go away. First he had shown up out of the dark at the caves, and then somehow he had arrived at the cabin so close to the time Dunn had gotten there that it almost seemed like the man was put specifically on the earth to thwart and taunt him, misfortune in the flesh. Dunn knew he was the better man, yet Clyde kept coming at him in ways that didn't give him a chance to return the fight in the way he knew he was capable.

Hiding in the thickets gave him time to analyze everything that had gone wrong with his plan, and each time that brooding came back around to Clyde. Not only did he blame Clyde, he also hated him even worse than the very first time Clyde had ever walked into the hotel more than a year before.

He would have killed Clyde back at the cabin, but everything had gone wrong that could go wrong. First Joe had failed to shoot the man in the checkered pants, then Clyde's posse had shown up and all hell had broken loose. And Dunn didn't wait around to buck the odds, not with so much lead flying. He had run back to his and Joe's camp, grabbed their horses, and ran.

Contempt, that was what Dunn sensed in the marshal. Contempt and a lack of respect, as if the fool thought he was better than him. But he wasn't better. He was simply a washed-up old lawman with an overblown reputation. The man couldn't even hang on to his wife.

Remembering how Helvina double-crossed him and then laughed in his face took his attention away from Clyde, at least temporarily. The gall of that stupid, rich bitch. Nobody laughed at him.

Dunn could stand it no longer, and he rode to a point on the far side of Cemetery Hill. He tied his horse in the trees and climbed the rest of the way up to the top. From that vantage point he watched the town throughout the day. And from there, he saw two men that he assumed were lawmen marching Adolphus Vanderwagen in shackles from the depot to the café for lunch, and he saw Dixie Rayburn and that red-haired whore going in and out of the hotel several times. But he didn't see Morgan Clyde, nor did he see Helvina Vanderwagen.

Come nightfall, he snuck down to the back of the hotel and waited until one of the maids came outside to take in some laundered bedding from the clothesline. He had once caught her taking home food from the hotel's kitchen supplies, and she was a girl who was afraid of losing her job or getting into trouble with the law. On more than one occasion he had used the threat of revealing her thievery as a means to get her to do what he wanted. In the past, when he had still been her boss, in order for him to keep her secret she had to meet him in that very same pantry and let him have his way with her. But this time it bought him information and the assurance that she wouldn't tell of his presence.

From her he learned of Helvina's death, as well as the death of the man in the checkered pants. And he learned of the two new marshals in town, and that there were other posses still out searching for him.

The news of Helvina's passing pleased him, but at the same time it was disappointing. He had so dearly wanted the pleasure of settling that score himself. But Clyde was staying in the hotel, and what's more, the maid said he was all but on his deathbed.

Dunn considered waiting until late in the night and then sneaking into Clyde's room and cutting him from ear to ear, but the maid told him that Dixie and Red Molly were taking turns sitting with Clyde. He weighed his options while the maid heated some leftovers from the evening meal on the cookstove and brought them out to him.

He thought about burning the hotel down while he waited for her to bring him the food. And while the flames burned behind his eyes, he also considered forcing the maid to pull her dress up for him one more time. She was a homely girl, but in the past he had pretended she was Helvina Vanderwagen. The urge left him almost as quickly as it came over him, and he let the maid go back into the hotel. He moved around the building to where he could see the dark window that was Clyde's room, stared at it for several breaths, and then slipped back into the shadows and was gone.

He was on his way back to Cemetery Hill when he saw the lantern burning in Hank Bickford's woodshop at the back of his funeral parlor and blacksmith shop. He moved closer and saw someone through the window. Hank was sanding a wooden coffin he had recently put together, and he was covered in dust and a pile of white pine shavings covered his feet. Stooped over the coffin like he was, he didn't see Dunn come to the door.

Dunn drew one of his pistols, tested the door latch, and opened it. He stepped into the room and let the door close behind him. Startled, Hank snapped upright.

"Don't you make a sound," Dunn said and cocked the pistol.

"What do you want?" Hank asked.

"Whose is that?" Dunn nodded at the coffin Hank had been working on.

"Nobody's, yet."

"Good. About how long is that box?"

"Six and a half feet, inside to inside," Hank answered in a shaky voice. "Why?"

Dunn rapped on the coffin lid, and the sound of the pale wood under his knuckles was as hollow as his laugh. "That's a mighty plain coffin. You ought to paint it black. Maybe tack on some brass hardware."

"I could do that."

"Take off that lid and get inside it."

"What?"

"I said get in," Dunn said. "I want to see you lie in it."

Dunn removed the lid and climbed into the coffin, taking care not to knock it off the sawhorses it rested on.

"Lie down on your back like you're supposed to," Dunn said.

"I got a wife and two kids," Hank pleaded.

Dunn jammed the muzzle of his pistol against Hank's chest. "Lie down."

Hank lay down on his back. He stared up at the ceiling as if he were afraid to look at Dunn or the pistol hovering over him. "Oh, Lord, you're going to kill me, ain't you?"

Dunn gave him an odd, thin smile "Close your eyes and cross

your arms over your chest. Isn't that how you do it?"

"Oh, Lord," Hank moaned.

"What's it feel like?" Dunn asked.

"I don't know. Like lying in a box."

"Have you got red velvet to line it with?" Dunn said as if he didn't hear Hank.

Hank took a quavering, deep breath like he was trying to gather himself, but he didn't open his eyes. "Never have used that before. Most folks around here don't have the money for such, but I guess my Lottie could sew some kind of lining."

"You do that. Make it shine. What about tombstones?"

"I got those, too. Not marble. Have to ship that in on the train and it costs to have my man up in Kansas City engrave it for me. But I've got plenty of good flat sandstone. Keep a stack of it up at the cemetery. I can scratch a few words on it easy enough with a chisel."

"Get out," Dunn said and stepped back from the casket.

Hank opened his eyes and climbed out of the casket slowly, lest his moves be misconstrued. "I don't mind telling you, Charlie, you're scaring the hell out of me."

"You call me Charlie again and those kids of yours are going to lose their daddy. Put out that lantern."

Hank took down the lantern from where it hung, raised the globe, and was about to snuff out the wick when Dunn waved the pistol at him.

"On second thought," Dunn said. "You better find your shovel before you put out that light. I got some digging for you to do."

Chapter Fifty-Two

A day later and Morgan was still confined to his hotel room. But he did feel well enough to get out of bed and sit in his chair where he could look out the window at the street below. He was sitting in the very same chair when Molly and Dixie saddled up and rode out of town headed for their farm. And he had been sitting there earlier that day when Cumsey rode out with the deputy marshals and their prisoner.

He was lost in his thoughts when somebody knocked on his door. It seemed lately that someone was always knocking on his door.

"Come in," he said.

It was Ben who came into the room. He was dressed once more in his uniform.

"Good to see you," Morgan said.

"I came to say goodbye."

"What about your mother?"

"They'll put her on the train as soon as it gets here. She told me once that when she died, she wanted to be back in New York. Maybe I can get more leave time to go back and see her buried."

"I would have liked to attend her funeral," Morgan said. "Though I doubt she would have appreciated that."

"I think you're wrong. You could go back. Put this territory behind you. Take her home on your way."

"No, there's nothing left back there for me."

Ben took off his hat and ran his fingers around the brim. "I never did feel like I really knew her. My own mother, and listen to me say that."

"She was complicated," Morgan said while looking out the window.

"Yes, she was."

"She always wanted the best for you and her. Remember that," Morgan said. "I think that's what got her in trouble more than once. Always wanting. Pushing."

"Don't," there was a warning in Ben's voice.

Morgan nodded that he understood.

"I didn't come here to talk about her," Ben said. "Didn't come here to talk at all. I simply wanted to say goodbye."

"Have you changed your mind about quitting the army?"

"I don't know. I'm going back to Fort Gibson for now. Maybe I'll stick, or maybe I'll muster out. I feel like my whole life I've been living in somebody else's story. I don't know what to believe. I need to go somewhere and get my head cleared."

"You'll figure it out."

Ben nodded. "Then there's Grandfather's trial. I'm assuming there will be a trial."

"There will be."

Ben started to go.

"I'm sorry, Son. Sorry for everything."

Ben said nothing to that.

"You could stay a few more days."

Ben shook his head. "No, I don't think that would be good. You know, I've still got a lot of hard feelings about you. I know Mother said things about you that weren't true, but she was right about some of it."

"I know. There's a lot of bad water between you and me."

"Well, so long."

"Write me a letter or something if you get the time," Morgan said.

"I'll think about it."

The sound of the door closing behind Ben seemed overly loud to Morgan. He stayed in his chair thinking about that sound until there came another knock on his door. He hoped that it was Ben coming back, but that hope was short-lived. It was Hank Bickford who came in the room.

"Did you come to measure me for my coffin or to bring me my bill for shoeing my horse?" Morgan asked.

"You won't be trying to be so funny when I tell you what I come here to say," Hank said.

"What is it that you've got to tell me?"

"Charlie Dunn came by my place and pulled a pistol on me."

Morgan's flint-blue eyes came alive. "When was this?"

"Last night," Hank said. "He made me go up to the cemetery and dig a grave."

"For who?"

"For you. Made me promise I would come tell you he'll be waiting up there this afternoon. Said to bring your pistol and you two could see which one gets the grave."

Morgan rose from his chair. "Have you told anybody else about this?"

"No," Hank said. "I just finished digging that hole a little while ago, and then I came straight here."

"Is he up there now?"

"He is. You want me to go fetch my gun? I'll gather some men."

"No, you don't tell anybody. This is my business."

"You're as crazy as he is."

"But you can do me a favor," Morgan said.

"What's that?"

"Ask the hotel girls to bring me up some hot water for a bath."

Hank gave him a confused look. Morgan ignored that look and went to his closet. From it he took out his black frock coat and the rest of what he called his town clothes.

"I wonder if one of those girls would brush my suit coat while I take a bath. It's starting to look a little road worn."

"Hell of a time to be worrying about a bath and a suit coat," Hank said.

"You're too much blacksmith to make a good undertaker, Hank."

"How do you figure?" Hank asked.

Morgan's blue eyes took on the same gleam they had earlier when Hank had first mentioned Dunn, but then he smiled. "Hank, you ought to know a man needs to look his best if he's going to a funeral."

Chapter Fifty-Three

Morgan walked down the street in his freshly brushed frock coat. The left side of the tail of that coat was swept back and tucked in behind his holstered pistol. Few saw him pass, but some of those who did paused what they were doing long enough to wonder where he was going. He ignored their stares and kept walking. When he passed the livery barn, he considered saddling his horse, but didn't. It was a short walk to the top of Cemetery Hill, and it was a way he knew well.

It was a pleasant day. The only clouds in the sky were as white as dogwood blossoms. There was virtually no wind to speak of other than a faint breeze occasionally tickling the highest tree leaves, and the gentle warmth of the spring sun felt good where his still damp hair lay against the back of his neck.

Pretty day, or not, he was far from healed and in no hurry. And he had a stop he needed to make.

Noodles was busy giving a haircut to an elderly man Morgan didn't know when he went inside the barbershop. The skinny little Sicilian nodded at him without stopping the snipping of his scissors.

"It's good to see you, Signor Clyde," Noodles said. "I see you are feeling better."

Morgan only gave him a return nod as an answer, and sat down in one of the chairs arranged for waiting customers. It felt good to rest his legs.

A stack of newspapers and various journals and other publications lay on a small table beside him. He picked up one of the newspapers and glanced at the front page to pass the time, but soon lost interest in reading anything and looked out one of the front windows where he could see a mangy old red hound with a missing back leg hobbling along the boardwalk. He could see every one of the hound's rib bones.

Morgan reached inside his coat and brought out his leather wallet. He laid it on the stack of newspapers. Inside that wallet was his portion of the McAlester reward, plus a few more coins and greenbacks. He patted the leather to make sure Noodles saw it, and then rose to go.

"Noodles, if I don't come back here today, would you do me a favor and send this to Fort Gibson?" he asked. "Send it to Lieutenant Benjamin Clyde. I've written his name on a piece of paper in case you forget."

"What's in it?" Noodles asked while he peered at the leather wallet.

"Not much," Morgan said. "Not much at all."

He glanced one last time at the newspaper he held and noticed the date. He read it out loud, "March 31st, 1876."

The edition was three days old, but something about seeing that date struck him, though he couldn't say why.

"Time flies, doesn't it?" the old man in the barber's chair said.

"Some days go slower than others, some faster," Morgan said. "I guess you're right when you go to adding them up."

"You get as old as me, and one day you'll look back and ask yourself how in the hell did you get so damned old. Of course a young fellow like yourself won't understand," the old man replied.

Morgan fished a pickled egg out of the jar Noodles kept on the counter, then he nodded his goodbye and went back out on the street. He thought about what the old man had said, and chuckled. *Like hell he didn't understand.* He was a few months short of turning forty, yet, at that very moment he felt like he was a hundred years old.

The three-legged redbone hound was standing nearby staring at him.

"What are you looking at?" Morgan asked.

The dog gave a faint wag of its tail, unsure about being spoken to.

Morgan pitched the pickled egg onto the boardwalk in front of the mutt, and the egg was gone almost as fast as it appeared. Again, the tip of the dog's tail quivered.

Morgan waved a hand at it to shoo it off. "Go on before somebody kicks you."

The hound stopped a few yards away, gave him another odd look, then moved on down the street towards the hotel and the train tracks.

Morgan straightened the hang of his coat on his shoulders and went in the opposite direction. He passed Hank Bickford's buildings, and then the last place he came to before coming to the foot of Cemetery Hill was the Methodist Church. He studied the bell hanging in the steeple of the little white building. Somehow, that steeple gave the town substance. He had no use for Reverend Pickins, but he had to give him that. The first time Morgan had come to the site not too many years before there had been nothing on the grounds except for construction camp tents and several hundred rough and rowdy workmen. Dixie was right, the territory was changing.

The climb up Cemetery Hill wasn't a steep one, but it was long. He went cautiously, not only because he was looking for Charlie Dunn, but also because his weakened body wouldn't allow him to go more quickly. He had barely topped the hill when he saw Dunn standing under a huge shade tree on the far side of the graveyard.

Morgan slowed his pace even more, and glanced at the sun, pleased to see that it wouldn't be shining in his face. His boots brushed through the spring grass and the first green shoots of wildflowers growing among the scattered tombstones.

He could see then the fresh mound of earth where Hank had dug the grave. Dunn stood on the far edge of that hole, and began to pace back and forth as Morgan came closer to it.

Morgan took out a new cigar and jammed it in the corner of his mouth. He didn't light it, and took two more steps and saw that Dunn had taken off his suit coat and had folded it neatly over a new tombstone set at the head of the grave. Hank hadn't mentioned a tombstone.

"I wondered if you'd come," Dunn stopped pacing and said.

Morgan kept walking and didn't stop until he was almost to the opposite edge of the grave. Barely ten feet separated them, and the grave was a dark shadow between them.

Morgan chanced a glance at the tombstone, but didn't linger long on it. It wasn't made of marble, but rather common red sandstone likely plucked from somewhere nearby. There was no engraving on it.

Dunn noticed him look at the tombstone and smiled and gave a slight shrug of his shoulders. "Didn't have time to put your name on it."

"Well, here I am," Morgan said around the cigar clenched between his jaw teeth.

Dunn tipped his head to one side and then the other as if stretching his neck. "Everybody is going to talk about this day. About you and me."

"I've come here to either arrest you or kill you," Morgan said. "Your choice."

"Arrest me?" Dunn's voice took on a slightly higher pitch and there was a quaver to it. He gave a bitter chuckle. "I think not. Hell, you look half dead already. I almost feel bad inviting you up here."

Morgan bit down harder on the cigar in the corner of his mouth and tensed his chest to keep from coughing.

"You know, Clyde," Dunn said in a quieter voice, and made another of those birdlike movements of his head and neck. "I've admired that fancy black hat of yours ever since I saw you wearing it back at Fort Smith. I'm going to be wearing it as soon as I put you out of your misery."

Dunn's eyelids flickered and he went for both of his pistols. He was incredibly fast, and he had both of them clear of their holsters when Morgan shot him in the stomach.

The little outlaw screamed and the shot he fired went off into the ground next to Morgan's left boot. He staggered back, sagged, and then tried to lift his right-hand gun once more. Morgan shot him a second time about a hand's width above where he hit him the first time, and then thumbed his pistol hammer a third time and shot him in the chest. Dunn toppled forward and fell into the grave.

Morgan moved until he could look down into the grave and saw the outlaw lying there on the bottom. Dunn was still breathing, but fading fast. Morgan ejected the empties out of his pistol cylinder and let the brass hulls fall into the grave. He reloaded the revolver and then tucked the hot steel back into his holster.

It took Dunn several minutes to die, and he lay there gasping with his wild eyes still flickering while Morgan struck a match and lit his cigar between his cupped hands. When he had taken several puffs of tobacco, he eased himself down into the grave and closed Dunn's eyes.

It took him a great deal of effort to climb back out of the grave, and that exertion left smears of red clay on the knees of his pants and on his coat. He walked a ways across the graveyard, but stopped at the lip of the hill overlooking the town. There he took a seat on one of the tombstones and blew a smoke ring into the air in front of his face. Inhaling that smoke caused him to start coughing. He coughed until his eyes watered, and he ground out the cigar on the tombstone beneath him and pitched it away.

Below him, men were coming from town to the cemetery, drawn by the gunfire. Beyond them at the depot, the train was rolling in, and he saw two workers carrying Helvina's casket out onto the decking beside the tracks. The locomotive's steam whistle gave a lonesome, long blast, and he got up and started down the hill.

HISTORICAL NOTES

1. Robbers Cave—"the caves," as I have called them, lie within Robbers Cave State Park near Wilburton, Oklahoma. Folklore has it that the sandstone ledges and jumbled rock formations were a hideout for Indian Territory outlaws back in the days before Oklahoma was formed. Jesse James and Belle Starr are said to be among the most famous of those who used the site. While there is no written record or other definitive evidence to prove that assertion, members of the James-Younger gang did spend time in the area both during and after the Civil War. Also, Belle Starr's final home place and grave lies not far to the north between Whitefield and Porum, Oklahoma.

2. James Jackson McAlester and Rebecca Burney McAlester—while J.J. McAlester's family was never kidnapped by outlaws, my fictional relation of his rise to prominence in the territory, and later the state of Oklahoma, is generally factual. He was a man of enterprise, a town builder, and one of the early movers and shakers with a vision of what the territory could be. The store he built along the Katy tracks still stands in the city bearing his name.

Historians often point out McAlester's marrying an Indian woman in order to gain tribal membership and access to the coal claims that helped make him wealthy. Yet, little has been written about his wife, Rebecca, other than to perhaps portray her as a victim. However, historian Malinda Maynor Lowery, while discussing Choctaw and Chickasaw capitalism and kinship in an article in *The Native South: New Histories and Enduring Legacies,* states, "Chickasaw and Choctaw women had a long history of incorporating outsiders to serve their economic and political interests." In other words, those women could be as ambitious as any man, white or red. The Chickasaws and Choctaws were both matrilineal in that one's heritage descended solely from the female. Children gained their status within the tribe from their mother's clan. As a result, perhaps those women were far more actively and openly involved in seeing to their family's fortune than most white women of the Victorian era. One of Rebecca's friends, Annie Ream, the wife of one of J.J. McAlester's business partners, was a major player in Indian Territory business, especially the coal business.

According to this line of thought, it is easy to believe that Rebecca realized that the Indian tribes would not be able to hold off the encroachment of the white settlers forever, and she chose J.J. as much as he chose her, seeking a long-term foothold for her family in both worlds. Rebecca McAlester became almost as much of a local legend in the city of McAlester as her husband. The mansion she and J.J. built became a landmark in their home city. I hope my fictional portrayal of her depicts her strength and the type of challenges she could have faced.

3. Judge Isaac C. Parker—Judge Parker, remembered in countless newspapers, movies, and novels as the Hanging Judge, is perhaps the most iconic judge of the Old West. He served twenty-one years on the bench for the Western District of Arkansas, a district that included the Indian Territory, an expanse of over 74,000 square miles. For fourteen of those years, those he condemned had no right of appeal. During his tenure, he sentenced 160 people to death, including four women. Seventy-nine of those people were hung on his gallows. Some of those early hangings drew massive crowds much like

modern sporting events, and the press coverage only added to his fame. His original courthouse in the old barracks at Fort Smith still stands as a museum and a National Historic Site. One of his mottos perfectly encapsulates the challenges of justice and peacekeeping during the era: "Permit no innocent man to be punished, but let no guilty man escape."

4. Black deputy marshals and outlaw marshals—my fictional depiction of Cumsey Bowlegs possibly becoming a deputy U.S. marshal could have happened. More than one black man rode for the Western District of Arkansas. One of those men, Bass Reeves, became one of the most effective lawmen in the territory. He is remembered by a bronze statue and monument erected in his honor in Fort Smith.

Additionally, the line between lawman and outlaw was often blurred during those years, so that a horse thief like Cumsey might get a chance to right his wrongs. Not only did many peace officers, such as Wyatt Earp and Wild Bill Hickok, sometimes walk dangerously close to the line separating bad guys and good guys, there were also many lawmen who started out as outlaws or wound up as one.

Grat Dalton of the Dalton Gang once served as a deputy U.S. marshal in the Indian Territory, and his older brother, Frank, was killed while also serving as a deputy marshal. Bat Masterson, famed Ford County sheriff during his Dodge City days, earlier was involved in a scandalous gunfight in Sweetwater, Texas, where he killed a soldier in an argument over a prostitute. Masterson was also once arrested and fined for helping a fugitive escape the Dodge City marshal's clutches. Henry Brown, city marshal of Caldwell, Kansas, first fought in the Lincoln County War out in New Mexico Territory and rode with Billy the Kid. Brown and his assistant marshal, Ben Wheeler, a former Texas lawman himself, were hung by a lynch mob for trying to rob a bank in Medicine Lodge.

ABOUT THE AUTHOR

Some folks are just born to tell tall tales. **Brett Cogburn** was reared in Texas and the mountains of Southeastern Oklahoma. He had the fortune for many years to make his living from the back of a horse, where cowboys still step on frisky broncs on cold mornings and drag calves to the branding fire on the end of a rope from their saddle horn. Growing up around ranches, livestock auctions, and backwoods hunting camps filled his head with stories, and he never forgot a one. In his own words, "My grandfather taught me to ride a bucking horse, my mother gave me a love of reading, and my father taught me how to shoot straight. Cowboys are just as wild as they ever were, and I've been fortunate enough to know more than a few."

Somewhere during his knockabout years cowboying, training horses, and working in the oil field, he managed to earn a BA in English and a minor in history. Brett lives with his family on a small ranch in Oklahoma. The West is still teaching him how to write.

The employees of Five Star Publishing hope you have enjoyed this book.

Our Five Star novels explore little-known chapters from America's history, stories told from unique perspectives that will entertain a broad range of readers.

Other Five Star books are available at your local library, bookstore, all major book distributors, and directly from Five Star/Gale.

Connect with Five Star Publishing

Visit us on Facebook:
https://www.facebook.com/FiveStarCengage

Email:
FiveStar@cengage.com

For information about titles and placing orders:
(800) 223-1244
gale.orders@cengage.com

To share your comments, write to us:
Five Star Publishing
Attn: Publisher
10 Water St., Suite 310
Waterville, ME 04901